Taking Body

K.A. Merikan

Acerbi & Villani Ltd.

TABLE OF CONTENTS

Chapter 1 - Caspian

"You can do this. You're twenty-three, a grown man. You don't care anymore how others judge you," Caspian told himself, staring at the newest Instagram photo of a bodybuilder he followed. The bastard had two women hanging off his flexed arms, as if he were a tree, and he'd surely eaten Caspian's daily calorie allowance for breakfast. Since everyone went low-carb nowadays, his diet was likely based on nuts—one of the many mundane things that could kill Caspian.

It seemed to come so easily to this guy, as if he actually enjoyed several hours of exercise per day and never got bored of grilled chicken. Perhaps Caspian was looking for excuses. Nobody had blocked his way into the college gym, but the shame of revealing his frail arms and legs to anyone there terrified him to the point where he never used their facilities despite paying for the membership each year.

He'd tried calisthenics and workouts utilizing everyday objects, but neither did anything for him, and after attempting a 'healthy' diet several times, even the scent of protein powder gave him nausea. Still, those were excuses.

So maybe he'd never grow taller than five-foot-three, but he could most definitely gain muscle mass, and exceed the hundred and twelve pounds he'd been stuck at since graduating from high school. If he was lucky, maybe he'd escape the purgatory called undateable while he was at it. Despite the dislike for his physique, Caspian could see he wasn't *ugly*. He did have a good enough face, with plump lips that could have been considered sexy, and if he gained weight, his large blue eyes would make him look attractive rather than childlike.

Tonight, he would stop holding himself back. He'd just obtained his bachelor's degree, chosen a specialization, and returned home to work at Dad's firm. And since he considered this the start of a new life, he was determined to make a change. To no longer be the nerdy kid who tried to fit in by means of self-deprecating humor. So he motivated himself with more photos from the same Instagram account and stepped into the dark parking lot, facing the sprawling gym across the street.

As soon as he spotted the bulky men in tank tops chatting in front of the entrance, his instincts screamed for him to hide in the vehicle. They told him that he could use his mom's kettlebells for at-home weight training. That he could eat two extra chicken breasts a day instead of putting himself through this grinder.

But what he needed wasn't a workout video on YouTube. Only real engagement, advice, and the motivation of being watched during exercise could change things. Maybe, just maybe, he'd even meet someone with boyfriend potential, but that wasn't his priority. No. This was Caspian staking his claim. Battling for ground in uncharted territory. Molding himself into the man he was meant to be.

Fortune favors the bold.

"Excuse me," he mumbled once he stood behind the man blocking his way into the gym.

Nothing.

"Excuse me," he repeated to no avail. "Excuse me?" Caspian tut-tutted in frustration and dared to tap the man in front of him on the arm.

The human tank turned his bald head in surprise. "Didn't see you there."

"That's okay." Caspian lifted his eyebrows expectantly and glanced from the guy's square face to the door.

It was only then that the living mountain stepped away from his two friends, creating a corridor for Caspian. Mumbling his thanks, Caspian walked in, assaulted by the bright lights revealing every detail of his small form. He always dressed in layers to create the illusion of more bulk on his upper body, but the LEDs were merciless and surely cast shadows on his narrow cheeks, making him look as if he were starving himself.

He didn't like it here. Unlike the sleek gyms in the city where he studied, this one seemed... unwashed, for lack of a better word. Like the kind of guy who maintained the very basics of hygiene but sported oily hair and wore the same clothes three days in a row. Ugly graffiti covered

the walls in the exercise space, and the floor had cracks no one had bothered to repair. Worst of all, it smelled—
of sweat, cheap male deodorant, and dust. Hint of mold maybe? But what was he to expect of Grit, Ohio?

The woman at the reception desk gave him a wide smile, which was more professional than he'd expected from this dump. But he still hated having to interact with her in a place where men like the three at the entrance passed through the door every single day. She might not see how bony Caspian was through his clothes, but there was no hiding the fact that she was taller than him.

Caspian endured a brief introduction, signed papers, paid, and accepted a key before hiding in the locker room. Relief made him exhale when he realized the small interior with light blue tiles on both the floor and walls was empty, even if a bit grimy. At least the faint scent of disinfectant promised he wouldn't be getting athlete's foot. Hopefully.

Farther down, a corridor led to another room, and the sounds of splashing water and someone's humming coming from there were Caspian's cue to hurry before the stranger finished his shower.

He took advantage of being alone and threw his duffel bag to the bench. If he was quick enough, he could avoid meeting anyone here, and get on with his training. He might have to discuss the use of weight machines with a member of staff, but he'd worry about that later. One thing at a time.

Working out wasn't a competition. He would do his thing and ignore the people who hadn't let their bodies down, and who'd surely believe he didn't belong there. But he did, and the bill in his pocket was the proof. He just wished his heart would stop rattling like a cow bell. The lockers reminded him of high school, but he'd grown up since then. If not in size, then in maturity, class, and determination.

He was no longer the short gay kid who used to be mercilessly bullied by a bunch of teen degenerates. He could still recall their mean faces and undeservedly strong arms. Tall like a bunch of trolls, sons of criminals, bikers, and trailer trash, they considered themselves so much better than Caspian just because he didn't have their brute strength.

Even at university, he'd been christened pocket-rocket as if it was somehow so cute that he was tiny but feisty. Because at his size, he wasn't *a force to be reckoned with*. No. He was *feisty*. Plucky. Spirited.

With silent fury burning his veins, Caspian squeezed the oversized T-shirt that still smelled of Mom's fabric softener, but he didn't get to change.

"The ladies' locker room is on the other side," a low male voice said, and as Caspian froze, the sound of flip flops tapping against damp tiles echoed in his head like a warning.

But while his throat tightened with shame and discomfort, he reminded himself that he'd paid for time spent here, and therefore had every right to be in the locker room, regardless of what some meathead thought.

"Don't worry, I'm not gonna stare," Caspian said and spun around, losing his breath when he realized the half-naked man stood closer than he'd thought. And that he wasn't a random stranger.

It was Gunner Russo.

The object of Caspian's hate, fear, and fascination all rolled into one big, tattooed body.

But while the Gunner Russo from high school had been a relentless shithead, much taller and stronger than Caspian, the Gunner Russo in front of him was... well, even bigger. At least six-five and ripped as if being dehydrated was his natural state, he had wide shoulders and biceps like bread loaves. His upper body, tattooed with a cacophony of skulls and predator animals, made Caspian's fight or flight instinct ring.

His hair had been styled into a crew cut, which left nothing to obscure Gunner's features. And his face wasn't one people could ignore. Not just because it was enviably symmetrical and belonged on the cover of a sports magazine with its striking dark eyes, and a big nose so unlike Caspian's button-sized one.

Caspian noticed all those because he remembered Gunner from high school, but what would've stood out to a casual observer was the animal skull tattooed over the left half of the ruggedly masculine face. He wasn't sure whether the outline of bones belonged to a wolf, bear, or some other creature, because regardless of what predator it was, its very presence would've made any normal person pause and consider Gunner's sanity.

Still, in his most secret fantasies Caspian had always cast Gunner as Ares in his personal Pantheon of male Greek gods. The man was *that* hot.

But Caspian didn't want to fuck him. He'd have given his left arm to *be* him.

"You're already staring. You expect a show or something?" Gunner growled and opened the towel, which had covered his crotch so far.

Caspian should've looked away. Not doing so would be suicide.

But he'd wanted to see Gunner Russo's junk throughout high school, so how was he to deny himself when it was so casually revealed to him? Thick and long like half a baton of French bread, it hung between the broad thighs along with a sac that was twice the size of Caspian's. Gunner's naked body was hairy too, with a dense thatch of pubes and dark strands peppering the skin in all the places where Caspian had only a soft dusting.

For all the anger and hate Caspian still harbored for Gunner's endless bullying in the past, he couldn't deny that Gunner had grown into a *damn fine* man who dwarfed him in every way. How different Caspian's life would have been if he were as tall as Gunner and as muscular as him? Nobody would have bullied him if he had a body like that.

Gunner's thick, dark eyebrows drew together just as the door behind Caspian slammed against the lockers.

"Whoa!" a man laughed, sending a cold shiver down Caspian's back.

"What? What's going on?" Another asked as the door shut again.

Gunner looked over Caspian's head, to the men who'd entered, despite still holding his towel open. "Little gay boy wanted to have a look. I'm a generous man, and he's never gonna see another cock this big."

Caspian had been out at his college, but now that he'd been trapped by these three gorillas, whose bulks blocked all exits, his survival instinct told him to deny everything he was. But before his mouth could have turned the whole thing into a joke, anger rose inside him again, because he hadn't asked for any of this.

"If that's how you see it. I'm here to work out, not ogle anyone."

One of the newcomers, who had a pot belly pushing at the front of his shirt, and dull skin that said a lot about his habits, gave a low chuckle that took Caspian right back to middle school, when even the word *sex* had made all the kids giggle as if they knew what fucking was about.

"Oh, Gunner, did you want him to see your schlong?"

It took Caspian a moment to recognize him, but the voice was distinctive enough to identify him as Bud Dorset. Literally named after the beer, as he'd boasted many times in high school, unaware that it made him pathetic instead of cool to anyone with half a brain.

Gunner shrugged and rearranged the towel around his hips. "Show's over."

The third guy, freckled, bald, and with a big red beard stepped right in front of him like a ginger wolf about to play with its prey. He wasn't as massive as Gunner, but then again... few people were.

"Wait. Aren't you... *Casper*, right? Like the ghost?"

Todd Brown. A bully even worse than Gunner. Back in high school the fact that he was a year older than the rest of his hyena pack had made him their informal leader, and it seemed he hadn't turned into a decent human being since.

Clenching his jaw, Caspian stuffed the T-shirt back into his backpack. "I see you really want this space to yourselves. I won't disturb you."

"Wait. We're not done here," Todd said and pushed Caspian at the locker so hard all of his survival instincts kicked in and... he froze, like a rabbit facing three wolves with nowhere to run.

He was sixteen again, small and weak. Defenseless against a pack of predators who didn't care about his valuable skills, or the fact that lots of people loved him. Civilization might have moved forward since the Stone Age, but those troglodytes hadn't gotten the memo.

Gunner laughed, leaning against the wall as if he were trying to lure Caspian in, not intimidate him. "What are you even doing here, shrimp?"

Bud rested against the door, as if to make sure Caspian understood he wasn't going anywhere until they allowed it. "I don't think it's fair that you got to see Gunner's dick, but we didn't see yours."

Caspian's head hurt where it had hit the locker, and he squeezed the backpack to his chest, as if it could stop his heart from going frantic. "I learned my lesson, all right? I'll just go—"

He tried to take a step toward the door, but Bud and Todd grabbed his arms and pushed him right back, as if they'd agreed on it telepathically.

He should have screamed then, called for assistance, but when he tried to rip his arms out of their grip and found out their hands were like shackles, his voice just wouldn't come out, leaving him vulnerable to whatever was to happen next.

Gunner groaned. "I really don't need to see his dick. Just kick him out."

Todd faced him with a scowl. "Stop being such a fucking spoilsport."

"Take off his pants, Gun. Let's see what this faggot has to offer." Bud laughed.

"No—" Caspian tried, but his voice came out tiny, like the squeak of a mouse. This was his nightmare come alive. The price he'd be paying for wanting to better himself. Who had he been kidding? He didn't belong here.

Unable to get away from the grip of sweaty hands, he shut his eyes and waited, listening to the slow clap of Gunner's flip flops. He couldn't think. Couldn't breathe. He wished he could leave his body and not have to go through this humiliation. But it was no use.

When big hands pulled on his pants and unceremoniously slid them down to his thighs along with his underwear, the seconds of endless silence were somehow even worse than the burst of laughter that followed. It meant that while they hadn't expected him to be big, they were stunned at just how small his cock was.

Bud was the first to voice it. "My thumb is longer than that."

Gunner backed off, and when Caspian dared to have a peek at the room, desperate for a way out, he saw that his tormentor was glaring at his crotch in silence. It was hard to say whether Gunner was about to kick someone's teeth out, or if this was his neutral expression.

Todd tut-tutted in mockery. "Dunno. About what I expected. Guess his ass gets all the action anyway."

Caspian shivered. He didn't know whether it was out of fear, anger, or disgust, but the cause didn't matter either, because he could do nothing against such brute strength. People like those guys deserved to die. They did not belong in society. They should be fucking shot or shipped off to some deserted island where they'd fight for dominance among themselves without bothering decent people.

If only he had Gunner's physique, he'd have broken all their noses and teeth, but he was nothing like Gunner. Small, frail, and weak, with a cock those gorillas felt nothing but contempt for, he was a sad excuse for a male.

Angry and proud, but with no physical presence to back it up. A top without the kind of tool his potential partner wanted.

"Get lost," Todd said, hauling Caspian forward hard enough that he smashed into Gunner with his pants still pooled at his ankles. The mountain of muscle didn't even budge, still damp from the shower and mocking him with the size of his pecs.

Caspian croaked an unnecessary goodbye and shuffled forward, stunned like a pig before slaughter. Heat ate him up as he continued toward the exit because he was too afraid to bend over and pull up his bottoms with those three watching.

A friend had once told him there was nothing to be afraid of. That everyone did their own thing at the gym, and nobody would pay any mind to the size of his body, but clearly that wasn't the case. Not in Grit, Ohio, where high school bullies never grew out of their shitty personas.

He was able to breathe again once he stepped between the two sets of doors dividing the locker room from the reception area and only then pulled up his pants.

He would never come back here.

Worse yet, he needed to leave town. He could never face Gunner, Todd, or Bud again after this.

He went outside, struggling for air when his windpipe suddenly became tighter, but he couldn't break down in front of all the strangers enjoying their favorite pastime. He didn't want them to hold back laughter and pat him on the back. He didn't want to answer any questions or lie to reassure them that nothing was wrong. And besides, the three brutes might come out any moment and tell everyone what happened.

And then, he'd *die*.

Like a zombie on the lookout for fresh meat, Caspian staggered along the building, far from the bright glow of the lamps. By the time he scooted down and leaned against the rough wall that smelled of piss, his body was warning him of impending doom, but this wasn't the first time he'd been close to a panic attack, so he tried to focus and breathed in.

Then out.

Breathed in.

Then out.

The rattle of metal startled him so much he opened his eyes wide and instinctively held his arm up for protection.

But while he'd expected a punch, a long, warm tongue licked his elbow instead, and a dog with an uncanny resemblance to a dingo stared at him with its ears up.

The rattle had been made by a shopping cart pushed by an elderly woman with a shock of pink hair tangled up on her head like a neon pretzel.

"Mad Madge," Caspian said, naming the town's most known eccentric without thinking. When the horror of what he'd just done occurred to him, he shot to his feet, the panic attack replaced by yet more shame. "I'm *so* sorry. I didn't mean to say that. I thought you were... someone else," he finished, staring at the large, round blots of rouge coloring her cheeks. They were dark enough to stand out against her skin even in the dark.

"Oh, yes, my sister, she's a right old wacko," Madge laughed and adjusted the glittery, heart-shaped glasses that were part of her unforgettable look. She rattled her cart closer and presented Caspian with a jar. "Can you help open it for me, sweetheart?"

That was it. The universe was mocking him.

But it wasn't like he could refuse help to an older lady, whom he'd called mad to her face. So he tightened his hands on the jar and tried to twist off the lid. To no avail.

He really was a loser.

A sob left his lips, and he pulled the glass container to his chest, unable to keep tears in once they started flowing. He gave up and sank to his knees.

The dog barked, and when it stepped closer to lick Caspian's face, he didn't fight it. He couldn't believe what had happened to him at the gym, and worst of all, that no matter how much he hated Gunner for what he'd done, admiration remained so tightly entangled with the disgust he felt.

Caspian didn't have a crush on the bastard. He didn't want to fuck him. He wanted to *be* him.

"Oh, honey... there's no point crying over a jar of moonshine. Here, maybe this one will be easier to open," Madge said and struggled with another container. She didn't even bother to give it to him this time, surely afraid he'd fail again.

The dog was licking Caspian's hands now, its whining like a lullaby to calm Caspian and stop him from embarrassing himself further.

"There. Have a sip. It'll do you some good," Madge said and handed him the open jar. The smell of the liquid inside made it obvious that this was homemade booze, produced with no certification whatsoever, but Caspian let it burn his throat as he imagined a life in Gunner Russo's body.

He'd be strong.

He'd be fuckable.

He'd get to decide his own fate.

Gunner had no idea how lucky he'd been to be born in that skin.

Chapter 2 - Caspian

Caspian's back clicked as he rolled under the covers, trying to amend the discomfort caused by the uneven mattress. The pull in his spine made him settle in a horizontal position, but between sunlight shining straight into his face and his butt sinking deep into the bed, the need to sleep soon became irrelevant.

He grunted with displeasure and threw his arms to the sides, scowling when he realized that the bedding was made with some kind of satin.

Had he hooked up with someone?

Impossible. That wasn't his *thing*. He wouldn't have bothered going to someone's place for a blowjob, and as much as he wanted to try anal, he would have liked to at least remember doing it for the first time. Had he really drank that much last night? He vaguely remembered getting back home, so why was he… here? And where was *here* anyway?

He sat up, alerted by a loud meow.

"Get up, Gun!" a female voice hollered as Caspian took in his surroundings, from the satin sheets sliding against his skin, to the sharp smell of bleach coming from not far away.

He was sitting in a small double bed by a curtained window of what had to be a trailer. There was only so much space beyond the reach of the mattress, and he froze, realizing that whoever he ended up in bed with had a woman living with him. *Shit.*

He looked around the pale walls and built-in cupboards covered with pictures of cars and chiseled, sweaty men staring at Caspian from behind boxing gloves. But as he moved to the narrow space at the foot of the bed, frantically searching for his clothes, the door opened, and a woman stepped in, folding her arms under a pair of large breasts that were about to pop out of her orange tube top.

She wore tiny denim shorts with white pockets sticking out at the front of her thighs like twin flags, and jewelry in a bright shade of gold that contrasted with the duskiness of her tan.

But just as Caspian stilled, readying himself for an onslaught of questions and fists, the woman offered him a bright smile and applied some lip balm to her plump mouth before dropping her pert behind in his lap.

"Good morning, McDreamy. Where did you hide your wallet?"

Caspian froze, raising his arms to avoid touching her by accident. "I... what?" He unexpectedly hit the wall, as if the space was closing in on him. How small was this place for him to feel like it was a trailer for dolls? He stalled with his lips parted, staring up at the arms that both were and weren't his.

Thick. Inked. Tanned and covered with dark hair. He wiggled the tattooed knuckles for good measure, and even though the hand was most definitely not his, it moved as expected.

"Your wallet, big man. I need to get some food for Fluffer and do some other shopping too." The woman smiled, and when she leaned in, Caspian could smell her fresh, minty breath. He froze when her breast, so big for her tiny frame, pressed against his shoulder, in a bid to distract him and make him do what she wanted. She hadn't taken into account that he might not have the slightest interest in what she offered.

Caspian's brain pulsed with unease when he looked down at thick, hairy thighs that weren't even close to his own slim legs. He needed a moment. He needed air and space. And maybe some water, because he'd clearly taken or eaten something he shouldn't have.

"I'm not giving you anything. I just woke up, and I need time. Okay?"

She frowned at him as if that was the last thing she expected to hear. "Rude! You can try sucking your own dick then." She rubbed her ass against his crotch for emphasis before jumping off his lap.

"I'll just find someone who doesn't want my money for it," Caspian snapped and shot up, dropping when his head smashed into the ceiling.

She frowned and reached up to pat his pec.

Reached *up*. For his pec.

"Um, honey pie? You sure you're okay? I know you can be a grump when you're hungry..."

Something was wrong about his size perception. The trailer was either tiny, or he had become a giant.

"*Honey*? What? I don't know you. Is this some kind of scam? Because if it is, it's not working," Caspian said, gently pushing her aside as he lowered his head to avoid hitting his forehead against the doorframe. Even out of the room, his head brushed the ceiling unless he hunched over, making his neck cry out with discomfort.

"Oh, my God, Gun! You're using again! I thought you said you never touched smack after getting your face tattooed." She took a deep breath and stepped back, rubbing away an imaginary tear. "I can't deal with you when you're like this. I'll be back later. Feed Fluffer."

"Fluffer?"

But she pushed past him and ran down a corridor that was almost too narrow even for her, toward a larger space at the end. Assaulted by sunlight streaming through a small window to his side, Caspian followed her past an open bathroom, which reeked of sewage and fruity deodorant, but before he could have reached the woman's side, she grabbed a pink handbag, glared at him, and let herself out.

"I expect you to be sober when I come back!"

He took a deep breath but gave up on arguing with her when he faced a kitchen area cluttered with dirty dishes, boxes, and multipacks of canned food. Beyond the counter that divided the kitchen from the living area was a stretch of old dark red carpeting and at the very end—a booth of sorts, with a gray sofa wrapped around a table, and a recliner that faced a TV hanging below the ceiling.

He'd never been this confused in his life. Not even when he'd had a concussion back in high school. He ran his large fingers over a photo stuck to the fridge with sellotape. It featured none other than Gunner Russo standing next to the woman who had just harassed him. In the picture, Gunner embraced her with one arm and showed off knuckles tattooed with a random assortment of letters that looked suspiciously like the ink on Caspian's hands.

Could... was it possible that—?

He spun around and faced Gunner. With eyes still puffy from sleep, scruffy cheeks, and short, messy hair, he wasn't nearly as threatening as he'd been the night before, but Caspian stepped back nevertheless, hitting the counter at the same moment as Gunner. Two mouths opened, but only one made a sound.

Caspian was facing a mirror, and the low, husky voice he'd spoken with to the woman was not his own.

His heart beat faster, its echo drumming in his ears, but he wouldn't blink, too shocked by what he was seeing. He ran his fingers over the ink covering half his face in an outline of a toothy animal skull. Was he to believe that his consciousness had somehow taken over the body of Gunner Russo overnight? Just like that? What kind of fucked-up dream was this? No wonder everything around him was small when he was a six-foot-five giant with arms like branches of an old oak and legs like tree trunks. Even his hands were massive, as were his feet—

Caspian pulled on the waistband of his boxers, and yep, his cock was a beast to be reckoned with too. Long. Thick. Powerful.

A flush climbed up his neck by the time he looked up again, facing the handsome brute who'd turned his time at school into a nightmare and had humiliated him last night. Oh, how easy his life would have been if this weren't only some strange dream that felt deceptively real. With a body like this, he could achieve *anything*.

He exhaled and faced the kitchen when his stomach grumbled, twisting with unfamiliar intensity. If this was a lucid dream, could he imagine a cute twink sitting on the counter and fuck him with the massive tool that was temporarily his?

Caspian lowered the boxer shorts, exhaling as the fat dong twitched, getting harder when he imagined his favorite singer sprawled in front of him and already pushing down his skinny jeans with a flush on his angular face.

Caspian exhaled and touched the table to make room on it, but something dark dashed from behind a plate at speed and sent him crashing back into cupboards.

"Was that a fucking cockroach?" he uttered, as if there was anyone here to answer that question.

Another, and then its whole family, rushed across the floor next. Caspian let out a squeal and jumped onto the sofa with his dick swinging between his legs. It might not have been dignified, but he didn't care, since no one was watching.

Something sharp hid between the cushions, and he stepped right fucking on it! A short examination revealed that it was the lid of a can, not a used needle, so he exhaled with relief and bent down, pulling his shorts back up. At least the dining table was clean, or rather cleared, because the dark circular stains left on the white surface weren't going anywhere. He rested his forehead against it, trying to breathe.

This wasn't right. He didn't know what day it was, or how he'd gotten here. Gray sweatpants rested on the sofa next to him, and he put them on after shaking them over the floor, to make sure no bugs hid between the folds of fabric.

Maybe he'd consumed some hallucinogenic drugs by accident?

The dark form of a smartphone resting next to a butt-shaped dip in the seat drew him in, and he picked it up, swiping his thumb across the cracked screen. The phone asked for his PIN, so he entered it, but the damn thing claimed it was incorrect.

Of course. Because it wasn't *his* phone. His was a brand new iPhone in a wooden case while the piece of junk in his hand didn't even have a logo anywhere.

Caspian's stomach growled, distracting him from the task at hand, and all of a sudden, he was not only still horny, but also *ravenous*.

His gaze swiped across the messy kitchen counter, but while there were no roaches in sight, he was barefoot. What if he stepped on one, and it wiggled under his sole? Or worse yet, what if its exoskeleton broke under his weight, and he'd end up covered with not only its juices, but also the eggs it carried?

Revulsion shook Caspian's entire body, but his stomach twisted again, and his brain buzzed with annoyance as he caught sight of an open cupboard and the bread stashed inside.

He hated white bread and its bland cotton-like flavor, but in this moment he'd gladly drench all the slices within sight with bacon grease, and then douse his thirst with a protein shake.

A ball of white fluff leapt between the crumpled paper bags on the counter and opened its flat face in a wild meow.

It seemed Fluffer hated roaches as much as Caspian and—

Caspian scowled. Who named their cat after sex workers preparing porn actors for a scene? Had names like *Fluffy* or *Snowflake* been taken?

The cat meowed again, then got down to the floor and circled its empty bowl before releasing a brutal sneeze that sprayed snot over the steel trash can next to his food. Caspian stilled, wondering where he could find some tissues, because yet more of the clear goo glistened under the pet's nose.

"I'm hungry too. I'll be with you in a sec," Caspian said. His voice was... sexy. He could work as a fucking sex phone operator with a voice this raspy and low, so unlike the sounds his own body produced.

But before he could have devised a strategy of protecting himself from roaches, someone banged on the door, making him still. Maybe the girl was back in an even more revealing outfit? Caspian was fine giving her Russo's money as long as she agreed to make him some food.

After a brief scan of the floor, he found it bug-free and strode to the door held shut by the kind of flimsy lock a petty criminal could have opened with a credit card.

A bit of plywood fell to the floor as he tugged on the handle, but it wasn't his shitty trailer, so he ignored it and stuck his head out into the sun.

The air smelled of eggs, bacon, and gasoline, but as he set his bare feet in the sparse grass outside, a large silhouette in a brown suit caught his eye. A man in his early fifties, with a pot belly stretching the front of his striped shirt, stepped closer, combing back his graying hair over and over, as if he couldn't get a leaf out of the short strands.

"Russo! How are you this fine morning?" the stranger asked, pulling close a folder, which crooked his tie to one side. The pale stubble peppered over the man's cheeks made the pinkness of his skin appear brighter, and his eyes wouldn't stop darting around, as if he'd drank several cups of coffee since he'd rolled out of bed.

"Good morning," Caspian said, unsure how he should act. This stranger had come here for a reason, but his appearance revealed few clues as to his identity. The man straightened up, as if surprised by Caspian's mundane answer.

"I'm happy to hear that. Let's make this quick then." He smiled and held out his hand.

Caspian squeezed it in greeting, but it earned him a frown.

"Russo. Stop fucking with me. I don't have time for this. Give me the money, and I'll be out of your hair. Surely, you don't want any trouble."

Money?

Was this scruffy guy some kind of debt-collector?

Caspian's stomach rumbled. "Oh... was it today? I must have confused the dates. I'm sorry," he said, because at this point he didn't know where Gunner's wallet was, and if *he* lived with a money sponge like that girlfriend of Gunner's, he'd have hidden a large sum where she wouldn't find it. Even a meathead would have taken precautions against robbery.

"Seriously? You think that kind of shit will fly?" The man shook his head. "It's five hundred tomorrow, or we'll be looking at higher interest rates," he said as if he were a hedge fund manager, not some lowlife in an ill-fitting polyester suit. "And with the amount you owe us, Russo, you don't wanna go there."

The hell?

Then again, it wasn't his problem what kind of trouble Gunner's stupidity had gotten him into. Gambling? Drugs? None of Caspian's business. Though the scent of cigarettes wafting from the debt collector did make his lip twitch with an urge he'd never felt before. Almost as if he... wanted to fill his lungs with calmingly warm smoke. But he would not do that, because it was a disgusting habit!

"Sorry. Should I expect you tomorrow *circa* nine?"

The man nodded, the frown on his face deepening. "Yeah. 'Circa' nine, Russo." He walked off, shaking his head.

A loud bark made Caspian glance over the shoulder, and only then did he realize Gunner's unsightly home was at the very edge of the vast trailer park, because the mesh fence and trees were just behind the nearest mobile home.

An orange dog sat in the middle of a cluttered lawn, between a pink flamingo that had long lost its bright color, and a garden gnome that missed half of its hat. When Caspian looked beyond the animal's curious ears, he saw no one other than Mad Madge sitting on the steps to the old trailer with a mug of coffee between her bony fingers.

"Hey there, honey!" She waved at him and smiled. "Will your brother walk Dingo for me tomorrow?"

"My brother?" Caspian asked before he could have bitten his tongue. Mad Madge wore a lush pink dress, and purple leggings paired with denim trainers. She didn't pick up on Caspian's blunder and exhaled, taking another sip of her warm beverage.

"Dingo really likes Noah. And I think walking the dog does him a lot of good too. Way more important than rehabilitation, if you ask me."

It seemed both brothers were bad eggs then.

"Sure... yes, I think he will," Caspian said, retreating to his trailer, but he didn't get to dive into the dingy old box. A strong hand fell on his shoulder and squeezed.

Caspian was out of patience at this point, but when he realized it was Todd Brown, he yelped in a pitch so high the menace actually stepped back with his eyebrows raised high.

"What's up with you, Gun? Did the Snowman scare you?" he asked, looking back at another man, whom Caspian also recognized as a member of Gunner's high school gang. Todd's younger brother, Ralph, had fiery hair and a long scar along the whole of his grim face, but he'd doubled in size since teenagehood, and his chest muscles and biceps threatened to rip open the flimsy T-shirt he wore.

Caspian stepped back, his stomach twisting as if Todd had stuffed his big hand through his navel and pulled at his guts. The horrible moment from last night came back, crashing into Caspian like a bottle smashed on the side of his head. He could feel hands holding him in place as his pants were yanked down. And then, silence. Mocking laughter.

Maybe this lucid dream was his chance to get back at them? In Gunner's body, he was taller than either of these bastards and just as big—no longer a tiny twerp, helpless at their feet, but a man who could smash his fist into Todd Brown's face so hard the creep could never again claim to be the *ginger Casanova*.

As he simmered in his fury, Ralph cocked his head, drawing more of Caspian's attention to the hairs growing between his thick eyebrows. "I texted you, Gunner. Did you get my message?"

Caspian took his phone out and put in the PIN number—the PIN number! It wasn't stored in his memory, but his fingers knew it, and the cracked screen revealed the picture of a boxing champion set as the desktop image. And over it, alongside information about a new message was today's date. Only one day had passed since Caspian's unfortunate gym visit.

"I haven't read it yet. My girl kept me busy all morning," he improvised, and the lie made both brothers grin.

"Fair enough. Just don't be like him and get tied down with three screaming brats," Todd said, and Ralph slapped him on the head.

"The meathead's just jealous my Trinny is fertile like a well-plowed field."

No.

Jesus Christ.

Caspian laughed with the two men, wondering what indecent comment he was expected to make.

You just make sure your plow is the only one digging into that fertile ground?

No. That didn't seem like the right thing to say at all. So he opened the message instead while the two brothers teased one another.

[*We comin to talk about the THING*] was all the text said, and Caspian couldn't help but feel the message not only didn't bring anything to the table, but was redundant altogether.

"So... the *thing*?" he urged when the brothers stopped bickering for a second.

Todd's face got more serious, and he nodded. "We move the drugs tomorrow. I know you need the money, so be there."

No more cryptology then.

Sweat beaded on Caspian's neck. "Oh. And the drugs are so heavy that I'm required...?"

Ralph regarded him with a scowl, but Todd laughed out loud.

"Always the joker, eh?" he said. "Dumbass. We need more muscle, just in case."

In case... what? But Caspian kept the confusion to himself this time. His gaze wandered to the cracked screen again, then to the bulge at the front of his pants, to the strong, tattooed abs, and as Todd muttered something in his low, rumbly voice, the words Bud had said to the real Caspian last night came right back.

My thumb's longer than his dick!

Caspian's head pulsed, and his hand trembled around the smartphone. The things he could do with Gunner's body and the right app... Nobody would ever dare mock Gunner Russo's size. And nobody would ever complain about the length of his dick.

But no matter how much his knuckles itched, he nodded, unwilling to get hurt over nothing when he could be downloading Grindr. "I'll be there," he said to end this worthless conversation. "See you later, gotta go to work."

Ralph blinked several times. "You got a job?"

Of course scum like Russo would be unemployed.

"Something like that," Caspian mumbled and rushed back to the trailer with his finger tapping the screen every now and then so he wouldn't have to guess the PIN again.

But as he shut the door behind him and opened the app store, a new thought appeared in his mind, inflating to a point where both hunger and lust diminished.

If he was in Gunner Russo's body, then where was Gunner?

Chapter 3 - Gunner

Gunner couldn't remember ever sleeping this soundly. Instead of the tap of cockroach legs marching over packets of chips, he could hear birds tweeting outside, and Sandy must have done the laundry for once, because the fresh scent of cotton lulled him into keeping his eyes shut for a bit longer.

He was also *alone*. Sandy didn't bother him. Fluffer wasn't meowing for food. No one knocked at his door. He actually enjoyed the furball cuddling up to him in the morning, but it was nice to just enjoy a bit of peace. The one thing that could make this morning better would be the sound of a piano, but he didn't feel like getting up to attach earbuds to his phone. He stretched and was surprised when neither his knuckles nor toes reached the walls.

But what made him open his eyes was the scent of pancakes coming from somewhere farther away, because it could only mean Sandy had done something so terrible it warranted a cooked breakfast to appease him. What was it this time? Had she stolen his credit card and maxed it out? Gunner was already knee-deep in shit, since he'd only managed to gather half the money he owed Snowman this week. His nerves became tight strings, and he sat up, ready to face another shitty day.

Instead of the formerly-white cupboards at the footboard of his bed, he saw flat concrete blocks attached to the opposite wall and windows hidden behind long black curtains reaching all the way from the ceiling to the floor.

It was bright enough outside that the light peeking in around the dense fabric revealed a large television hung across from the bed, with display cabinets on one side and shelves full of DVDs on the other. Under the screen was a modern-looking media unit boasting at least two game consoles along with some more tech. As Gunner took in the room larger than his entire trailer, he noticed a fitted wardrobe taking up the entirety of the side wall, and above the wooden headboard—a massive painting depicting a sports car racing on a white background.

Where the hell was he, and who had he cheated on Sandy with last night?

He rolled out of bed, already dreading that he might bump into the woman's husband or boyfriend, but the longer he took in the interior, the more confused he got. Nothing about the space could be considered even remotely feminine.

The lump in Gunner's throat obstructed his airways when he considered that he might have gotten drunk enough to drive to another town and somehow hook up with a man.

And didn't remember it.

He opened the curtains in an effort to get in more light and make the search for last night's clothes a bit easier, but he froze when his gaze fell on the long, slim fingers of his hand.

His tattoos were gone, and the dense dark hair covering his forearms had been replaced by a sparse dusting, barely visible on pale, smooth skin. A garden extended beyond the window with a green lawn while across the street, a house straight out of affluent suburbia blinded him with its white walls and shiny golden gate

But his whereabouts no longer mattered, even though the wooden floor felt so clean and pleasant under his bare feet.

Struggling to find breath and increasingly agitated, he pressed his palms to his face to find it without a hint of stubble. His lips were narrow yet soft and plump. His small nose had a cute upturned tip. Even his hair was the wrong length and would have been so easy to grab, unlike the short crop he sported.

Something was wrong.

Terribly wrong.

He ran over to the wardrobe because that would be the logical place to keep a mirror. He swung open its door and—

Gunner screamed, because no other course of action would do at the sight in front of him. Caspian Brady stared back at him from the mirror, dressed in a gray pajama set worthy of a middle-aged man, and with his mid-length brown hair still messy from sleep. He was the perfect little twink, with smooth limbs and big blue eyes that shone like the Swarovski crystal pendant Gunner had gotten Sandy for Christmas when things had still worked between them. Breathless, Gunner leaned in, enchanted by the smooth texture of the skin on Caspian's cheeks, which made him look way under his real age of twenty-three.

Did Caspian have to shave in order to achieve this boyish radiance, with rosy lips opening above a chin that had the faintest dip in the middle? When Gunner tested a smile, his fake grin turned real at the sight of adorable dimples. Whatever this messed-up dream was, he wasn't in a hurry to wake up, so he stood still, captivated by his reflection.

As one of the smallest guys Gunner had ever met since his teens, Caspian was a source of fascination, and even though Gunner hated himself a little for what he'd gone along with at the gym, he'd have lied if he claimed he hadn't been a little bit curious of the dick that went with the smooth twinky body.

With the stupidly cute grin still on his face, Gunner pushed down the pajama pants and bit his lip when he revealed the lovely pink cock he'd now get to ogle at his leisure. He was getting horny just thinking about being the one *inside* this body. Even Caspian's—*his* balls were fuzzy like two tiny peaches.

He turned around to get a peek at his buttocks, and his ears went aflame when he pondered whether the rumors about Caspian were true. Did he really fuck around with men? Did he let them use this pert, hairless ass? Gunner pulled on one of the butt cheeks, and his brain stalled at all the things he could do in Caspian's life. No one would expect him to make tough decisions, fight for dominance, or always make the first move. He was the prey. The temptation. A single wink of his jewel-like eyes would send guys into a frenzy and make them dream of pinning him down with their cocks.

A hot shiver shot up his spine, and his prick twitched as a ghost of hot breath made the baby hair at the back of his neck rise.

A sharp knock on the door froze him to the floor. He frantically adjusted his pajama pants, but with the cock already up and interested in Gunner's secret fantasies, he made a dash for the bed and rolled into it to cover his crotch with the checkered comforter in the most boring navy shade of all.

"Yes?"

Oh, even his voice was perfect. Smooth and sweet like the expensive milk chocolate he'd once gotten for his birthday from Mr. and Mrs. Wagner.

But he didn't get to focus on how it sounded, because the door opened, revealing a short man with graying hair cut in a tidy style. He wore slacks and a dress shirt, with the tie tucked between the buttons at the front, and as Gunner looked on, the resemblance between Caspian and the stranger was impossible to overlook.

"Morning, son! Your mother wants you at the breakfast table, so get up *pronto*," Caspian's father said with a wide smile that revealed that he also had dimples. He tapped both his hands against the doorframe, as if suggesting that he wasn't moving without his son.

Gunner shifted under the covers, relieved that his boner was going down. "Oh-okay... I'll be right with you," he mumbled.

"It's not like you to sleep in like this. But I guess last night was out of the ordinary. Right?" The man raised his eyebrows expectantly, prompting Gunner to nod.

He had no idea what the fuck he'd done last night—or had it been Caspian?—to end up here, but it must have been 'out of the ordinary' for sure.

"Don't be long. Pancakes will cure your hangover."

Gunner watched Caspian's father disappear behind the door and then sat up in stunned silence. He was piecing together that Caspian must have come home drunk. His father knew of it, but hadn't yelled at him. And Caspian's mother was making him pancakes, because they presumed he wasn't feeling too fresh.

No wonder Caspian was such an entitled little prick when he'd grown up with two loving parents, abundant food, money, and a TV larger than Gunner's bedroom window. All this was so very unlike the childhood filled with yelling and violence Gunner had endured.

Whether this was a dream or not, Gunner would be taking advantage of it for as long as it lasted. He would have started off by finding out how much spunk that cute dick produced if it wasn't for the fact that Dad might come back if he didn't hurry.

He got out of bed, found black slippers that fit Caspian's small feet perfectly, and peeked into a hallway that intimidated him with its elegance. Stretching endlessly from the window by Caspian's door, it belonged in one of the grand, old-fashioned houses featured in every meet-the-parents movie. The wooden floor had no scratches in sight, and fresh flowers in a vase on a side table perfumed the air.

As he made himself move along the two rows of doors, his gaze locked on picture frames hung on the way to the staircase. Some featured larger family gatherings, but most were only of Caspian, his dad, and a plump blonde woman, who was surely Caspian's mother. Images from a happy childhood flashed in front of Gunner's eyes like stills from a cartoon that didn't reflect his own reality.

Caspian and his parents sitting by the Christmas tree in matching pajamas and surrounded by piles of gifts. On a trip to Disney World. Making s'mores by a campfire. A graduation photo with proud Mom and Dad.

Gunner didn't get to finish high school, but now that he looked at Caspian's adorable pout he almost wished he'd been there just to watch Caspian receive his diploma.

"Caspian! Come on! We're leaving for work soon!" A female voice resounded from below, so he peeled his gaze away from the life he could never dream of having, and padded down the stairs that were wider than his bathroom.

The stairs spat him out into a large hallway featuring a massive mirror in a wooden frame carved into a complex tangle of fruit and leaves, but the scent of pancakes drew him straight to the kitchen, which looked suspiciously similar to the one in a suburban villa he'd broke into with the guys two months prior.

"Good morning, mother," he said, but when her brows rose, he figured this wasn't the way Caspian would address her. "I mean, *Mom*." Maybe silence was the key until he got his bearings.

Three pendant lamps hung above a massive kitchen island with shelves full of cookbooks on one end and a row of four bar stools standing along the outer edge. The dominant color of the cupboards was a pristine shade of white, but the warm hue of the wooden floor, and the little herb garden set up on shelves by the window made it cozy despite the restaurant-sized cooker and an equally large hood above.

"Go on now, sit. I made you coffee," Caspian's mom said, adjusting the pink apron that protected her neat blue dress as she flipped one of the pancakes with a spatula. Even while cooking, she was the epitome of understated elegance with makeup that was barely visible and hair styled into a roll at the back of her head. She couldn't have looked more different from the women in Gunner's life.

After a moment of hesitation, he took the seat next to his new father, still dazed by the unfamiliarity of it all. This strange morning had to be part of some odd dream, even if it didn't *feel* like one, but he could go with it. Especially since fresh pancakes were on the menu.

Several bowls of toppings to choose from stood in front of them next to chocolate, caramel, and strawberry syrups. And it wasn't cheap shit either. Each product had the kind of classy branding that would have told Gunner he couldn't afford it without the need to check the price.

"Must have been a rowdy party with your friends last night," Fake Mom said and even winked at him as if they were in on the same joke. "Don't make that face. I work in event planning, honey. I see things."

Gunner stared at the selection of fruit, sprinkles and sauces he could add to the pancake Fake Mom put on his plate, and wondered if this was how Caspian ate each day. Since for some inexplicable reason Gunner got to experience this breakfast, he'd enjoy himself and forget that cereal or sandwiches purchased at the gas station were his usual morning fare.

He topped the pancake with bananas, chocolate chips, and strawberry jam with huge chunks of fruit, then finished his edible artwork with a dollop of whipped cream and caramel before digging in.

Fake Dad laughed. "Someone's got an appetite for once."

Gunner stalled with his mouth full. This couldn't be how they worked out he was an impostor, could it? But Fake Dad went on.

"We're happy to have you back, and I'm sure it will take you a few days to settle in, but consider looking at the courses we talked about. They're the sensible next step now that you have your degree, and you'll be able to do them while gaining experience at the firm."

Oh, so this wasn't a normal breakfast after all.

Gunner swallowed and was more careful with the next bit he cut, because Caspian surely didn't gorge on food like a pig. "I'd have to consider how much they cost first," he uttered, but Fake Mom gave a little chuckle and dug into a pancake of her own on the other side of the counter.

"Nonsense, honey. You know we'll help you. You need to keep studying if you want to be successful in the future."

Which in this case clearly meant they'd pay for the course. Caspian had been born into a golden cradle! The proposition was overwhelming, and while this wasn't *his* life, and those nice people weren't *his* parents, he offered them a smile and continued eating dainty pieces of the dessert-breakfast as his mind entertained what his life could have been if he hadn't been born to Leo Russo of the Rabid Hogs MC and a woman who disappeared from their lives so early Gunner had no recollection of her.

"Of course. I met some of my high school friends at the gym, but today might be the day to read up on the courses." He had no idea what degree Caspian had, but there would be clues to find in his bedroom.

Fake Mom groaned, taking off her apron. "Why would you waste time going to that dirty place when we have machines at home?"

"Or is there some high school sweetheart you left behind, hm?" Fake Dad tapped Gunner with his elbow. "We wouldn't be offended if you brought her here. You're an adult now. Just make sure you give us notice—"

Fake Mom shook her head. "Only if it's serious."

Gunner felt the food rise in his throat from a surge of anxiety. Oh. So Caspian wasn't out. Come to think of it, Caspian might be straight. Nobody had seen him with a guy, and all the rumors started because he was so small, pretty, and quiet. Gunner's dirty mind did the rest, creating a guy who might have very little in common with the real Caspian Brady.

"N-no, there's no girl," he muttered, realizing in frustration that after eating only three pancakes he was so full even the caramel sauce had lost its appeal.

"Better to wait than date the first girl that comes along," Fake Mom said and reached across the counter to pat Gunner's cheek. Maybe he should've been offended by the gesture, but it felt nice to be in someone's care for once, so he smiled back at her and put down his cutlery, so very sated he feared walking might be an issue.

"There's a perfect person for everyone," Fake Dad said and gave his wife a kiss on the cheek.

Gunner rarely met couples who actually got along, and his disastrous on-off relationship with Sandy was just the tip of the iceberg. He hadn't noticed *when* she'd moved in, and didn't know how to get rid of her, because when he got drunk enough, her blowjobs did take the edge off. She was a glimpse of possibility that he might be bisexual not *gay*.

Caspian's family would probably accept him as a gay man, even if it created a bump in their dynamic. Could Gunner hijack this life and start over? His existence would have been as full of joy as his plate had been of carbs.

Fake Dad walked out first, but Fake Mom wasn't far behind and grabbed a pair of nude high heels on the way. "Remember to get your car washed, and practice the piano. *Usus est magister optimus.*"

Gunner nodded slowly, even though he had no idea what language she'd just used, let alone what the expression meant.

"Have a good day, Cas. Put the dishes into the washer, will you?" Fake Dad asked, and moments later Gunner was alone in the huge, beautiful house, staring at a stack of pancakes this new body couldn't fit in.

The silence was disturbed by a bird trilling outside, but it was oh-so-quiet otherwise. No children shouting. No arguments. The cooking enthusiast from the trailer on the left of his wasn't here to disturb his peace with her hand mixer, and Mad Madge wasn't playing her TV too loudly.

Even the constant whizz of the highway was gone.

For once, Gunner was alone with his thoughts.

He knew it would have been best to clean up first, but his stomach might rumble in an hour, so he left everything on the counter, picked up the cooling mug of coffee and headed to the closed door on the side of the kitchen.

It led to a smaller living room decorated in cozy shades of red and furniture in dark mahogany. A big window let in lots of light, and a piano stood by a set of leather armchairs and a matching sofa. A knot formed in Gunner's stomach at the sight of several framed diplomas boasting about Caspian's achievements. Could a person claim brain damage to explain why they couldn't play music anymore?

Gunner hadn't touched a piano since he was twelve, and even then, it had been just for fun. He'd already grown tall, and Dad wanted to groom him into an enforcer at his motorcycle club, so he'd set Gunner up with a boxing trainer. Gunner had expected the same kind of punch-or-be-punched schooling he got at home, but Mr. Wagner had been a different kind of man than Dad and his friends.

The Wagner house hadn't been as grand as the one belonging to Caspian's family, but it was clean and cozy, with a small garden where Gunner got to train most days. Mrs. Wagner filled it with music whenever she had students over, but she played for fun as well and encouraged Gunner to improvise sometimes. The streams and rivulets of classical music would often flow through the open windows when he trained with Mr. Wagner, and it hadn't been love at first note for him at all.

If anything, he'd initially found the music jarring, as if it wasn't meant for him and represented a world where he wasn't welcome. He'd been an angry child, an angry teenager, and hadn't grown into the most well-adjusted adult, but Mr. Wagner had recognized his attitude off the bat and had become a mentor Gunner's dad could never be. He sneakily introduced Gunner to classical music by convincing him he'd be a better boxer if he used it to clear his mind and stay calm under pressure.

Mr. Wagner had taught him to store his fury for the fight and to focus his thoughts on technique instead of unleashing the storm raging inside him at a whim. Gunner never quite mastered those lessons, but he tried his best, and the stillness he experienced when secretly listening to Beethoven or Mozart remained his anchor to this day.

Classical music reminded him of being invited to family dinners with the Wagners, and getting to press keys on the piano to make sounds—because what he did couldn't be called playing. Of meals that didn't come from a microwave or a blender, of getting to play with their cat, and being allowed to decorate cookies, because in the Wagner household it wasn't considered a *woman's job*, but a fun activity for the whole family.

His friends wouldn't have understood his taste in music, so he kept it hidden. But no matter how much he loved the brilliant tone of the piano, he couldn't *play* it.

Still, with no one to watch him, he might as well press some keys before he got inevitably unmasked as a fraud.

The instrument called to him without making a sound, and when Gunner sat in front of it and saw his reflection in the polished oak, memories took him back to a moment when Mrs. Wagner had sat on a cushioned bench alongside him and taught him how to perform a simple duet. His own digits had looked so clumsy in comparison to her long and narrow fingers, but he'd learned to play that melody by heart and had performed it for Mr. Wagner's sister when she came to visit from Florida.

No one ever shouted at him in their home. And he'd never left hungry, as if they knew his father didn't always remember to keep the fridge full. They'd been the best people Gunner had ever met, but they'd moved away when he was only fifteen, and the lifeline they offered had broken.

Still, he was overcome with a sense of nostalgia as he uncovered the keys and put Caspian's graceful fingers on their smooth white surface. He still remembered how to play the C-major scale and smiled when his index finger pressed the keys one by one, making the instrument sing. Its sound wasn't as clear as it ought to be, just off-key, as if it hadn't been tuned in a long time, but the tremor that accompanied each note was almost welcome. Even if Caspian himself were here to play, the music wouldn't have come out perfect. Gunner picked up a thin book of sheet music from a stack that lay on top of the piano, alongside a metronome and a wooden bust of Frederick Chopin, and opened it on the first page.

It was Beethoven's 'Moonlight Sonata', but what he saw below the title wasn't just a meaningless tangle of symbols written into rows of staffs.

When he took in the sheet, the music spoke to him as if it were an alphabet of sounds, as easy to read as a short newspaper article. His heart skipped a beat in reaction to the melody already playing out in his mind, and he put his fingers on the keys without needing to look down. His body knew exactly where to start the soft, melancholic tune, and he didn't need to question the score in front of him.

Then again... he didn't need to *read* the sheet music, because he knew this piece by heart, and the body he occupied could bring it to life. He closed his eyes and tuned into the soft sounds echoing in his heart. A minute later, he stopped thinking at all, and his fingers produced music as refined as the piano players whose recordings Gunner kept in a secret folder on his phone. Even as the pace picked up, challenging his small hands, he didn't make a single mistake, lost in this impossible dream where his whole life was as refined as the music he loved.

Both peaceful and passionate. Removed from grit and grime. Fulfilled, overwhelmingly beautiful. There was nobody to stop him. He had no debt, no tattoo covering his face, and no girlfriend whose company he didn't even enjoy.

In this new world where his fingers glided over the keyboard, he wasn't a hulking brute you sent to make your neighbor give back that toaster they borrowed, but a graceful boy who could openly walk down the street holding his boyfriend's hand. Because no one would question him about it. Being gay wasn't a thing in Gunner's world. But Caspian? He was slender, cute, polite, and played the piano.

Caspian *could* be gay.

As the tune changed, turning into a wild, speedy chase of fingers along the keys, each inhale pulled Gunner higher. Off the chair. Off the ground, as if he were floating up to another dimension while his body stayed behind, as alluring as it was material.

But an erratic *ping* made him drop right back to the bench, and to a reality where Caspian's elegant iPhone called for his attention.

The fog of music hadn't yet settled, but he picked up the device and opened the screen with a swipe of his thumb. The message wasn't meant for *him*, but in this moment it felt like he could steal Caspian's life and remain in this amazing dream forever.

The content of the notification threw him right back to the gutter.

[Let me suck your balls]

He stilled with his cheeks flushed, and stared at the message that didn't sound like something any woman would say to a random stranger. Seconds later, he received a picture of a mouth that most definitely belonged to a male. The young guy in the picture was showing off his tongue, as if begging for something to lick.

Gunner curled his legs and could hardly breathe as he scrolled up the chain of filthy messages on the same app. Caspian went by Chris in all the conversations, and the photos he attached didn't show his compact body but bulging muscles belonging to someone else.

A part of Gunner thought that maybe Caspian had just bought a stolen smartphone, but people who lived in such a massive house had no need for second-hand electronics.

The messages were all Caspian's, and the dirty, dirty things he wrote to a whole array of men who clamored for the attention of the fake person Caspian masqueraded as, had Gunner's body burning.

[I'll bend you over the hood of my car and fuck you so hard I'll have to drive you home.]

[Finger yourself, slut. Open up that hole.]

[I want to see my spunk clinging to that stubble. Are you gonna be my bitch?]

The dissonance between the person he knew and the things Caspian had written to strangers made Gunner's head hurt.

Caspian wanted to be dominant, as hard as it was to imagine. But then again, he was impersonating a different guy, and always avoided meeting guys in person. Was he getting off on the catfishing?

Gunner bit his lip, mesmerized by the filthy nature that apparently hid in this small body.

How many guys had touched it? Did Caspian have sex with a condom or without? Did he kiss his hook-ups? Even though he lived with his parents now and wasn't out, he'd just graduated from university. He'd surely fucked around while he was away. Maybe he even had boyfriends there?

Gunner's frantic search through Caspian's regular text messages found nothing, but he was done reading anyway. He needed to get a better look at Caspian's body now that he was alone.

He sent the piano a kiss before rushing up the stairs with the phone in hand. Could he find a man to fool around with before this madness ended?

He'd never tried searching for someone, but fantasies about strong male hands, broad chests, and cocks with balls full of cum had always lingered at the back of his brain, trying to creep out whenever he got drunk. At times, he imagined himself as this cute twink with long legs, narrow hips, and soft lips, but he could never be that boy, and the idea of looking for men he could have sex with was so illicit he wouldn't dare go through with it. In his world, there was no room for weakness or otherness.

He was big, inked, the son of a biker, and enjoyed boxing.

His massive body might be imposing but not graceful.

His face handsome but not tempting.

Even his cock was of an intimidating size.

But all those things weren't true today. Today, he had this new, perfectly lovable body, and as he pulled off the ugly pajamas to reveal pale, smooth skin in front of the mirror in Caspian's bedroom, the cute, uncut prick responded to the fantasy of a man breaking into this house and finding him like this—naked and vulnerable.

With a face that many *girls* would envy.

He turned around to get a better look at his round butt.

"Anyone want a piece of this?" he whispered, testing his voice. "You have to earn it."

God, even his voice sounded seductive!

He laughed out loud and rearranged his hair. Then rearranged it again. The smooth brown haircut was a bit boring, but Gunner could work with it. He'd seen boys with mid-length hair, who were absolutely stunning. And who knew what the future held? Maybe he'd get enough time to grow it out?

The longer he watched his reflection in the warm rays of the morning sun, the more certain he was that any guy with even the remotest interest in men would be up for the cutie in the mirror. Gunner would shave off the mess of pubes to showcase his cock, and maybe get rid of the leg hair, but if he were to wish upon a star, he couldn't have asked for a nicer form to inhabit.

A sudden urgency twisted his chest, and he took in the open wardrobe, at shelves stacked with boxes and a row of identical drawers. What kind of underwear did Caspian wear? Would it be colorful and fun or sexy, with sheer panels of mesh?

But when he opened the top drawer, it revealed neatly folded pieces of fabric in various combinations of black, brown, navy, and gray. Dirty red was the most daring shade in the collection, and as Gunner picked out a checkered piece, it unfolded into loose boxer shorts that were less inspired than Gunner's own underwear.

This couldn't be all of it. Could it? Caspian surely had something he wore when he intended to have sex.

Annoyed, Gunner pulled the long drawer all the way out and grinned when he found a wad of cash hidden at the very bottom, but his attention was soon drawn to a stack of white undershirts covering an uneven shape. A secret stash of sexy undies Caspian hid from his mom?

But the smile dropped from his mouth the moment he pulled the fabric aside to reveal twin silicone globes.

He wasn't sure what he was looking at for a while, so he pulled the thing out only to stare, stunned, because there was no denying what it was now.

A fake butt.

A silicone, peachy, fake butt.

Squishy to the touch, with a hole for fucking and a set of artificial balls sticking out from between the legs that ended just below the pertest ass. As he breathlessly held the globes open, a crack appeared in the artificial skin, but before he could have gathered his thoughts, the door slammed against the wall, and a cool breeze touched his skin as a dark silhouette towered in the corridor.

A part of Gunner believed for a moment that his home invasion fantasy had come to life the same way the one about a perfect twinky body, a loving family, and playing the piano had, but then the intruder screamed, and his voice sounded familiar enough to shatter his hopes.

Gunner he was face to face with... himself.

Chapter 4 - Caspian

The damn pickup choked again. The transmission needed fixing, and judging by the stale smell in the cab, the air-con needed work too. Caspian couldn't believe even someone as slovenly as Gunner Russo could have neglected his vehicle so badly. The repairs would take money, but clean-up was free. There was no excuse for the crumbs littering the dips in upholstery nor the beer cans and other trash piled up on the floor.

The state of the car made Caspian think of the man himself. Mother Nature had given Gunner the body of a god, yet he'd wrecked it by inking his face, smoking cigarettes—which sadly Caspian now craved—and living in a hovel. The things Caspian could do in life with a body like Gunner's...

And the worst thing was that among all the litter surrounding Caspian wasn't a single snack to stifle the ravenous hunger that not only twisted Caspian's insides but also sat on his skull and squeezed his brain, so he pulled into a gas station the moment he spotted it. The real Gunner could wait while Caspian stuffed his face with junk.

He managed not to hit his head this time and rolled out of the old truck with eyes already set on the Doritos he'd spotted through the shop window. Pulling out the wallet he'd managed to track down once he found the clothes Gunner had worn the previous night, he sped through the automatic doors, his feet carrying him to the snack aisle when he walked straight into someone.

Caspian stepped back, instantly focused on the collision. "I'm so sorry. My mistake."

The other participant, a middle-aged man with a prominent bald spot at the top of his head, stalled at first but then laughed nervously and backed away, raising his hands. "No harm done, I have to pay more attention to where I'm going."

"Have a good day, sir," Caspian said, but before he could have made his way to the blue bag of crispy tortilla goodness, a low laugh made him glance over the shoulder and freeze.

Bud Dorset was approaching him with a wide grin that had meant mockery just last night at the gym. His pot belly stretched the front of the graphic tee with a message too indecent to be worn at work—or anywhere, if Caspian had something to say about it—but the name tag attached to his top meant that he was in fact employed here.

The open can of beer in his hand signified he wasn't fazed by the possibility of being fired.

"You surprised me there, Gun. Thought that bastard would have left trembling, but you seem in a real good mood."

Caspian needed to breathe. This guy might have overpowered him with ease any other time, but today he had access to every weapon in Gunner Russo's arsenal and could use all this strength to his advantage, as if he were wearing a military-grade exoskeleton. There wasn't a person in this town that could have intimidated Gunner, so Caspian should act the part.

"It's my girlfriend. She's a star," he said.

Bud grinned, showing off the unusually white teeth that didn't go with his grey complexion or puffy eyes. "Sandy? I bet her *star's* good and tight."

Caspian spotted the opportunity and he'd grab it. He slapped Bud's forehead hard. No one could blame him for defending his woman's honor, even in this world of degenerates.

"That's my girl you're talking about, asshole!"

When Bud raised his hands and smiled apologetically, Caspian walked off to the aisle of junk food with a spring to his step. He normally had this kind of food on special occasions. But in Gunner's body? He wanted to stuff his face with it. The blue packet of Doritos evoked a visceral feeling in the pit of his stomach, but he also grabbed two chicken sandwiches on the way to the cash registers. He could only hope the pittance in his wallet was enough to pay for the food, because his mind was too scrambled by hunger to count his funds.

He exchanged a few meaningless words with Bud and was off, packing his mouth full of Doritos while he sped away from the trailer park and toward the lovely suburb where he'd grown up. He finished the bag before he reached the right exit but still didn't feel satisfied enough and glanced at the cold sandwiches with longing, even though they likely tasted like salt and cardboard.

He supposed mayonnaise would make up for the flavorless iceberg lettuce isolating the chicken salad from bread, but it wasn't something to eat while driving, so he paced himself and followed the familiar route through a woodland separating the residential area from the highway.

It was only once he drove past the stone marker at the entryway to Wild Oaks that he realized the old pickup with rust peeking out from under its white coat and a sticker of a busty skeleton woman on the window of the passenger's side didn't quite fit the vibe of this neighborhood. Oh, how different this piece of junk was from the vintage Southfield, which Caspian had renovated last summer. The old car was one of only twelve ever made by a genius mechanic dedicated to craft rather than making money, and one of the very few things his friends envied him for. But one couldn't have everything.

He grunted, speeding up on the empty road winding between homes tucked among trees, in hope that none of his parents' neighbors would call the police to report him as a suspicious individual.

His parents should be at work at this time of day, but worry still settled in his chest when the pale walls of their sprawling home emerged from the greenery. He'd have parked in the driveway any other time, but a vehicle like Gunner's was bound to raise eyebrows, so he ended up pulling into a narrow service alley in the bushes behind the house.

He needed to find the dumb gorilla before he stole all of Mom's jewelry!

Getting into the house was a breeze since he knew the entry codes, but what he wasn't prepared for was the smell that hit him the moment he stepped inside.

Pancakes. Fresh, delicious, Mom's pancakes, which she infused with a tiny bit of Bourbon vanilla. He could barely handle three most days, but his hunger knew no bounds in this overgrown body, so despite being here to confront the menace who had taken over his identity, he made a U-turn for the kitchen with saliva already pooling in his mouth.

He narrowly avoided hitting the shoe cupboard with his hip, but the open doorway was what ended up confusing him, because he almost hit his head. Again. He knew this house by heart. He'd grown up here, yet everything seemed different now that he was so much taller and broader in the shoulders. It was as if he'd walked in wearing a muscle suit and with two ladders attached to his legs, but those pancakes? They were familiar despite looking so small from high up.

The chicken salad sandwiches lay forgotten in the dirty truck as he packed cream, sauce, and fruit between two pancakes and ate them that way before chugging milk straight from the bottle. He wished he could have tried them with peanut butter, but because of his allergy, Mom and Dad didn't keep any in the house.

He repeated the process with different pancake-sandwich fillings three times before he was full and sat in the barstool, patting his belly with a blissful smile. His happiness didn't last long though.

Someone was speaking upstairs!

Right.

Gunner.

Who on earth could he be talking to? Judging by the three plates still on the counter, the wolf in sheep's skin had sat with his parents at breakfast, and Caspian cringed at the thought of how that conversation might have gone.

But it didn't matter. He was here to find out what had happened and put an end to this bastard's stay in his home.

The carpet dulled the sound of his steps on the stairs, but he didn't waste a second and headed straight for the end of the corridor in the second floor. Whoever was in Caspian's bedroom with Gunner would fly out of here faster than he could apologize for invading someone else's home!

Caspian pressed on the handle and entered his bedroom, but where he'd expected to find Gunner with a crony of his, already counting money from the things they'd collected since Mom and Dad had left, he saw his own naked form.

But that wasn't the worst of it.

Gunner was holding Twinkie, Caspian's favorite sex toy.

Caspian screamed.

The big blue eyes widened, narrow shoulders stiffened and Gunner dropped Twinkie with a shrill cry.

"W-what are you doing?" Caspian uttered through his choking throat. His gaze settled on the slab of silicone and then wandered up the slim legs, the lean torso, all the way to Gunner's horrified expression.

Gunner's expression. On *his* face.

Caspian could hardly stand this mindfuck.

Gunner wouldn't take his eyes off Caspian even as he grabbed a blanket. "I... I... What is that?!" he demanded, holding the checkered fabric in front of himself with one hand and pointing to Twinkie with the other. "I sure as hell wasn't fucking it!"

Fire burned in Caspian's massive form, and he slammed the door shut, approaching the tiny man, who was both him and *not him* at the same time. "None of your damn business! Who told you to rummage through my stuff, Russo, huh?" he roared and pushed at his chest. There was no resistance to his force, and Gunner dropped on the bed, clutching the blanket to his chest.

So this was how easy he'd been to overpower. He both resented knowing it and revelled in his newfound force. Yesterday at the gym, he'd been so furious, so angry, yet so very helpless and meek. Or so he'd thought, because it seemed he was only now realizing what true anger meant. His whole body buzzed as if he were a human tuning fork, and Gunner—the object hitting it with his sole existence. An unstoppable force raged in him with glee when he noticed the wide-eyed look of *fear*. Like a shark sensing blood in the water, he followed.

"I didn't! How did you do this? And that thing has balls by the way! Are you gay, *Casper*?" Gunner asked with a mean twist to his lips, but his hitched breath and the pitch of his voice told Caspian everything. Gunner could at best be an angry Chihuahua while Caspian had turned into a wolf.

He loved it.

"Why? You afraid of gay cooties, Russo?" he asked with a wide grin and grabbed the slender ankle, pulling Gunner off the bed with a single tug.

It was easy to feel unstoppable being this tall and strong. To a man like Gunner, other people didn't matter.

He didn't have to take their opinions into account, because if someone confronted him, he could beat them into a pulp. Gunner probably bench pressed more than Caspian weighed.

"Who's got a small cock now, huh?" he asked, ripping the blanket off Gunner's naked body.

Understanding flashed through Gunner's eyes, and he covered his crotch in panic. "I didn't say that!" he yelped. Was *this* pathetic squeak really how Caspian sounded?

Either way, the sad excuse of *wasn't-me* wouldn't help Gunner after the torment he'd put Caspian through back in high school.

It was his turn to be afraid, and Caspian pulled him up by the arm. "Yes, I am gay, and I'll enjoy being your gay *alter ego*," he purred, staring straight into the wide-open eyes.

It was funny how different his face looked now that he didn't see it in the mirror but through another pair of eyes. The delicate lines of his jaw were youthful rather than emasculated, and his lips—so plump he kind of wanted to check whether they'd feel different against Gunner's rough fingers. And he could check, because Gunner wouldn't be able to stop him.

"N-no! Don't you dare be gay in my body!" Gunner yelled in the sweet voice that made Caspian increasingly amused. Gunner writhed against him, but even when he punched Caspian's forearm again and again, the force behind it was laughably small and couldn't stop the assault.

For once. For the first time in his life Caspian held all the cards. He shook Gunner for good measure.

"Remember that time you slammed me against the door, and I got a concussion, huh? You grew up so strong, and tall, even though you've done nothing to deserve it, and you used it against all those who were weaker than you. You still do," Caspian growled, and when Gunner tried to hit him again, kicking around with both legs, he pushed him down and squeezed his pale, delicate throat.

Blue eyes opened wide, staring straight at him, and as the naked form under him arched, seeking a way out of the trap of strong arms, a jolt of heat passed through Caspian and left his balls throbbing. He'd hated his old body when he'd lived in it, because it held him back, but it was now impossible to ignore the rosy nipples perking up toward him like raspberries that would release sweet juice if he bit in.

So it was fucked up, but no one needed to know.

It wasn't his fault that his new body was guided by hunger and too much testosterone.

"You've got no idea about me!" Gunner whined and in a bid to free himself, pressed his palm against Caspian's chin.

Caspian roared with laughter and grabbed the slim wrist before pinning it down and leaning over Gunner, whose lips trembled as he looked up, squirming. "Pretty interesting experience to walk a few miles in my shoes, isn't it, Russo?"

His grin might have split his face in half when the big blue eyes glossed over with tears. He refused to see the body under him as his own, and the more he adjusted to the new one, the more he rejected the one he'd been born with, as if it were a transplant from the wrong donor.

His dick might have twitched when a tear slid down the flushed cheek, but... oh well, if that scared Gunner—all the better.

"You're a sick fuck! How did you do this?" Gunner choked out when Caspian loosened his hold on his throat to allow it. Because *he* was in charge. *He* decided who talked and who didn't. Who walked and who got their legs broken.

In this new reality, he had all the assets.

"Me? I didn't do a damn thing. It's you who attacked me for no reason. Maybe there's a God after all, and he's fed up with your shit, Russo!" he uttered, increasingly breathless as Gunner's knee trailed up his inner thigh.

He was so tiny. Compact and defenseless.

Caspian could do anything to him, and Russo would have no way of stopping him.

The teary eyes looked up at him as though they were about to pop out of Gunner's new head. "You're... hard," he whispered, as if afraid to complain more loudly. "Get off me." Gunner must have realized that his position in the food chain had changed, because he was pleading, not demanding. He might be a rabid animal, but he learned fast.

"You're one to talk," Caspian purred, noticing the stiff prick resting against Gunner's flat stomach. Funny. It wasn't that small or *pathetic* when not attached to him.

The blue gaze was off him in an instant, and Gunner covered his crotch with his free hand. "It's your fault! It's *your* gay body!"

Caspian laughed and, at last, let go of Gunner, but he didn't deny himself another glance at all that smooth skin. He'd always been attracted to small guys with cute faces. He just didn't want to be one himself, and now, in some fucked-up fashion, the world had responded to his wishes.

There was no guarantee he'd stay this way, so he wasn't about to waste this opportunity. "Enjoy the soft bed and pancakes. Don't eat anything with nuts. Don't kill my parents, your EpiPen is in the top drawer in the closet," he said, rising to his feet.

Gunner instantly grabbed the blanket and covered himself, as if that could offer any protection if Caspian chose to hurt him. "You can't be serious. We need to do something about *this*."

"I'm good."

Caspian enjoyed the way Gunner stared at him without comprehension before wiping away what was left of the earlier tears.

"Your parents are nice. The pancakes were delicious. The soft bed gave me the best sleep of my life, and I don't even like peanuts. So fuck you sideways." Gunner showed him the finger but the scowl on his face was adorable rather than threatening. "Go deal with *my* life if you think I had it easy."

Caspian stopped smiling the moment he remembered the confrontation from earlier. "Actually, your buddies want me to move drugs. You're seriously worse than I'd thought. I don't believe in drugs!"

Gunner's pink lips twisted into an ugly smile. "You figure it out. Or you won't have anything to eat. Up to you really."

Caspian laughed in his face. "You're what? Twenty-five? And you haven't achieved a thing. A smarter man could milk so much more out of the assets you've been born with!"

That rubbed the smirk off Gunner's face, but he remained still under the blanket, which meant that this morning's lesson must have sank in. Good.

He licked his lips. "And you're supposed to be gay? Your wardrobe sucks ass. I could live your life so much better. You got everything handed to you on a platter." A weak comeback, but what could one expect from the likes of Gunner?

"Oh, really? We shall see what I can turn your miserable existence into with some intelligence and skill."

Gunner got up and walked over to the bedside table with only the bottom part of his legs showing from under the blanket cape. Caspian seriously needed to get laid because even the pink toes were getting him horny. To his disbelief, Gunner pulled out the small wad of emergency cash he kept in the underwear drawer and held it out to him.

"Feed my cat. Pay Snowman. This will get you through two weeks of debt. You pick up the drugs at the Coconut Bar. The password to get to the basement is *air fryer*."

"I will not pay off your debt with my hard-earned savings!" Caspian said the moment the money was in his hands. He couldn't believe this bastard's audacity!

The smug smile spreading on Gunner's youthful face made Caspian want to punch the fucker. "You don't want the fallout, but suit yourself. Do you think I'll just get pancakes for the rest of my life if you go and get yourself killed in my body?"

"How much do you even owe?"

Gunner shrugged. "A hundred grand or so."

Heat burned the back of Caspian's neck. "'Or so'? You don't even know exactly how much? I could just beat the fucker up and be done with it. Why haven't *you* done it?"

Gunner shook his head. "You've got no idea how this works, do you? The Snowman is just the collector. You touch him, and you're dealing with bigger fish. Seriously, just pay the man if you don't want to spend the time you got in my body in a hospital."

The sense of safety Gunner's body had given Caspian was slipping from under his feet. Russo might be fucking with him, but he was correct when it came to one thing—Caspian didn't know how the criminal underworld worked. Not beyond the things one could see in stupid crime shows with holoscreens and instant lab results. And if he was to survive his first clash with it, before he learned his way around, his only choice was to trust Russo's word.

"Fine," he said and spun around, heading off to meet his destiny. His new body might have come with problems, but he'd untangle them all.

"Fine!" Gunner yelled after him. The damn gorilla always needed to have the last word.

Chapter 5 Gunner

Gunner was so tense he expected his tendons to break like threads that had been stretched too thin, and the relief at the sound of the door slamming downstairs was so great he collapsed onto the bed in a state of shock.

His heart still thudded like mad, and even though he'd tried to put up a front, the encounter with a man so aggressive and so much bigger than him left him sitting motionless and unable to calm down. Terrified.

He'd been in some nasty fights since his teenage years, but had forgotten how it felt to be this frightened. No matter how much he'd writhed and kicked, it had done nothing against Caspian when the fucker was armed with Gunner's body. It took him back to being a ten-year-old boy, at the mercy of a father who was not only twice his size but also often came home drunk, or on drugs.

While it was obvious being small had some disadvantages, Gunner hadn't expected it to affect him so viscerally.

And as if being squashed like a bug hadn't been humiliating enough, he'd gotten a boner on top of it all.

If he made his mind blank enough, could he forget that embarrassing moment ever happened?

Not really, because every time he tried to *not* think about it, he saw the scene unravel in explicit detail. Him. In Caspian's body. So small and helpless. Trapped under a man twice his size. A strong, massive hand against his throat. The other holding his wrist down. And a big dick he knew all too well pressing against him through thick denim.

Gunner curled his toes and laid back in the bedding with a soft groan. Was he *still* hard or had he just gotten another erection? He wasn't sure and it didn't matter, because he was alone and no one needed to know what he was about to do. He pushed down the blanket to look down the body he was yet to discover. While slim, Caspian definitely worked out in one way or another, because his muscles had a hint of definition. But Gunner's one-track mind led him straight down the treasure trail of hairs, to the cock resting on a bed of dark pubes. While indeed on the small side, the shaft had some girth, and Gunner wrapped his slim fingers around it, both horny and confused by how different it felt in his hand in comparison to the thick sausage he was used to carrying in his pants.

And unlike his, Caspian's prick was uncut.

Would there be any difference in how it felt to the touch? He spat in his hand for good measure, too horny to search for lube, and flushed when his fingers pulled on the soft hood, exposing the head. He rubbed the tip, like usual, but the sensation felt almost too intense, so he touched the damp slit and only then glided the digit around while his balls heated. Small tingles trailed up the backs of his legs as he let his head fall back, drawn to the scary moment when the hulking body had stretched over him.

The memory of his own face staring back at him with anger burning in eyes he so often saw in the mirror was a bit of a cold shower, so he replaced it with another one. Mike Choi was the sole gay man Gunner knew, and he too was seriously ripped, with massive guns for arms and pecs like huge, juicy steaks. Yeah. This would work.

Mike straddling him and opening his pants to present his firm dick. He was a no-nonsense kind of guy, and he'd show Gunner his place by shoving that stiff tool down his throat from the get-go.

Gunner had never tried using any toys to play with his hole. It didn't feel right, even if he were to plan going somewhere truly private for such an experiment. He was afraid he'd like it too much, that it would change how he perceived himself, and he shouldn't want to get dicked in the first place. But was it something he should try now? No longer constricted by who he ought to be or what he should represent, could he explore a part of himself he never dared to acknowledge?

Maybe. He'd need to find out if he had it in him.

For now, he was far too engrossed in the fantasy of submitting to another man to bother working out the technicalities of anal.

He glanced down his smooth chest and pinched one of the pink nipples, imagining not the real Gunner, but this body being teased and grabbed by a hot, muscular guy like Mike Choi. For once, he didn't want to close his eyes and drift off while jerking off. He wanted to see every detail of his own trembling thighs, tiny feet and slim fingers around a cock that barely peeked from out of his clenched fist when he stroked it.

His toes curled when he imagined the weight of Mike's hand on his head, the scent of male arousal, and above all—the cock forcing its way past Gunner's gag reflex. It would move, caressing him from the inside, and within moments he'd be red-faced and damp with spit, but he'd let Mike use him however he pleased anyway.

To be desired like this, touched, rubbed and squeezed, was a need that always penetrated Gunner's secret fantasies. He moved his hand over the pulsing cock, raising his hips as the lewd scene playing in his head intensified and the imaginary balls met his chin.

Heat flashed through his body, and as phantom cum splashed down his throat, the scent of his own filled the air, and he shivered with pleasure, rocking in the middle of the bed until his balls dried.

He lay in the soft sheets for a while. This was exactly what he needed to take the edge off after confronting Caspian. It would had been amazing to take a nap, but he wasn't sure how much time he'd be given in this body, so he intended to make the best of this fuckery. He just needed to make sure he stayed away from fights.

He took a shower in Caspian's en-suite bathroom, which was half the size of Gunner's whole trailer. The water never changed temperature when he washed, covering him in a steady stream from the square rain showerhead above. Just like Caspian's boring room and wardrobe, the interior of the bathroom was an expensive-looking mix of white, greys and blacks in a variety of textures. Gunner had actually gone over to one of the other bathrooms to pick up a shampoo that wasn't mint or sandalwood. And what was Caspian's obsession with tea tree anyway? It didn't even smell like *tea*.

With his hair refreshed with the scent of raspberry and banana, Gunner was ready to take on the world, so he opened the closet with a wide smile that faltered as soon as the sea of gray, black, brown, and navy blue swallowed him like a tsunami of dull. The situation went from bad to worse when Gunner started laying the garments out on the bed, only to discover that monotonous colors weren't the biggest issue about Caspian's wardrobe.

Everything was two sizes too big. The suit Gunner found in a remote corner was the single tailored piece that might showcase the narrow lines of Caspian's body, but where Gunner had hoped to emerge from the house like a butterfly about to have the time of his life, he now feared he might end up looking more like a moth.

In his own life, Gunner didn't have money to spare and was far from being flashy in his fashion choices, but even he incorporated more fun in his clothes than... whatever this was. No sane guy would as much as glance at him in any of the things filling up the two rails in the vast closet, which meant that he had one option—to let Caspian's credit card take him out for a shopping spree.

His hands trembled when he realized that the best spot to go through with that plan was the mall in one of the nearby towns located along the highway.

The same one where Mike Choi had his sports nutrition store.

Was that destiny, or what?

A cold shiver went all the way to his stomach when he remembered the ease with which Caspian had pushed him over, but he couldn't live guided by fear. Mike Choi was rough around the edges, but surely wouldn't be aggressive toward a gay man he could fuck?

Or date.

Would they date?

Gunner stared into the tall mirror. He was cute. Why wouldn't another guy treat *him* for once? When he dated girls, it was his job to pay for them, but shouldn't *he* be the one getting treated when he was this motherfucking adorable?

The strands on his head barely reached the ends of his earlobes, but that was still more hair than he was used to dealing with. Should he splurge on a visit to the barber's? Caspian didn't have any jewelry either, only a fancy oversized watch that had extra holes punched in to fit his slim wrist. Even in his old body, Gunner liked to sport a bit of bling and could get away with signets, but there was nothing to put on his long, slim fingers in any of the drawers. He could only hope Caspian had lots of credit.

He ended up putting on a pair of torn jeans he'd found tucked at the back of a drawer, because while worn, they were small enough to kind-of fit Gunner's new body. There was a hole on one of the legs, but it looked like some pathetic accidental rip, so he tore the denim all the way to the seam for it to appear more deliberate. There was nothing to be done about the tent-like tops though, so Gunner resigned himself to one of the white polo shirts, hoping he'd get to replace it with something more interesting soon enough.

Five minutes later, he opened the garage door and hardly believed his eyes when he found a beautiful vintage car waiting for him. The dragon logo at the front of the hood told him nothing, but the shape of its body was reminiscent of luxurious cars from the 1950s. Painted a cherry red, it had an interior furnished with cream leather upholstery and marbled wood. And while obviously an antique of sorts, it was in excellent shape, polished to perfection as if it had been deep-cleaned last night.

The driver's seat was comically close to the wheel, but Gunner realized how much sense that made with Caspian's short legs the moment he sat inside the vehicle, rubbing the thin steering wheel as if it were a sacred artefact.

Now that he got to see the console from up close, he decided that the car wasn't just clean. There wasn't a scratch or imperfection in sight, as if it were either new or recently renovated. He didn't think he'd ever sat in a vehicle this flawless outside of a showroom.

It took him a while to find the keys attached to a laser-cut token shaped like a pony car, but he screamed in glee the moment he realized how smoothly the vehicle ran. Not a single issue with this pristine mechanical beast, regardless of how old it was. Oh, how he wished to show off this beauty, and flaunt it in front of the Brown brothers. Then again, those two fucks meant nothing in his new life. In this car, he was the king of the road even with the unruly damp hair that kept getting into his eyes.

He might not get to enjoy this forever, but for as long as this craziness lasted, he'd live Caspian's life to the fullest. Only it would be a better version of it. With fun, and color, and his pert ass turning heads.

Getting to the mall was a breeze, and he entered its hallways with a spring to his step and a smile on his face as shop windows passed in front of his eyes, trying to tempt him inside. He was on the lookout for the perfect clothes, but fifteen minutes into his spree, it was starting to become clear that while he had a vague idea what kind of clothes looked attractive on the pretty twinks he'd been so often envious of, he had no reference where to find them.

Prone to distraction as he was though, he drifted off to get himself the biggest strawberry Frappuccino topped with extra cream and sprinkles. Just because he could. Usually, he'd consider it a wasteful thing to buy on his tight budget, but Caspian's account could take that hit. The guys would have given him shit for buying a *girly* drink as well, but that didn't matter when he was a tiny speck of a boy no one paid mind to at the mall.

For once, he wasn't making any waves, he wasn't gathering wary glances, and wasn't followed by security. He could sit by the fountain with his pink drink, unnoticed, and not worry that someone might bother him.

He could just *be*.

He drifted through the corridors, surrounded by shops he'd only ever entered when carrying Sandy's bags, still too intimidated to go into any of the ones that might stock the kind of clothes that would complement his new slender body. But as he stepped into a large circular interior that was often used for special events at the mall, his feet grew roots into the fake marble floor.

The clear song of a piano was out of sync with the pop music blasting from the speakers, but even before Gunner's gaze drifted to the large white instrument standing next to a fountain on the side of the hall, he'd been briefly taken back to his late childhood and the lunches eaten with Mr. Wagner after boxing practice while Mrs. Wagner played the piano in the other room.

Several people stood still and watched the performer play, but most didn't pay him any attention, going about their business while the stranger's fingers danced over the keyboard like ballerinas repeating the same performance for the hundredth time. There wasn't a hint of discord in the music, and when the man rocked, as if hypnotized by the melody he produced, Gunner found himself gravitating ever closer to the grand piano.

The player had longish wavy hair, which he styled back, a graceful profile, and the slender body of a model. He moved with the music, as if it was carrying him to a different world altogether.

Gunner's fingers itched to join the musician. He could imagine himself playing alongside the stranger, showing off his new-found skills and flowing with the music they created together.

In a burst of courage he couldn't comprehend, he approached, put his drink by the music rack, and sat by the man, who looked back at him with a frown of surprise.

But he didn't stop playing, so Gunner closed his eyes and joined in, letting his fingers guide him over the keys. He was intimidated at first, but once he tuned in to the unknown melody, his hands found their rhythm, producing a background tune that elevated the piece, making its sound yet more refined.

The other man's knee pressed against his in appreciation, and they moved together, floating on the waves of classical music, as if it was for everyone, not just wealthy people who could afford fancy instruments and visits to the opera.

They didn't have to discuss anything, and the music came to an end without one awkward note, as if they both implicitly understood it needed to happen, based on prior knowledge.

Adrenaline rushed through Gunner's veins, and he smiled widely as the small crowd that had gathered around them erupted in applause.

Gunner's mouth stretched into a smile, even though he wasn't sure what would have been the appropriate reaction. But when the other guy rose from the bench and bowed, Gunner hurried to follow his example and bask in the appreciation of perfect strangers.

People had cheered him on when he boxed for money. But not like this. Not just because they appreciated the performance. When Gunner entered the ring, bets were made, and whether he won or lost, someone always left with a scowl. But those people? They simply enjoyed the beautiful sound of the piano.

The stranger stared straight at Gunner, adjusting his crisp green shirt before putting on a sleek leather jacket.

Gunner got a bit nervous, suddenly worried that he'd messed up the guy's moment. "That was fun, right?"

"Why? You've grown out of hating it, Cas?" the other man asked, pinching a mole on his chin, which was the only imperfection on his pristine face.

Oh, so Caspian knew this person? Did all piano players know one another? There couldn't be that many of them around.

Gunner grabbed his drink, because he wasn't sure what to do with his hands. "People change."

The stranger shrugged and stepped away from the piano, which saved Gunner the effort of tilting his head all the way back in order to see his face. "Is that why you've changed your style, Cas? Ripped jeans?" A wide smile stretched the handsome mouth, but the question made Gunner self-conscious.

"I... I don't know really. I'm shopping for some new stuff. I just came back to town, had a look at my wardrobe, and I'm thinking I need something more... current, you know?"

The other man took another step back and watched Gunner in a way that made him feel like a bug pinned under a microscope. They weren't... exes, were they?

"That shirt isn't doing your frame any favors."

"Hey Alex, amazing performance!" A young woman smiled in passing and tapped Alex on the shoulder, but didn't acknowledge Gunner, as if he wasn't even there.

Not that Gunner wanted to be noticed, and by a woman at that, but it still stung a bit. He pulled on the front of the polo shirt with a scowl. "Do you have time to help me look for something more appropriate? You seem like you've got your shit together." He hoped the compliment could win him a competent advisor.

Alex went quiet, and just as Gunner was about to retreat, embarrassed over wasting this guy's time, Caspian's friend offered him a wide smile and squeezed his shoulder. "Oh, yeah. I lead such a busy life in Atlanta, but I'm here just visiting my parents, so I have lots of time. You must tell me about your plans for the future. Where should we go first?"

Put on the spot, Gunner wasn't sure, but he did have Caspian's credit card to boost his confidence. He thought back to Caspian's boring wardrobe. "I'm done looking like my own dad, you know. I wanna feel fresh."

Alex's smile widened. "Of course you do. I know just the thing. With your height, we should probably hit the teenager section though. If I do a good enough job, maybe you'll reconsider and sell me the car."

Gunner chuckled when Alex put his arm over his shoulders. Surely with the help of a friend so stylish, everything would work out for him. This day would be *good*. He'd make himself into the perfect bait for Mike Choi.

Chapter 6 - Caspian

Snowman had to count the money three times, as if his racing mind couldn't cope with the job at hand. He only succeeded once he divided the cash into five piles accounting for a hundred dollars each. His face was dark pink, like some extravagant kid's drink from the nineties, and his short, white hair hung over the prematurely-wrinkled forehead like a torn spider web.

Caspian's feet kept tapping the floor of the dingy office as he watched his hard-earned money disappear into a safe, but Gunner suggested the person he was actually indebted to—the man behind Snowman—was a dangerous character, and Caspian wasn't willing to suffer the consequences of Gunner's disastrous financial decisions.

Unfortunately, since he now inhabited Gunner's body, the bastard's problems had become his own, and unless something changed, he'd have to visit the cramped office in one of the buildings by the entryway into the trailer park many more times in the future.

"Pleasure doing business with you," Snowman said and took another gulp of coffee that smelled so sharp it could have risen the dead.

"So we're done?" Caspian asked just to confirm what he already knew.

Snowman nodded. "For two weeks."

What. The. Actual. Fuck.

"And when will I be done paying this off?" Caspian asked, trying to keep his voice steady, because if he was to deal with the pressing financial issues and move on, he needed to make plans—something Gunner apparently wasn't very good at.

Caspian didn't know how long he'd get to live as this alpha guy, and he wanted to enjoy it to the fullest, without worrying about a debt he knew nothing about!

Snowman chuckled and rubbed his scruffy cheek. "I'm not the person to discuss the terms with. You know that."

It seemed he'd need to have another chat with Gunner then. And soon.

"Fine. See you in two weeks," Caspian said, cursing when he rose and hit his head on the lamp. Being tall had its downsides too.

He walked out of the office and toward his new home with shoulders squared and mind clouded by rage he couldn't pinpoint. It was like smoke in his brain, obscuring all logical thought and making his fists clench. Nobody paid him any attention as he made his way down the narrow asphalt road winding through the trailer park. He took his time to spy on the unfamiliar community and get to know his neighbors. Some of the residents kept their places tidy and even owned small gardens, while others had literal trash piles around their homes, as if the owner of the grounds didn't care about everyone's health and hygiene.

He put on a pair of sunglasses to protect himself from the sun and fed his curiosity from behind the reflective lenses. A couple fought nearby, shouting at the tops of their lungs. An older gentleman made a table in a makeshift carpentry workshop set up under an awning in front of his trailer. A mom watched her kids play outside, sitting on the steps of her home with a thick layer of green cream on her face and a magazine in her lap. It was the society in microcosm, with its own heroes and villains.

And a bunch of lazy asses who did nothing useful with their time.

He scowled when Sandy lifted a pair of bejeweled shades from her eyes and waved at him from a sun chair. She was chatting to a bunch of female friends, who'd gathered by a trailer near the road, drinking cocktails and making full use of the sun in their bikinis.

"Hey! Gun-gun! Wait up, we need to talk!"

"I'm not giving you money," Caspian said, heading straight for Gunner's place and the truck parked next to it. He needed to get away from here. From the cockroaches. From Snowman. From the thugs dumb luck had cast in the roles of his friends. And from Gunner's girl.

At least hunger was no longer a problem, since he'd stolen provisions from his parents' fridge, but who the hell knew how long those would last? This wasn't the life he'd imagined when he dreamed of having a body like this. He'd been dealing with problems all morning when he could have been looking for a sweet piece of ass to pin.

"Asshole!" One of Sandy's friends yelled. "This woman could be carrying your baby, and you're making her pay for your cat's food? What kind of man are you?"

"But she's not," Caspian said, hoping that Gunner didn't in fact owe anyone child support. He went faster as he approached the beat-up truck and slid into the cab, muting the squeaky voices of Sandy's friends with loud music. In the corner of his eye, he saw one of them hurry his way, but he had no intention of letting anyone berate him. He might have to deal with the debt, but considering that Gunner had mentioned his cat, but not his girlfriend when they'd met, Caspian assumed she wasn't that important, and he wouldn't jump through hoops to please her. She had her own two hands and could search for a job instead of sitting around in the middle of the day if she needed cash.

He only relaxed once he could no longer see the gate of the trailer park in his rearview mirror. The road, and the familiar buzz of the engine made him relax. He glanced at the thick fingers resting on the steering wheel and imagined what those massive hands could do to a man... The right kind of guy would also think so. Maybe Caspian didn't even need Grindr to hook up? He was hot now and could surely find someone willing to bend over in no time.

His face heated when he remembered finding the cute barista from his favorite coffee shop on the app, and since he knew where the pretty boy worked, he could just go there and casually propose a date while he placed his order.

His wallet might have gotten lighter by five hundred dollars minutes ago, but he still had enough cash on him for a coffee. Or two, if the barista agreed to a *rendezvous* after work.

In his mind, he was already pressing the blond cutie against the wall at the back of the building, smelling the coffee and sugar in his hair, and lowering the pale jeans to expose the round globes of his buttocks.

He stepped on the gas with fire burning in his veins, but just as he was about to make a dash toward the cafe, a red Porsche blocked his way, changing lanes as if its driver hadn't noticed that Caspian had picked up his pace. He punched the horn, getting agitated when the rude fuck refused to go faster and rolled forward at the pace of a turtle, laboriously overtaking the car on the other lane, as if it were a long-haul truck, not a sports vehicle.

And unless it was only Caspian's imagination sparking with anger, the fucker had slowed down, as if trying to punish him for daring to honk at a fancy car with obnoxious personalized licence plates—*ALEXG*.

Caspian knew an Alex who never failed to mention that his parents named him after Alexander the Great. *That* Alex's parents owned a large funerary company with shops all over the state, earned a crazy amount of money on pushing unnecessary products on bereaved people, and he wasn't better himself. For whatever reason Alex had decided he and Caspian were mortal enemies back in middle school, when Caspian won a piano competition, relegating Alex to second place.

They'd never fought or openly spoke against one another, but while their rivalry remained implicit, even Caspian's parents had caught its scent and kept mentioning a start-up Alex had presided over, as if they hoped it would motivate him.

Caspian really didn't care what Alex did with his life, or whether he'd won any more piano contests for amateurs. The fact that he'd grown so much taller than Caspian, however? *That* shit was pissing him off to this day. Especially since the fucker never failed to mention it. At least he still had the beautiful, cherry-red Southfield to flaunt in front of the bastard. Caspian would make sure Alex didn't get his hands on the vehicle, even if he offered millions of dollars for it.

Caspian rolled down his window and looked out when the car in front of him came to a standstill at a large crossing. "Just move the damn thing! Can't you see the green light?" he yelled despite knowing that the traffic lights at this particular intersection were kind of confusing, and he'd fallen victim to it several times when he'd first learned to drive.

A head stuck out of the Porsche, and Caspian stilled when it turned out that it was none other than his frenemy Alexander the Not-so-Great.

"Oh, I'm *sorry*. Are you in a hurry?" the bastard shouted back but didn't move despite the light for their lane still being green! Cars in the other lane kept passing them now that their lights changed, and he could have technically just maneuvered around Alex, but at this point, it was a matter of principles

Caspian's hand went for the horn before he could have thought his reaction through, and he drove closer to Alex's vehicle, stopping two inches away. "Are you blind? If you can't read traffic lights, get a fucking taxi!"

"Learn some manners." Alex shook his head and showed him the finger, but there was an attentiveness in his eyes that Caspian had never seen before.

Yeah, asshole, you just flipped off a dangerous motherfucker, and you'll regret it.

Caspian opened the car and dashed toward Alex's vehicle, slamming his hand on the roof so loudly Mr. Not-so-Great flinched in fear. Here was to hoping he'd pissed his pristine slacks.

"Get out of my way or I'll slash your tires!" Caspian roared, and hit Alex's side window to make his point. The bastard was lucky he'd closed it.

Rage burned through his veins, growing, like a bonfire fueled by gasoline, and this was as good an opportunity as any to unleash it. He was finding out what it was like to make Alex pay attention, and he was getting weirdly horny because of it. His hook-up couldn't come any sooner.

"Get lost, or I'll call the cops!" Alex yelled from inside the car, but he was leaning away ever-so-slightly, as if he were afraid that the muscular giant might smash his window and drag him out.

Caspian didn't think. He reached for the key in his pocket and showed it to Alex before lowering his hand, ready to spoil the pristine red paint.

The pure, unadulterated terror in Alex's eyes was the sweetest ambrosia for Caspian's heart.

"No! Oh, my god! Are you insane? Don't! Sorry, sorry! Jeeesus!" He raised his hands for good measure.

"Fuck off then. Go! Go," Caspian said and kicked the bastard's wheel, breaking into ecstatic laughter when Alex rode off with a squeak of tires, dashing through the intersection. The fumes he'd left behind smelled like spring sunshine. The lights had changed during their exchange, but Alex always had more luck than reason, and he hadn't collided with anyone on the way.

When Caspian turned around, satisfied with this victory, his gaze lingered on the old car behind his truck and he felt a pang of guilt when the elderly lady hunched over behind the wheel, as if she expected him to yell at her next. She must have watched the fight and hadn't even bothered to use her horn to break it up. She'd done nothing wrong and shouldn't have to fear a stranger, just because he was bigger and stronger than her, so he saluted her with a manic grin and got back to his car with adrenaline flushing his body.

Was *this* what life was like for Gunner Russo? Undeserved respect? He might have to deal with debt, with the gang shit, and share his trailer with an extended family of roaches for as long as this crazy dream lasted, but people at last paid attention to him. Caspian was used to being invisible, to people's eyes sliding past him as if he didn't matter, but now he could feel the weight of his bulk in every step he took, and he would enjoy it.

Starting now.

Once the light changed to green again, he drove straight into the swath of gray emptiness that made up the town centre. Dotted with warehouses, old shops, and bungalows, it was a landscape of long-lost prosperity. But when Gunner drove past the small church, which stood out with its elegant white facade, and the school, the red brick of the county library called out to him. It used to be his favorite place in this town, and had become more so since a modern café opened within its walls. Mom had told him the locals initially predicted its failure, but turned out even a town as insignificant and drab as Grit, Ohio, needed a place for casual dates and meetups with friends that were a bit classier than sitting around on the bleachers.

His skin itched in anticipation, even though he didn't yet know whether the pretty boy he had in mind was working this afternoon. He slammed the door shut and was about to march straight at the door to present his new improved self, but stepped back to check himself out in the rearview mirror. Gunner kept his hair in a crew cut so short Caspian didn't have to worry about any of it being out of place, but he did make sure his ears were clean, and that the front of his shirt wasn't stained.

The eyes looking back at him had the color of milky hot chocolate, and they shimmered when he smiled, making the expression as charming as he'd always wanted to appear. Even the face tattoo couldn't spoil the perfection of Gunner's masculine features, so Caspian smoothed out his clothes once more and entered the café.

It was modern yet not pretentious, spacious but cozy, with pale wooden chairs and green plants on shelves, tables, and in strategic spots on the floor.

Whenever he visited his parents, he loved to come here and sit by the window with a flat white and watch people or read. The chatter of other customers created the right amount of white noise to calm him, and the staff was both proficient, polite, and eye candy.

But as he stepped through the door, something was noticeably different in the atmosphere that greeted him inside. The pretty barista stood behind the counter, but something was off about the smile he greeted Caspian with. Since everyone was allowed to have a bad day, Caspian ignored the way the barista whispered something to his co-worker and captured the blue gaze from afar.

He could sense many pairs of eyes sliding across his tall, muscular form, but he hadn't come for the patrons. He was here for the boy with the septum ring and silvery hair.

"Didn't know Grit had places like this," rolled off his tongue effortlessly as he stuffed his hands into his pockets. He used to hate the low, rumbly tone of Gunner's voice when the guy had intimidated him with it, but now that it wasn't being used against him, he recognized it as capable of charming pants off pert boy asses.

The barista, whose name tag read *Adam* wouldn't stop smiling but his gaze drifted off to the ordering screen in a way it never had when Caspian came over in his own, insignificant body. Was he shy? Caspian could work with that. In fact, he wouldn't mind doing all the heavy lifting. He'd love to be the man who asked out, the man who made the first move, and the man who pounded his partner into the mattress.

Though he was getting ahead of himself.

"Yeah, it's been here a few years. What can I get you?"

Caspian toyed with having his usual order, but instead grinned, hoping to engage the barista. "What's your favorite?" he dared to ask in a flirtatious way. Short and small, Caspian had always been too self-conscious to flirt with the guys he liked and settled on whoever seemed least choosy, but he was no longer the shy man no one wanted. Today, he walked the world as a muscular hunk that wouldn't be crossed or overlooked.

The question made Adam look up, and a deep flush colored the boy's cheeks when their eyes met. How amazing was it that his sheer presence could do that?

"I... um, the mocha is the best in town. Would you like to try one?"

Emboldened by the sight of Adam's tongue touching the corner of his lips, Caspian leaned forward and winked. "How about I pay for two and we drink them together?"

When Adam glanced up at him again, Caspian could have sworn he heard the boy's speeding heartbeat. "I'm sorry, I can't... I'm at work, you know. Sorry," he mumbled. "Mocha? Extra sprinkles on the house," he added as if wanting to... finish the transaction even though Caspian's presence at the counter wasn't blocking anyone else from placing their order.

But it then occurred to Caspian that maybe Adam's boss was a hardass who didn't want his employees flirting with customers. Would the boy write his number on Caspian's receipt, like people did in the movies?

Either way, Caspian hadn't come here to walk away empty-handed.

"When do you get off? I could wait," Caspian said and rubbed the boy's finger on the counter. The brief touch sparked arousal in his balls, as if his libido were out of control. They could fuck in Gunner's old fucked-up truck, if the boy were up for it, because no one in their right mind would care about the vehicle being a piece of junk when such prime dick was on the line.

But Adam froze, sucking on his bottom lip in a way that sent Caspian's mind down the rabbit hole of cocksucking.

A man in a suit and tie approached the counter with a smile. "Is everything okay?"

"Why wouldn't it be?" Caspian asked, taken aback by the intrusion. It wasn't as though Adam had other customers to serve at the moment.

"I just noticed you haven't yet received your drink, sir. Would you like me to take over, Adam?" the man asked, and to Caspian's frustration, the boy nodded and stepped away from the register as if he were fleeing.

He walked off with a mumbled "Sorry, I mean, thank you."

The fuck was *that*? Why would the pretty boy miss out on the dick ride of his life? Caspian might not have any experience topping, but it wasn't like he'd never had sex, and what he didn't know he could surely make up for in enthusiasm.

"Since when is it not appropriate for staff to chat with customers? Is that some new policy I'm not aware of?" Caspian asked, fighting the boiling heat under his skin. He'd spent his life as a permanently pissed-off guy with no muscle to enforce his will, and yet despite now having this large, imposing body, he didn't know how to fight such rudeness when the people involved weren't scum.

"I could see my barista getting uncomfortable. Please just order your coffee and—"

"What was there to be uncomfortable about? I wasn't being unpleasant."

"You are being unpleasant now, sir. Please don't cause a scene."

He wasn't causing a scene! What on earth was this about?

It was as if someone had injected adrenaline straight into Caspian's veins. "What's your problem?"

He could sense at least a dozen eyes sticking to his back in unhealthy curiosity. Of customers, and even of the other staff as if he were a freak show just because he looked imposing. Of course Gunner would have marked his perfectly handsome face with an ugly tattoo. The bastard had no future beyond bars, orange jumpsuits and an early grave, and therefore no reason to keep such natural perfection unspoiled.

Fucking idiot.

The manager raised his hands, but frowned. "There will be no problems as long as you leave peacefully, sir."

Caspian's own body wouldn't have had long enough arms to grab the huge jar of roasted coffee beans standing by the espresso machine. But Gunner's did, and Caspian grabbed it before tossing the entire contents at the manager. "Congratulations. You've just earned yourself a ton of reviews, but for now this is me throwing pearls to the pigs," he growled and spun around, storming for the door.

He hadn't been insulted like this in his entire life! These people treated him as if his sole presence was an infection that needed to be contained with a cocktail of vodka and antibiotics. Un-fucking-believable.

And even though he was in the right, his head boiled with embarrassment at the sound of whispers meant to chastise him and chase him farther away. Worst of all—it was working.

And Adam, who had always been polite, had turned out to be a prissy, elitist fucker, who dismissed a guy just because he looked as if he might have been born on the wrong side of the tracks! So he wasn't good enough to plow that precious ass, because he had old shoes and a rusty truck? There wasn't enough money in Caspian's wallet to splurge on a new wardrobe right now, and he had no doubt that this massive frame was as difficult to shop for as his own tiny one. Couldn't he just enjoy this fucked-up dream for what it was?

He hit the roof of his truck a dozen times, but that didn't quite take the edge off his anger. Apparently, he was now too intimidating for real-life hook-ups, so Grindr it was.

And he was *hungry*. Again.

He could only think of one place in Grit where he'd get a plateful of filling food on the cheap *and* have the peace and quiet to browse a dating app.

And yes, he'd have peanut butter, because he now wasn't allergic to it.

Chapter 7 - Gunner

The new clothes hugged every line of Gunner's body. He hadn't been sure about the sizes at first, but Alex had insisted that they fit so much better than the baggy outfits Caspian had always hidden behind. It only made sense to listen to the advice of a man who looked so good himself. Because what did Gunner know about fashion? He wore the safest possible options and clothes that showed off his muscular form, but the body he now occupied was short, slender, and would be complemented by different styles.

Most of the load he now carried in several plastic bags came from the teenager ranges of popular brands. All of it, really, apart from the high-tops in a pretty lavender hue, which were the smallest men's size in the large store specializing in sneakers. Their color had intimidated Gunner at first, but Alex convinced him it was okay to wear for young men, and he'd ended up putting them on right away.

The shade of the trainers went surprisingly well with his new green tie dye T-shirt and jeans, both of which were a skin-tight fit. Walking around in such snug clothes made Gunner self-conscious, but the longer he wore them, the more he liked his own reflection in shop windows. He was getting some eyeballs from strangers, even a couple of smiles, and when Alex suggested that he should think about getting his hair done in order to match the new style, Gunner didn't hesitate and reached for Caspian's credit card.

Alex had to be a very good friend of Caspian's to be so supportive and spend so much time on the wild shopping spree. When Gunner wasn't sure about going blond, Alex reassured him about it, and then talked Gunner into being bold, grabbing life by the balls, and so... Gunner now sported a crystal stud at the top of his ear. Because it was his body now, and since he was no longer an imposing, hulking presence, no one would care that he experimented with his looks in a way that would have made people in his past life question his masculinity.

There was only one question left to answer—was he as fuckable as he considered himself to be?

He was almost regretful when Alex needed to go home, but maybe it was just nerves. With his new/old friend gone, Gunner no longer had an excuse to delay the planned visit to Mike Choi's store, but maybe his worries were unwarranted now that the new style had transformed him into someone this sexy. And the bright hair color made his face so much perkier than Caspian had ever seemed.

There was no point in overthinking all this when he knew for a fact that Mike was gay and therefore up for what Gunner was currently offering.

Gunner walked into the store stocked with shelves of energy bars and protein shakes with confidence, but his energy depleted with each step, because the customers, who were mostly buff gym bunnies, gave him curious glances. He didn't belong here anymore, and his skin crawled with the realization that he was no longer sure *where* he belonged.

In his old body, he'd felt right at home here whenever he shopped for supplements, or just stopped by to chat to Mike about his workout routine. But he was a different person now—not the regular known to all the staff but a pretty thing with a juicy ass presented in tight jeans, and a face to turn heads. He hadn't come for healthy snacks or advice. He was here for Mike.

The familiar tattoo of a stylized dragon crawled up Mike's arm as he leaned over the counter at the back of the store, writing something down in a large notebook. He wasn't very tall, and in his own body Gunner easily towered over him, but still seemed like a giant compared to Caspian's form, with thick biceps, a big chest pushing at the front of the black muscle shirt, and smooth black hair pulled into a ponytail at the back of his head.

Gunner felt as if he were in a video game, wearing a full-body VR set. How should he act to attract a man like Mike? In porn, guys always went straight down to business, and while Mike never hid his sexual preferences, it wasn't like he ever talked about that side of his life in Gunner's presence. But he was a business owner, always well-groomed, and drove a nice car. Gunner would be intimidated approaching a guy like him if he didn't know that Mike was cool, and mingled with all kinds of people.

"Hey," he tried when Mike hadn't noticed him standing there for at least half a minute.

Brown eyes looked up, but the handsome face that always had broad smiles for Gunner froze in a neutral expression. "Can I help you?" Mike asked, straightening up, as if he wanted to show off his superior height. Now what he was *available* to Gunner, it was impossible to miss the sexy way his upper lip protruded ever-so slightly.

Gunner glanced over his shoulder, suddenly self-conscious about what he was about to do. Not just because this was the first time he intended to approach a guy he wanted to hook up with but because he didn't want to out Mike to customers. But no one was close enough to hear a hushed conversation at the counter, so he raised his chin and met Mike's gaze to the intense drumming of his heart.

"You look like the kind of guy who knows about all these protein powders and workouts. Do you offer *personal training*?"

So it was suggestive. And bold. But also dressed up in enough lies to keep Gunner from running off in embarrassment.

Mike's brows rose, and he let the silence hang in the air as if it were a dead mouse stinking up the place. "Sorry, I'm not a trainer. But if you tell me what you want to achieve, I can tell you which products to use."

He clearly didn't catch the suggestion, which meant that hiding behind indirect propositions was dead in the water.

Gunner licked his lips and leaned against the counter. Even the fresh hole in his ear seemed to throb with worry and excitement, but in this body, he could do such things. He could pursue these illicit needs. Nobody would recognize him behind the big blue eyes and blond hair. In this body, he was safe to truly be *himself*. "I'd like to achieve you on top of me," he whispered, too nervous to blink.

Mike snorted, then tried to compose himself, only to laugh again, hiding behind the notebook he'd been writing in. "What? Is this a joke? Have you seen yourself in the mirror, kid?"

Gunner stared back, not sure what to make of this. Yes, he'd glanced in the mirror hundreds of times today, and he was super fucking cute. *And* he hadn't been called *kid* since his early teens. Caspian was twenty-three!

"No. And I know you're gay, so I don't see what your problem is." It came out more harshly than he'd wished, but while he looked very different on the outside, this new body hadn't changed his personality.

"There *is* a problem. You'd break in two if I poked you with a finger, and you look like you've stolen those clothes from your younger brother. Come back when you grow some muscle, and then maybe I'll consider taking another look at you," Mike said, staring straight at Gunner, as if he wanted to see him crushed.

The body that attracted such vicious words wasn't even his, yet it still stung. Clearly, just because he thought he was a cute twink, didn't mean everyone shared the sentiment.

Someone behind him snorted. "Won't you even give his mouth a test drive, Mike?"

Gunner's lips parted in shock at the indignity of it all, but Mike answered first.

"Nah, he wouldn't fit it all in."

Gunner squared his shoulders and turned to face the other guy. "The fuck did you say?" As much as he enjoyed being compact, having to look up to meet the bastard's eyes doused him with a sense of humiliation.

He vaguely knew this guy but wasn't sure of his name. Doherty?

Whatever Doherty's actual name was, he wasn't hesitant about showing his true colors to someone weaker than him. "She's a feisty one, isn't she? Is that a sock?" he asked, gesturing at Gunner's crotch with a leer that told him that perhaps this guy would have been up for giving Gunner a go, were they alone. But only as long as no one found out.

Gunner wasn't a blowjob vending machine.

Mike shook his head. "Get lost. Don't proposition people in my store. Gays like you give us all a bad name," Mike said in a low voice, staring at Gunner from under lowered brows.

Gunner opened his mouth, but someone grabbed his arm and pulled him back. His first instinct was to lash out, so he swung his fist and hit someone's pec.

"Ow!" Noah scowled at him, and a lock of brown, coily hair fell into his face as he took a step back. "I was just gonna ask if you're okay..."

Mike spread his massive arms. "Psychoslut-boy is clearly fucked in the head. Get him out of here!"

Gunner stilled, staring at his half-sibling with a growing sense of doom. He'd been found out. His little brother, the only family Gunner still had left, had seen him proposition another guy, and their relationship would be ruined forever.

But all of Noah's attention was on Mike as he stepped forward with a flush darkening his tan skin, which made the lightning-shaped scars spreading across his cheek appear even paler than they were. The terrible accident that had drowned Gunner in crippling debt and tied him to Snowman and the gang he worked for left scars all over Noah's body, and even on his face, but he seemed stronger and healthier than ever when he stood in front of Gunner with both hands on his hips.

"This is really uncalled for. Give the guy a break!"

Only then it occurred to Gunner that to Noah he was just a stranger, not the older brother he was meant to look up to.

Mike rolled his eyes. "*You* should take your *break* now. Maybe he'll suck your dick as a thank-you."

Noah scowled and rubbed his wide, freckled nose. "See you in fifteen. Let's go, hm?" He pointed to the door, and Gunner took this opportunity to exit, but there wasn't much dignity to it.

He might still have his personality, but what was that good for when he couldn't challenge neither Doherty nor Mike? His pride was deteriorating, and he questioned every fashion choice he'd made today.

"Thanks for butting in," he mumbled as they left, his gaze stopping on the store's logo at the front of Noah's T-shirt. Had he recently started working for Mike?

Noah was such a good kid. He didn't have to step in but had still chosen to challenge his boss to help out a perfect stranger. The brown freckles sprinkled across his nose and cheeks made Noah look very young, but when he met Gunner's gaze, walking him out of the store and into the afternoon sun, he seemed so put together it made Gunner ashamed of his own lewd actions.

Suddenly, he wanted to cover himself with something big and baggy, straight from Caspian's ugly wardrobe, but Noah made him sit on a bench in front of a fountain close to the mall entrance and rested alongside him. Even seated, the seventeen-year-old who usually reached up to Gunner's shoulder, was taller than him.

"I'm really sorry. They're douchebags."

"I can see. I don't know what I was thinking." Gunner hid his face in his hands as dark thoughts swirled in his head, replacing the earlier cotton candy. He'd been so preoccupied with presenting cute and getting his belly full of pancakes that he forgot all about his responsibility to Noah.

With their father dead and Noah's mom earning peanuts at her two jobs, Gunner had been the one to take on the burden of paying for Noah's medical bills, and the physiotherapy that had brought him back into shape and prevented him from having a limp for the rest of his life. The massive sum Gunner had borrowed from Snowman and his boss paid for it all, but it kept mounting up, and who would take care of it if not Gunner?

Who would make sure Noah had a chance for a better, more honest life when the accident had already put him at a disadvantage financially and with school? Caspian was too self-absorbed to continue paying off the debt and would surely disappear on Noah and his mom, leaving them to deal with the fallout.

Noah's hand moved up and down Gunner's back. "Don't worry. Mike's super-hot but has the personality of a turd. You're better off finding someone else."

Gunner's self-flagellating thoughts came to a halt, and he looked up, meeting his brother's dark brown eyes.

Had Noah just complimented Mike Choi's physique? What?

"I just... I thought I had it in the bag. I don't know what I was thinking. I'm sorry. I'm wasting your break." Gunner stared at the lilac shoes he'd considered cute only an hour back yet now wasn't so sure about.

Noah patted his shoulder and got up with a snort. "It's okay. Plenty more fish in the sea. I heard Grindr is where it's at." He winked at Gunner and walked off, leaving him stunned.

How did his little brother know such things?

From Mike Choi, no doubt, but there was no point in focusing on that when Gunner didn't know how much time he still had in this new body. Maybe he should listen to Noah and... take the plunge?

He decided to forget the hurtful words and ignore the intrusive thoughts about whether his new style made him ridiculous or sexy in a "gay" way, and stared at Caspian's expensive phone. He'd seen Caspian's message exchanges on the hook-up app before, but now that he was considering finding a partner for *himself*, he wasn't sure how to approach that daunting task. Taking new photos, ones that presented his real self, should be a good start.

But all plans died in his mind when he entered Caspian's profile on the app and saw that the bastard had replaced the unknown hunk that had featured there before with photos of... Gunner. Or himself. However that worked now.

Gunner's heart pounded as if it were trying to crash its way through his ribcage. Swept up by growing panic, he was about to delete the photos and change the password to block Caspian out of it, but an incoming message made him freeze. He tapped it only to find a whole conversation Caspian was having with some horny stranger, and it seemed they'd be hooking up… right… about… *now*.

Gunner took a screenshot of the address, jumped to his feet and ran.

"Not in my fucking body!"

Chapter 8 - Caspian

Anticipation buzzed in Caspian's veins as he sipped coffee in a booth at the back of the diner. Unlike at the cafe he'd lost some of his warm feelings for, in the dingy box of concrete, glass, and plastic everyone was equally welcome as long as they paid for their orders. Not a single person here piqued his interest, but he hadn't come to eat or chat with the server.

He'd come here to get laid.

The box of condoms and lube, both of which he'd got at the nearby gas station, burned through the pocket of his jeans like a constant reminder that this was it—he'd finally have anal. His new tattooed face didn't have as many takers as the photo of the handsome blond guy Caspian had stolen off the internet and used on Grindr since he'd first downloaded the app, but following the confrontation at the café, he decided to be upfront about the ink, because having someone run off would have been much worse than getting fewer messages. Not to mention, less productive in the hook-up department.

What counted was that he was about to hook up, and while he did have stage fright, he kept telling himself that it didn't matter if he fucked up with a stranger. So what if he came too soon or made some other blunder? He didn't know the man he was about to fuck, so even if something didn't go according to plan, he could just forget it and move on.

It was safe.

Easy.

It would be fun.

"Here we go," the server said with a smile and placed a juicy burger in front of Caspian. He was so girly-looking with his painted eyelids and small frame that Caspian had mistaken him for a woman at first, but his chest was flat as the table, and his voice, while high in pitch, sounded male.

Caspian had gotten hungry. Again. He'd never considered how many calories a body as big as this burned through, but at this rate, he'd be spending everything he earned on food.

"Getting ready for a long drive?" Gale, the server, asked, which made some sense considering how many trucks were parked close to the diner.

Caspian shrugged, smiling up at the guy as he dug in, eager to sate his hunger before his hook-up called him over to the motel. He groaned in pleasure as beef, chili jam, and peanut butter combined in his mouth. Yes, he could finally have peanuts, and they were fucking glorious.

"No, I'm local. Are you sure we've never met?"

Gale snorted and tugged on his short blond hair. "I would have remembered."

Was he flirting? Caspian wasn't very good at telling, but he could see how this new body could attract attention. It was everything he wanted—big, firm, tall, with ruggedly masculine features. Only the big face tattoo spoiled the perfection of Caspian's current form, because the other ink, while not perfect, gave him that hot and dangerous vibe he was going for without being *too much*.

The server wasn't quite his type but maybe they could meet up some other time? No reason to be overly choosy when Caspian didn't know how long he'd get to enjoy Gunner's body.

"I would hope so. Will you give me your number?"

Gale bit his lip, shifted from side to side, then wrote down something in his notepad and passed it to Gunner. "Enjoy your meal, and call me over if you need anything."

The piece of paper had Gale's number written down along with *'I finish at 10pm'* and a heart. Living as Gunner was that easy. A wink. A direct question, and—boom—he had a potential date set up for the night while *he* hadn't dared to approach guys until college, and his first sexual experience was blowing a classmate at a drunken party. To this day, Caspian wasn't sure whether the guy really hadn't remembered a thing or had chosen to pretend it hadn't happened. And even after that, Caspian struggled to find hook-ups so much he didn't bother to try *dating*. Clearly, there were no takers for someone his size.

The ease with which he obtained someone's phone number kept niggling at the back of his head, and he couldn't decide whether he was glad or frustrated to see the insecurities that plagued him since puberty proven true. So what if some guys passed on him because he looked intimidating when others flocked to his muscles and ink like cats to a bowl of fresh milk?

He used to be invisible, but now even the strangers sitting in the other booths took notice of his presence, regarding him with respect and a drop of suspicion. As if he were potentially dangerous.

And he liked that, no matter how humiliated he'd felt at the cafe.

Maybe one couldn't have everything?

He wasn't yet certain if he'd call Gale, but knowing he had the note in his pocket was enough to ease some of the worries knotting his insides.

It would be fine. He was horny and ready to finally *fuck* a guy. What was the worst that could happen? One had to start somewhere, and his experience in giving and receiving blowjobs, while not extensive, proved that one learned best in practice.

He finished his food and was still nursing the coffee when his phone chimed, kick-starting his usual insecurities. He opened the message, worried he'd find it full of excuses from the Grindr guy, but his hook-up only wanted to let him know he awaited Caspian in room number fourteen at the Karma Motel.

Heat shot to Caspian's face, but this was his sink-or-swim moment, and he wasn't about to drop to the seabed before he emptied his balls.

He placed cash on the table, waved at Gale, and left the diner, facing the expanse of the vast parking lot filled with trucks. The afternoon sun colored the massive vehicles with gold, but it also shone straight into Caspian's eyes, so he lowered his gaze to the asphalt and breathed in gasoline-scented air as he walked along a patch of dry grass separating the truck stop from the road.

The motel, a three-story monstrosity of concrete, was easy to spot from afar when the landscape was so flat, but he couldn't have been more excited even if he were to enter a luxurious hotel in Paris. He was about to get laid. And for the first time it didn't feel like being picked because there was no one else around.

Number fourteen was on the first floor, and he could enter it straight from the parking lot located between the arms of the horseshoe-shaped building. Regardless of how hot he now was, the anxiety over this being his first time to top remained a steady presence at the back of his mind. But he was determined to go through with his plans and knocked on the wooden door that had paint peeling off at the edges.

His hook-up opened right away, as if he were a dog waiting at the door for its master to return home. The guy was average-looking, like a semi-handsome accountant in his thirties, with short dark hair and a clean-shaven face. He was the kind of person whose features would have been impossible to describe accurately, but Caspian already knew that he'd never forget the first person he'd fuck. So what that he wasn't Caspian's type and wore a white T-shirt with gray checkered shorts? His ass would feel as good as that of the hot barista's would have, were the kid not so stuck-up.

The stranger smiled and took a few steps back to make room for Caspian. "Wow. You weren't joking about six-foot-five."

Caspian's balls tightened, and he gave the man a little push, entering the small room with only one window by the bathroom door. Curtains with a vintage-style flower pattern blocked most of the daylight, but enough of it seeped in to reveal a large bed and a collection of simple furniture. It was an ugly, forgettable space that surely cost very little money, but it would serve its purpose just fine.

The room smelled of cotton air freshener, as if someone had tried to mask the odor of old carpets or mold, but Caspian didn't care. He wasn't here to relax.

"Jordan, was it?"

The guy's eyes widened, and his flush became a dark red. "Y-yeah."

Yes, Jordan, you're about to get the ride of your life. Caspian might not have the physical experience, but he knew what he wanted, and for once, his body wouldn't stand in the way of his fantasies.

He might have never done this, but he'd researched what to do and watched tons of porn. It would be fine.

No. It would be amazing.

When Caspian stepped closer, thinking was no longer necessary. He caught the whiff of soap on the other man's skin and took hold of his throat, leaning in to smell his warm neck. Jordan gasped, and the way his Adam's apple bobbed under Caspian's massive palm made Caspian's underwear feel tighter, just like it had when he'd held Gunner down that morning. So maybe it *was* fucked up that he found promises of violence a turn-on, but he refused to feel guilty about it after years of living as the underdog everyone overlooked.

Not anymore. Jordan's breath trembled as he slid his hand across Caspian's pecs, and his eyes clouded with admiration for the hunk he wanted to submit to. At very long last, Caspian was right where he was supposed to be, in the skin he deserved, following the needs he'd ignored for most of his life. *This* was his moment.

"I'm going to bend you over that bed. And I'm going to make you beg for my dick," he uttered, tightening his hand on Jordan's throat as they gravitated through the dusky room, toward the place where Caspian would become the man he'd always wanted to be.

Jordan's consent was a broken mewl, but as he touched Caspian's groin, a rapping at the door startled them both before they could have made it to the bed.

Caspian looked over the shoulder, but he wasn't expecting anyone, and Jordan wouldn't have invited any friends without asking him first, so he pushed his hand under Jordan's top and pawed at his to-be lover's smoothly shaven chest. A jolt of arousal made his toes curl when he buried his face in the hot neck, but the knocking wouldn't stop, intent on breaking them apart.

This couldn't be Jordan's wife, or girlfriend, or something, could it?

"I know you're fucking in there!" said a high-pitched, but male, voice. "I do not agree to this!"

Jordan offered Caspian a confused stare. "Mistake?"

But Caspian froze when he realized how familiar the voice was, even though it always sounded slightly different when he was the one using that same mouth.

It couldn't be.

He couldn't have come here!

"Go away!" he roared and spun around, banging his fist against the door. That did shut up Gunner, but his silence only lasted for a second.

"You want me to make a scene? I can make a fucking scene! That's *my* dick, *my* body, and *my* face!" He started kicking the door so hard it rattled.

Jordan stepped back, and his face fell as he adjusted his clothes. "Err, sorry, I don't want any boyfriend drama."

"He's not my boyfriend. He's—" To make his point, Caspian moved his hand to the side of his head and made a cuckoo sound.

He couldn't fucking believe this. Jordan had been so pliant and ready, yet now he smiled in an awkward, apologetic way and went for the door as soon as he was dressed.

"Let me know when you work it out. I really wanna try this again."

"Open the fucking door, or I'm gonna break it down!" Gunner yelled as if he still had a body that could break anything sturdier than thin plywood.

And as if Gunner wasn't being pathetic enough, Jordan opened the door at the very moment the little shrimp chose to throw himself at it, and he fell inside, straight to the dusty carpet.

Confusion stopped Caspian from lashing out at the nosy fucker when he realized that the person picking themselves up from the floor did not match the voice he'd heard. Where there should have been brown hair, was a pale blond mane, and the garishly colorful, tight clothes revealing how tiny the intruder's frame was didn't resemble a single piece Caspian owned. But when the guy looked up, Caspian saw the soft features he'd been stuck with until today.

Caspian's ears were drumming so loudly he couldn't hear anything beyond the echo of his heartbeat.

"Is that a piercing?" he uttered and grabbed Gunner by the nape to better see the crystal glinting in Gunner's ear.

"So... bye, we'll be in touch," Jordan said and shut the door behind him before Caspian could have said a thing.

Maybe it was for the better that he left. If Caspian murdered Gunner and permanently took over his body, there would be no witnesses.

"What—what the fuck have you done to me?" Caspian uttered, pulling Gunner up to his feet in a single yank.

He made a ridiculous picture in clothes that seemed to have shrunk in the washing machine, and with the ear stud, but the platinum blond hair he was sporting weirdly complimented Caspian's face, which bore an unfamiliar expression.

This was the ugly scowl that had twisted Gunner's mouth when he'd yanked Caspian's backpack off in high school, or pushed him into the swimming pool. Only that it looked much less threatening on the gentle features of Caspian's own face.

Almost *cute*.

Gunner frowned and glanced all the way down to the lilac high-tops he wore instead of normal shoes. "I made you presentable, so you look your age, not like a middle-aged accountant."

Caspian tightened his hands on Gunner's shoulders—or were they his? He wasn't sure anymore—and frowned at him. "Those tight-fitting clothes. That hair... are you trying to hook up with guys? Are you gay?"

For a moment of hesitation Gunner seemed so lost Caspian almost patted the fucker's shoulder in support, but Gunner was right back to his shitty attitude. "N-No! But you are, so I just... like... I had to go with the flow. Your friend Alex helped me pick it all out, and he knows you, so it's for *you*."

Caspian's mind came to a halt before exploding with rage so hot Gunner might find himself burnt. "Alex is *not* my friend! He made you wear that? And dye your hair?" he asked, tugging on a fluffy strand so hard Gunner flinched.

He slapped Caspian's hand away as if he weren't a tiny pup barking at a Doberman. "I chose it all, because it's cute. Alex just gave me the confidence to do it."

Caspian stalled, because when Gunner glared at him that was exactly how he looked.

Cute.

Adorable in his anger.

"Yeah? That's what you wanted? To show off your ass like this?" he whispered, mouth dry as he slapped Gunner's buttock and saw it jiggle in the elongated mirror on the wall.

Gunner's face went aflame, and the pink flush only made his eyes bluer. Had they always been so bright, or was the pale hair bringing out their color? "Hey! It's not for you to touch, you... big gay!" Gunner choked out and pushed at Caspian's chest, but he could as well have been a kitten trying to pounce on its mom.

Caspian shoved him at the wall, his nerves stretched thin in anticipation, and he grabbed the slim neck to make sure Gunner understood his place in the food chain. "No? It's my body. My ass. My mouth," he whispered, standing right in front of Gunner. His head was boiling. He could hardly think, but when Gunner looked up, his pink lips open, Caspian pushed in his thumb and pressed down on the soft, wet tongue.

His dick twitched.

It was fucked up. Insane.

But he couldn't make himself pull away.

The pink of Gunner's face turned into a bright red, and it hit Caspian how fuckable he was in comparison to an average Joe like Jordan. The big blue eyes betrayed tension, but instead of biting Caspian's finger and running to safety, Gunner stood still like Caspian's twinky wet dream and stared back.

There had to be a reason for this crazy body swap, so what if the universe had realized it made a mistake and put them back in the bodies they should have been born in? If Caspian was now a buff giant with a big dick, maybe Gunner was a gay little bottom, and his outside finally matched his inside? Why else would he have chosen to dress like the hotties Caspian watched on social media?

"You chased off my hook-up. I think you should pay up," Caspian whispered, shocked yet increasingly aroused by the blurry gaze Gunner met his with. So maybe it was fucked up to lust after his own body this way, but it no longer *felt* his. Gunner wore it differently, as if it were a shabby jacket he'd found in the thrift store and upcycled with sequins.

He said nothing, and his passivity only fueled Caspian's fire. He moved his thumb in and out of that warm mouth. Gunner raised his eyebrows and pointed to his chest with a question. Oh, the things Caspian could do to that slim body…

"Yes, you little slut," Caspian said, so hot the air coming from his lips felt like smoke. He grabbed Gunner's hand and pressed it to his crotch, gasping when his dick twitched in response to the touch.

Gunner melted against the wall, and the tight bright top clung to hardening nipples. He lowered his gaze, as if he were shy, but his soft lips tightened around Caspian's digit, and... he sucked on it before squeezing Caspian's growing package with a bit more boldness.

Gunner Russo was gay.

A revelation that made Caspian both giddy and horny for so many different reasons.

"All this time, you've been hiding in plain sight. You've been after me and called me slurs, and you're gay yourself?" Caspian asked, pressing his thumb to the flesh under Gunner's tongue and pulling him along as if his finger were a hook lodged in flesh.

His brain was turning into mush. Hatred, anger, and lust spun together, creating an intoxicating concoction that made his balls throb in equal measure to his fists. The need to dominate this man was so primal that bending him over felt like the only logical choice to make.

Gunner mumbled something, but with Caspian's finger in the way, it came out unintelligibly. Since it sounded like excuses, Caspian didn't care to listen and held Gunner by the jaw even as the slim fingers wrapped around his wrist. He'd show Gunner Russo what it felt like to be small, powerless, and forced into submission.

The clothes that would have seemed so alien, so wrong for Caspian emphasized how available Gunner was. And to think that all this time he'd kept the girlfriend as a beard and fucked around in secret.

Caspian shoved Gunner onto the bed the moment they reached it, already kicking off his shoes and climbing after him. His gaze licked up the line of Gunner's ass, which the tight jeans showed off so perfectly. So shamelessly. He slapped it hard. "Take off your top."

He sounded raspy.

Sexy.

Like he'd always wanted to.

His hand was so big when compared to the pert backside, and he couldn't look away from this proof of his dominance, so aroused it was making his vision blurry. He could snap this guy in two, but chose to fuck him instead.

Gunner glanced from side to side, and some of the blond stands fell into his face. "Are you sure you w-wanna—?" he asked, but was taking off his shoes.

That was it. He didn't want to wait any longer.

Caspian ground his hips against Gunner's ass and reached to his front, pulling at the T-shirt. The bright fabric clung to the flushed face, but once it was peeled over his head and remained only on his back and shoulders, Caspian twisted the top to secure the slender arms covered with a dusting of hair. Gunner made a small, soft sound but didn't fight him, and even tilted his hips so Caspian's groin rubbed against the balls trapped in tight denim. Regardless of the fake hesitation, the dirty boy wanted this as much as Caspian.

"Yes. You have to pay for what you've done. And all those tight clothes you're wearing gave me just the idea."

When Caspian pushed Gunner's knees apart to make room for himself, the slender back arched when Gunner hid his face in the pillow. Which was for the better, because this way Caspian wouldn't have to confront who he was about to fuck. The blond hair, the clothes, and the submissive way Gunner acted would be enough to hide the strange truth. Because if destiny chose to give Caspian this big, strong body to play around in for a while in an act of cosmic justice, he would not turn his back on what he'd been offered.

He grasped Gunner's hip with the big, tattooed hand the size of Gunner's buttock, and even though he hadn't been the one to choose the ink covering his arms, he'd never felt more comfortable in his body. For once, it was Caspian who called the shots.

He was *the man*. And he'd conquer the body trembling under his touch.

Without thinking twice, he stretched over Gunner and bit into his shoulder blade. The soft gasp muffled by the pillow set him on fire, and he reached to his belt, fumbling with it as he tasted smooth skin, rolling the flesh between his teeth and then teasing the shallow bite marks with his tongue.

"I should have known this was what you wanted all along. You hard yet, Russo? Hard for a cock deep inside you?" He slid one hand between Gunner's legs to find an erection. When Gunner wiggled, releasing a little moan, his ass pressed against Caspian's cock, as if he were trying to tease the shark floating in the water with him, not escape.

His belt fell open, and he yanked it out of the loops, rocking his painfully stiff prick against Gunner. The worn leather went around the slender wrists, tying them together, and only once Caspian was certain his lover would stay put did he free his own erection. Cool air felt like a pinch on heated skin, but he ignored it and opened the skin-tight jeans keeping him from seeing Gunner's goods.

He no longer could think of all that smooth skin as his own, and eagerly peeled the denim off the waiting ass, exposing tight boxer shorts made of neon-blue fabric with a print of pizza slices.

His mouth watered. His brain buzzed, and all of a sudden he was starved enough to bite off a chunk of flesh through the underwear and then drag the flimsy piece of clothing with his teeth.

"I'm gonna make you my bitch, and you're gonna love it," he whispered against the gooseflesh on Gunner's naked buttock.

There was so much to love about a small frame and smooth skin. As long as it wasn't *his*. But fate fixed its mistake today, and he could be the stud he'd always wanted to be. A man allowed to do whatever he wanted with the pliant body shivering under him.

He plucked the lube and condoms out of his pocket and went straight for the virgin hole winking at him when Gunner hugged the pillow and tilted his hips a bit more. One touch was enough, and Gunner raised his feet with toes curled in pleasure. He looked so obscene with pants and boxers lowered just enough to expose his ass yet still hiding the balls and cock in shadow.

He was everything Caspian had always wanted in a hook-up, and as his slickened finger dove into the tight channel, discovering how hot it was, his thoughts caught fire and filled his head with fragrant smoke.

"Did you not hear me? What are you?" he asked and slapped Gunner's buttock, leaving a pink impression of his massive hand.

Gunner yelped and peeked over his shoulder with wide blue eyes partially covered by the blond hair. The dissonance of seeing so much beauty in the body he'd always judged made Caspian stall, but the choked words coming out of Gunner's mouth brought him back to life.

"I'm your bitch," he whispered.

"Hell yes, you are. That's why you're gonna take my cock," Caspian rasped, slamming his knuckles against the hole as his entire middle finger went in. He was surprised to discover that the channel wasn't snug and smooth all the way in, and licked his lips, probing at the flesh beyond the sleeve of tight muscle. He couldn't believe this was happening. That he was about to not only fuck a guy for the first time but also do it with someone so damn pretty.

If he could have been certain of Gunner's health status, he'd have ditched the rubbers, no questions asked, because just thinking about filling up this lovely ass with his cream and marking his territory had him shivering in anticipation.

God, he couldn't wait much longer!

"Oh yeah? I'll screw you so wide open with my big dick," he gasped and slapped his tool against the same buttock that still bore the mark of his palm. The slender arms tied with the shirt and belt were the picture of submission, and the ragged noise of Gunner breathing into the pillow made Caspian's heart pound in his chest like a machine. He was no longer a twig of a boy but a beast to be feared.

"Yes. Fuck me," Gunner uttered and spread the trembling thighs wider while his little hole tightened around Caspian's finger in a promise of what it would soon do to his dick.

His cock had a mind of its own and wanted to dive in already, but Caspian would do it right and distracted himself by counting flowers on the curtains as his fingers stretched the tight hole until Gunner no longer tightened up.

But once he decided that this delicious ass, framed by lowered underwear and a leather belt holding still a pair of wrists, was ready, he pulled on the condom, and pushed his dick at Gunner's hole. The muscle didn't give in right away, and the entrance dipped under pressure, which only aroused him more.

"Yes. Fuck. Take it."

The little moans and mewls Gunner uttered were ambrosia to his ears, but he could barely think straight when the tight ring of muscle relaxed enough to accept his cockhead. Having a man under him like this had always been an unfulfilled fantasy of Caspian's, and he held his breath, watching the rigid length sink between pale buttocks, one of which was still flushed from the single strike. He hoped the faint hand imprint would mark Gunner as his forever, and while this was in no way a rational wish, he still indulged in the fantasy of owning this boy.

"Fuck, fuck, fuck..." Gunner uttered, rolling his face over the pillow as sweat beaded on his back. He was tense but didn't try to pull away when Caspian took hold of his narrow hips and made shallow thrusts, pushing farther past his partner's resistance each time. Gunner's channel felt like a vice made of hot silk, but Caspian didn't want to finish yet and alternated between staring at the glorious flesh under him and closing his eyes to let excitement dim just enough that he could continue.

He felt like Alexander the Great conquering Persia.

Begging for more dick with each movement of his hips, Gunner seemed to relax. His fingers kept twitching and squeezing the brown leather tightened around his wrists, and if it were doable, Caspian would have loved to nip and suck on each digit as he jackhammered the tight ass.

"Too much for you, virgin boy? Too bad you no longer have a choice," he whispered, moaning when his cock went in farther and finally bottomed out. "You're mine until you milk my cock, get it?"

Gunner gave a frantic nod, and squeezed his ass on Caspian's cock without even being prompted. "Yes. Please, use me."

Never before did Caspian have such ultimate control of anyone. The boy under him voiced his submission with every little moan, and Caspian could've gotten high on the sounds alone. It didn't matter which body was whose and why. He, Caspian, was on top and giving his lover cock while being encouraged to fuck harder.

He'd never been this wanted, this desired, and the feeling was already sinking its teeth into his flesh. He wanted to always feel like this.

"Yeah? Gunner Russo loves my cock up his slutty ass?" he uttered, squeezing his hands on Gunner's waist as he entered him ever faster.

The other body no longer resisted, and his dick moved in and out freely, a fat baton stabbing into the soft, warm hole over and over. As he picked up his pace, Gunner's buttocks shook every time Caspian slammed home, his entire body yielding to the force behind

Caspian's thrusts. The moans escaping Gunner's lips went straight to Caspian's balls, so every now and then, he gave Gunner a little slap on the ass just to get a reaction.

But what aroused him most was feeling the difference between their bodies, so he dropped to all fours, locking the smaller man under him and fucking Gunner like the bitch he was. He even grabbed his throat for good measure, loving how the pulse quickened under his touch.

"That's it, you'll be riding my cock every day until I'm done with you," Caspian growled and bit on Gunner's nape like a wolf pinning his prey.

Gunner's moan sounded like a confirmation, but Caspian wanted to see proof and sat back on his heels taking his boy with him so they both kneeled, with Gunner sitting in Caspian's lap.

Blue eyes peeked at him from a flushed face, hazy as if Gunner were drunk on the thick dick drilling his ass. Caspian pushed two fingers into the soft mouth and shivered when the boy sucked on them right away, greedy for more. Harder. Faster.

"Go on. Milk me. You better hope that condom doesn't break, slut, or you'll be leaking cum all the way home," Caspian growled and rolled his teeth over the exposed throat.

When Gunner started pumping his cute round ass against Caspian's groin, heaven opened above them. What was supposed to be a hate fuck, a way to get off and punish Gunner at the same time, was turning into an addictive feast for all senses. He'd wanted sex before, but until now he'd had no idea just how hungry he'd been for this exact meal.

Gunner rolled his narrow hips at a quick pace, legs spread wide to accommodate Caspian's thighs, rising and falling as if his life depended on it, and he sucked on Caspian's fingers while mumbling something. He squeezed the tight channel of muscles as if the only thing that mattered now was Caspian's pleasure.

When the tied hands pressed to the bare flesh of Caspian's stomach, he was lost.

Pleasure buzzed at the base of his spine before jolting up and down his body as he pushed his hips up, thrusting into Gunner until his balls emptied. The world spun, and he already knew that he needed to buy the very same brand of cotton-scented air freshener that hung in the air, so it would always remind him of this moment.

Spent, he pulled Gunner close and dove his hand down the slender body, capturing the hard cock and pumping it at a merciless pace.

Gunner's mouth was free again to make those painfully arousing noises, but those didn't last long. He cried out, and hot spunk covered Caspian's fist like the physical manifestation of pleasure leaving his body. The tight hole started throbbing with heat around Caspian's cock as if it didn't want to let go yet.

Caspian could well have been called Zeus, because he felt like a god when he lazily lapped at the bite mark he'd left on Gunner's shoulder. As he pushed the boy forward, and the warm ass slid off Caspian's softening dick, he found himself staring at the hole, which now shone with lube.

"Fuck... that was—" Hot. So very hot. The hottest thing on the planet.

But instead of the horny promises he was expecting, Caspian heard a sob. His brain stilled. His bones turned into ice, and the lingering arousal into confusion. Hadn't Gunner come while asking for more?

The boy curled up, rolling his face into the pillow, and Caspian stared at him as horror took root in his flesh and chased away the pride he'd felt moments ago.

He did hate Gunner. Always had. But he'd also wanted to excite him and fuck him more thoroughly than any man before. This was supposed to be his moment of triumph.

Uncertain, Caspian touched Gunner's side with the back of his hand. "I... are you hurt?"

"N-no, just take this off," Gunner said between one sob and another, hiding his face, but awkwardly holding out his bound wrists to Caspian.

Caspian's head throbbed with static as he released Gunner from the belt and T-shirt. Had he done something wrong? The sight of tears streaming down the reddened face didn't give him the rush of power they'd had in the morning. His sexual fantasies could get a bit violent, but not because he wanted to *hurt* anyone. Even Gunner.

"Are you sure you're okay?" he tried in a softer voice as he watched Gunner pull up his pants and hide the flesh still marked by Caspian's slaps.

"Yeah, I'm fine, I just—never with a man—" Gunner looked around the floor, as if searching for something, but got up while Caspian was still processing what he'd just heard.

"But you're gay. And had this hot body." He pointed to his chest, not bothered to zip up, but he did throw away the condom.

Gunner ran his fingers through the blond hair, and Caspian once again marveled at how it suited his blue eyes. "I'll... see you around," Gunner mumbled, and Caspian frowned in shock, but Gunner opened the door and bolted.

Barefoot. In only his jeans.

No.

This wasn't over!

Chapter 9 - Gunner

Gunner collided with the door and fumbled with the broken handle, his mind screaming that the predator who'd just sampled him was about to bite in again. He managed to open the motel room and stumbled outside when his stomach twisted in discomfort. The sun was still up and shone straight into his eyes as he ran into the parking lot, trying not to think about the forbidden thing he'd done. And with Caspian of all people.

What the hell was wrong with him?

Had the lack of opportunity really been the only reason stopping him from having sex with a man before? Impossible. This body must have been what made him lose all inhibition. Just like he couldn't control his new eyes, and they kept leaking tears when his real body seemed to be made of stone.

He didn't know where he was going, he was barefoot, and had left his phone in the room, but none of it mattered. The urge to run was too great to ignore. He needed to escape what he'd done.

Gunner hadn't just let Caspian fuck him. He'd ridden the guy's dick. Said he was Caspian's *bitch*.

And the worst thing was that in the moment, he hadn't cared about what all of it meant, too lost in pleasure of those massive hands holding him down and dirty whispers in his ear. He'd let Caspian show him his place using Gunner's own flesh against him!

And he'd gone with it like a cheap whore. He wasn't normal. None of this was normal.

He wanted to disappear.

A loud honk tore through the air, and Gunner looked left in time to see wide eyes staring at him from behind a windshield. The car came to an abrupt stop, but its hood still pushed at Gunner's hip. With his head spinning and legs far from stable, he didn't manage to remain standing and fell onto the asphalt.

Caspian—in Gunner's old body—slammed both his hands on the roof of the car, his neck and face blooming with a dark flush. "Are you fucking blind?" he roared in a low voice that sounded as if it had come from a rusty pipe. "You just hit him! If there's a single bruise on that boy, I'll find you, and I'll break your neck!"

Gunner got up on shaky legs, unsure what to say, but just as he turned around and was about to run into oblivion, Caspian grabbed him from behind and threw him over his shoulder as if he weighed nothing.

"You're not going anywhere," he whispered, and the vicious tone in his voice prompted Gunner to curl his toes. Was *this* how he sounded to others? Like a lion purring at his mate? That did explain why so many girls leaned closer when he spoke to them and why Sandy stuck around.

The guy in the car didn't even care to shout anything back and drove off with a squeal of tires.

Gunner's head throbbed with questions he had no way of answering. "I... We don't have to talk about it!" He wiggled in the hold, but it was like steel. He shouldn't have been surprised. He knew his body was strong. He'd worked all his life to make it so, and still, to be on the receiving end of that force was both thrilling and terrifying.

"We absolutely do," Caspian said and carried him toward the open door to their motel room as if Gunner were weightless. But as the asphalt and trash littering the parking lot passed under Gunner, it occurred to him that his hole felt damp, and a bit sore, and that he *needed* to be alone. Process everything that happened and clean up without anyone staring at him. Especially not *Caspian*.

But shock kept him quiet and clutching to the other man's massive form.

"Hey, where are you taking him?"

Caspian spun around, and when Gunner crooked his neck, he saw a woman staring at them with a stern expression. And while Gunner saw her upside-down, he recognized the body language of someone ready to run. Or call the cops.

He wanted neither to happen. This was between him and Caspian. Their situation was fucked up enough without the interference of an outsider.

"It's okay," he laughed nervously. "Just a game we play."

The woman's shoulders relaxed, and she took a step back, adjusting a large weekend bag on her shoulder. "If you say so—"

She let her gaze linger on Gunner, as if offering him another chance to ask for help, but Gunner's indecision was put to rest when Caspian gave him a slap on the ass—a callback to the glorious moments from fifteen minutes ago when Gunner's skin had burned with blows much harder than this one.

"You're coming with me, boy. Brace yourself," Caspian said so loudly it could only be for the benefit of strangers, and Gunner found himself cooking on the inside.

Caspian put him down once the door was locked behind them, and Gunner's stomach cramped at the discomfort of the upcoming conversation, because he didn't want to have it. He'd never even told anyone of his gay feelings, and had only tried to get together with Mike because it couldn't be traced back to him once he returned to his own body, and he'd somehow ended up submitting to the one person who knew the truth.

He'd let a man fuck him. Call him slut. Slap his ass.

And he'd begged for it.

He covered his face with both hands and kept them there when Caspian grabbed his forearms and steered him back until Gunner's calves hit the bed. With hope leaking out of him like air from a slashed tire, Gunner sat down, resigned to his fate. He parted his fingers enough to glance at Caspian.

But instead of rolling him over for another round, Caspian took a cautious step back and crossed his arms on his chest, just staring. Gunner wasn't used to being in the presence of someone who could overpower him with such ease, and he couldn't help but peek at the massive tattooed pecs that, unbelievably, still felt like a part of him. He'd chosen that ink to look dangerous, to intimidate, and it was working even though he knew it was Caspian Brady on the inside.

The silent scrutiny felt like a hand tightening around Gunner's throat, and he wished for his body to cave in on itself, so he didn't have to confront the reality of what happened. But there was only so long the truth could be avoided, because Caspian knew all about Gunner's shame.

"I don't know how to do this, okay? I don't know how to be gay!" he choked out breathlessly. "I can't blame it on your body, since you're in mine, and you've clearly got a mind of your own. So I guess this is me. A faggy fag." He sobbed, too overwhelmed to fight it.

"Jesus, don't say that," Caspian muttered and dragged over an old chair, which he sat in back-to-front. He even put on his T-shirt as if they needed decency all of a sudden. He then speared Gunner with an inquisitive gaze that didn't belong on the boorish face. It was so strange to see someone else behind features Gunner had seen in the mirror all his life. Not just because he wasn't the one *inside there*, but because Caspian's body language and expressions were so different to his own that they transformed the familiar physique into something unknown.

Gunner spread his arms, helpless against the interrogating gaze. "Well, it's true. I just let you drill me like I didn't have a brain anymore. And now I'm crying about it like a wuss! Can I just stop fucking crying?" He grabbed a tissue from the side of the bed and rubbed off the tears that kept coming.

Caspian remained silent, his thick, handsome brows lowering, as if he were taking his time to think over what Gunner said. "Is that something you wanted? You know… before?" he asked, and while the question was intrusive, there wasn't even a hint of a mocking smile tugging at the corners of his mouth.

Gunner needed to take a deep breath to stop his teeth from clattering. There was no point in lying, was there? "Y-yes. But I've never done it. And then you put your hand on my throat, like you owned me, and I fucking lost it."

Caspian cleared his throat and moved in the chair, as if he were attempting to lessen the pressure of fabric on his crotch. Was this awkward conversation turning him on?

"That's okay. People have all kinds of fantasies. Maybe you just felt free to go with what you wanted because… you're not yourself? Does that make sense?"

Gunner gave a weak nod, because just like he'd felt more confident about drinking a girly drink in public in this new body, the desire to submit no longer felt as jarring as it had in his own hulking form. He took a moment to assess this new situation and looked down at his curled toes. Even his feet were cute now—narrow and nearly hairless. "I guess. Those things are just… not something I should even consider."

"Why?"

Gunner groaned in frustration. Why did he have to explain this? "'Cause you don't get any respect if you are that way. You've got no idea about my life, so please make sure to keep your needs on the down low while you're in my body." Though it seemed that Caspian's needs were exactly what Gunner's body was made for.

Caspian shifted, as if Gunner's response made him uncomfortable. He embraced the back of the chair and rested his chin on the wood. "I used to be out in college, but no one in this town knows. No one needs to know what we do in bed, right?" he asked, and his brown gaze pinned Gunner down, as if he were an insect on a board, not yet dead but already knowing its fate.

Heat climbed Gunner's neck when their eyes met. Was Caspian suggesting they'd fuck again? Gunner's stomach clenched at the memory of being under all that bulk, his hands twitching in bondage while a thick cock pounded him like a jackhammer.

"You'd want that? Just until we err... work out what happened..." Gunner's heart started rattling the moment he realized that he could finally explore the desires he'd kept secret all his life. Temptation was being handed to him on a silver platter, and he suddenly wished to be much closer to the man who'd taken him with such ferocity.

Caspian stretched and cleared his throat before meeting his gaze. "It makes sense, doesn't it? You want to explore your fantasies, and I want to—enjoy having this body," he said, pointing to his chest as he rose, towering over Gunner even from two steps away.

When Gunner hadn't managed to produce a sound, Caspian sat next to him on the bed, legs spread so his knee poked Gunner's. How strange was it that he was aroused by his own body when it wasn't his anymore? Had it been this sex or masturbation?

"And... no hook-ups with other people," Gunner muttered, daring to run his fingers over Caspian's sturdy thigh. "We've got reputations and stuff."

A scowl passed through Caspian's face, but after a tense second, he offered Gunner his hand. "But I'm seriously horny. You need to be around if we're not gonna see other people."

Gunner squeezed the massive fingers as if they were his lifeline. It felt so strange to shake on something and feel so small when compared to the other guy. The fingers touching his were thick, and rough, and so very hot to the touch. And he liked it. Being small. Being weaker. Being the object of another man's lust.

"Yeah. We'll make it work. I know what you're talking about. Like if you don't get your dick sucked, you might just punch someone."

Caspian broke into a chuckle and leaned closer, bumping his head against Gunner's with a smile so friendly it transformed the familiar features into those of a stranger. A very handsome one at that. "*Yes*. Very much yes. How do you deal with this?"

Gunner's heart fluttered. "I guess I'm just angry very often. I box— but also... Have you met Sandy?"

Caspian groaned. "Right. Your girlfriend."

"No, she's... I mean she *was* my girlfriend. We're kinda on-off. Like, mostly off, but I let her stay at mine. Don't know how to get rid of her."

"So I *can* kick her out?"

Gunner shook his head. "You can try. I haven't succeeded. She always turns it around somehow. Point is, sometimes, if I got really horny, it worked with her. But never *really*, you know?"

Caspian nuzzled the bridge of Gunner's nose. "Because you're gay."

Gunner swallowed. "Yeah. Probably. Only one way to check, right? Can I kiss you? Or is that too weird?"

Caspian licked his lips, and his hand moved over the mattress to rest behind Gunner. "I might have gone about this the wrong way. And I might not be the uber-gay you always thought I was, but I do have some experience. I could teach you," he said and moved his finger up Gunner's throat, eventually pulling on his chin as he leaned in and pressed his lips to Gunner's.

Gunner had kissed quite a few women in his life. Mostly when drunk at parties, but this couldn't have been more different. This was the kiss he wanted. He closed his eyes and in this body, with this man, didn't feel the pressure to take over. He didn't know what was expected of him, and instead of stressing out about it, he embraced being passive and let Caspian guide him.

The arm behind him pressed closer, providing support to his back, and Caspian's other hand moved to his neck, so very warm as it squeezed his throat. Caspian opened Gunner's lips and teased them with the tip of his tongue.

A giddy smile spread Gunner's mouth as he let it happen. For once, he didn't have to make decisions and call the shots. He was free to go with the flow and that gave him the confidence to kiss back. He let his fingertips travel up the large forearm of the man who'd already fucked him once and *would* do it again.

It gave him such a thrill to know this for certain, and when Caspian nipped on his lips, pulling away, Gunner leaned in, trying to capture that stubborn mouth. Caspian grinned at him.

"Say it."

Gunner had a vague feeling he knew what this was about, but feigned obliviousness. "Say what?" He attempted to distract Caspian by sliding his hand between his legs, but it wasn't as effective as he'd hoped, and Caspian grabbed his jaw, forcing Gunner to meet his gaze.

"Say that you're my bitch," he whispered with a wolfish smile, and the raspiness of his voice sent a shiver all the way to Gunner's cock.

It would have been easier after a few colorful shots, but Gunner still did as told, because Caspian's confidence was too hot to resist. "I'm your bitch," he whispered and cupped Caspian's package, elated at being allowed to do such a thing.

This time, the distraction worked, but was it really a distraction at that point? Caspian let out a soft gasp and covered Gunner's cute palm with his paw while rocking his hips up. "This is lesson number one, bitch. Undress me," he whispered, pulling Gunner's hand to the hem of his shirt.

Gunner shouldn't enjoy being humiliated with words, nor serving another man, yet here they were. For as long as this craziness lasted, he would be bold and take life by the balls.

Drunk on the freedom to touch another man, he climbed into Caspian's lap and pulled up his T-shirt, amazed by the powerful chest and arms as if they hadn't been his own only yesterday. He would often worry whether he shouldn't bulk up more, but seen from the perspective of someone else, his old body was huge and oozed danger out of every line of ink. Gunner trailed his fingers over the tense stomach, and couldn't help but feel a prickle of arousal at the scent of sweat that had seeped into the T-shirt Caspian had worn during their first fuck.

"Do you like it? Touching a man?" Caspian asked, resting his fingers on Gunner's hips but not yet moving them anywhere else, even though the chub in his pants made his excitement obvious.

Gunner nodded and put one of his arms around Caspian's shoulders as he unzipped Caspian's pants with the other hand. "I'm fucking overheating," he rasped. "It's not too weird, right? I look at you, and I don't see... myself, you know?"

"So weird. But me neither. You're—" Caspian licked his lips and pushed his thumbs up Gunner's chest. "The blond really suits you," he said, rolling his hips up to rub his underwear against Gunner's hand. How had this much confidence hidden in the tiny frame Gunner now lived in?

He sighed with relief. "Yeah? 'Cause I thought it was cute. And then you said Alex isn't your friend, and I was like... *fuuuck*!" He leaned in for a quick kiss, just because he could.

Caspian growled but didn't push Gunner away and lifted his hips so Gunner could pull the jeans off. "He's Judas incarnate. A real snake. But dealing with him will be on my *agenda*," he said, almost as if it excited him as much as the touching. The desire for revenge looked so sexy on those stern features, wrinkling the broad nose and twisting the lips that had called Gunner such derogatory things.

Gunner sniggered at the unfamiliar words. He hopped off Caspian's lap to take his pants off with more ease. There, he'd undress him and be *his bitch*.

The ugly word floated in his head like fizzing candy—sweet, sour, and provoking constant excitement as he rolled his hands down Caspian's thighs and watched him like a good boy.

"Are your parents immigrants? They say shit in strange languages too." His eyes glided over the thick package, and he curled his toes at the memory of that dick sliding up and down his crack. He could still feel the burn it left behind. And now he wished to make the discomfort even more aggravating.

Caspian didn't answer right away, but he rolled his knuckles down Gunner's cheek in an unusually affectionate gesture. "It's Latin. Mom's in the habit of using some proverbs and the like, and I picked it up from her."

"Oh," was all Gunner had. He'd never graduated high school. But it wasn't as though Caspian needed a conversation partner. Their exchange would be physical. That much he could offer.

After a moment of hesitation, Gunner kneeled in front of Caspian, sliding his fingers over the thighs covered in short dark hair. He'd always wanted to know what it was like to suck cock, and now he could try it without fear or shame. Caspian was gay and probably saw nothing humiliating about what Gunner was about to do. He was safe to experiment with for as long as their strange situation lasted.

"You want to taste it?" Caspian asked and pressed his heel against Gunner's back, bringing him closer to the stiff length filling the front of Caspian's underwear.

The aroma of cum still hung in the air, and Gunner's ass throbbed when he remembered coming in the crumpled sheets less than fifteen minutes ago.

It was insanity, yet he wanted to continue. To now taste Caspian's—or was it his own— cum. "It's not weird, right? That I want to?" he asked, looking up from the floor at the powerful man above. In this new body, he could be completely submissive and hand over the reins to someone else. Without worry or fear.

Caspian shook his head, staring at Gunner with eyes so dark they were like twin wells in the middle of the night. He covered Gunner's hands with his own and pulled them up his thighs, as if he wanted Gunner to feel how muscular and hairy they were. "You're doing good."

While Gunner regretted getting the face tattoo, he did like the other ink on his body, and it took on a different meaning to him now that he saw it as an outsider. The man he was about to serve with his mouth had threats pushed into his skin, and every dark line, even the ones forming the grotesque skull shape on the right side of his face, communicated to the world that he'd crush anyone who dared challenge him.

To be of interest to a man like that was both frightening and exciting. The strength packed into the thick muscles meant Gunner could be easily carried, overpowered, but if he belonged to such a stud, he'd also be protected, cared for. In his fantasies at least.

Gunner had butterflies in his stomach as he pushed Caspian's briefs down enough to see that his cock was hard for him again. His female partners liked its size, since, while large, it wasn't too big to handle, and thank fuck for that, because it still left his ass aching a bit. But when he leaned in to lick the tip, it occurred to him that he wasn't sure how much of it he'd fit into a mouth so gracefully small.

How perverse was it that it made him even hornier for dick?

Caspian's hand felt so big against his face. The thick fingers that used to be so familiar pushed into Gunner's hair, caressing his scalp as he rolled his tongue around the head like a good boy.

"Just... go slow first. Taste it," Caspian whispered, watching Gunner like a hungry wolf about to pounce its meal. The large teeth tattooed above and under his lips on one side transformed him into a beast that might rip out his throat if he didn't service its cock well enough.

It gave Gunner a thrill to wrap his slim fingers around the hot girth and lick the drop of pre-cum glinting at the pisshole. His own dick throbbed in anticipation, but what he wanted was those dark eyes on him, and fingers squeezing his hair to make him understand that he wouldn't get to touch himself until he served his purpose.

"Like this?" he whispered with his lips lovingly pressed to the cockhead.

Caspian's dick was salty and tasted of the cum it had shot into the condom. Touching it made Gunner's own cock twitch in his pants as he closed his eyes and focused on all his other senses while Caspian petted his head.

"Lick it. Like it's a popsicle and it's so hot you're craving it more than anything."

The fantasy Caspian presented was so very close to Gunner's desires, but if he was to avoid staining his new jeans, he needed to release the pressure on his groin. Relief flooded him along with the excitement when he pushed the denim lower, but while it aroused him that his ass was again exposed, the only desires that counted were Caspian's, so Gunner got right back to the dick in need of attention.

He first sucked in the bulbous head and closed his eyes with a groan as his fingers once more found their way to Caspian's sturdy thighs.

"That's a good boy. Feel it. I want to shoot down your throat and see you swallow all of it. My cum belongs inside you," Caspian whispered, spreading his legs farther and pushing up his hips.

How had this much erotic energy hidden in Caspian's small body all this time?

Gunner was so eager to suck in more of it he quickly leaned in, testing how much he could take. His ears burned when he imagined himself on his knees, with cock-sucking as his one obligation.

Caspian's hand tightened in his hair, holding him down when the cock rolled up Gunner's tongue and pushed at the back of his throat. It felt so big in his mouth already, but despite instinctively wanting to pull away, he couldn't, or didn't want to, resist the dominant gesture and tightened his lips on the girth, sucking on the thick meat.

Caspian uttered a low grunt and raised his knees on either side of Gunner's head. "Fuck... yes. You like how it tastes, little cocksucker?"

Gunner grunted his enthusiasm and ran his hands up to Caspian's tense stomach. All the muscles he'd worked so hard to chisel were now available to his touch, so he closed his eyes and inhaled the musky scent clinging to dark pubic hair. If Caspian wanted to come down his throat three times a day, he'd just need to call, and Gunner would be there to provide his services.

He was so masculine, and decisive, and each ugly word coming from his mouth went straight to Gunner's balls. Their fantasies were perfectly aligned, and whatever power had made them swap bodies intended to give them both what they wanted.

"Touch my balls. Gently," Caspian said and made a little stir with his hips, which pushed the head of his cock past Gunner's gag reflex, making him choke ever-so-slightly.

He followed the request, petting the tight sac, as if he wanted to coax cum into his mouth. He was so horny for this. For this man. For what Caspian offered. Not only for the body he could experiment with, but also the aura of dominance that stroked Gunner's dick without touch.

Another moan. Gunner loved how it sounded—somehow both needy and masculine—and he sucked on the hard prick with more force, rubbing his tongue against the shaft until Caspian pushed him lower.

"Look up. Look at me."

Gunner's eyes darted to Caspian's dark gaze and the smile of a predator on his lips.

"That's it. Let me see that mouth full of cock," Caspian purred in a low tone that made every hair bristle on Gunner's body. And then Caspian pushed up his hips while firmly holding on to Gunner's hair, and drool rolled out of Gunner's mouth down the thick shaft as if he were an animal, helpless against his desires.

"I'm not sure if you can fit in all of it. You're so small," Caspian said with a mean smile stretching his mouth. His cock rocked back and forth, riding Gunner's tongue and hitting the back of his throat each time, as if he were preparing ground for his next move.

Gunner frowned, straining with the effort to stop gagging, yet Caspian's distracting touch made him shiver and lose focus. The stiff cock throbbed in his mouth, and he traced every ridge with his tongue as his heart rattled in fear and anticipation.

"If only I'd known back in high school that Gunner Russo would be sucking my cock with so much devotion... Would have made my days so much sweeter. Go on. Take it. I'm not letting you go until you swallow my cum," Caspian rasped and made an abrupt thrust with his hips, making Gunner gag as the cockhead slid past his soft palate and forced its way into his throat.

Panic struck, flashing white in Gunnar's eyes as he trembled and tried to pull away. But Caspian held him steady and made a little shushing noise. "Breathe. I'm not gonna hurt you," he said in a voice so different from the vicious yet exciting tone he'd used before. But he didn't move, keeping his prick somewhere *inside* Gunner's neck, where it provoked the gag reflex and uncontrollable drooling.

Gunner took several long inhales through his nose, then looked up into Caspian's face despite the dampness in his eyes. He shouldn't trust Caspian. Not after high school. And especially not after what had happened at the gym yesterday. Yet here he was. Still on his knees, still caressing Caspian's cock with his tongue.

He wanted this so bad. Wanted *him* so bad that he couldn't help himself and eventually calmed down, swallowing when instructed. Once he relaxed, the intrusion no longer felt so threatening, and he even leaned into the fingers rolling across his scalp.

"I know you can take it. I *know*," Caspian said, and pushed Gunner's head lower as soon as he finished filling his lungs with air.

Gunner's cock twitched when yet more of the length dove into his throat, and this time he managed not to gag. He was Caspian's bitch and didn't have the right to refuse him. In this warped world of arousing humiliation, his mouth only existed for Caspian's pleasure. Losing the control over his access to air was damn scary, but he needed to trust that Caspian wouldn't choke him to death and just needed to wait until his master chose to let him breathe.

Maybe it was a fucked-up way to think about this, maybe trusting the guy he'd bullied made Gunner a fool, but he was getting dick for the first time in his life and couldn't be expected to make rational decisions. He reached between his own legs with a choked moan.

"Keep those hands on me," Caspian said in a voice so demanding Gunner didn't dare refuse him and embraced both of the firm thighs keeping him trapped. His mind heated, screaming that he might start choking soon, but Caspian mercifully pulled out, letting his cockhead rest on Gunner's tongue. The salty aroma filled his mouth, heightening the anticipation building in his body. He'd swallow cum. Finally, after all the years of dreaming about it, he'd taste the real thing!

"Open wide. I want to see everything," Caspian ordered, and kept speaking as he watched his own cock leaking pre-cum into Gunner's mouth, beautiful and scary like a beast that held Gunner's life in his hands. "I'm gonna fuck that hot little mouth hole of yours now. Tap my thigh if you need air, but you better not."

Gunner whimpered, and Caspian didn't give him any more warnings. He pulled on Gunner's hair, holding him in place and sawed his cock into Gunner's mouth, forcing the thick meat down his throat every other thrust. Just like he'd promised.

Gunner was scared at first, despite knowing Caspian wouldn't hurt his own body, but when Caspian eventually pulled his cock out to let him breathe, the fear transformed into lust so primal he wished Caspian had a twin to fuck Gunner again while he sucked.

Not allowed to touch himself, he was reduced to being a willing tool. A hole Caspian could use for sexual relief however and whenever he wanted. Gunner used to fantasize about his friends getting him drunk and having his way with him, since it had seemed like the only way he'd ever get to experience sex with men, but this was a hundred times better. The humiliation came with a sense of safety, since Caspian didn't seem like a bad person, and as Gunner got used to the prick pushing into him at the angle Caspian chose, the thrusts became hypnotic. His skin burned. His head was a mess of random thoughts and images, but he floated beyond it all, focused on the strong, steady hands and the dick *taking him* again.

He'd never produced so much saliva, and each time Caspian pulled out, threads of thick spit stretched between the cock and Gunner's waiting mouth hole.

Mouth hole.

In this moment, he wished it was his *name*.

"That's good. Keep that pretty little mouth open," Caspian rasped and slid one of his massive hands to Gunner's throat, making him mewl.

The next few thrusts were brutal, but felt almost *necessary*. A predator like Caspian couldn't come without drawing at least a bit of blood, and when he reached his high, the nails digging into the side of Gunner's neck were the confirmation of his nature as prey.

He swallowed when the first gob of spunk hit the back of his throat, ready to do whatever Caspian required. His head spun. His back was damp with perspiration. He was shaking.

Caspian let out a sequence of low, raspy grunts as his balls emptied down Gunner's *hole*, but once he was done, he cupped Gunner's heated face with both his paws and held it up, with his cock softening on the soft, damp bed of Gunner's tongue.

"Did you like it, bitch?" he whispered, struggling for breath while Gunner kept his thighs wide open to avoid putting too much pressure on his own dick and coming all over his pants.

He nodded, a shivering mess with his neck still aching where the nails had bit in. This was madness. Pure fucking madness. Yesterday, he'd reluctantly joined in on the taunting at the gym, and now, here they were, with Gunner swallowing Caspian's cum in apology.

"Thank you," he slurred around the cock in his mouth. All this time, he'd been hiding the nature of a slut, and he could finally let his freak flag fly.

Caspian's eyes brightened when he smiled, so very handsome it was making Gunner's erection painful. "You ever had a man give you a blowjob?"

Gunner shook his head with air caught in his throat. "I've never done any of this with a man," he uttered once Caspian finally removed his cock.

Their eyes met, and the dangerous glint in those brown eyes made Gunner shiver even before Caspian threw him onto the bed as if he were a ragdoll. The crumpled sheets dug into Gunner's back, but he didn't dare move when Caspian rolled over him, and licked Gunner from his balls to the tip of his dick.

"Oh God!" Gunner whimpered and bit down on his fist. This man was a beast. He *should* have been born in Gunner's body.

Would have made so much better use of it. But as Caspian took in the entire dick with no issue, Gunner questioned how much practice Caspian had at this. How many cocks have already come inside this small, elegant body before Gunner got to live in it?

It turned him on that he didn't know. As if he'd been used by anonymous men while wearing a blindfold.

It only took several bobs of Caspian's head and a few licks for Gunner to come with a ferocity that shook his whole body, and he cried out, curling his legs and grabbing at Caspian's head.

No thoughts existed in his mind for several seconds, only pure fulfillment. He clutched Caspian's short hair, worried the other man might pull away too soon, but he stayed, caressing Gunner's cock with his tongue and stroking his bare skin until waves of pleasure left him adrift.

There was a squashed fly on the ceiling above the bed.

But it didn't matter that the air smelled stale, or that no one had bothered to properly clean the room when Gunner had just had sex with a man for the first time.

Caspian looked up and let Gunner's cock drop with a wide smile. "You were so turned on."

Gunner was still barely breathing and too tired to feign coyness. "I'm such a fucking slut," he said with resignation. He loved it. How would he deny what was obviously true?

"A very sexy one," Caspian said, grinning as he crawled up the bed and rested his head next to Gunner's. His arm was heavy as it lay across Gunner's chest, but while their bodies cooled, there was nothing but pleasure in the loose embrace.

Gunner hesitated, but eventually turned to Caspian and hugged him. He fought the overwhelming feelings drowning him when Caspian held him in a way so different from short bear hugs and pats on the back. The embrace offered comfort that made the rough sex they'd just had seem less illicit. A sense of melancholy flooded him the moment he came and threatened to drown him, but Caspian's presence was the life jacket keeping his head above murky waters of regret.

"Do you know if this hotel works by the hour? Not sure when we should leave," Caspian said and yawned, lazily rubbing Gunner's back.

Gunner put his cheek against the meaty pec with a smile. "We need to go soon anyway. You're giving boxing lessons at seven."

Caspian frowned. "What? I know nothing about boxing."

Gunner bit his lip and pulled on Caspian's nipple with a silly smile. "It's important, okay? I'll go with you and coach you through it."

Caspian rolled his face into the covers. "Okay. Fine. But we'll eat some real food right after. I'm already starving."

Gunner considered that for a bit, but he was still stuffed since having pancakes and the sweet coffee drink. "I could eat…" he paused, and when Caspian looked up at him with raised eyebrows, he finished. "Dick."

"Idiot."

Chapter 10 - Caspian

Caspian would have never admitted it to Gunner, but he was sweating bullets. Just twenty minutes after their quick shower at the motel, his T-shirt was starting to stick to his back, but he'd used some Old Spice he'd found in the glove compartment of Gunner's rusty truck, so there was at least a chance that no one would smell the fear on him.

It was one thing to carry his head high and send people menacing stares. Teaching a skill he didn't have—quite another. He was setting himself up for failure, but he figured it might be all right if the lesson happened in private.

No such luck. Gunner drove Caspian's lovingly-restored Southfield to the same goddamn gym where Caspian had been put through the worst humiliation ever, and while it now felt like a lifetime ago, he'd only woken up in Gunner's body this morning. He'd been on edge on the way there, but Gunner turned out to be a surprisingly good driver, so he didn't have to worry about his rare vintage baby at least.

Though, considering the vehicle was fully insured, that was still the least of his worries.

The gym was swarming with people, and by the time Caspian stepped out of the truck and faced its bright lights, his legs felt as if they were made of cotton, no matter how muscular they now were.

He was glad that Gunner's presence provided him with a distraction, because he looked stupidly cute in the oversized hoodie he'd borrowed from Caspian. He'd gotten self-conscious about the tight, colorful T-shirt he'd worn to the motel, and said he needed to rethink his style after all. Caspian hoped the tight jeans weren't going anywhere though. A part of him regretted that the hoodie obscured Gunner's ass, but another part, one weirdly primal, was glad that no one other than him would get to see it.

"So... who am I looking for? I know this is short notice, but can you actually tell me if there's an easy way of training someone without actually showing everyone that I don't know what I'm doing?" Caspian waved back at two massive men, who gestured at him from a bench by the gym's front door.

"The kid's fourteen and only started a few months back, I'll guide you through it. You'll only be training one move today to perfect it, and I'll show it to you before he comes."

Gunner put his hands in the pockets of the hoodie, leading the way as if this place wasn't a sanctuary for monsters. Caspian had been picked apart by them just last night, and Gunner was obviously aware of the risk of showing up here in Caspian's body, so fuck only knew how he managed to stay so confident.

Caspian followed him inside like a sheep, confused as to why Gunner Russo would be training *kids*. Did he intend to pull them into some kind of gang activity Caspian didn't yet know about? He did vaguely know most criminals started out early in their lives.

As the two of them approached the entrance, he cringed, already anticipating that Gunner would get the same treatment he'd had last night, but when he gave a loud whistle, the two guys blocking the way noticed him right away and stepped aside, parting like the Red Sea had for Moses and the Israelites.

How was the little shrimp doing that?

He nodded at the guys and followed Gunner into the bright front room, but while he'd expected having to chat to the receptionist first, Gunner headed for the locker room, as if it were a safe place for him to be.

Maybe he still didn't realize how others saw him? Or did he rely on Caspian's protection?

Or maybe he knew some moves he could pull off even in a body with short and thin limbs.

"I'll show you the move in the lockers," Gunner whispered and blew air at the strand of hair falling into his eyes. It was still hard to comprehend how different he seemed despite wearing Caspian's own skin.

Inside, a tall meathead with a tattoo on his bald head sat up on the bench and followed them with his gaze, frowning. "Come to grow some *inches*?" he laughed, and Caspian stopped in his tracks, mortified beyond reason.

But Gunner just spread his arms with a stupid grin. "What? You don't recognize me? I'm the extra weights. A hundred pounds, so you better get lifting."

A hundred and twelve, actually, but Caspian bit his tongue. No matter how big he now was, he didn't want to fight the other guy. But instead of getting angry at the impudent answer, the man laughed out loud.

"I could lift two of you on each arm!"

Gunner smiled even wider, and answered as he walked on to the locker rooms. "Okay, okay, I'll get my three brothers next week."

Why was Gunner lying? He didn't have any brothers, or siblings for that matter. But the muscular stranger seemed amused and offered Caspian a smile as he followed Gunner past a set of lockers, where they'd have enough privacy to practice the move he was to teach Gunner's fourteen-year-old student. It was called the lead hook and involved rotating his body, shifting his weight and jabbing his fist at the right angle. He wasn't sure how he was to teach this to anyone when it felt so very awkward to *him*, but several tries later, Gunner assured him that he was doing well.

Whatever the teacher said.

"You'll get the hang of it. I just don't want the kid feeling like I bailed on him," Gunner added for encouragement and clapped before spreading his legs and resting his hands on his hips in a very masculine gesture that seemed surprisingly natural.

Sexy.

Yet it still felt weird to Caspian to see *himself* doing it.

"If you say so. I'm afraid there's only so long I can pretend I know what I'm doing," he whispered, leaning to Gunner's ear. The pale hair still looked good, even after all the tumbling at the motel, and it smelled nice too.

Gunner bit his lips with a grin and stroked Caspian's side. "You seem to be a fast learner."

A deep shudder went from the tips of Caspian's toes to the top of his head, and he captured Gunner's gaze, embarrassed that he didn't remain the steady presence to command the room. But the touch felt so good.

"So I've been told. Now... where's that student of yours?" he asked and cleared his throat to get rid of the raspiness.

Gunner led him to a room with mirrors on one of the walls and a whole stack of mats in the corner. Every glance at his new reflection was both confusing and exhilarating, but there was no time to ogle himself as they approached a boy roughly Gunner's size. His black hair could have used a wash, and Caspian cringed at the severity of the poor guy's acne, but before he could have decided what to say, Gunner extended his hand to the boy.

"Hey! You must be Brian. Gun's told me all about you."

Brian's grim face lit up, and he smiled at Caspian, like a puppy eager for praise from his new master. "He did?"

Caspian shrugged and stuffed his hands into his pockets. "Sure. He's another student of mine and was really eager to meet you."

The way Brian stared at the jeans leaving nothing to imagination when it came to the shape of Gunner's legs told Caspian he might have blundered. But despite now having a body that didn't fit in with the dirty walls and the smell of sweat hanging in the air due to insufficient ventilation, Gunner took everything in stride.

"It's a bit difficult sometimes, because Gunner's so much taller than me. He said it would be easier if I got to train a bit with someone closer to my own size. So the angles are right, and all that."

"Yeah, but first, the lead hook," Caspian said, deciding it was time to grab the bull by the horns and step into the shoes he now needed to inhabit.

Gunner gave a brief shake of his head, but Caspian stepped closer to Brian and explained the move like Gunner had to him earlier, word for word, making sure to show each element several times, so that Brian understood what was expected of him.

But as Caspian looked up and asked if his protégé had any questions, Brian cleared his throat and uttered. "I mean... I know this one already."

Fire ate the skin of Caspian's face and reached his mind, making him stutter when his brain stalled. "I-I... yeah. Just w-wanted you to perfect it. That's all."

"So we can practice," Gunner added quickly. "Gun was telling me it's time to test your progress with someone in a similar weight category." He took off his hoodie without even a hint of worry about his new body being tiny.

Brian seemed to accept that explanation and soon enough entered the boxing ring in the gym's largest interior. Despite the high ceiling swarming with pipes and AC ducts, the air smelled of sweat and rivalry, and Caspian tried to ignore the crowd of massive guys training in small groups all around him. They might not see him as an intruder, but he sure as hell knew that he didn't fit in, and in the new body—neither did Gunner.

Caspian wasn't sure what he'd expected to see in the ring, but when Gunner focused on his opponent as if this was a real fight, his stomach suddenly felt heavy. Gunner had only taken over Caspian's body earlier today, but when he moved, avoiding Brian's jabs or making strikes of his own, it seemed that nothing at all was left of Caspian in the slender shell of flesh and bone. Gunner might not be as strong as he was used to, but he knew how and when to jab at Brian to hit him with gloved fingers.

Caspian had never much cared for boxing, or any other combat sport for that matter, but as the two boys in front of him locked eyes, searching for weaknesses in one another's guard, he felt weirdly engaged. Brian might be small, but he had more muscle on him than Gunner, and Caspian wasn't even sure who he was rooting for more. The younger boy to show Gunner that size was a challenge, or for Gunner to show *him* that one could win with more than brute force.

The hour passed like barely minutes, and while Caspian spent most of that time ogling Gunner and remembering how that slender body had taken his cock, he made sure to offer Brian praise whenever it seemed that the boy had done something right.

To Caspian's relief, Brian didn't seem to notice anything was off, and left after fist-bumping Gunner.

Caspian leaned over the ropes with a smile. "And how does it work? Does he pay the money straight into your bank account, or...?"

Gunner stretched, as if he wanted to show off his body—the same one Caspian had been so focused on hiding. How did this guy manage to *wear it* with so much confidence? "No, no! Don't mention cash to him. He's got a tough situation right now."

Caspian frowned. "But you made a big deal over not losing this client." And where was he supposed to get money for food and bills? Wasn't *this* his part-time job?

"Yeah, he is. He's a good kid, and if things get better, he'll pay me in a month or two. His dad lost his job, and it's all a bit shit for him right now."

Caspian frowned, self-conscious about all the other men training in various spots around them, even though nobody tried to approach him beyond offering nods or brief waves.

"But... you're poor. And you have that debt. You need all the money you can get."

Gunner deflated as if Caspian had punctured him. "Well, yeah. So?" he snapped. "So I can't do a good deed because I'm poor?"

Caspian took a step back and would have fallen off the edge of the ring if he hadn't grabbed the thick, stiff rope that surely had never been cleaned. "No... it's just that you could train someone else instead of Brian. Someone who could actually pay you for your work."

Gunner scowled and wouldn't even look at him. "Clients aren't exactly busting my door, *Casper*."

"You know my name."

Gunner shrugged. "Whatever."

What the hell?

Caspian grabbed Gunner's shoulder and pulled him so they faced one another across the ropes. "I don't like this attitude."

"So stop pointing out what a failure I am!" Gunner scowled, showing his teeth like a rabid dog. His muscles went so rigid it seemed that only the public setting stopped him from roaring.

Caspian counted to five and took a deep breath, meeting Gunner's gaze, meeting the same icy shade of blue he used to see in the mirror.

"I don't know your life, okay? But that debt thing needs to be dealt with. That's not an opinion but a fact."

Gunner sighed, as if the weight of the world had dropped onto his shoulders. "I've got some business lined up. But there was this boxing teacher that used to be really kind to me when I was a kid and had a shitty home life, and I wanna give back, you know? We're all in the same boat on this side of the tracks."

"Oh." Caspian stared at him, his mind wiped in the face of something he'd never associated with Gunner— compassion for another person. How could this guy taunt him without blinking an eye, and then work for free, just because he felt sorry for a kid. It didn't make sense. "But I'm from the other side of the tracks, and that made me fair game?"

Gunner shrugged and removed his boxing gloves. "Kinda. You've got the fancy car, the pancakes Mommy made for breakfast—" He stalled and bit his lip before shaking his head—"but I'm still sorry about yesterday, okay? It was shit of me to provoke you and then let my buddies do that to you. And for the record, your dick is perfectly fine."

Caspian stalled when his mind went aflame with the realization that the cock he'd enjoyed sucking earlier was the same one he'd resented all his life. So maybe it was on the smaller end of average, but when he'd taken it in his mouth, it had been smooth, and warm, and tasty. There was nothing wrong with it.

Nothing.

He was so confused he'd only noticed Gunner fighting for his attention when an open hand waved inches from his face.

"Are you there?"

"Yeah. But I'm still angry. You could have just told them to leave me be!"

"Like that would have worked on those idiots. You don't know them like I do—" Gunner stalled with his gaze fixed on something to their right. "Goddamn it."

"What the fuck, slut boy? You stalking me?"

Caspian was startled at first, but when Gunner's nostrils flared as if he were a bull about to charge, Caspian followed his gaze across the floor, all the way to a corner where a buff Asian guy stepped in front of a swinging sandbag he must have been hitting, and laughed, peeling the sweaty front of his T-shirt from his torso.

"Get over yourself, Mike. Like I did," Gunner said, bristling. He grabbed the hoodie and slid off the ring.

Slut boy?

Slut boy?

What did you call him?" Caspian asked, jumping off the platform and already heading in Mike's direction as sparks exploded under his skin. He didn't know what this was about, but the scraps of information he already had were enough fuel for his anger.

"Gun? What's up? Why are you hanging out with that piece of trash?" Mike asked, intent on not reading the room.

"Let it go, Gunner," the *actual* Gunner said, following him, but Caspian was already making his way toward Mike, who seemed to have realized the tables had turned only when Caspian shoved him back so hard the bastard barely kept himself upright.

"Who are you calling trash, huh? Do you have a death wish?"

Mike frowned, but raised his hands. "Wait, wait, I don't get it. He your cousin or something? He tried to make a move on me at the store today, so I thought maybe he followed me here. Boy's too thirsty for his own good."

Frost cut into Caspian as he looked back at Gunner, so tense he felt like his ligaments might snap from the pressure.

But he couldn't start a fight. Not when he didn't know what the fuck he was doing. So he rolled his head over his nape, to loosen up the tension there and was about to dismiss the whole thing and walk off to have a serious fucking chat with the little flea.

But as he opened his mouth to speak, Gunner roared and charged at Mike. "Says the fucking king of one-night stands! It was just a fucking offer!" he yelled and before Caspian could have grabbed him, Gunner climbed the guy like a tree, using his arm as leverage, and punched the side of his head.

Mike hadn't anticipated this and fell under the unexpected weight on top of him. Their altercation could no longer be ignored, and the other guys stopped their training, gravitating closer like crows to a bagful of crumbs

Fumes of heat and blood-scented smoke filled Caspian's head, but he only moved when Mike jabbed Gunner's side with his fist. He grabbed the boy from behind and yanked, peeling him off the other man as if he were plucking a baby out of a burning building.

"What the fuck are you doing?"

Gunner stilled, clutching at his side. "He fucking started it. I know he's gay, so what's the big deal in me hitting on him? Big fucking *whoop*! You're not even all that anyway!" He showed Mike the finger.

Mike's face was red as he rolled back to his feet, fists already rising, but Caspian turned around so Gunner's opponent couldn't easily reach him. "I'm training him now, so if you touch him again, it's gonna get personal," he bluffed, struggling to keep his body steady with all the eyes pushing hooks into him.

Those guys could've ripped him to shreds if they smelled that something was fishy about him, and in an instant, he understood why it might have been hard for Gunner yesterday to stand up to his pseudo-friends who *also happened to be* drug dealers.

Mike took a deep breath and pointed at Gunner, but didn't step any closer. "You talk to me again, you come to my store, or as much as make eye contact, you're *dead*, you little shit! Understood?"

Gunner waved his hand. "Fine, whatever."

He was at least sane enough to leave before things could have escalated and walked toward the exit as soon as Caspian put him down. Caspian had never seen a more volatile twink.

"See you," Caspian muttered to Mike, because it felt like the thing to do, and followed Gunner while someone else asked the men to go back to whatever they'd been doing, since the show was over.

But it definitely wasn't over for Caspian.

What the fuck had Gunner been up to while he hadn't been looking?

"You have some explaining to do," he whispered and grabbed Gunner's arm as soon as they were in a dusky corridor, out of everyone's sight.

Gunner groaned, but didn't fight Caspian the way he had Mike. "I was just trying things out, okay? He's the only gay guy I know."

"You just walked into his shop, and what, offered him a blowjob? Maybe you should carry around a price list, while you're at it?" Caspian forced out through his tightening throat and shook Gunner.

"It wasn't like that! I thought we could, like, date or something..." He didn't sound convinced himself, but when a woman passed them and barely hid a smirk, Caspian knew they should continue this conversation out of sight.

"Take me somewhere private. Now," he said, burning with the desire to break Mike's jaw himself.

Chapter 11 - Caspian

Gunner groaned and led the way down the corridor, to a large storage closet filled with metal shelves stacked full of protein powders. "He pissed me off, okay? He made me feel like shit. Like I shouldn't have even asked, and I'm fucking adorable."

Caspian's hand stopped on the lock, which he hastily turned as soon as they were both in. "So he's a douche, I get it! Believe me, I get it! You can't go around offering yourself to randos! This is mine," he growled, gesturing at Gunner's compact form in the tight jeans that looked so cute with the oversized hoodie.

Gunner hesitated, and his blue eyes met Caspian's. "What if I'm really horny, and you're not around?"

Liquid fire rose in Caspian, and he grabbed Gunner's shoulders, bringing him closer. He couldn't even think of what he'd do if he found Gunner flirting with some other guy. That wasn't what they'd agreed on.

"I don't care if you're too horny to wait. Come and see me or fuck your little boy hole with a dildo!"

Gunner had the audacity to laugh. "You mean the rubber one in your closet? I don't know how that will help with *my* need." He stood on his toes and pulled Caspian a bit lower to lick his lips.

Oh Damn. He might have as well grabbed Caspian by the balls.

The moment when he'd walked in on Gunner holding Twinky would forever be one of the most embarrassing in his life, but he couldn't let the boy take charge of this moment and pushed him at the wall. "Then I'll get you a dildo, and you'll ride it whenever I can't be there to satisfy you."

"And should I make videos of me doing it, so you can watch them later?" Gunner ran his fingers over Caspian's forearm, and his touch was like a match setting Caspian's skin on fire. Never before had his cock hardened so fast.

Gunner was a shameless slut, and Caspian wanted him all to himself.

He'd had crushes before, mostly on cute twinks who seemed so unattainable. But he'd never felt so jealous. He wasn't sure whether it was because Gunner was his first bottom, or because Gunner was a sexy firecracker, but Caspian wanted to keep him.

He wanted to get tested now and cream his tight hole as soon as he made sure this body had no STIs to pass on.

"Yes. But no face," Caspian added, because the last thing he wanted was to deal with the potential fallout, if the recording got into the wrong hands.

"Why? Is my come-face ugly?" Gunner purred and ran his hands up Caspian's chest, all the way to his neck until he wrapped his arms around it. He truly was fucking adorable in the big hoodie, which only reinforced the idea of him being small when compared to Caspian's hulking form. Yet that didn't stop him from knowing how to tease a guy like a pro.

Caspian had already fucked him twice today, but his dick was *throbbing* for more.

He needed the release more than he needed food, despite being so perpetually hungry, and he grabbed the slender neck, trapping it against the wall as he nipped on the smooth skin of Gunner's jaw and smelled his hair.

"No, but I'm the only one allowed to ever see it."

Caspian had told himself fucking Gunner was about scratching a physical itch, yet here he was, becoming obsessed with the person who'd bullied him for months back in high school. Gunner's Adam's apple bobbed against Caspian's palm, like a reminder that he was now in a position of power and could have put pressure on that delicate neck, if his intentions were any different. He had no desire to frighten Gunner, but it gave him a thrill to know that he was the predator. And when Gunner's eyes glazed over in response, it became clear they both appreciated this new reality in equal measure.

"You wanna see it now?" Gunner whispered, and the nostrils of his small nose flared with each quick inhale.

"Fuck," Caspian whispered and clashed their mouths, sliding his other hand into Gunner's mane and holding on as if it were reins. His lips tingled with the need for more, and he poked the soft mouth with his tongue just as his knee pushed between Gunner's thighs.

Yeah, he did want to see *it* now.

How was that even a question?

"You dirty little slut. You wanna do it here? There's people who have keys to this room," he whispered, but for once the perspective of being walked in on aroused rather than scared him.

"You gotta be quick then," Gunner whimpered and arched his neck instead of trying to free himself from the hand collaring his slender neck.

His stare was filled with lust, as if Caspian were the hottest man on the planet, and that was exactly what Caspian had always wanted to see reflected in the eyes of his partners. He now had the body to get him what he needed, and he'd make the most of it.

"Take my cock now. I wanna see you holding it."

Gunner immediately cupped Caspian's crotch with so much affection it felt like a hug, but he didn't stall for long and unzipped Caspian's jeans soon after.

His small, slender hand felt so damn hot, and when it rolled up and down the shaft, Caspian could have sworn that his balls cooked in response.

"I'm gonna destroy you. Right here. In this room where someone could hear us," he uttered in a heated whisper and rolled his tongue along Gunner's ear.

He'd seen Gunner fight that Mike guy and run his mouth at people with such ease, yet in Caspian's hands he became putty, as if he had special powers to transform the little bastard into a lustful kitten. Nobody had ever made Caspian feel so wanted. So powerful.

Gunner let out a little whimper and squeezed Caspian's cock. "I'll be quiet."

"You won't be able to keep it in when I drill you with this," Caspian said and thrust his stiff cock through the tube made by Gunner's hands. Arousal crawled up his back, buzzing ever louder, and when Gunner met his gaze, once again blushing like an innocent, Caspian squeezed his neck and gave him a hard, breathless kiss.

The soft lips were so pliant for him, and he could just see himself becoming addicted to their eagerness. He might see himself as the one in charge, but was he really when Gunner's wanton gestures and looks baited him as if he were a tomcat called upon by a female in heat?

It didn't matter where they were, or that the room had a stale scent to it, or that the wall had patches of dirt in places people regularly brushed against. He could sense Gunner's desire in every shiver going through his delicious body. He could feel it in the hard-on rubbing his leg, and see it in the way eyelids lowered over the blue gaze.

"Jesus. You're such a fucking honeypot," Caspian rasped and reached under the loose top, quick to unzip Gunner's pants. He didn't want to wait any longer than necessary and swiftly lubed himself up, dropping the tube to the floor as soon as he had a generous amount of the gel in his palm.

"Then lick me..." The spaced-out smile when Caspian pulled Gunner's pants down told him all he needed to know about the connection.

He ran his tongue up the scratches on Gunner's neck, his jaw, and all the way up Gunner's cheek. The little moan escaping those tempting lips made Caspian breathless with the urge to drive his cock into the slutty boy. He would. Any moment now.

Without thinking much, he leaned down, grabbed Gunner under the knees, where his jeans pooled, and lifted him against the wall, because he *was* strong enough for this now. Oh, yes. He'd be looking into Gunner's eyes this time, because he was no longer afraid to see his own face as he drove his cock in. While his new, massive body already felt like home, the old one no longer did, and when he met the lustful gaze, all he saw was Gunner... or rather, a version of him that was delicious instead of threatening.

Gunner wrapped his arms more tightly against Caspian's neck. When Caspian pushed Gunner against the wall, his cock slid into the welcoming valley between the pert buttocks, right where it belonged.

They both gasped, lips joining as Gunner clawed his fingers and massaged Caspian's flesh through the clothes. There was an unexpected tenderness to the touch, but Caspian's dick was throbbing for release already, and his balls felt so tight he could barely think.

Folding Gunner in half, he reached down, grabbed his shaft and changed the angle of his hips, pushing the head at the sweet dip in flesh that promised him heaven.

And when the hole twitched, opening up to the pressure, butterflies fluttered in Caspian's stomach, making him shiver.

"Oh, baby... that's so good."

Gunner whimpered and squeezed him tight when Caspian pushed just enough for his cockhead to pass the ring of muscles. Gunner had lost his anal cherry only earlier today, so this surely hurt or was at least a bit uncomfortable, yet instead of trying to make Caspian go slower, he let his head drop against the wall and fought for air, rosy as if he were already about to come.

"That's it, such a horny boy. I bet you can't wait for me to be balls-deep in you," Caspian cooed into Gunner's ear, and it sparkled back at him with the new piercing. How could a body be so well known to him, yet feel so new?

Gunner let out a soft groan that went straight to Caspian's balls. "Fuck. It's so thick."

"It is. *So* thick, and you'll still take all of it, because you're my bitch," Caspian said, but despite the arousal cooking his brain, he kept his eyes open and held still, watching his boy's face for signs of discomfort.

Gunner's top lip trembled, his brows drew together, but instead of asking for Caspian to slow down, he leaned in for a quick kiss. "I'll take anything you want me to."

How had this guy lived so many years and stayed a virgin? He clearly had a desire for sex to match Caspian's own.

"Tell me why," he rasped, watching the flushed face without blinking, while his cock sank farther into that hot, willing body. It didn't matter that someone could walk in, or that they were doing it in an ugly, badly lit storage closet. All that mattered was the boy in his arms, taking his dick and asking for more. He'd never felt this validated as a man.

"'Cause... Cause I'm your bitch. And I'll only take your cock. Only suck yours. Swallow only your cum. And film myself only for your pleasure."

This was the fulfillment of all Caspian's fantasies, and as he pushed up, burying his prick deeper and deeper in the snug hole that wouldn't stop sucking him in, he captured Gunner's lips and traced them with his tongue before diving in. He'd penetrate both of his holes as often as Gunner wanted. He'd keep him for as long as he could, because their sex was something out of this world. So good that the memory of Gunner's past actions paled like an old photograph left in the sun for too long.

So what if he used to be a bully when now he'd become this pliant, sexy boy who offered himself to Caspian as if he really had no shame. That was all the atonement Caspian needed, perhaps because his dick was doing the thinking.

He picked up pace with every thrust of his hips, so focused on the radiant face in front of him that he barely broke a sweat despite carrying another person's weight and moving at the same time. He was the king of the fucking world.

His kisses muffled the little moans Gunner made every time Caspian pumped his cock into the searing heat of the compact body folded between him and the wall. Just yesterday, he'd been an unfulfilled guy who'd never topped and doubted he'd ever find a bottom willing to give him a chance. Today he was on his third fuck and had a slutty thing spreading his legs in the supply closet because he couldn't fucking wait for Caspian to fill him with spunk.

They worked together like a well-oiled machine, and while it was a tight fit, and the friction became hotter with each thrust, Caspian let himself go and drilled his prick into Gunner's body like a piston. His blood bubbled with joy when his balls pulled closer to his body, and when he knew it was almost over, he bit down on the boy's lips to stifle the grunts pushing at his mouth as he trembled, shoving his cock as deep as he could.

"Oh!" Gunner's eyes flew open and his moan became louder. "Oh, fuck, fuck, fuck! Right there!"

Spurt after spurt, Caspian planted his load, but once his climax was over, Gunner suddenly felt heavy, and Caspian found himself sliding to his knees. With ecstasy painted all over Gunner's face and biting his pink lips, Gunner rode Caspian's cock in a frenzy, and Caspian barely had enough brain power to cover the boy's mouth when he cried out. Hot, damp breath tickled Caspian's hand as he slumped against the wall, flushed and heaving.

The dark stain spreading at the front of Gunner's grey hoodie told Caspian his boy had come too.

"How are you so damn hot? I want to keep you in my closet," Caspian whispered, kissing his way up Gunner's throat, which smelled so delicious he wished he could carry that scent with him wherever he went.

Gunner grinned with his eyes still closed in the afterglow. "Maybe you should. You could then pull me out and use me whenever you need to nut."

Caspian might have just come, but his dick still gave a little twitch. "You're trying to kill me. Suck out all my juices like a little cum vampire," he whimpered, pushing his hands under the hoodie so he could touch the pliant flesh he was already addicted to.

"We're at a gym. Wanna go shower and pretend we're just two bros casually washing next to each other?" Gunner wiggled his eyebrows. How were his features so playful, so alive when Caspian had often felt like the dullest guy in the room?

How had he not noticed that his face was quite handsome when he smiled?

Out of breath, he gave a quick nod and reached down to keep the condom from slipping off his shaft, but when he touched Gunner's hole, reality smashed into him like a glass bottle.

"I didn't rubber up..."

Chapter 12 - Gunner

Gunner's mind was still hazy after the earth-shattering orgasm when he met the dark eyes that seemed to scorch him.

"I mean, we're gonna shower anyway." Gunner shrugged. His ass throbbed around the softening cock, yet he wouldn't have had it any other way. The pressure inside made him feel like a new person, as if taking Caspian's cock was starting to transform him into someone much closer to his true nature than he'd ever been.

Caspian took a deep breath and looked away, as if he'd just swallowed a fly. "No... I mean... aren't you worried about STDs?"

Gunner shrivelled up a little on the inside, frustrated by this change of topic when they'd been engaged in perfectly good teasing. He stepped away from Caspian, and while he was annoyed Caspian brought the real world into their cocoon of lust, he couldn't stop thinking about how much he loved being Caspian's spunk hole.

"Dunno. Not really."

Caspian exhaled, pulled up his pants to hide his junk, and showed him a packet of condoms. "I've been educated about safe sex *ad nauseam* and I had condoms right there. I could have used them. What the fuck is wrong with me?"

Gunner kissed his pec, eager to go back to the relentless flirting. "Because you're a horny stud?"

Caspian stilled, staring at him with an unreadable expression. "I'm sorry. I should have asked, but it's like my brain's just boiled over." He rubbed his face up and down. "We need to get tested."

Gunner rolled his eyes and rearranged his clothes, though he wasn't sure how to deal with the cum inside him. Should he keep his buttocks squeezed tight until they reached the shower?

But then his brain glitched, and he looked up at Caspian. "Why? How much do you sleep around? I've only got Sandy. *Had.* I suppose."

Caspian's frown was so deep it might have dug into bone. "What? You mean that girlfriend of yours? You only ever slept with her?"

He made it sound like a bad thing.

Gunner led the way out of the closet to avoid Caspian's gaze. "Not like 'ever', but nowadays. How's that so strange?"

Caspian shifted his weight and wrapped his fingers on his nape. "It's not bad. It's just,.. that you're so hot. How do you not bang everything that moves?"

Gunner glanced over his shoulder as they made their way down the corridor. He just hoped they wouldn't meet anyone on the way to the showers, because he felt like he had *filled-with-cum* painted across his face. And a stain of his own spunk on the hoodie. Fuck. Did Caspian's mom do his laundry for him?

"'Cause I don't wanna. It gets so complicated. I only fuck Sandy sometimes to take the edge off. I don't think she cares for it, and I kinda like it that way." Gunner shrugged at how pathetic that sounded.

They both stilled when one of the regulars walked past them, acknowledging Caspian with a nod, but once the coast was clear, Caspian leaned down to whisper. "So you really never had a guy? Not even a drunk blowjob?"

Gunner sped toward the lockers with his ears on fire. "Maybe it's easier to slut around with guys in your world," he grumbled. "You don't have a boyfriend, do you?" Changing the subject was a go-to strategy that never failed.

Caspian stilled and stayed behind before catching up with Gunner. "No. I'm just surprised. But how can you be sure Sandy isn't sleeping around? Have you ever been tested?"

"Stop grilling me like I'm some disease-riddled maggot! And Sandy's too lazy to cheat on me anyway. Even with us not being together anymore."

Two women who'd passed along the corridor at the bottom of the stairs gave them brief looks of disgust before hurrying off. Just great.

"It's not like that," Caspian said, grabbing Gunner's arm and pulling him back.

"What's it like then, huh? No, I haven't been tested, but I'm *fine*, okay?" He didn't know whether he wanted to shower with Caspian anymore. His feelings were as erratic as the exhaust on his old truck.

"Don't be like that! We can just go together. Do it as a team," Caspian tried, but it

was obvious that he feared he'd accidentally soiled his pristine body with trailer trash cum. Joke was on him, because he was the one in said body now.

Gunner slipped out of Caspian's grasp and jogged until he finally reached the locker room. "We're all gonna die someday anyway."

The door slammed shut behind him, and before he knew what got him, strong hands grabbed his shoulders, spun him around, and pushed him against the wall so he had no choice but to meet Caspian's dark, inquisitive gaze.

How was it that Caspian seemed so hot to him now when Gunner had so often felt like an awkward lump of flesh when interacting with people in that same skin?

"Do not walk away from me. Is that clear?"

Gunner's heart throbbed, and he had to take a deep breath to calm down. He wasn't afraid of Caspian anymore. Not so soon after they'd fucked like bunnies on speed. But whenever Caspian got this dominant, his behavior pushed all of Gunner's buttons at once and left him confused as to whether he should run or pull down his pants.

"Fine," he mumbled.

The wide shoulders relaxed, and Caspian leaned closer, watching Gunner as if he were examining a particularly interesting beetle specimen. "If we're to be exclusive, it makes sense to discuss such things. I've been regularly tested. Just in case. I expect you to do the same if you want to ditch the rubbers." He cleared his throat and blinked, because he must have realized Gunner had said nothing of the sort.

Oh, this is fun.

Gunner smirked. "Aren't you gonna invite me to dinner first?"

Caspian stretched and looked around, as if he were suddenly afraid they might not be alone in the locker room. But no. There was no one else present.

"Okay. But... do you? Want to not use condoms, I mean," he said and stuffed his massive hands into his pockets, back to his sexy confident self.

Gunner ruffled his hair to obscure his face. "Y-yeah. It's hot. Like you're marking me. Breeding my tight ass like that..."

The way Caspian's Adam's apple pushed at the skin of his throat, going up and down, had Gunner's toes curling.

"I like that too. It's so damn erotic. I already know I'm gonna jerk off thinking about it later," he said and cupped Gunner's face with one hand, rubbing his coarse thumb across his mouth.

Gunner bit his lip, fighting a silly smile. That hand was so *big*. It turned him on just how small he was in comparison. "So you get tested frequently?" he mumbled. "Is it expensive?"

Caspian cleared his throat, averting his gaze. "I— maybe not *a lot*, but I've done it several times. And some places even test you for free, since it's a public health issue."

Gunner grabbed a clean towel from the shelf by the wall and led the way to the showers. "So how many guys have you slept with?" he asked, while secretly sizzling at the thought that the body he now inhabited had been touched by strangers, though he wasn't sure whether this aroused or horrified him.

Caspian shuffled behind him in silence, as if he wanted to leave Gunner in suspense and never satisfy his curiosity.

"Not that many. I don't know... ten?" Caspian said in a voice so quiet it barely sounded like the rich baritone that had sent shivers down Gunner's spine minutes ago.

Gunner processed that with a frown as he pulled off his hoodie. "Okay, so... you're not as slutty as your Grindr suggests?"

Caspian pushed the fresh towel against his face and screamed. The fabric muffled the sound, but it was loud enough for Gunner to take a step back.

"Oh no. You saw it. Please, tell me you haven't actually read any of it!" Caspian uttered, still keeping his face hidden in rough fabric that had long ago turned grayish.

"Sorry, it was too juicy to pass on, but there was so much it'd be hard to read all of it. Bet those ten guys had the ride of their lives." Gunner rushed to take all of his clothes off and surprise Caspian with his nakedness by the time he looked up again.

"You got it all wrong. Sorry. I got to be honest with you, I—" Caspian stalled when he lowered the towel just in time to see Gunner's jeans sliding down his ass. Was he thinking about there being his cum deep inside it? Because Gunner totally was. "What I mean is... I had the wrong body for the things I wanted to pursue."

Gunner pushed off his clothes while meeting Caspian's gaze. He could relate to that. He hated the need to voice those embarrassing thoughts, but three fucks in, they were way past being strangers. "I think I know what you mean. I never even considered searching for guys, 'cause I feel like there's all these expectations when you look a certain way. I live where I live, and... it was just easier not to face the reality of who I am."

He'd never shared that with anyone. Hell, until today, he'd never told anyone he was gay, but if there was one person he didn't need to pretend for, it was the man standing in front of him.

Caspian went still and rubbed his massive chest. "Yeah, but... you could have gone to another town. You're so handsome any gay guy would have wanted you. And I was just this... shrimp," he said with a twist to his lips, using the same comparison that had been thrown against him last night.

Gunner stepped closer over the cold tiles and pushed Caspian's T-shirt off him, then ran his fingers over the tattooed chest. Skulls above the collar bones, barbed wire becoming a snake with a large knife stabbing its head, its long body winding all the way around the torso as if it originated in the navel. Spiders on a web adorned his forearms along with a scorpion reaching onto one of his hands. Insects and reptiles. Poison and death. All saying *do not approach*. The ink had been his armor, a deterrent to make him appear more threatening than he was. But the story told by the designs was only skin-deep and kept Gunner's secrets in the dark.

"It's a nice, muscular body, but won't attract people who want to pick me up and roll me over. You've fucked me enough times to know what I like. Those muscles come with expectations. This?" Gunner looked down his new frame and gently stroked the flat chest with smooth skin and little definition. "This is perfect for me. Just not for what *you* wanted."

Caspian's nostrils flared, and he shrugged, visibly uncomfortable. He cleared his throat, took off his remaining clothing, and headed for the showers. Unbelievable. Was he running from this conversation after starting it *himself*?

Gunner rushed after him, and since there wasn't a soul around, he didn't have qualms about pouncing on Caspian. He grabbed his shoulders and pulled himself up on Caspian's back, while wrapping his short legs around Caspian's waist for stability.

He lowered his voice to a rasp, imitating Caspian. "*Do not walk away from me. Is that clear?*"

Caspian looked back, his arms spread for balance. Oh, he was *so* firm to the touch!

"Sorry. It's just embarrassing," he said and continued toward the row of identical showers that had fixed showerheads and brown tiles to hide dirt for as long as possible. Grabbing Gunner's knees helped him carry the additional weight with more comfort.

Gunner laughed, stupidly exhilarated. He hadn't piggybacked on anyone since he was a kid, instead always being expected to give rides. Clinging to the fragrant body, he kissed the side of Caspian's neck. Just because he could. He'd been hiding those secret needs for so long, but Caspian allowed him to spread his wings and fucked him until Gunner was happy like a teen who'd gotten his braces taken off.

"What's embarrassing, is the rubber boy toy in your closet. Better tell me about the guys you'd fucked. Was my new ass *virginal*?" he teased.

"I've never done any anal," Caspian muttered in a small voice and stepped on wet tiles, straight into a cloud of vapor scented like someone's shower gel. There was also a hint of moldiness in the air, but the sandalwood notes hid its presence well enough.

Gunner kissed him on the back of the head. He was getting some seriously tense vibes from Caspian and was eager to soothe him. "I've only done it with this one girl a few years back, 'cause I was curious, but fucking her just wasn't what I wanted. And she was all like, 'yeah, slam that big dick in, stud', and that was a massive turn off for me. Barely kept it up really, so we've all got some skeletons in the closet."

"You don't mind? That I'm not experienced?" Caspian uttered and scooted down so Gunner could get off him.

Gunner jumped down and shrugged. "Not really, no. You, like... *seem* to know what you're doing." He couldn't get over how amazing his old body looked from the perspective of someone much shorter. Gunner had always felt too big for any space he entered, but Caspian carried his form with a silent strength that was somehow both imposing and calming.

"I suppose I should be glad you'd worked up some stamina while you still had this body. It's probably the only reason why I hadn't come the moment I pushed into you the first time," Caspian said, spreading his firm arms. He stopped with his mouth open and met Gunner's gaze. "It was everything I ever wanted."

"Me?" Gunner could only hope this wasn't some elaborate dream he'd wake up from any moment now. He knew Caspian meant the body he'd got to fuck three times already, but the acknowledgement still felt good. Gunner had dreams of being wanted this way, of a man stronger than him putting him in his place and breeding him over and over while he mewled in helpless pleasure.

His stomach fluttered, and he could sense the heat rushing to his face, so he turned on the water with a quick flick of his hand.

They'd been naked before, but this wasn't a private space. Someone could come in at any moment, but instead of frightening him, it gave Gunner a thrill to stand so close to Caspian. Whoever might enter would immediately notice how small and cute he was compared to the massive guy under the other showerhead.

A smile pulled on Caspian's lips, and while he too switched on the flow, he remained close to Gunner. The warm water splashed his bare chest and drizzled lower, to the cock that had been inside Gunner so recently.

"Yeah. You, you nasty little sexpot."

Gunner turned around under the water and pulled his butt cheeks apart, looking over his shoulder to catch Caspian's expression. "I'm the nasty one? Look how filthy you made me."

The predatory stare that stabbed into his flesh when Caspian faced him was worth the risk of acting so lewdly in a gym bathroom. He wanted to be the center of Caspian's wet dreams and with each hour, he was finding his feet as the manic pixie twink.

"You better watch out, or I might just bend you over my knees and spank you."

Gunner got himself some mint-scented soap from the dispenser on the wall and started lathering up. This was all fun and games, but it was late, and he had cum to wash off.

"What if I like it?" he teased and splashed some water on Caspian, who delivered a fast hit to Gunner's ass with the back of his hand.

"Then I'll have to come up with a different way to punish you."

While his old body was a handsome cage with a face marked by mistakes of his past, in the new one, Gunner felt free for the first time in years. As if he could do anything. Reinvent himself and explore his identity without boundaries.

"I am a free-spirited twink, and I will not be constrained," he said with feigned seriousness and lifted his chin.

Caspian grabbed Gunner under the armpits and lifted him up. Their bodies collided under the steady stream of the shower, and by the time Gunner crossed his ankles on Caspian's ass, he was sandwiched between the strong chest and the cold, cold wall anyway.

"How am I supposed to let you sleep in my old bed without me?" Caspian rasped and licked the side of Gunner's face, making him shiver with the heat of his tongue.

Gunner chuckled feeling shy, even though he literally had Caspian's cum inside him.

He wanted to come up with some witty, erotic remark, but then a door opened, letting in a whiff of cool air, and he pushed at Caspian's torso with so much force he ended up slipping out of his partner's grasp and falling to his poor aching ass under a stream of water.

Noah stood in the doorway with his mouth open, but he ignored Gunner and instead focused all his attention on Caspian. Of course.

Fuck.

"Err... Gunner?" Noah choked out.

Chapter 13 - Gunner

Caspian stood still at first, but then offered Gunner his hand and faced Noah, unaware of who that was. "We're busy."

Noah spread his arms, and his dark brows lowered. "What?" His attention finally drifted to Gunner. "And what the hell are you doing with my brother?"

Gunner got to his feet and rushed out from under the water. "It was just a prank—dare—thing..."

"Brother?" Caspian uttered, staring at Noah as if he'd never seen anything freakier in his entire life.

Noah swallowed and rested his hands on his hips, his face going slack. "Are you okay?"

"He's fine. Perfectly normal," Gunner said, searching for a way out of this madness.

The showers, which only moments before had been the stage for Gunner's self-discovery, now felt oppressive, and he grabbed the towel off the hanger to wrap it around his hips. He knew he needed to come up to an answer that made sense, but all coherent thoughts had evaporated from his brain, leaving him drowning without anything to keep him on the surface.

Noah spoke again before Gunner could have come up with an idea for damage control. "Gunner. Do you want to tell me something? Or is this a bad time, or—"

Gunner rubbed his face in frustration that seemed to have no end. But if he was to tell *someone* about what was going on, it would be his little brother. "I will talk to him," he said to Caspian. "Go on, tell him it's fine."

Caspian's big, tattooed chest grew as he inhaled. "I think it's best if he waits for us outside. We could go somewhere private and discuss this."

At this point, Noah's eyes were the size of saucers, and if Gunner didn't do something fast, he might end up with a psychiatrist knocking at his door.

He turned to Caspian and shook his head. "No, no, no, I said I'll handle this."

Noah took a strangled breath and kneaded his face, as if he were trying to rub off his freckles. "Is *this* how you paid off Snowman this week? I came to ask because I was worried. I mean… I'm not judging, but you don't have to do this. I'll take on some extra shifts—"

Oh Jesus.

Caspian frowned and raised his hands, finally settling into his role. "Look, I know it might be a shock, and I didn't want you finding out this way, but I've been living with this secret for some time—"

"No! You have not! Shut up!" Gunner yelled and pushed at the massive chest, which barely budged at the pressure. He looked back at Noah, because it wasn't as though Caspian would slap him back. "We're gonna talk, and you'll understand. And *he* will stop talking shit." He gave Caspian a warning glare, because coming out in Gunner's body wasn't his decision to make!

"Hey, don't shove me," Caspian growled, and his hand went straight for Gunner's throat. The collar of fingers didn't hurt, but its presence still shocked Gunner into a stupor. Hadn't they flirted a minute ago? Hadn't they just fucked? Hadn't Gunner given Caspian pleasure?

In sex that same hold had driven him frantic, and his body responded to the memory by flushing him with heat.

Noah stepped closer and put his hand on Caspian's arm. "Hey, Gunner... It's okay, whatever's going on, we can talk it over."

No. It was *not* okay.

Caspian leaned in to meet Gunner's eyes. "Did you hear that? He says it's fine. Calm down, let's dress, and we can figure this thing out together."

There was something calming about the steady way he spoke, but everything Gunner was, everything that made him, rebelled against the idea of his little brother knowing about his secret cravings.

Gunner stepped away as soon as Caspian let go. "No. I need to tell him stuff, and you're not part of that. Stop confusing him!"

Noah raised his hands. "What the hell is going on?"

Caspian's mouth pressed together, and he took a deep breath. "He already saw us. Don't you see he's fine with it?"

Gunner shook his head. He'd gotten caught up in a fantasy that had no place anywhere near his real life. "No! It might be fine to be a faggot in your world, but this is out of control. I need to talk to my brother, and you don't belong in that conversation! Don't know what you thought this was, but you're wrong."

Caspian frowned, taken aback, and his mouth twitched into a bitter smile. "I thought you wanted to be my bitch."

An involuntary whimper escaped Gunner's mouth, but before he could have spoken, Noah stepped in between them with a twist to his full lips.

"I don't know what's up, but don't speak to him like that. I met him today, and I think he's having some kind of mental breakdown." Noah glanced back at Gunner. "Do you have any family I could call for you?" he asked softly.

This couldn't be happening.

"You know what? Fuck you," Caspian said, his patience finally snapping. He glared at Noah. "Sure, take him with you. He'll explain and lie, or whatever."

Shame seeped into every pore of Gunner's body, but Caspian's anger was preferable to getting his real life wrecked. His shoulders slumped as Caspian stormed out, a bulldozer of a man with clenched fists.

"I'll see you later!" Noah yelled after him, but then looked back at Gunner with questions in his brown eyes. "What's your name?"

Gunner gave a deep sigh, and once he heard the locker room door slamming hard, they walked out of the showers so he could get dressed. "It's complicated."

"Your name is complicated? Shoot, I'll do my best not to mispronounce—"

"It's *Gunner*, okay?"

Noah frowned. "Okay, that's confusing."

"Tell me about it," Gunner grumbled, but Noah didn't say anything more and just waited for him to get dressed.

Now that Caspian was gone, Gunner was feeling as if someone had taken away his anchor. They'd spent the whole afternoon together, discovering each other's bodies, they'd had lunch, and then gone through the boxing together, fucked *again*... He shouldn't have snapped like that, but he'd panicked. He didn't know how to navigate being gay, not to mention the insane body swap situation.

The wait was painful, and Gunner hoped to gather his thoughts while it lasted, but by the time he and Noah left the locker rooms and headed toward Gunner's fancy vintage car, he hadn't come up with any revolutionary ideas on how to deal with this mess.

"Are you sure you can drive?" Noah inquired, getting a step ahead and having the audacity to stare at Gunner's eyes in the light of the streetlamps, as if he were checking for signs of drug use.

"Yeah, I'll take you home, and tell you everything on the way."

It felt strange to be smaller than his seventeen-year-old brother. Noah had really grown up in the past two years despite spending months in the hospital after his accident. And yet Gunner was responsible for him, and had vowed to give Noah the support *he'd* never had growing up.

The way he'd stood up to his own brother to protect a perfect stranger spoke volumes about the kind of person he was growing to be. Maybe his life would be less burdened with sadness and failure than Gunner's had been.

"Uh... okay. This is weird though. Why isn't Gunner with us? I get it that he's embarrassed, but he's still my brother, and I don't know you," Noah said but opened the passenger door of Caspian's fancy car, suddenly stilling. His gaze slid over the pristine leather upholstery and cream and cherry red, over the wooden steering wheel, the shiny dashboard... and he didn't get in, as if he were afraid to do some damage to the expensive car and end up liable for repair costs.

Because he couldn't be afraid of *Gunner,* could he?

"I'm not a serial killer, okay?"

Noah's lips pressed together. "That's exactly what a serial killer would say."

Gunner groaned. "Fine. There's no sane way to say it. I'm Gunner. *Your brother Gunner.* I know it's hard—"

"What? You're making less and less sense."

"No! It's true." Gunner looked around and slid into the seat, forcing Noah to bend down in order to keep seeing his face. "It's one of those body swap things."

Noah crooked his head like a befuddled cartoon character. "Say what?"

"I'm Gunner."

Noah wrapped his arms on his chest and lifted his chin, exposing the long scar running up the side of his throat. "Oh really? Then prove it. Tell me something only my brother Gunner, would know."

Gunner growled to himself and leaned against the steering wheel, racking his brain. He bit back a smile when he found the right memory. "Remember after your accident, when you first woke up—"

Noah dismissed him with a gesture. "My accident's no secret."

Gunner grinned. "No, no, stay with me here. When you first woke up, you were so drugged up you couldn't feel your body well, and you couldn't move much either, so you asked me if I could check if your dick was okay. And I did. 'Cause that's the kind of big brother I am."

Noah slid into the seat, shut the door, and turned his head to stare at Gunner, his face tense. "What the fuck?"

Gunner had to take a deep breath before starting the car, because the tension in his muscles was making him overheat. "I know. It happened today. I woke up like this. It's been... a weird day. Do you think it will wear off overnight?" Being able to discuss this with someone other than Caspian was such a relief he melted into the seat, breathing deeply for the first time since Noah had walked in on them in the gym.

"I—I don't know. This is some sci-fi shit," Noah said and closed his seatbelt, never looking away from Gunner. His bright eyes shone in the dusky interior, peeling the protective layers Gunner tried to establish. "And... your secret..."

"It's not what you think!" Gunner said as they drove off, and he was annoyed that it was now dark, and he couldn't excuse putting on shades. "I was just... confused at the mall. Because of this body. The other guy, Caspian, he's gay, and his body is—it has these *urges*." He was ashamed of throwing Caspian under the bus like that, but what was he to say to Noah after all that he'd seen today? It wasn't like he'd care about the sexual habits of a stranger.

"Yes, but you don't have to sleep with people you don't like. Anyway, it's okay. I don't mi—"

"Well, you should mind! 'Cause I'm not gay." Gunner snarled, keeping his eyes on the road as the deliciously filthy things he'd done with Caspian sizzled in his memory.

He hadn't simply *allowed* Caspian drill him, but he'd been a willing participant. Thrice. Just today.

Noah looked out of the window and rubbed his hands together. His left ring finger was slightly crooked, but it was amazing how well the surgeons had managed to mend his broken body following the accident. "But it doesn't matter. Clearly, you want to explore this now."

Gunner went silent. Could *this* be a loophole he could exploit? His way to have his cake and eat it? Then again, what if Caspian was pissed off at him and wouldn't want to fuck anymore? After today, Gunner couldn't imagine having sex with anyone else but the beast of a man now living in his old body. They might not know each other well but they'd understood *things* about each other no one else could.

Caspian wouldn't have gone to find another hook-up, just to go against Gunner's wishes, would he? It wasn't like he'd have that much stamina left after coming three times already.

"So who's the other guy?" Noah asked, pulling Gunner out of his chaotic, needy thoughts.

"Caspian. I knew him back in high school."

"Oh… so he was the one who paid Snowman. And… this swap thing… how did it happen. Why him?" Noah asked, watching Gunner as if he really expected a coherent answer when the situation Gunner was in had no place in the real world. It was some movie shit, but he hadn't accidentally broken an ancient statue, or whatever else caused people to swap bodies in wacky comedies. He'd met Caspian at the gym, then had beer with the guys, and fallen asleep.

"I don't know. He doesn't either. But maybe it's some kind of punishment from the universe. I... might have done a shit thing to him yesterday." He blinked, staring ahead as the car passed trees on the way to the trailer park at the edge of town. "Oh. Maybe I need to redeem myself somehow."

Noah leaned back in the seat. "Gunner... *no.*"

"No?"

"Why do you pick on people?"

The judgement in Noah's voice made Gunner shrink. "I don't know. I got caught up in it, and Todd was there, spurring me on. I didn't mean to hurt him. If anything, I kinda just wanted it to be over, so I went with it. Okay, maybe I was a bit—" *curious to see his dick.* "Never mind. What's done is done. The universe is telling me to live a day in his shoes. That's it. We'll be back to normal tomorrow. For sure."

"So how was it?" Noah asked as they drove past all the fast food joints and toward the scorched remains of the Rabid Hyenas biker club.

"Hm? How was what?" Gunner looked at the road in front of him to avoid the dreadful memories of the fire that had taken their father. He'd been a bad man, but their financial situation had been better when he was still around.

Noah cleared his throat. "You know, touching another guy."

Gunner's face went aflame. *Everything I ever wanted and lusted for.* "Weird. Especially since it's *my* body."

"So a bit like masturbation?"

"No! Jesus. I guess... I kinda felt free to go with it, since this isn't *my* body, *my* life, you know?"

Gunner drove past the sign welcoming them to the trailer park and headed for the bungalow where Noah lived with his mom, Zahra. Their home was only a fifteen-minute walk away from the trailer park, but any reason to avoid confronting Caspian just yet was good enough.

Noah licked his lips. "So it's something you might do again? Once you're back in your own body?"

Gunner scowled. "You're such a fucking smartass. No, it's not, and I won't. Don't you ever do shit in a dream that you wouldn't do in real life, but then you wake up and think to yourself, oh, okay, so that was a thing?"

Noah shrugged, in no rush to leave when Gunner stopped in front of the white bungalow. What could he possibly be thinking about? "Depends on the stuff. I guess if I had like… a sex fantasy, I'd like to try it out in real life."

"Well I don't. End of story. You don't always get everything you want in life, and you should know that."

Noah slumped against the door, making Gunner regret his words. Maybe he'd been too harsh, but it was for Noah's own good. Living in fantasy land of big dreams was what had gotten Noah into his car accident in the first place.

Noah chewed on his lips for a while. "And you'll be going back to his house?"

Just thinking of the mansion of a house made Gunner relax. His life in Caspian's body might be temporary, but he'd enjoy it for as long as it lasted. "Yeah. I'll just go check on Fluffer."

"Okay, but I'll see you tomorrow, and if nothing changes, we'll investigate, right?"

Gunner didn't want to think that far ahead when his life was already chaos. "Yes, Noah, you can become the paranormal detective tomorrow. If I'm not back to normal. Which I will be."

Noah hesitated but then rolled out of the seat and waved. "Need to go. Mom's gonna be mad if I'm late."

Gunner waited until Noah disappeared from sight and let out a scream of anguish while banging the steering wheel.

What a fucking mess.

It took him several moments to calm down, and once he felt ready to face the world, he headed for the trailer park. Sandy wasn't always responsible enough to feed Fluffer, and even though he'd told Caspian to do it, it was better to be safe than sorry.

He parked not far from the entrance, to avoid meandering among the trailers when someone's car was already blocking half the driveway. He was used to people giving him looks, but while in his own body he was a predator everyone watched out for, *Caspian* was prey, and he sped up when a group of teen boys noticed him from afar. Darkness hid him from sight as he made his way through the labyrinth of mobile homes, cars, and sheds, and he was relieved that there was no menacing laughter or hurried steps behind him.

The disappointment in Noah's voice came back to him the moment he felt relatively safe from the kids.

Why do you pick on people?

Was he too impulsive? Or just mean to the bone? He'd always had a bit of a grudge against Caspian over things that had happened in high school, but that was some bullshit drama that should have been long left in the past. So was he jealous? Being born into a rich and loving family wasn't an achievement, but it wasn't a crime either. It wasn't Caspian's fault that Gunner's life had been filled with anguish and violence.

"Hey sweetie," he cooed when he spotted Fluffer's big, inquisitive eyes reflecting lamplight. "It's me."

The cat opened its mouth and rose from its place on the step leading to the trailer. Did he recognize who Gunner truly was, even though the fancy cologne he'd used this morning smelled nothing like his former self?

Speeding up, Gunner was about to run up to his pet when someone grabbed his forearm and tossed him at the nearest wall.

"Who do we have here? Are you here to spy on Gunner?"

Ice weighed on Gunner's stomach when three shadows closed in on him, like demons in some dumb paranormal TV show.

But this was real, and his heart thudded.

He wanted to speak up, to tell Todd to go fuck himself, yet his voice got stuck in his throat, because unlike at the gym, where there had been too many witnesses for Mike to inflict any serious damage, the dark alley between trailers was a place where anything could happen. A woman had been murdered on the other side of the grounds just two weeks ago, and her killer hadn't been found.

"Hey, shrimp, he's talking to you." Bud slapped him, blowing out fumes of beer, and even though it didn't hurt much, the humiliation of being prodded like this hit Gunner like a truck.

"I was just..." What would be the best lie in his position? If he were in Caspian's shoes—fuck. He *was* in

Caspian's shoes. "To talk about his cat," he blurted out. Reason had clearly left his body.

"What do you want with it? Maybe we should take your wallet? Provided there's enough dough in there, the puss can be yours. Maybe," Todd said with a mean chuckle.

Bud frowned. "Gun wouldn't sell his—"

Ralph shoved at him without saying a word.

This might be his end. Those three vultures would rip him apart and consume all the juiciest bits, leaving only blood and bones. But then hope filled his lungs like fresh air. He dashed forward, slipping out of Bud's clutches and hit the living room window with both hands before two pairs of arms roughly dragged him away from it.

"Gunner! Help!" he cried, but his voice broke when a hard kick to the back of his knee sent him into the dirt.

"Where do you think you're going, huh? We were talking to you," Todd hissed, shoving Gunner to his hands and knees.

Darkness had settled on the trailer park, and the music coming from a nearby home would obscure his screams. He knew this, because he'd been on the other side of that situation many times, and those were things one needed to consider to avoid getting caught.

He wouldn't get his redemption, but what was about to unfold would be punishment he'd never forget.

"Let go of me!" he yelled, because any noise he could make would work in his favor. Bud tried to silence him with a kick to the stomach, but Gunner grabbed his leg and bit the fucker on the calf like a rabid dog. So he was small, but he wouldn't go down without leaving his tormentors with battle scars.

Something collided with his ribs, and he might have rolled over twice before he landed on his back, with pain radiating all over his slender body, which didn't have the protective layer of dense muscle he could tighten in order to lessen the blow.

The world around him trembled, and he tried to get up, but when his gaze passed over the window of his trailer, he saw an eye looking at him from behind the curtain, and realization stabbed his heart

Caspian was here.

Yet he stayed hidden and refused to help.

Chapter 14 - Caspian

Caspian went straight back to the trailer park. His blood buzzed with fury, and he'd almost driven a slow car off the road when it got in his way, but all he could think about was Gunner and the casual way he'd dismissed him, when they were in this hell together. If anyone else was to know of their situation, Caspian should have been a part of that conversation too. He'd known what the bastard was doing—trying to shift all the blame for what Noah had seen to Caspian. Just like when they'd met in the morning and Gunner had claimed Caspian's body was 'gay'. It was such a shitty thing to do. Especially after everything that happened since Gunner had hounded Caspian down at the motel.

Bitterness tingled at the back of his tongue and trailed to the pit of his stomach where it slowly turned into an inferno that had him hitting the horn and driving way too fast in Gunner's useless piece of junk.

He was gay. So was Gunner. They'd both enjoyed each other's bodies throughout the day, and there was nothing wrong about that. To have that thrown into his face as an insult made him want to find the piece of shit and charge at him.

But when he parked by Gunner's trailer and saw that the lights were on inside, he knew there was another problem he needed to face.

The ex-girlfriend Gunner couldn't get rid of. Caspian left the vehicle with a sense of purpose and jumped up the three steps with his blood already pumping faster. Enough was enough.

Sandy was sitting in front of the TV and eating chips as he entered, but her face twisted the moment she spotted him. She looked like a demon about to pounce him and eat his soul.

"You can't watch *The Beach Bachelor* with me. You've been a shit all day, *and* left me with no money."

"Why didn't you go get yourself a job and earn some yourself? You sit on your ass all fucking day," Caspian barked, taking in the messy kitchen. If Gunner was the one bringing money home, shouldn't she at least have the decency to keep the small trailer relatively clean?

Sandy threw the chips to the sofa, and Caspian cringed when some of them scattered and rolled to the floor. "Oh yeah? And who fed Fluffer, huh?" She got up, spreading her arms, as if she were the threat, and he— someone who should cower.

Had Gunner really been such a pussycat with her? Caspian bet she was staying here rent-free too.

"You fed a cat. That's the only thing you've done all day long? Are you high?" he asked, staring her down, because while Gunner might not have known how to deal with this cash-sponge, Caspian had no fucks left to give.

She shifted her weight and cocked her head as if she were seeing him for the first time. "Well, yeah. But just on weed."

"This isn't working for me. Pack your bags," he said, guided by the fury singing in his veins. He wanted to smash something, but getting rid of this annoying fly was the next best thing.

She folded her arms on her chest. "You've gotta be kidding me! I put up with your bullshit for a year, and you're throwing *me* out?"

"Evidently."

"Oh yeah? Just watch me then! This is the last straw!" She licked the orange chip dust from her fingers and scooted down. With one tug, she pulled the TV cable out of the plug.

"Hey, what the hell do you think you're doing?" Caspian asked, thrown off guard.

"This is mine. You told me to pack my bags, and that's what I'm doing," she said and dragged over a chair, which she climbed on so abruptly the top of her nipple peeked from above the tube top she was wearing, as if her breast were fighting for its freedom.

This made zero sense. Gunner would have had a television of his own. And even if it belonged to her, for reasons he could only speculate about, Gunner had earned it back ten times over, if he'd been supporting her unproductive lifestyle all along.

"I'm vetoing this. Leave the TV, or we're gonna have a serious conversation," he said, unsure how to act. He could have just punched another guy, but what was he to do about a woman? He'd been taught to be respectful, but it wasn't working.

"You barely use it" she yelled, not caring that the neighbors would hear her through the thin walls. "If you want me out, you can live without your precious *British Bake Off.* And by the way, I know you've been using my shampoo, and I'll be taking that too!"

She slid off the chair and walked straight at Caspian with the screen tucked to her chest.

He did the one thing that came to his mind and blocked her way. "You will place the TV back on the table and go pack your personal things. Do not play with me," he added, because it seemed like the right thing to say.

Sandy pursed her lips, turned around, and... *threw* the TV at the table. The flat screen landed on the edge and cracked in the middle, while a piece of black plastic broke off its frame when it collapsed to the floor.

"There! Your precious TV! All yours! And on the table, like you always wanted," she screeched and grabbed the packet of crisps. "I guess these are yours too, huh?"

Before Caspian could react, she dipped her hand into the packet, then threw crushed chips at him.

What. The. Fuck. This woman was feral!

But he couldn't bring himself to just grab her, even as she went red and pouted at him like an overgrown child. *This* wasn't who he was.

"I said pack your bags. *Now.*"

"Or what? Like it can't wait till morning?" She shook her head with a smirk.

Gunner must have let her walk all over him. But *he* wasn't Gunner and wouldn't be convinced by the incentive of sex, which was surely what she intended to hold over his head next.

"If you don't go now, I will make you leave."

She rolled her eyes. Actually *rolled her eyes* at him. "Oh, come on, Gun. You can posture to your friends, but I know you're a marshmallow, so cut this shit out and we'll talk in the morning." She turned around and walked off toward the bedroom at the end of the trailer as if she hadn't just trashed the TV.

Caspian's hesitation only lasted a moment. He didn't want to manhandle her, but there was no other way, so he caught up, grabbed her by the waist and lifted her as if she were a large teddy bear and weighed close to nothing.

"That's a goodbye."

"Let go of me!" She screeched and pounded on his arms with her fists, but while it hurt, it couldn't make him let go, nor deal any real damage. "Or I'll tell everyone you liked a finger up your butt when I blew you!"

"Nobody's gonna believe I'd want you to do it with those sharp nails," Caspian snapped back, but his mind instantly went to territories it didn't belong. He opened the door and put her outside, by the steps. "If you won't pack your stuff, I'll just have to do it for you," he said and shut the door in her face, heading straight for the bedroom.

Enough was enough, and Gunner would thank him once they were back in their respective bodies. Sandy hollered outside, likely cursing him with all the black magic she knew from TV shows, but he grabbed a trash bag, and stuffed it with all the clothes and trinkets that looked like hers. On the way to the door, he also visited the bathroom, swept all her toiletries in too, and then grabbed her handbag from the kitchen counter.

Two of her friends had joined the sad scene outside by the time Caspian opened the door and threw two bags of her shit to the ground, drunk on his victory. "And take the damn cat too," he said, glaring over his shoulder to find the flat-faced furball on the table.

All three women stared at him, but Sandy was the first to speak. "I'm not taking the ugly stinker! You wanted him, so keep him and wipe his leaky nose!"

Oh. Ooh. So the cat was… Gunner's?

He flinched as something touched his calf, but when he looked down, the pet's big eyes met his before it gingerly leapt down the steps and laid on the one in the middle.

"Just… get lost. Don't wanna see you here again, lazy ass," he muttered, glaring at Sandy and her crew.

"Well, same here, asshole! You don't know how to treat a lady right!" She grabbed one of the bags, leaving the other to one of her friends.

"Don't worry about him, Sands, you can stay at my place," said a woman who could have been Sandy's twin before glaring at Caspian as if he were in the wrong.

A short examination of the door told him there was a cat flap at the bottom, so he petted Fluffer and left him outside, breathing a sigh of relief as the sense of justice settled in his chest.

But he was still left with a mess.

Caspian approached the broken TV set with a soft sigh. "Well, I didn't need you anyway, but Gunner's gonna be livid."

Fatigue got to him when he parked his ass on the sofa. But there was nothing strange about being tired after swapping bodies, fighting, topping for the first time, and eating for three people. All that since morning.

With a sigh of mindless exhaustion, he switched off the light and curled up on the seat, his eyelids heavy as if they had weights attached.

It seemed he'd only shut his eyes for a moment when someone called out Gunner's name in a shrill voice. Caspian didn't react at first, but when more voices joined in, and the distressed tone of the first person got through to him, he rose to his knees and pulled on the curtain, peeking outside in time to see Gunner close his teeth on Bud's bare calf while a dog barked as if it were about to cough out its lungs.

He was about to do a slow clap, but then Todd took a step closer and kicked Gunner in the ribs so hard the small body rolled over like something that shouldn't be that weightless.

Rage burned Caspian's insides, because it was still his body, and he'd be the one to bear all the bruises once his mind returned where it belonged. But while witnessing the attack made him stiffen with discomfort, it was obvious the bullies were just toying with their prey and had no intention of really hurting him.

He could break it up. He could step outside, claim Gunner as his boxing student, like he had at the gym, and put an end to the pathetic spectacle, but an ugly part of him wanted to see Gunner get a taste of his own medicine. And to suffer for saying all the mean things he'd had after Noah walked in on them in the shower. If he was so eager to avoid any association with Caspian, why was he expecting help?

A third shadow emerged, and Caspian recognized Todd's brother, Ralph. Hyenas always travelled in packs.

"I'll go take his car for a spin in the meanwhile. You won't mind, lil' Flea, will you?" Ralph didn't touch Gunner, but watched on as Todd stepped on the boy's back in order to pin him in place.

The lesson Caspian hoped Gunner would learn definitely did not include his one-of-a-kind Southfield getting scratched by this maniac!

He rolled off the sofa and burst outside, jumping down the steps to avoid Fluffer, who gave a little hiss when he opened the door.

"What the hell is this racket?"

"Just having some fun with our little friend over here," Todd said, his green eyes shining with glee, as if life didn't offer him worthier amusements. "Said he wanted to buy your cat or some shit."

What an asshole.

Gunner remained on the ground, defeated by a pack of wolves he'd never had a chance against. Guilt seeped to the back of Caspian's throat when the boy scrambled to his knees, visibly shaking. Some of the neighbors stepped out of their trailers or opened windows, and watched the situation unfold, as if Gunner's real-life misery was better entertainment than trash TV.

"Don't touch him again. He's my new student."

Bud laughed. "Student? Of what?"

When Gunner tried to use the opportunity to rise to his feet, Todd shoved him right back to the ground. "Where do you think you're going? We're not done."

Hot rage burst into Caspian's skull, and he smashed his fist against Todd's head, sending him crashing into the wall of the nearest trailer.

Nothing had ever felt this good. Well, at least since coming inside Gunner's tight little ass.

"Am I not speaking clearly? Fuck off and don't touch him again."

Todd stared at him as he slid to his ass, holding his head. "What the fuck, man?" he choked out.

Even Bud stepped away from Gunner, letting the boy scramble to his feet. He might have tripped several times, but this *was* Gunner, so he glared at Caspian with glossy eyes as soon as he felt safe enough to do so.

"So you only come out when they threaten the car? Fuck you!" he yelled and spat Caspian's way, even though he was too far away for the glob to reach him.

It wasn't untrue, and while just moments before it had felt right to let Gunner suffer for the way he'd acted, the straight-up question stabbed Caspian with guilt. He should act like the real Gunner would have and break the little fucker's nose, but even in this body, Caspian couldn't let himself become the kind of piece of shit Gunner had been to him in school. But it wasn't as though he could explain himself in front of all the onlookers. Even Mad Madge was enjoying the show, sipping off-brand root beer in front of her home. They needed to get away.

"Wait for me in the car," Caspian said, meeting Gunner's eyes.

Gunner opened his loud, vulgar mouth, about to spew more venom, but then hesitated, and finally closed it. He turned around and limped away, holding onto his stomach and for once doing as he was told. He was like a wounded puppy, eager to go lick his wounds yet in too much pain to run.

Gunner deserved a lesson, but maybe not one this violent. What if he had cracked ribs, or something?

Caspian had to take a deep breath before he faced the three bullies who'd ganged up on a guy who couldn't have taken on even one of them. "I said don't touch him. How hard is that to understand, Todd?" Caspian asked with pent-up rage coursing through his veins. He wished he could've twisted off this bastard's balls for everyone to see, just to make him feel a fraction of the fear and anguish Caspian himself had been through because of people like him. The adrenaline of being stronger than Todd still buzzed in his veins as he zeroed in on the guy.

"Since when do you care about people like him? He must be paying a lot for those boxing lessons." Todd scowled, but didn't try to fight Caspian.

"Since when do I have to explain myself to you?"

Ralph shook his head and stood by his brother, opening his mouth for once. He sounded as if his throat were covered with rust. "I'm gonna let this slide, 'cause I heard you broke up with Sandy. Get a grip, man. I just hope you're less unhinged on the job tomorrow."

The job.

The thing.

The fucking drug-muling.

What the fuck had he gotten himself into?

"You bet I did. Gonna find myself a real woman this time," Caspian said.

Bud laughed like a cartoon villain. "So you broke up for real this time?"

So Gunner couldn't even get himself a girlfriend who'd win the approval of his deadbeat friends? How pathetic. "This whole thing's really making me rethink my priorities. You guys do the job tomorrow without me. I'm done. *Satis est satis!*"

It was as if even the birds had stilled at those words.

Bud cocked his head with his lips parted. "What?"

Caspian spread his arms in frustration. "Enough is enough!"

Todd stared at him without a hint of a smile. "The fuck are you talking about?"

"Oh, so I've punched you deaf?"

Todd straightened up, and while Caspian remembered him as a tall guy, he was of an average size when seen from Gunner's perspective. "No, I'm just worried, you know? We'd be one man short, but I guess we can take your brother instead. He doesn't have your muscle, but I'm sure he can be persuaded."

Caspian wanted to say that he didn't have a brother so the joke was on them. But then he remembered the kid with a brown mop of curls, dark eyes and freckles, who'd left the gym with Gunner, and his lips clamped shut.

He shouldn't have cared, because Noah wasn't really *his* brother. But he seemed like a good kid and wasn't even eighteen yet. Things like that mattered. "Leave him out of it," he said, and the way Todd's face relaxed told him it had been blackmail all along.

Caspian itched to break the fucker's nose to make him look more distinctive from the twin brother, but there would be a better time for such pleasures. Right now, he and Gunner bore one another's responsibilities, and that meant no matter how much he disagreed with drug use on principle, or how much everything in him balked at the idea of committing a crime, he'd need to go through with *the job* this once, because there wasn't enough time to get himself out of it.

"Fine. I'll go."

Bud was already walking off, but Ralph shot Caspian another grim look before turning away. "See you tomorrow," he said in a tone that sounded like a warning.

Fuckers.

Caspian didn't yet know how, but he would make sure those three bastards paid for all the things they'd done. To him. To Gunner. And everyone else.

"Show's over," he shouted to all the not-so-discreet spectators and picked up Fluffer, who stared up at him, confused like a person who'd just been woken from the REM phase of sleep. "And you're under house arrest until your master's back," he whispered and put the cat inside before locking the door, the cat flap, and heading toward the gates of the trailer park, where he expected to find Gunner.

He didn't pin the big, burly guy as someone who'd own cats, especially fluffballs who spent their days grooming, but what did he know? Maybe it used to belong to an ex of Gunner's, and he'd gotten attached to the thing?

Even though midnight was approaching, in his new form, he wasn't afraid to walk up to a stranger smoking a joint in front of his home. The guy had a ZZ Top beard and wore sunglasses despite it being so dark.

"Hey, have you seen a guy in a vintage car? It's dark red."

The man took a long drag of smoke with a thoughtful expression. "Oh, yeah... Little guy, big car. He drove away."

Caspian's arms dropped in helpless anger, but he bit into his lip to stifle the roar pushing at his mouth and faced the open gate.

Gunner was going against him *again*. But this time, Caspian wouldn't let him get away with it.

K.A. Merikan | **211**

Chapter 15 - Gunner

The bastard had watched it happen. Just hidden away behind the curtain and let those fuckers kick Gunner about, as if none of what had happened between them earlier mattered. Maybe it didn't, and Gunner had gotten ahead of himself thinking that he and Caspian were on the same team. Caspian had seen glimpses of it when he took charge in sex, stripping Gunner of his armor, but he didn't seem to understand what those moments meant to Gunner and had only seen being in charge as a power trip. Was this all there had been to their frantic, lusty encounters?

So maybe Gunner had been a bit of a shit to Caspian in front of Noah, but he'd panicked. Wasn't he allowed some slack?

Unwilling to face anyone, he ended up parking in front of a bar, frustrated and hurting. The bright moon illuminated him like a spotlight and pushed Gunner's thoughts farther down the rabbit hole of fantastical events that he'd woken up to. He'd turned on his favorite rendition of Mozart's 'piano concerto no. 24' to get lost in the music and calm down, but his mind raced with questions.

If he died, would he go back to his body, or would Caspian end up in his skin forever? Would their brains remember what each of them did once they swapped? Would he go back to his own body once the clock struck midnight, like Cinderella?

He didn't deserve a prince though. He didn't even deserve a good, guiltless dicking for the way he'd treated Caspian, and maybe the universe wanted to prove this to him today? The humbling experience of fearing people intent on hurting him for no reason would stay with him forever, as would the memory of having a bite of the forbidden fruit.

He'd been allowed a peek at what his life could have been if he'd been born someone else, and losing that new identity after just one day would be his punishment. Because Caspian's actions at the trailer park proved that he'd never forgive Gunner.

He shot a longing look at the broken neon above the entrance to the bar. A drink or two would have made everything better. And who knew, maybe not all the patrons were straight and Gunner could bask in male attention for a few hours more, forgetting the bitterness at the back of his tongue.

He was psyching himself to leave the car when his cell phone beeped. He glanced at it to make sure it wasn't Caspian, but no, the screen read *Mom*.

He answered with a heavy heart. He'd barely known *his* mom, but this one made him pancakes and was so nice he didn't want to worry her by ignoring the call.

"Hey, what's up?" Gunner asked, not sure if that was what Caspian would have said, but staying silent would have been even weirder.

After a short silence, the voice he'd first heard that morning spoke. "We're worried about you, Caspian. Will you be home soon? It's almost midnight."

Gunner rubbed his face, but his gaze followed two men leaving the bar. Both were tall, and he was almost certain he'd seen them around. One had long hair and a guitar on his back, the other wore a distressed leather jacket. Gunner would have forgotten all about them if the first one hadn't pushed his friend at the wall for a kiss that most definitely shouldn't have been happening in public, Gunner looked down at the phone, embarrassed as if he'd walked in on two people having sex.

"Caspian? Are you there?"

"Yes, Mom. Sorry. It's been a rough day."

He stole one more glance at the couple, but they didn't stay and were headed toward the Karma motel. He was already missing Caspian's touch, regardless of how betrayed he still felt, but good things had always been temporary in Gunner's life. Tomorrow, he'd wake up in his old body, and he'd be grateful for getting to experience one day in someone else's shoes, even if right now his ribs ached.

"It's okay. Come home and we can talk about it." Fake Mom fumbled with something. "Yes, he says he's coming," she said, likely to Caspian's dad.

They cared. They wanted him aro— No. They wanted Caspian. Gunner was an impostor in their son's skin.

"See you in a bit," he said and ended the call.

He might not have been who they were expecting, but they'd been kind to him and deserved a peaceful night, so he started the car and spent the next half an hour on autopilot, which switched off only once he arrived at Caspian's massive family home and realized he didn't know how to open the garage. Fortunately, his fake parents must have noticed his arrival, because the gate lifted, allowing him to park.

He sat in the dark for a whole minute, unsure how to deal with confrontation as Caspian, but he couldn't spend the whole night behind the wheel and eventually arrived at the front door, which opened before he could have started worrying about not having keys.

Caspian's mom already wore a dressing gown over a satin pajama set, but her eyes widened when she spotted him. "H-hello, dear," she said, and while it was obvious she didn't want to show the extent of her shock, her gaze slid up and down Gunner's body in silent judgment.

Right. The new clothes. The tight jeans, the lilac shoes, and the massive hoodie that clearly didn't belong to him. He should have thrown it in Caspian's face. And yet here he was, curling his fingers around the long sleeves and wishing he could just hide inside it and soak up Caspian's scent.

"Hi, I'm sorry. I left the keys home."

Caspian's dad walked up to the door in plaid pajamas that resembled the ones in Caspian's drawers. "You haven't been drinking, have you? I wouldn't like to see you making a habit out of that. Not to mention that you were driving—"

"I'm sober, jeez!" Gunner pushed past Caspian's mom, rigid with frustration, his leg and ribs aching from bruises that were developing on his body.

"What are you wearing? Where are your clothes?" Mom asked as the door shut.

Caspian had intended to go straight to his room, but knew he couldn't leave such questions unanswered, so he spun around and spread his arms wide.

"This is me now. Take it or leave it."

Caspian's dad frowned as they all walked farther into the grand house. "No need to be rude." He turned to his wife. "Look, Barb, we had all sorts of fashions back in our day."

Fake Mom—Barb—shook her head. "Yes, but I'm not recognizing my son anymore. What's gotten into you, Caspian?"

A big bad motherfucker with a chip on his shoulder, Gunner wanted to say but bit his lips and mumbled, "I'm just experimenting."

"Oh, so you want to change your style... start fresh?" Barb asked, cupping her cheek with one hand with concern painted all over her face.

"Is that color on your hair permanent? Why didn't you do any of this in college, like everyone else?" Fake Dad inquired, frowning.

Gunner ran his fingers through his blond hair. He'd loved it at the barber's, and the large mirror confirmed that he still looked cute. "I wanted to switch things up."

Barb cleared her throat. "Some men dye their hair now. At least it's a nice natural shade," she said, but then her eyes went wide, and she stepped up to Gunner. "Is that a piercing in your ear? Caspian! Are you seeing this, Thomas?"

Gunner spread his arms. "I'm not a child! If I want to get a piercing, I will. Who knows, maybe I'll do my nose next!"

"Are you not too old for this kind of rebellious phase?" Barb asked, gesturing at Gunner's ear. "It looks unprofessional. What if some of your clients dislike it?"

Gunner clutched at his hair. "Looks have nothing to do with doing my job well!" he said, even though he still didn't know what degree Caspian had.

"Tell that to all the people who won't ever get employed because they'd tattooed their hands or faces."

The words struck Gunner harder than Bud's steel-capped boot had. He clenched his fists, breathing hard. "Sure, just write people off based on their looks! You don't know their lives or what led to some of their—"

Thomas rubbed his grey moustache and spoke. "Caspian, I've got work tomorrow. I don't have time for these theoretical constructs. I understand you're adjusting to life after college. We'll iron out the wrinkles with time. If you're looking to reinvent yourself, tomorrow is a good time. You need a new suit for our garden party, and your mom's taking you shopping. You'll be meeting Mr. Sadler and the rest of the firm as a future employee, and need to make a good impression if you're to put your best foot forward for the job."

Gunner screamed out in helpless rage, because there was nowhere else he could channel it. "Fine!" He took a swipe at a notebook resting on the edge of the side table, and sent it to the floor with a clatter.

"Caspian!" Barb held her finger up in warning, but Gunner was already running upstairs. While he wouldn't have to worry about any of those expectations come tomorrow, they now felt oppressive and very much real. The demands of Caspian's parents were a bitter reminder that he wasn't good enough, even in this body, with a smooth face that didn't carry the mark of his worst decisions.

His fake parents must have given up for tonight, because he couldn't hear any shouting or footsteps banging on the stairs as he stepped into the dark bedroom and turned the key to lock himself in. He was midway through a frantic inhale when big, strong hands closed around him and pulled him against a sturdy body. He wanted to scream out, but a meaty palm closed tightly on his face and would block any sound.

Was it Bud? Todd? Had they both snuck in here to finish what they'd started?

Panic sank into his muscles when he realized he couldn't breathe, but before he could have thrown the first ineffective punch, ready to fight for his life, a familiar voice whispered straight into his ear.

"What the hell was that downstairs, huh?"

He should know his own voice, yet it sounded different when he heard it through someone else's ears. Deep and raspy, it sent chills down his back. He stilled at the realization that the massive hand against his face and the body squeezing him from behind weren't a threat. The scent of cologne he didn't know enveloped him in a confusing mix of fear and excitement. Caspian must have been there for a while and used a perfume from his own collection instead of the cheap cologne Gunner had at

218 | Take My Body

home. It had a thrilling, spicy quality that made Gunner's toes curl in his pretty new shoes, even though he was still angry at the treasonous bastard.

"And don't you walk out on me again. I told you to wait in the car," Caspian said. When he inhaled and the breath tickled Gunner's scalp, it felt like being smelled by a predator who still considered whether he wanted to eat his prey now or leave it for later.

He whimpered and tried to fight the firm hold of steel-hard arms, but his struggling achieved nothing. A jolt of arousal ricocheted in his balls the moment he remembered Caspian tying his wrists back with the belt.

But Caspian didn't try to undress him and took his warm hand off Gunner's lips before spinning him around so they faced one another in the dark. He loomed over Gunner like the hottest manifestation of danger.

Gunner didn't want to show how much Caspian's presence affected him, but he didn't manage to keep his lips from trembling. He could have screamed, and Caspian's parents would have come running, but he wasn't in danger and had no right to chase Caspian out of his own room. "I didn't wanna wait, and I still don't want to see your traitor face."

Caspian snorted. "I thought you wanted me to have a good relationship with those fuckers you call friends."

Gunner's mouth went dry, but Caspian held him by the shoulders when he tried to step back, away from that inquisitive gaze. "Yeah, but... not like that. Like, I'm really small now, okay? Everything hurts."

Caspian went still, his face stern like that of some old sculpture. "You're right."

Gunner frowned. "I am?"

Caspian sighed and spread his arms. "Yes. I wanted you to learn a lesson on how it is to be in my shoes, but it was also cruel and unnecessary."

Gunner took a few steps back and hugged himself, unsure what to do with this declaration. He wasn't used to talking about feelings honestly. "And you regret it?"

Caspian rubbed the top of his head, chewing on his lip before he spoke. "Yeah. It was a shitty thing to do, but I got so angry that I just went with what my gut was telling me. And I acted like a terrible person. I'm sorry," he said, stuffing both hands into his pockets.

"You don't... You don't think I deserved it?" Gunner mumbled and turned on the bedside lamp, just to do something with his hands, but as his adrenaline levels dropped, every movement reminded him of what had happened, creating a cycle of discomfort.

Caspian's lips twisted, but he stood in the middle of the room, rigid like a statue. "I did. But you were defenseless. It wasn't fair. I thought I was the better man, but maybe I'm not," he said, exhaling as he met Gunner's gaze.

"I told Noah. About the *thing*."

"That you're gay?"

"No!" Gunner whined and pulled off the hoodie to hide his face in its folds, even if just for a moment. "About the body swap. I'm pretty sure I convinced him, and we kinda talked about some things I did in the past. And how maybe this situation is my fault. That maybe the universe is trying to tell me I need to change my ways or whatever." He took a deep breath and looked Caspian's way with a heavy sensation in the chest, "I'm also sorry. For yesterday. I shouldn't have let them do what they did. I see that now."

Caspian might've honestly regretted the way he'd handled the situation at the trailer park, but the truth was that it allowed Gunner to understand the terror he'd put Caspian through the previous evening. They'd surrounded him, and he'd been unable to fight back. Gunner could only imagine how Caspian had felt when the guys pulled his pants down just to mock him.

With eyes stubbornly welling up in a way they never did in his own body, Gunner shoved the hoodie at Caspian for distraction. But before he could have gotten away, Caspian grabbed his wrist and stared at a bruise forming above his elbow.

"Shit. How hurt are you?" he asked in a voice that was oddly soft for a man his size.

"I don't know. What I'm saying is that I probably deserved it anyway."

But Caspian wouldn't give it a rest and urged Gunner to take off his top. There had been quite a lot of pain since the altercation with Bud and the Brown brothers, but the sight of ugly bruises forming on his side and stomach still came as a surprise. His arm didn't look much better.

Caspian's face became grimmer with every new mark discovered on Gunner's body, and he kneeled by the bed, gently touching the bruises with his fingertips in a tender way that didn't seem even remotely sexual. Yet the gentleness of his hands still made Gunner close his eyes. Sandy had never done that when he'd come back from a boxing match with the taste of blood on his tongue and a swollen face. As if the discomfort he'd suffered was just a fact of life and didn't need any special attention. But

Caspian was there for him, worried as if Gunner had at least suffered a broken bone.

"I know, I know, I injured your body. I'm sorry. I should have been more careful."

Caspian swallowed and faced him. "Bruises will fade. But you had to be in this skin when it happened, and I could have helped. It's my fault. Lie down," he said and walked to the ensuite.

"You're not mad about it?" Gunner mumbled and did as told.

Fatigue settled in his muscles the moment he rested his head on the pillow, as if the stress of this past day had only caught up with him.

"It's not your fault those damn gorillas targeted you," Caspian said, reappearing with a plastic bowl of water and two dry cloths. "I know how it is. You're doing your own thing, and some asshole just chooses to fuck your day up out of boredom." He sat on the bed, dunked the pieces of fabric in the water and placed them on Gunner's ribs and stomach, where he'd gotten hit the hardest. Cool yet not unpleasantly so, the damp compresses offered instant relief.

In the faint glow of the lamp, the frown on Caspian's face appeared deeper, and he was so focused on his task Gunner chose to stay still and let him do his thing.

The heavy silence must have weighed on them both, because Caspian finally spoke. "I won't let this ever happen again. No one's gonna hurt you on my watch."

Gunner choked up. He'd learned to fend for himself at an early age and had been his dad's pushover, Noah's protector, always on his toes around 'friends' to avoid showing weakness. No one had ever promised to keep him safe, but despite the grudge Caspian held toward him, he was being sincere.

"Why?" was the single thing that came to Gunner's mind as his heart drummed at a frantic pace, desperate to communicate that it wanted to believe those promises, even though they were made by an almost-stranger who'd been Gunner's enemy only a day ago.

Caspian cleared his throat, looking away, but the twitching at the side of his jaw betrayed how nervous he was. "Because it's right. And because I can. And because I want to," he said, his gaze spearing Gunner's bruised chest.

Gunner knew he shouldn't, knew he ought to be angry, but he couldn't help himself and ran his fingers over Caspian's thick, muscular forearm. The temptation to roll into bed with the man who promised to protect him became too strong.

"We'll change back tomorrow. The universe, or whatever, has taught me my lesson."

Caspian's shoulders sagged, and he entwined their fingers.

"You really think so?"

Gunner nodded. "It makes sense. Happened after I… hurt you last night."

Caspian mumbled something and rubbed his face. "Back to the drawing board, huh? At least I won't have to transport drugs and pretend I know how to box."

"And I won't have to work out what suit to choose for a party where I don't fit in, to secure a job I can't do. I don't even know what you used to study."

But for all that talk, Gunner was missing this new body already. He squeezed Caspian's hand, but instead of giving it a shake, Caspian pulled it to his face, pressing a kiss to the delicate skin at the inner side of Gunner's wrist.

"It doesn't matter now."

How was Gunner to let go of this gentle touch? Sure, he liked the pancakes, the big house, and comfy bed, but *this*? What he'd shared with Caspian today? He mourned the loss already.

"It doesn't. I don't need to pretend when I'm with you."

Caspian nodded, rubbing Gunner's arm. "Can I stay here tonight?" he asked, as if it wasn't his house, his room, and his bed. But he wasn't asking for a more comfortable sleep. Like Gunner, he didn't want to let go of this strange dream yet.

Gunner pulled him onto the bed. "Yeah, Sandy can be loud in the morning and you need the rest." A stupid excuse to be close. He had no idea how he would live on in his old body after today.

Back to being a big bad bastard with a tattooed face.

Back to 'friends' whom he didn't trust.

Back to constant financial worries and the ever-looming threat of Snowman's boss sending Gunner to the bottom of a lake with sandbags attached to his ankles.

But tonight, he could be the sweet boy Caspian desired, and when the other man leaned in, Gunner shut his eyes before warm lips touched his in a soft, soothing kiss. So unlike the greedy ones from before yet just as delicious.

He wrapped his arms around the thick neck, and even the pain in his ribs subsided when Caspian slid his thigh between Gunner's legs. Their earlier conflict didn't matter, and all of it would unravel tomorrow anyway, so what would be this one more indulgence? Until the dream lasted, Gunner chose to believe the big guy stroking his side was his man and his protector. It was okay to be vulnerable and sweet with him.

Neither of them was in a hurry this time, and even when Gunner's cock hardened from all that touching and kissing, he didn't try to push for more and raised his chin in submission, accepting each and every peck Caspian showered on his neck, then down his chest. He opened his eyes and peeked down in time to see Caspian rub the tip of his nose against Gunner's nipple before teasing it with the underside of his tongue.

The unexpected pleasure of the caress made him gasp, and he petted Caspian's nape before glancing to the door. "Are you sure your parents won't—"

"Their bedroom is on the other side of the house, and they respect the locked door."

Of course. Because they were *nice*. Nothing like Gunner's father had been.

Caspian returned for a kiss that was gentle but sparked something inside Gunner, prompting him to arch his body against the muscular form above.

"It's just us," Caspian promised before returning to Gunner's nipples, squeezing both between his fingers, then sucking on each one and rubbing his rough tongue against the sensitive flesh.

He was such a beast. He could have rolled Gunner over and fucked him again, and Gunner would have let him. But that wasn't what this moment was about. For the first time, Caspian was taking his time to explore every bit of the wonderful, smooth form. And Gunner wanted that too.

"It's nice to be in your body, but not have to pretend to *be* you. Does that make sense?" Gunner ran his fingers through the short hair on top of Caspian's head and met the dark gaze. The faint light of the bedside lamp blurred the edges between their bodies and cast long shadows, creating an intimate atmosphere.

"Yeah. It is," Caspian agreed and blew hot breath on Gunner's skin as he moved lower and pressed his mouth to the bulge at the front of Gunner's jeans. He kept staring up too, as if he wasn't in the least bit embarrassed by this gesture.

Gunner groaned and spread his thighs in invitation. "How are you this hot? I had no idea I was so irresistible."

Caspian laughed and moved like a rattlesnake, biting Gunner's left nipple, and then resting his weight on top of Gunner as he nipped on his lip. "Right back at you. Such a fine piece of ass. And only mine," he said, rocking his hips against Gunner's.

Gunner slid his fingers up Caspian's T-shirt, pulling it up as he trailed each rib. This was what he wanted as a gay man. Not to go on Grindr and hook up with strangers or find new dick each day. He craved to belong, to be the apple of another man's eye.

He wanted to be Caspian's.

He chuckled and kissed Caspian under the stubbly chin. "You like touching yourself?"

Caspian swallowed, staring back at him with slack features. "I think I'll like it more from now on," he said and moved back down, settling between Gunner's thighs and opening his skinny jeans. "Even my cock looks better on you."

Gunner snickered as he pulled the T-shirt off Caspian, ready to indulge in whatever this stud wanted to unleash on him. "I felt amazing when you had it in your mouth. It's so pink, and fits this body."

The smile stretching Caspian's face was genuine and so warm even the hyena skull tattoo looked exciting rather than menacing. Gunner whimpered when the denim was peeled off him, but Caspian didn't intend to wait and removed Gunner's underwear too before gently tapping the swollen cockhead.

"Tasted pretty good too," he whispered. When he lowered himself, resting his elbows between Gunner's thighs, Gunner's flesh became so sensitive he could feel the gentlest breeze, and his skin broke out in goosebumps when Caspian licked his way from Gunner's balls to his shaft.

The illicit pleasure of watching his own face sucking cock was as arousing as it was confusing. "All yours," Gunner whispered, because saying it any louder would have felt too real. But in the world of his fantasies, on this big, comfortable bed, they belonged to one another forever.

Thick, warm fingers dug into his thighs, and he shuddered when Caspian rubbed his stubbly chin against their sensitive insides. But then he leaned forward and rolled his tongue over Gunner's balls before sucking the wrinkled skin as if he'd never sampled anything more delicious.

When the universe had decided to teach him a lesson, had it known he'd be craving to stay in the body of the man he'd hurt? Even being so short, so much weaker than he was used to, and too dumb to understand anything about the job Caspian was to take on, he would have chosen to stay like this. Desired. Protected by a man who was truly *good* at the core.

He moaned and clenched Caspian's shoulder, his cock throbbing with the desire to come already.

He hadn't known just how much he needed for someone else to take the reins. To set the tone and take care of him. Tomorrow morning, he'd be back living his shitty life, but didn't want to focus on that when Caspian touched him with so much hunger, licking, rubbing, and sucking without shame.

He looked so damn hot when his cheeks hollowed around the hard prick in his mouth, but it was when their eyes met that Gunner really couldn't stop himself from squirming with lust. Rough fingers ghosted in the crack of Gunner's ass, and one of them slid in, reminding Gunner of the times he'd been fucked today, the slight burn added to the pressure mounting in his balls.

He was such a fucking slut for getting dicked.

When the teasing took him over the edge, he grabbed a pillow and put it over his face, arching violently as orgasm ripped through him in hurried waves.

Caspian didn't pull away, didn't resist when Gunner rocked against him, fucking the wet, hot vacuum of his mouth, and only let the cock out once it started to soften. He pulled the pillow off Gunner's face, as if he wanted more than just a pliant body to fuck. The room was still spinning around Gunner's spent form when Caspian straddled his hips and freed his fat dick with a groan of relief. He spat on his hand, squeezed Gunner's nipple and grabbed his own cock.

"You're so hot."

Despite barely catching his breath, Gunner squeezed Caspian's thigh. "Come here, I wanna see it up close. I want it so close you drizzle my face with spunk when you come." His cheeks were on fire when he said it, but this was his one night in the small body, and he would not censor himself.

Yes, he did want cum shooting from that dick on his lips and cheeks. He wouldn't shower after it happened, and tomorrow, Caspian would wake up with the memento of crusty, dried spunk.

The brown gaze flickered with arousal, and Caspian rolled his hips forward, pointing his meat straight at Gunner as he started jerking off. The thick, purple cockhead kept disappearing in his fist, only to reveal itself again, deliciously slick with pre-cum Gunner wanted to gather with his tongue.

"That's what you want slut? For me to turn your face into abstract art?" Caspian growled, his cheeks a dark red.

Gunner locked his eyes with Caspian with the thick cock right above his face. "Yes. Go on. Fill my greedy mouth." He spread his lips and rolled his tongue out in invitation. He'd never been in such a sexual frenzy. Caspian had opened him as if he were a shaken bottle of champagne, and there was no end to his fizz.

Caspian's thighs tightened around his chest, trembling, and his body stiffened in preparation for what was to come. He let out a frantic grunt and covered Gunner's eyes with one hand.

Gunner wanted to protest and see the prick erupt straight at him, but when the first splash of salty cum hit his mouth, he held it open, anticipating each and every string of sticky heat marking his flesh.

"Oh fuck. Oh fuck," Caspian hummed, and his thighs trembled under Gunner's fingers.

Gunner exhaled when Caspian took his hand away, and once it became clear there was no more cum coming, he stuck his tongue out as far as it could go and scooped the musky liquid. He gathered some cum off his cheek with his fingers and sucked that off too while glancing at Caspian from under lowered eyelids. If only he had a few more days, he'd make Caspian as obsessed with him as it already was the other way around.

"Happy, stud?"

Caspian was still catching his breath when he nodded and leaned in, offering Gunner whatever was left of the cum at the tip of his prick. "Fair warning. Don't get cum in your eyes. That stuff stings like a motherfucker."

A ball of cotton candy sprouted in Gunner's stomach. It wouldn't stop rolling around and releasing butterflies as Gunner sucked Caspian's cock clean, wordlessly thanking him for taking such care not to hurt him.

"And you know that from experience?" Gunner teased, stroking up Caspian's treasure trail and licking spunk off Caspian's hand when it was offered to him. The salty flavor spread over his tongue and covered his entire mouth, leaving him purring.

Caspian chuckled and rolled to the mattress, lazily trying to kick off his clothes. "It's a rite of passage," he said, his eyes flickering with humor as he glanced at Gunner.

"Let me do this for you, since you're such a gentleman." Gunner grinned and pulled Caspian's jeans and underwear off, before relieving him of socks too.

Gunner folded it all on the chair, weirdly emotional about the whole thing, but as he returned to bed, Caspian was already waiting for him under the covers, one arm lifting the comforter in invitation.

"Come here."

Gunner was so eager to be back in the safety of those big arms he tripped and fell right into the embrace. A part of him didn't want to sleep and let this day end, but his eyelids felt as if rocks were attached to his lashes.

Caspian dropped the comforter and stretched on the bed, pulling Gunner close, until his head rested on Caspian's thick bicep and his leg straddled one of Caspian's.

He fell asleep so fast he didn't even know when it happened.

Chapter 16 - Gunner

The harsh beep of the alarm clock startled Gunner so much he almost sat up in bed.

Almost.

Because a heavy arm kept him down as if he were a kitten stuck under a Mastiff's paw. He blinked several times, trying to work out what was going on when reality struck him like lightning. This was Caspian's room.

He moved his head over the pillow and stilled, looking at the handsome profile that used to belong to him. The facial tattoo side bared its teeth at him, but he wasn't sure whether the hyena skull was snarling in warning or grinning.

Caspian rubbed his cheek, frowned, and stretched his arm while rolling to his side so he could reach the offending alarm clock. The screech stopped like a bird that had been shot off a tree, but Caspian yawned and rolled back, pressing his face to Gunner's hair, still half-asleep.

Gunner was about to wake him, but the presence of someone else in his bed must have been alarming enough, because Caspian's brown eyes flew open, and he blinked, sucking in air as if he expected a stab in the chest.

"You're here!"

Gunner slipped out from under Caspian's arm, all too aware of the crustiness on his face. Leaving it on had seemed like a good idea last night. Now? Not so much.

"Yeah I'm here! What the fuck?" He jumped out of bed and spread his arms.

"You said we'd be back to normal by morning. And I didn't question it, like the idiot I am," Caspian mused, sitting on the edge of the bed with his head hung and tense shoulders.

"I don't know. Aren't you the one with the college degree and shit?" Gunner's lungs were working overtime, and he couldn't focus, too overwhelmed by the unknown.

They were stuck, and while he loved being in Caspian's skin, this fantasy needed to end. He had a brother to take care of and didn't know a thing about the fancy life he'd be supposed to lead if he stayed like this. He hadn't even finished high school, so there was only so long he could pretend he knew what was doing at Caspian's shiny new job.

"I don't have a degree in fucking magic," Caspian said and stood, rubbing his palm over the top of his head.

Gunner stalled, unable to take his eyes off the V-shaped muscles he'd worked so hard to maintain. How was he to think with all that hotness on show?

"I'll think about it in the shower." He shook his head and dashed to the en suite bathroom. The banging of heels made Gunner speed up to escape the giant chasing him, but

Caspian blocked the bathroom door with his leg and wouldn't let him close it.

"Don't run from me!"

This was starting to become a pattern. Gunner took a deep breath and turned to face Caspian. "I'm not!" He so was. "I just... I'm not gonna greet your dad with cum on my face, am I?"

Caspian's brows rose and he pushed the door open, stepping right into the bathroom. No privacy then.

"We can talk about this while we shower." He walked straight into the large stall in the corner, offering Gunner an excellent view of the tattooed shoulders, but also the broad, muscular back and strong legs.

The bathroom was as gray and stark as Caspian's bedroom, but there was a serene quality to it, which complimented Caspian's tall, masculine form. In this space of glass and tile, he didn't hit the ceiling with the top of his head, and the stall was perfectly suitable to fit them both.

Gunner followed Caspian like the horny sheep he was. "Okay. But... you know this can't go on, right?"

Caspian stilled and glanced over his shoulder as the first droplets of water from the rain shower hit the floor. "It's not that bad."

Gunner stepped in, watching Caspian in confusion. "What? You must want your life back." He'd be getting cramps in his neck from looking up. Was Caspian this tall or *he* this short?

Caspian adjusted the temperature of the water and stepped under the stream, releasing a soft exhale. "I mean... I now live with an extended family of cockroaches, and there's this debt I need to take care of, but I could work things out. Just look at me. Look at this body." He spread his long arms and made a slow turn, presenting his godlike form while warm droplets cascaded down the bulging muscles.

Gunner could barely breathe, so he washed his face, standing on the very edge of the stall.

"But—"

"No 'buts'. I've got the perfect dick, don't you think?"

Gunner bit his lip as he glanced at the thick tool, but then compared it to the one attached to his own new body. "I'm not... too small, right?" he asked, suddenly self-conscious.

Caspian stalled, and his gaze slid down Gunner's stomach, to his soft cock. It was unnerving to see him take his time with the answer, but he shook his head in the end and took Gunner's hand. "No. It fits you. And it tastes good too. We don't all have to be the same," he whispered, pulling Gunner under the artificial rain, which sank into Gunner's fluffy blond hair and drizzled down his body.

Gunner hesitated, but wrapped his arms around Caspian's waist, putting his cheek against the meaty pec. "I have... obligations in my life. I can't just become a happy-go-lucky twink. That's not me."

But when Caspian's arms locked around him, there was nothing he wanted more than to remain his sweet, pliant boy. To let Caspian take care of him. To sleep in a soft bed and no longer worry whether he'd have food on the table next week. To no longer feel the weight of the world on shoulders that, while strong and sturdy, always felt like they were about to crack.

Caspian kissed the top of Gunner's head and reached for the shower gel. The fruity scent of the soap

Gunner had brought here yesterday perfumed the damp air. "There's the debt and Noah. Anything else?"

Gunner could have melted into Caspian and the comfort he provided by suggesting that no problem was without a solution. "It's not that simple. I have to make the payments on time, and I don't exactly have a steady job. The debt keeps coming at me like a wave that can't be stopped. And then I don't know how to handle Sandy, even though I don't think she even likes me."

"You no longer need to worry about her."

Gunner stopped breathing and looked up into the dark eyes. "You killed her? No! She's annoying, but not—"

Caspian frowned. "What?" He stepped back before Gunner could have reacted. "What the fuck? I just made her move out. Did *you* kill someone that it was even an idea in your head?" he asked with a squeaky note in his voice.

"No!" Gunner said quickly. "I just...don't know you that well, and thought maybe you wanted to kill someone without consequences. Since it's not your body..." Caspian's deepening frown made him shut up. "I got it. I'm happy you don't."

Caspian blinked, resting his hands on his hips with his gaze stern as if he'd been born to become a drill sergeant. "You better not, because bullying and dealing drugs are one thing, but murder crosses the line of things I could live with."

Gunner spread his arms, frustrated by how short they were. The come-at-me! gesture didn't work so well when he was five-three. "I've done some bad shit, but I'm not a murderer! Wait. Sandy. She didn't take my cat, did she?"

Caspian shook his head and stepped closer, rubbing his soaped-up hands down Gunner's shoulders. "No. She said he was yours. Does he need to see a vet over this leaking nose?"

Shame hit Gunner like a bag of bricks, and he lowered his gaze, but that resulted in even greater awkwardness when he zeroed in on Caspian's dick. "I can't afford it right now..."

Caspian was silent as he massaged the sweet-smelling foam into Gunner's neck before moving his hands to the smooth chest. "Actually, you can."

Gunner stroked up all the way to Caspian's pec and put his hand over his heart. "I can?"

Caspian exhaled but didn't stop lathering Gunner's body. "I won't lie that I'm not dreading my credit card bill for after the spree you've had yesterday, but Fluffer needs some help. We'll make it happen."

Gunner smiled and arched into Caspian's touch like a happy cat. He'd sometimes dreamed what living as a pet would be like. Taken care of, fed, and free to lounge in the sun all day. "Thanks. I love the little fucker," he admitted.

"What about your brother though? What did you end up telling him?"

Gunner closed his eyes when Caspian went on to wash his hair and soapy suds slipped down his face. "A thing only I'd know, and he believed it was me. Maybe he'll be able to help us. Don't... I didn't tell him I'm gay though, so keep that on the down low."

He sensed Caspian's judgment in the way he slowed down the scalp massage, and while he braced himself for the questions coming his way, he still felt defenseless when Caspian spoke.

"Why not? What's the big issue? He seemed fine with it when he saw us."

Gunner huffed and ran his palms up and down Caspian's sides. "'Cause it's not... It's not like me. We'll work out what's going on with us, and I don't wanna deal with yet another issue when I'm back in *there.*"

"I'd say it's very much like you. Being gay really suits you," Caspian whispered, pushing back Gunner's lathered mane before directing him under the stream of water, so it would all wash off.

"For now just let Noah think it's the body. I don't know how to talk to him about it. It changes everything he knows about me. I'm his big brother. I'm supposed to protect him. He's been through enough shit."

Caspian let go of Gunner and handed him the pink bottle before grabbing one from his own collection. The brown shower gel disturbed the perfect sweetness of the air with a spicy, wood-like aroma. "He's got scars. What happened?"

"He was in a car accident two years ago. His passenger didn't make it. He survived but spent months in rehabilitation and still has issues. It's..." Gunner took a deep breath of the scented air. "I went into debt so he could get the best care, but I don't exactly have a good credit score, so it is what it is."

"Oh... so the only way you could pay for it was to borrow money from a loan shark?" Caspian asked. Gunner shrunk under the weight of shame, but there was no judgment in Caspian's gaze. "I didn't... I didn't think you'd do something like this."

Gunner stepped out of the shower and grabbed a towel softer than a kitten's fur. "Why? 'Cause I'm a shitty person?"

"What would you have thought if you were in my place?" Caspian asked, quickly washing his body.

Gunner thought back to how he'd felt yesterday, helpless against three guys who'd shoved him around and kicked him. He stilled, wrapping himself in the massive towel. "Yeah, I wouldn't expect much of someone like me."

"Maybe you should? Who knows how long we'll live in these bodies. We need to work something out."

"We can't stay like this! What's that amazing job your parents keep mentioning?" Gunner rubbed his face to hide it for that bit longer. He couldn't handle Caspian's life no matter how exciting living in this body was.

"I'm an accountant," Caspian said with a little smile stretching his lips as he switched off the water and grabbed a spare towel. "Scared of numbers?"

"Fuck!" Gunner raised his hands in frustration. He didn't bother picking up the towel as he walked back into the room to get dressed. "I could wing being a manager or something, but I don't know shit about accounting. Noah's mom does my taxes, for fuck's sake. I kinda... I kinda thought you might be a piano player."

Caspian blinked. "That's... obscure. How do you know I play the piano?" he asked and wrapped the towel around his hips, following Gunner into the bedroom.

Gunner put on one of the new pairs of boxers he'd gotten yesterday, with a pattern of ice cream cones. "I was just... Your parents might have said something. And when I touched the keys, there was this feeling that I could."

Caspian rubbed his head and picked his clothes up from the floor. "I learned to play because it's a tradition in Dad's family. Everyone needs to learn how to play an instrument of their choice. And they were very proud of me winning some contests, but I don't really enjoy it and rarely play nowadays."

"Well, then we're fucked, because I don't know how to be gay, don't know how to do accountancy, and your parents already noticed that there's something fishy about me. What about you? You seem strangely chill about all this." Gunner pulled on the new jeans and hesitated, holding up the big hoodie, but handed it to Caspian.

"Because this is what I wanted. I no longer have a reason to be scared of other guys. I am a stud!" Caspian gestured at his broad chest with a wide smile.

Gunner watched him in disbelief. "So you just wanna take over my life?"

Caspian pulled on his jeans and shrugged. "I'm gonna *fix* your life. *Carpe diem*, Gunner!"

His confidence was both infuriating and arousing. Gunner bit his lip, about to speak when someone knocked on the door.

"Honey! We're leaving in a bit!" Barb yelled from the other side, and Gunner's eyes went wide.

"I'm supposed to choose a suit," he whispered to Caspian in panic, out of breath as if he'd just run a marathon. "What am I supposed to pick?"

Caspian froze, staring at the closed door with shoulders so stiff it looked painful. "Just... a nice suit," he said, swiftly putting on the remaining clothes while Barb knocked once more. "Whatever you like. It's your life now."

He smiled and planted a sweet kiss on Gunner's lips before climbing out the window.

Was it? Was *this* his life now?

Chapter 17 – Caspian

Could a man get high from handling drugs? Or inhaling invisible particles floating through the air? His mind denied it, but the sense of weightlessness that transformed his head into a balloon filled with helium screamed that his system had somehow absorbed whatever substance they'd been moving.

He'd been on pins and needles throughout the long drive between Grit and Columbus, wary of every siren, every police car spotted on the way. But no one stopped them, and the exchange of drugs for money went as smoothly as any other transaction. Buying a television set took longer.

And now what? Caspian had no idea who he worked for or how many times Gunner had taken such risks to pay off a debt he'd taken on to help his little brother. What was the protocol? He remained quiet while their— What? Customers? Partners?—packed up and left the dark street in the deserted industrial area on the outskirts of the city, but once they were gone, he was stuck with the people he hated, didn't trust, and without his own truck.

"Jeez, I'm tired," he said, watching Bud and the Brown brothers for cues.

Despite them having a fight the previous night, Todd patted him on the back. Maybe in the world of thugs little scuffles were a daily occurrence, like in a pack of wolves.

"I bet you're not too tired for a visit to Tiffany's," Todd said, and his silent brother grinned with appreciation.

Caspian frowned. "I don't think they're open at night." Or was it their idea of fun to rob a jewelry store now that the drug deal had been finalized?

Bud laughed. "Tiffany's Babes keep their legs open at all hours."

Oh goddamn it.

"Not feeling it tonight. Next time?" Caspian proposed and yawned as realistically as he could. "I feel as if I'd been knocked out in the ring."

Todd shrugged. "By who? Your tiny student? I mean, he's tall enough to punch your dick, so I guess it would make sense, but it's our tradition. We gotta go see the girls while we're here with all this fresh cash."

"We're not married to tradition. Let's just go home," he said and moved toward Bud's van as if it was a done deal. He sure hoped confidence would be enough to put an end to this stressful night. Transporting drugs had been enough excitement for one evening, and he definitely didn't want to sit on his ass and feign interest in strippers.

Bud snorted, following him toward the van parked in front of a massive warehouse. "If you don't want to go to Tiff's, get yourself an Uber. I'm not wasting the trip."

Caspian's fate was sealed then.

He had a hard time keeping distaste out of his voice, but he was still reliant on those fuckers, so he took the wad of cash Todd pushed at him and stuffed it in his pocket. "Fine. Lead the way to the pit of Jezebels."

"Pit for jizz more like," Bud laughed, toying with the shirt stretched over his pot belly. Caspian was getting a growing feeling that he was most eager out of the three, but the brothers went off to their car, and so Caspian was stuck with Bud.

When the door on his side shut, locking him in the messy cab. The air inside smelled sharply of pine-scented air freshener, which barely obscured a stale odor that reminded Caspian of the funk clinging to the bottom of dirty trash cans.

So here it was. He'd just handled Class-A drugs, and as if that hadn't been bad enough, he'd have to now pretend to have an interest in women.

When the car moved, following the vehicle belonging to the Brown brothers, the inevitability of a couple of hours more in the company of those three troglodytes made him want to scream. How the hell was he supposed to act at the club?

Bud went on about his inappropriate fantasies on the way there, but Caspian only tuned in when Sandy's name popped out of Bud's mouth.

"I wanted to know if that's okay with you."

"What?" Caspian squinted, unsure what he'd heard.

"You know, to ask Sandy out. She's not like some of those other gold-digging whores. That girl's really something, and since you're not..."

Caspian wouldn't have pegged her for wife material, but he supposed that to someone like Bud she was the pinnacle of feminine charms, especially that he'd badmouthed her just the day before. Also, she was most definitely a gold digger, but that wasn't his problem anymore.

"I have nothing against it. Things burned out between us, you know. Go ahead."

There, Gunner had tried to get her out of his hair for God-knew how long, and Caspian had managed to do it within a day.

He mentally patted himself on the back.

"You're a real friend, Gun," Bud said and gave his shoulder a brief squeeze. Caspian still couldn't comprehend that he'd had several fights with Bud since yesterday, and the man still didn't consider him an enemy.

By the time they arrived at the club, Caspian knew all the strippers' names, their specialities and how big their breasts were. Bud had ranked them too, and didn't spare Caspian the details.

He wondered how Gunner had managed to fool his friends into believing he enjoyed outings like this, but it all became clear when they entered the club buzzing with loud, pulsing music. It was large, but not glamorous in the slightest, with all the spotlights focused on the girls, which left everything else in shadow.

Nobody would see just how uninterested his shlong was in the lady swirling around a pole in latex boots with heels so high they forced her feet into a shape reminiscent of a tiptoeing ballerina.

The air smelled of the smoke swirling through the air around the dancer, beer, booze and sweat, and the colorful lights didn't even reflect off the dark walls and platforms, as if this place were a black hole. How long would they stay here? Until Bud got off? Caspian could only hope it would be a quick affair.

"Hey there ladies," Todd smiled and opened his arms, staring at two women in skimpy gold bikinis. They must have known he had money on him, because they flocked to him like wasps to a donut dropped in the park.

Bud pointed out a Black woman with long braids and yelled, so Caspian could hear him over the music. "That's Ralph's favorite. 'Cause she's mute. Get it?" he whispered to Caspian, and it took a while to understand the joke. Right. Because Ralph didn't speak much.

"Isn't he married though?" Caspian asked. He realized he'd said the wrong thing the moment Bud frowned, so he laughed out loud and slapped the dumb bastard's back. "Got you!"

Okay then. Caspian shouldn't be surprised that these guys were cheaters on top of being bullies and drug dealers, but he sure hoped Gunner didn't share *that* habit. Just thinking about Gunner being with another man right now, behind Caspian's back, made liquid fire pump into his veins and he stopped listening to the conversations around him.

He followed Bud in the dark, but just as he was about to reach for his phone and check on Gunner, a slender hand slid around his, and soft flesh clad in thin fabric rubbed against his skin.

He froze and stared at the busty woman clinging to his arm. What was the code of conduct in this place? In movies, customers were never allowed to touch the girls, though technically he wasn't the one doing the touching.

"Hello there," he said and cringed at the stupidity of this line. Then again, he had no idea what was expected of him here, and maybe by holding on to this lady, he'd be left unbothered by anyone else.

Women had never expressed interest in him, so he easily flew under the radar when it came to being gay. This was literally virgin territory for him.

Todd patted his shoulder from behind but spoke to the woman. "This one broke up with his girl yesterday, I think he needs some comfort."

Bud snorted. "Yeah, in her tits."

Caspian glanced at the breasts covered in tattoos of state flags and instantly knew from Bud's earlier descriptions that this had to be Marvel, which was most definitely not her real name.

Could he spend time with this one sitting next to him while other girls danced? Or would she soon need to get up on one of the stages and leave him to fend for himself? There were fewer customers around than he'd expected, but the crowd of guys cheering on the girl in ballet shoes was large enough to liven up the space, even though the rest of the club was sparsely peppered with men sitting alone or in small groups.

Gunner knew those women, but Caspian was stuck wanting to ask how she'd been, because what if that was too personal of a question? On the way here, Bud had talked about the girls as if they were friends, but what the hell could he know if he only came over once or twice a month to get a lap dance? Gunner should have warned Caspian of the tradition he observed with his buddies and told him how to act around the girls.

As soon as they all sat in a booth, Marvel straddled Caspian's lap so unexpectedly, he leaned back into the plush upholstery.

"I bet you deserve better than her anyway," Marvel said and winked at him as she wrapped her arms around his neck, suffocating him with the strong scent of perfume.

The other guys had girls vying for their attention too, so this tradition likely involved leaving large amounts of cash at Tiffany's, but as Caspian tried to come up with something to say, Todd's gaze swept over him for an uncomfortably long time.

Just watching.

Could he... suspect Gunner was gay? Or just wondering what was off about his buddy's behavior tonight?

Sweat beaded on Caspian's back when he met Marvel's gaze, unsure what was expected of him. In the movies he watched, lap dances happened somewhere private, not in the middle of the room while another girl bowed onstage, gathering her tips to an applause so loud it could be heard even over the roar of music.

"Can I touch you?" he asked in the end, because while Ralph was already waiting for his favorite performer in front of the vacated pole and Bud had his face between the breasts of a blonde girl with no distinguishing features, Todd *would* become suspicious if Caspian couldn't get his shit together.

He could do this. It wasn't like he'd have sex with her.

"Sure thing, big boy!" Marvel laughed and to Caspian's horror, she started rocking over his crotch as soon as a new song flowed from the speakers.

Bud pulled his face out from between the other lady's breasts to laugh at Gunner. "You shy, Gun?"

Marvel's butt was clad in golden shorts so tight they should've been considered panties, and he froze, stuck in a hell a lot of men would've loved to spend an eternity in. But this was just a performance for the benefit of the other guys, so he looked past Marvel's face, at the pipes crowding the ceiling, and imagined a hot twink in her stead. Dressed in a crop top and jean shorts, the boy would rock against him like she did, his palms rolling down Caspian's chest, only to move back up the moment they got anywhere near his dick.

That twink had Gunner's face, of course. *His* face. Which was fucked up, but no one needed to know what hid in Caspian's brain. Gunner was the sexiest, sluttiest little cocksucker. And when he came...

Lord have mercy.

In Caspian's fantasies, the vanilla-scented hair that swept across his face was blond and much shorter than Marvel's. He saw fluttering lashes, trembling lips, felt slim fingers clutching at Caspian's T-shirt just as tightly as Gunner's hole hugged his dick—

Marvel laughed, spoiling the imaginary perfection. "Someone's ready for more," she said and slid her hand to the zipper of his jeans.

There were many things Caspian was willing to do in order to avoid suspicion, but sex with a complete stranger wasn't one of them.

"Maybe we should go somewhere private," he whispered, already plotting to tell her a sob story so she'd play along and pretend *something* happened. Because while he didn't find female bodies unpleasant in any way, he would not force himself to fuck one. Especially not for the sake of satisfying someone like Todd Brown, the big bully who deserved a fork in his knee for all the things he'd done to Caspian in the past.

"Sure, babe." Marvel squeezed his cock through the fabric with a wink, but Todd wouldn't give it a rest.

"Oh, come on! We're celebrating. She can blow you under the table," Todd said and handed him a beer. This wasn't a legit club, was it?

"You want that, sweetie?" Marvel asked as if there was nothing wrong with Todd's suggestion, but Caspian spotted the stiffness of her smile right away. Did Gunner go along with this pressure? Had he lied about only having sex with Sandy?

"You want to see my dick that much, Toddie?" Caspian asked, giving Marvel a gentle nudge, so she'd slide off him. His cock had gotten hard from the mix of touch and imagination, but he refused to be uncomfortable about it.

When Bud snorted, pulling his own lady closer, Todd slapped the back of his head. "It's not me who's besties with the tiny gay boy."

Bud frowned, looking up from between the two large breasts. "It's not *not* true."

Marvel had enough experience to smell trouble from a mile away and fled the booth, but Caspian feared no one and let the adrenaline flooding his veins take over. "You expect me to have gay cooties, like I'm a twelve-year-old?"

Todd's lip curled as if he were a ginger wolf and he spoke loudly enough for Caspian to hear him despite the music. "I expect you to be on our side. *Are you* on our side, Gun? Or is there another team you're playing for?"

The question was like a piece of plutonium dropped to the middle of the table, and Caspian felt his stomach tighten with worry, even though he was a big bastard, taller than either Todd or Bud. He might be able to break both their jaws now, but these crazy motherfuckers wouldn't let it go and could mess with his life in the future. The desire to knock teeth out burned in his gut, but he couldn't let his instincts guide him down a path of mayhem.

"I just wanted to enjoy a girl in peace. It's you who's being a prima donna!"

It was as if he'd thrown a piece of venison at a wolf. Todd shoved the table away, sending bottles to the floor, and went straight for Caspian.

"What'd you call me, bitch?"

Caspian's fist collided with Todd's jaw in a split second. The bastard hadn't expected him to act so fast, because he hadn't put up his guard and spun like a rag doll, hit his head on Bud's knee, and slid to the floor.

Caspian went still, staring at the carnage in front of him, and then at his fist, which didn't even hurt. His mind had been hesitant about getting into a fight, but Gunner's body knew exactly what to do in order to keep itself safe. Muscle memory had taken over just like it had when he'd unlocked Gunner's phone without knowing the PIN number.

Todd got to his knees with blood dripping from his nose and fire in his eyes. "I'm gonna fucking kill you!" he screamed, but when he attempted to reach Caspian, Bud, who'd also lost his girl, pulled him back.

"Come on man, cool off!"

Caspian's fists itched for more action, but despite the unexpected rush coursing through his veins, his mind grasped the reins again. It made way more sense to pull back now.

"Some celebration, Todd!" he said, spreading his arms.

"What's going on?" Ralph asked, coming over, even though his favorite girl was still on stage, rubbing her behind against the pole.

Caspian was so done with this bullshit when he had a perfectly horny twink waiting for him at home—his old home, but still—and he wasn't about to waste any more time in this shithole. The last time he'd seen Gunner, he'd been stressed out about the swap, about the new life and body, and instead of talking to him about it, Caspian was stuck at a shady strip club.

Bud shook his head. "Nothing, I think I'll take Gunner home. He's had one too many."

Gunner hadn't had any booze at all, but he wasn't about to point that out. "Thanks, man," he said while Ralph offered Todd a crumpled handkerchief in order to stop the blood drizzling from his nose. The tissue was used, which made Caspian hope the bastard ended up with gangrene and lost his nose altogether.

Or better yet, died in a ditch. Gunner might have done terrible things to Caspian, but he was at least remorseful. Maybe Todd would swap bodies with the stripper and get a taste of his own medicine. Caspian just didn't wish it on the poor girl.

The Brown brothers didn't bother to bid him goodbye, but Caspian didn't care and followed Bud to the van, somewhat surprised the vulgar bastard cared about his friends enough to stop their fight.

"Sorry about that. Don't know why he's on my case," Caspian tried as they both sat in the vehicle, because the silence was already making him uncomfortable. As rotten as Bud was, he remained on Caspian's side, and until this was over, Caspian needed all the support he could get, because he had no doubt Ralph would follow his brother's lead.

"Just be fucking normal," Bud grunted and hit the steering wheel with both hands. "Have a beer, get your dick sucked, and don't pick fights with Todd. It's not that hard. You don't want to be his enemy."

Caspian used to think that a tall, strong body capable of easy violence would keep vermin like Todd out of his sight, but it seemed that staying afloat in the murky world of crime and degeneracy involved way more than that. He'd judged Gunner over not wanting to come out to his brother, but Noah was still a kid and might accidentally spill the beans to someone who shouldn't know.

Caspian didn't even want to imagine what would have happened if those gorillas found out the truth, and in Gunner's world being alone meant becoming prey.

He might have had the body of a bull and its strength to match, but there was only one of him and hundreds of Todds, for whom a gay man like Gunner, one of their own, posed a threat. Caspian didn't quite understand the mindset behind it, but the possibility of Gunner not being into chicks was very clearly a stab at the twisted system of values those people lived by. And unless he removed himself from their company altogether, he too would be forever bound by those same rules.

Caspian spent the drive dwelling on the difficult choices Gunner had been forced to make all his life, but they arrived at the trailer park before 11pm, and despite fatigue weighing down his muscles, he got into his truck the moment Bud disappeared from sight.

He needed to talk to Gunner and point out all the things he should have warned Caspian about. But the anger he'd felt at some point had evaporated, replaced by the dull need to see him and relax in the company of the one person who understood what Caspian was going through.

He parked in the service road, just like before, and was baffled to see lights on in the living room. His parents were usually in bed at this hour. Were they entertaining? He couldn't see any cars in the driveway.

Caspian wondered whether he shouldn't send Gunner a message, but the open window in the first floor drew his attention before he could have done that.

The old Caspian would have never climbed to the second floor, even at the back of the building where none of the neighbors could have seen him fail, but this new Caspian had done a drug deal tonight and punched Todd Brown. What was a little risk to him now? Having long limbs and enough strength to hold on to the drainpipe helped too.

He climbed to the protruding roof above the home office and from there, getting into his bedroom was a piece of cake.

The sound of the piano lured him through the dark interior, all the way to the door. His dad played the violin, and while mom loved classical music, she'd never learned to play this proficiently, which meant that the person producing the sounds downstairs would have to be a guest.

Unless...

Caspian squeezed his fist, remembering how instinctual the punch in the strip club had been. His body had led the way even though his mind had no framework for striking an opponent or defending himself, and it surely worked the same for Gunner. But wasn't the simple instinct to protect himself different from playing elaborate pieces of music? Gunner had mentioned that he'd felt as though he could play when he touched the keyboard, but the complex melody coming from downstairs sounded lighter and more passionate than anything Caspian had ever played.

Was it possible that Gunner had talent for this, and could express it in a body that knew the right moves?

He didn't remember the title of the melody, nor its composer, but it felt like sunshine on a summer morning and soothed the aches in Caspian's body as he leaned against the door to hear it better. Like a heart, it beat evenly, making him relax as he slid to the floor and listened to all the nuance he'd never have been able to bring out from sheet music. But passion led Gunner's every finger.

The overwhelming harmony of sound brought him to dark shores when the tone of the piece grew deeper, sinking him in peaceful warmth. When the music wound down in an improvised ending to the sonata Caspian had finally recognized, he found himself amazed and filled with questions. But his mood soured minutes later when the house erupted with yelling.

"What if I don't want to?" Gunner raised his voice and Caspian struggled to hear the muted conversation, but still cringed when he heard his father's response.

"...rethink your priorities!"

Dad was understanding, and barely ever angry. What was Gunner doing down there to cause such a ruckus?

Caspian found himself scratching the door in frustration, but he couldn't go downstairs and berate Gunner, because in his parents' eyes he'd be a stranger who'd invaded their home. A stranger with a tattoo on his face and of a threatening size.

So he stayed still, shaking his head at Gunner's audacity. His parents were kind, and loving, and always had his best interest in mind, so why would Gunner talk to them with so much anger? That guy needed a talking to.

This was yet more proof that the swap could not go on. Gunner needed to sort out his own problems, and as much as Caspian enjoyed this new body, his family was more important. He couldn't lose his parents over some muscle.

The quick footsteps thudding on the stairs told him Gunner was coming his way, and Caspian wasn't looking forward to the conversation they needed to have.

Chapter 18 – Gunner

Raw fury replaced brains in Gunner's head as he ran up the stairs. He'd done nothing wrong. As a young man, Caspian had every right to question the direction he wanted to take his life in. So maybe his time at university cost a lot of money, but if Caspian didn't want to go back to his body and take over, then Gunner needed to act before he messed something up in Thomas's company.

He'd been afraid to broach the topic, but when both of Caspian's parents praised his skill at the piano, he blurted out that he'd rather make music and teach for a living. And that was when all hell broke loose.

How the hell was he to pursue a career in accounting? All the relevant knowledge and manners were Caspian's, not his. After Caspian had left in the morning, he'd experimented with some math challenges on his phone to check if the new brain would do the work for him the same way it helped him play the piano.

No such luck.

How was he to navigate this? Not only was he not particularly good at math but also didn't know the tax laws. He didn't even know how to act at the fancy party he was supposed to attend in two weeks.

He opened the door to his room and barely held back a scream when his gaze zeroed in on a tall figure leaning against the window. But when the intruder didn't charge at him and instead made a slow turn, moonlight caught the skull outline on his face.

It was Caspian.

Without thinking, Gunner locked the door, rushed across the room and hugged him, hiding his face between the firm pecs. Caspian smelled faintly of smoke, but despite the distress raging inside Gunner, the familiar scent didn't awaken the need to ask for a cigarette.

For a moment, Caspian remained stiff, but before Gunner could have questioned him, thick arms settled around him like an impenetrable ring of safety.

"What was *that* about? Why are you yelling at them?" Caspian asked.

"I... I just..." Gunner rubbed his cheek against Caspian's T-shirt as he fought through the tightness in his throat. "I suggested I might want to develop the piano thing," he mumbled. "They sent you to the lessons. Shouldn't they be happy for me?"

Caspian's shoulders slumped. "Yes, but they're your parents now, so don't raise your voice at them. Put yourself in their shoes. I've been excited to start working with Dad, and I told them that many times. It's a good job. Good money. Then, all of a sudden their son starts acting like a different person, so cut them some slack."

Gunner stepped away with guilt chewing at his insides. "I don't know how. My dad was a mean son of a bitch, and we always yelled at each other. And they're just... just so nice. I don't know how they manage to keep their cool like that."

Caspian bit his lip, watching him without a word. His mouth went slack, and he frowned but no longer seemed angry.

Gunner didn't need his pity. He opened his mouth to say something mean, but Caspian offered him a smile that warmed even the cool moonlight. "You play beautifully. You told me you knew how to play, but I wasn't expecting *this*. You gave quite the concert."

Gunner bit back a shy smile, struck by a compliment that for once wasn't about his physical attributes, and ran his fingers through his hair. He'd been worried about the drug deal going wrong and started playing to soothe his nerves, and... well, it hadn't been meant for Caspian's ears. He'd half-expected for Caspian to laugh at his attempts at the piano, but got praise and validation instead.

"Thanks. I... I always wanted to be able to play. I mean, not *always*-always. But when I was still a kid I used to have this boxing trainer, Mr. Wagner, and his wife taught piano lessons. Their house was always filled with classical music, and they got me into it. It was something that was only my own, you know? I never told anyone, not even my girlfriends."

Caspian frowned. "Why didn't you learn?"

Gunner stared at him. "What? You know where I live. If anyone found out, it would hound me forever. Also, I don't have access to a piano. Even if Mrs. Wagner wanted to make me her charity case, they eventually moved out. And when would I even find the time for practice? I was always doing shit for my dad, and had to take care of Noah once *he* was gone."

Caspian scowled, but he shook his head moments later. "It's a shame. You have real talent. When I play, I just follow the notes correctly, but you bring the music to life. It's incredible."

Gunner huffed, unsure whether he should beam with pride or punch something. Because yeah, it *was* a fucking shame. Not much he could do about it now. "I just imagine things that fit the melody and let my feelings take over. I listen to classical music when I need to calm down, when I'm happy, when I'm sad. It's... like I can feel it flowing through me. And for the first time, I can add some value to it too. Interpret it in my own way."

Caspian's Adam's apple bobbed, and he sat on the edge of the bed with a slight frown that was barely visible in the dark room. "I wouldn't have pinned you for the type to do that. Since you always seemed to value everything that was hyper-masculine. If you believe it's okay to be a slim artistic kid, why did you bully me so much?" he asked softly, keeping his gaze on Gunner's chest. In that moment of vulnerability, even the facial tattoo couldn't hide who he was.

Gunner twisted his fingers, uncomfortable with the memories flooding his head as if the dam keeping them out of mind had broken down. "Remember that motorcycle club fire years ago?"

Caspian shrugged. "Who doesn't? Bunch of low-lifes got burned to a crisp. Why?"

Gunner squinted and crossed his arms. Memories were in freefall and cut his soul with their sharp edges. "Yeah, pretty much what you said back at school. That they deserved it and that no one would miss trailer trash scum. One of those bikers was my dad. And yeah, he was *not* a good guy, but when I heard you trash-talking him like that at school, laughing about his *death*, I lost my shit. You became my target, and that was that. So yeah, being small didn't win you favors with me at the time, but you crossed the line. Because I was jealous. Because I was that scum, and didn't even have a dad anymore, when you had *everything*."

Caspian went very quiet, but then pulled Gunner to sit in his lap and squeezed his hand. He took in air, as if he wanted to say something, but in the end just shook his head and rested his forehead against Gunner's shoulder. It took him another three seconds for him to open his mouth again.

"I'm so sorry. I had no idea."

Gunner took a deep breath and pressed his face to Caspian's cheek. Tears burned his eyes, but he wasn't ashamed of it for once, because Caspian wasn't like the other men in his life, and wouldn't judge him for a moment of weakness. "My life went off the rails after that. I missed school, I was on drugs half the time. I shouldn't have taken it out on you anyway, but I couldn't stand the look of you. And yet I wanted to be you."

"You didn't. I was miserable," Caspian said in a tight voice and squeezed his hand on Gunner's knee. "Scared of going to school."

Gunner wrapped his arms around the thick neck and breathed in the faint aroma of cologne and smoke that still clung to Caspian. "I don't know how to fix that. I'm sorry. Hope college was better for you. You no longer had to mix with the likes of me." Maybe the universe was actually playing a joke on Caspian, not him, by forcing him to interact with the man he wished to forget.

But Caspian swallowed and met Gunner's eyes. "The world must have really turned on its head. Because I like being around you. Don't know if it's this body, or if you've been hiding who you truly are, but you're not how I remember you at all."

Gunner hesitated but ended up leaning in for a kiss, charmed by the softness in Caspian's voice. "Right back at you. You're kind, not snotty. How did it go tonight? You paid Snowman for the next two weeks, but time's always ticking. I'm sorry you have to deal with this."

Caspian let out a groan. "Why didn't you tell me about the strippers? Todd started a fight because I didn't want to have my dick sucked in public!"

Gunner's shoulders sagged. "Right. *That*. I had a busy day. I didn't think about it."

Caspian shook his head. "You need a better job."

"I've got a tattoo covering half my face. Who's gonna give me a sensible job around here, huh?" He wished he wasn't sitting in Caspian's lap, being grilled about things he didn't want to discuss.

"Why did you get it in the first place?" Caspian asked, sliding his arms around Gunner and pulling him closer. As unnerved as Gunner was, with Caspian holding him like this, a real conversation didn't seem impossible. As if he didn't have to shrug off uncomfortable topics or get defensive.

"It's… I was going through a bad time after Dad's death, I dropped out of school 'cause I couldn't keep up anyway. I don't remember that time very well, because I was on drugs, but I had the smart idea to commemorate the club. They were called Rabid Hyenas. So here we are. A hyena skull on my face." He sighed and stroked the ink etched into the left half of Caspian's face. "I don't dislike it on you. The design's cool, just like the others on my body… but it's closed a lot of doors."

Caspian sighed, moving his hand up and down Gunner's back, as if he wanted to soothe him. "Must have been really hard without your dad…"

Gunner swallowed, hugging Caspian tightly. No one had ever spoken to him about it this way. He'd gotten a few silent pats on the back with a bit of sympathy, but never this kind of acknowledgement, because he'd always been expected to 'take it like a man'.

"He wasn't a good guy. A part of me was even relieved that he was gone, because he could get really violent when things didn't go his way, kicked me out whenever he brought women home, but… I was seventeen, my brother was eight, so I had to fend for myself. Making sure I seemed tough to everyone around was the only kind of survival I knew."

"I'm sorry, I can't imagine what it must have been like to have a parent like that."

Gunner shrugged. "It's no big deal. Lots of people—"

Caspian grabbed his jaw and forced Gunner to meet his gaze. "It's not fine. No kid deserves to be treated like that."

Gunner took a deep breath, taking it in and realizing he'd never really dug this deep into the rotting truths about his past. "I suppose they don't. He was getting me ready for only one kind of future. I knew I'd be a biker, I knew I had to be tough, I knew I couldn't be gay."

Caspian watched him, *listened*, without a hint of judgement in the deep brown eyes. It was a strange feeling to be acknowledged like this. As if he were looking in the mirror, and telling himself all this for the first time. Admitting to himself just how shitty his life had been.

"I hid in plain sight. Covered any attraction to guys with fighting a lot, fucking girls, and getting tattoos that made me look dangerous, so no one dared mess with me." Gunner ran his fingertips over the lines of ink on Caspian's face. "But that also meant normal, nice people avoided me. I got so angry that no one would give me a chance when I managed to get off drugs. It really hit me hard when I was applying for jobs after Noah's accident, and then I stopped trying, 'cause what's the point? I am what I am. "

"Would you consider removing the face tattoo?"

"I don't have money for that."

"But I have credit. And some more savings," Caspian said softly.

Gunner stared at him, not sure what to say. Caspian wanted to offer him the cash just like that? "Until I pay off my debt with Snowman's boss, no other expenses matter. And then I'd still have scars on my face. Can't win really. Wait." He glanced at Caspian and wiggled his eyebrows. "I can think of a few ways to make money in *this* form."

Caspian's brows rose. He loudly sucked in air and squeezed Gunner's shoulder. "This is my body, and only I get to fuck it," he said in a voice so raspy it sent shivers down Gunner's spine, all the way to his hole.

If only it weren't just about that.

It would have been so hot to see Caspian's eyes burn with real jealousy. To feel desired in every way by a guy who saw him as something more than a piece of ass.

"I'd make sure you didn't find out," Gunner teased and pulled on Caspian's ear with his tongue. "I'd have a sugar daddy on the side."

"I'm a drug runner now. Can't I be your sugar daddy?" Caspian asked, watching Gunner as he produced a fat wad of cash. "How about you show me the pretty things you'd gotten yourself today? Might just tip you."

Gunner tried to take the money, but Caspian was faster, so he ended up empty-handed. "Fine. But don't laugh, okay? I spent all day in the store with your mom so they could adjust it all. Close your eyes."

He jumped off Caspian's lap and ventured to the bag hiding his new suit.

"Oh no, what did you get? A dressy romper?" Caspian asked, laughing, but he did shut his eyes like a good boy.

Gunner had never considered himself ugly, but Caspian smiled a lot, and it somehow made the same features more handsome, as if the satisfaction he felt inside radiated over his face. He'd also got himself a switchblade when he was out. Next time people like Bud or Todd wanted to assault him, he'd be drawing blood.

"Dumbass. It's a suit. Your mom's holding a garden party in two weeks, and she insisted I don't have anything appropriate. She wasn't wrong." Gunner undressed and pulled out his new treasure.

The clothes Alex had helped him choose had felt like a bit too much from the start, but the outfit Barb had advised on inspired confidence. The restrictive nature of fitted clothing made him feel like even more of an impostor though.

He hadn't thought he could pull off a suit before they'd arrived at the store, but Barb had guided him through the process, and listened when he'd suggested he'd be happy to experiment with color and get something more suitable for summer.

She even reassured him in his choice, saying that suits in brighter colors were getting increasingly popular at weddings. Barb helped him choose a shirt with a faint stripy pattern and a green tie to go with the light blue set, which suited him perfectly.

"I bet you look real hot in it," Caspian insisted, grinning.

"Promise not to laugh," Gunner said as he adjusted his tie according to Barb's instructions and glanced at the mirror. He looked like he had his shit together, despite his knot-tying skills remaining questionable. Elegant, pretty, confident—the person staring back at him from in the mirror was definitely not trash.

"I can't promise you anything," Caspian said and tapped his feet against the floor. "When can I look?"

Gunner cleared his throat and took a deep breath. "Now."

Caspian's eyes flew open, and the silly smile dropped from his face almost immediately. Seeing him like this had Gunner's stomach filling with ice, but before he could have dismissed his clothing choice or run off to the en suite, Caspian raised both hands and spoke.

"Wow. You look... different."

Gunner grabbed a pillow from the chair and threw it at him. "Different good, or different bad?"

Caspian chortled and pulled out a twenty-dollar bill, which he waved in front of Gunner. "Come to daddy."

Something flipped in his stomach and went straight to his balls. He had to take a deep breath to calm down first, and only then walked up to Caspian, imitating a male model coming down the catwalk to the best of his ability. Caspian taking care of him, and making life smooth as they fucked each other brainless? That would have been the life.

"You like it? A classy boy with a dirty mind?" Gunner grinned and patted his pocket when he stepped close enough.

Caspian pushed the money in, but then dove his fingers deeper into the pocket, touching Gunner's cock.

"I like him doing his job."

"Didn't you say you refused a blowjob tonight?" Gunner arched to the touch, putting his hands on Caspian's shoulders. He couldn't get over the size difference. His brain still remembered that he used to be this massive, fearsome guy just two days ago, yet now perceived Caspian as much larger and stronger than he'd ever imagined himself.

"It was *your* mouth I wanted on my dick," Caspian said, pinching Gunner's chin between his thumb and forefinger.

"You know I'm a slut for my sugar daddy," Gunner said, shocked at how comfortable he was speaking like this when they were alone. He felt neither shame nor awkwardness, only arousal. "But I don't wanna get my new suit all wrinkled." He pulled on the tie to undo it.

Caspian cupped his crotch, which sent yet more shivers over Gunner's skin. "Then take it off."

Button after button, Gunner opened the suit jacket, then the shirt, showing off just a peek of skin. Last night's fuck felt like something that had happened centuries ago and there was nothing Gunner wanted more than to feel Caspian's dick inside him again. He had no idea where this would lead them, or when the unexplained change would end, but he'd enjoy the ride.

"Is this what you want? A sweet guy?" he asked with a bit of trepidation, because he wasn't sweet. He had a softer side, sure, but was far from an innocent twink, and hoped it didn't put Caspian off.

Caspian's teeth sank into his lip as he watched Gunner strip and place garments across a little stool, so they wouldn't wrinkle. The warm glow of the bedside lamp softened his features when he grinned and took off the hoodie. "As long as he leaves his morals at the door when he comes to me, ready to take my dick in his tight, greedy hole."

Gunner should've felt offended, but the dirty talk made his heart flutter. "Think I can do that..." He ran his thumb along the waistband of the white boxer briefs Barb had insisted to buy for him earlier, even though it had been embarrassing as fuck.

"Then say it." Caspian hooked two fingers under the fabric and pulled Gunner closer, devouring him with his gaze alone. "Tell me how much you missed my dick all day."

Gunner bit his lip and stroked Caspian's ears with his thumbs. "What if I'm too shy?"

"Then I'll have to make you," Caspian said and gestured at Gunner's feet, which were still clad in socks. A chuckle left Gunner's lips, but he placed one of his feet on Caspian's knee, as if he were wearing high heels. A gasp left his lips when rough fingers massaged his calf and then peeled the fabric off him.

Gunner couldn't wait for Caspian to squeeze the confession out of him, to lose control under the force of those strong hands. He pretended to zip his lips and challenged Caspian with his eyes as the other sock followed its partner to the floor

Caspian's hand went straight for his throat. "Oh, I can make my little bitch talk."

With his other arm, he swooped Gunner off his feet and pulled him into bed, leaving no doubt that soon enough, Gunner would be singing to Caspian's tune.

Chapter 19 – Gunner

Gunner enjoyed many things about his new body. How smooth it was, how nonthreatening he seemed, and how beautiful it made him feel. Just two weeks since the unexpected swap, he sometimes forgot the flesh that seemed so very right for him was actually Caspian's. He felt so very at home in it he struggled with the idea that he shouldn't get used to it too much.

But regardless of how many things were easier with a fresh face, a credit card, and a cushy home, he still had the responsibility to take care of his family, and it unnerved him that he currently needed to rely on someone else to handle his debt. And Noah. So far, both of them succeeded at living one another's lives, but there would come a time when feigned confidence and looks wouldn't be enough to make up for the lack of experience. And then, everything would fall apart.

Gunner frowned, rising to his toes in an attempt to grab his favorite protein powder off the shelf, but no matter how much he strained his calves, it remained out of reach.

So yeah, there were disadvantages to being cute and tiny.

"Let me help you with that," Caspian said, standing right behind Gunner as he effortlessly picked up the plastic container. He wore his own expensive cologne, and its spicy aroma overwhelmed Gunner's senses when they stood so close.

Little things like this were what made Gunner's heart float. Caspian was there for him whenever possible, and they couldn't take their hands off each other. Gunner didn't even care that it was freaky anymore, because the pure joy of being with a man overshadowed the concerns he should have had.

Caspian was an unstoppable tide not just because of the size and strength of his new body, but because he exuded confidence Gunner would have never imagined hiding behind Caspian's original features. He was cockier each day, and Gunner couldn't help but be drawn to his attitude. For once, he didn't have to make all the decisions, because Caspian was more than willing to take charge. Like yesterday, when Caspian had taken them to the clinic for an STD test. Despite protesting the very idea just two weeks prior, Gunner did what Caspian wanted, because that was how they rolled.

It was a little late for that, really, but Gunner kept that opinion to himself. What mattered was that it was important to Caspian. Their relationship was tainted by bad blood and ugly events from the past that couldn't be changed, but their connection already felt as if it had been tattooed into Gunner's flesh with ink only he could see. The intensity of their time together made Gunner realize that if they figured out how to swap back, removing that emotional tattoo would leave him with scars.

He smiled back at Caspian, thrilled over having such a massive man at his side. "Thanks. Could you carry it? I'll write down how much and how often you should have it." Because Caspian had no idea about maintaining muscle mass.

Gunner used to be obsessed with keeping his body as large and intimidating as possible, since in his world that commanded respect, but his new form offered a new perspective, and he realized that losing a couple of pounds while being six-five wouldn't make that much of a difference in the grand scheme of things.

But Caspian was on board with both training and nutrition, excited about the size of his biceps, and eagerly listened to everything Gunner had to say on the topic.

"I could even carry *you*, if that's what you want," Caspian said with a wiggle of his brows and slid his hand along Gunner's shoulders.

They were at a big supermarket out of town where Gunner got his supplies in bulk, so while he wouldn't kiss Caspian in public, this casual closeness didn't petrify him as much. His fear had two dimensions now. Of being out as Caspian, but also of someone spotting Caspian being sweet with him. The big body with an inked face didn't allow much anonymity in a town like Grit, Ohio.

He playfully shoved at Caspian with his shoulders. "Show off."

"You know me. Always eager to show my boy his place on my dick," Caspian whispered, leaning in so his breath tickled Gunner's ear.

Heat climbed up Gunner's neck. This did not get old. Caspian had the filthiest mouth, the meanest hands, the best cock, and Gunner loved everything about his company. The constant excitement between them made Gunner lose his breath, *and* his mind.

"Not in the store..." He laughed, but didn't miss the opportunity to squeeze Caspian's pec when he gave his chest a playful shove. It was such a delicious slab of meat.

"Are you sure? You don't want everyone to know you're taken?" Caspian said and led Gunner forward by pressing his palm to his back, as if he wanted to make sure at least Gunner realized whom he belonged to.

Hot cotton candy sprouted in Gunner's chest as he lifted his eyes, staring at Caspian. "I kinda do."

Never in a thousand years had Gunner imagined any of his gay fantasies would come to life, yet here they were, and he had no doubt they'd be fucking on some side road within minutes of leaving the store.

And while he loved drinking cum, gagging on Caspian's dick, and getting drilled from behind, there was also a softer side to Caspian's desire.

He was an amazing kisser and could be so gentle and sweet when the mood was right. No one had ever been so tender with Gunner before, and it was as if in those new bodies, they'd become one another's perfect partners.

A part of Gunner, which wanted to remain cautious, suggested that maybe he was just drunk on being with a guy for the first time, but did the cause of his affection matter when Caspian pulled him close, making butterflies flutter in Gunner's stomach until his knees got soft?

Caspian always caught him in such moments of weakness.

"We could, you know. I was planning to tell my parents sometime," Caspian said.

Gunner laughed, but stilled the moment Caspian's brows gathered in a deep frown. "Oh. You're serious. Me? As in... this body? You would introduce *this* guy," he poked Caspian's chest, "as your boyfriend to your parents?"

A scowl passed through Caspian's features, but he wouldn't let go of Gunner and led him into the main aisle of the supermarket. "They'd need some convincing, but we could make up a story about me overcoming the challenges of my upbringing and all that. Then, I wouldn't have to sneak in and out through the window every night to get to my *boyfriend*."

Gunner's toes curled inside his new grey-pink sneakers, but he tried to sound casual when he spoke. "Yeah? We're a thing?"

He hadn't been sure, because their relationship had gone from vengeful to caring so fast his mind was barely keeping up with it. They'd come a long way since agreeing to fuck for practical reasons on that first day.

He liked being in Caspian's company, and while at times he didn't get Caspian's jokes or misunderstood the meanings of difficult words, Caspian always explained them to him or changed the topic before Gunner could have felt inadequate. Gunner, on the other hand, had introduced Caspian to the joys of *'90-Day Fiancé* and it turned out Caspian wasn't above enjoying trashy TV shows. They now even had an inside joke about the universe giving *them* a ninety-day trial run.

While their lives had been nothing alike, none of that mattered when they were together, joking around or *being there* for each other, as if fate itself was pointing out that they were way less different than it seemed on the surface.

"Of course we are, so you better not flirt with anyone else."

Gunner loved how confident Caspian was about this. He wanted them to be together and said it so plainly, without any ifs nor buts.

The shrill ring of Gunner's phone spoiled the perfect moment between the cereal aisle and the checkout, but he picked up the video call as soon as he saw Noah's name on the screen.

"What's up?"

His brother kept one of his eyes shut to protect it from bright sunlight, and wind swiped his coily hair into his face, but that stopped once he went into shadow. "You must hear thi—are you with Cas?" Noah asked when Caspian peeked over Gunner's shoulder.

"Yeah, I was just showing him where to get the good protein powders."

Nothing to see here. Your brother isn't a little cum bucket.

"That's good," Noah said, undisturbed. "You won't believe this. I just came over to Madge's, and she told me there's more people in town, who've been affected by some weird magic!" he said, and the video shook before showing Mad Madge's bright pink cheek from way too close. Noah helped her adjust the phone, and she cleared her throat, offering Gunner a smile.

"What a pretty boy! Is that your friend, Noah?"

"Hello," Caspian said, resting his hand on Gunner's shoulder.

"So what's the magic, Madge?" Gunner asked skeptically because everyone in town knew her as the local eccentric, and she didn't make any sense half the time. He was inclined to believe she was just imagining things, but since Noah was so eager to help, Gunner didn't want to dismiss it.

She exhaled and pulled off her pink shades to reveal watery blue eyes weighed down by dark brown eyeshadow. "See, a few years ago, those two men came to my trailer and accused me of witchcraft. They said I made them feel each other's pain, and they showed me that when one was cut, the other got the same wound out of nowhere. It was really strange."

Gunner stilled, catching Caspian's serious expression in the corner of his eye. "Are you sure this happened when you were sober? Do you remember who they were?"

Noah pushed his way into the screen. "I know one of them. I mean not *know*-know, but Madge told me who he is. He's a musician and does gigs at Tony's bar on Saturdays."

Madge pushed him out of the way and pointed her finger at the phone. "Wait, wait... I know you. You're that boy who wanted to be bigger. Couldn't open my jar—"

Gunner frowned. "Say what?"

Caspian reached over his shoulder and ended the call. "I wouldn't have believed her if this weird thing hadn't happened to *us*. It's Saturday. We could go straight from here."

Gunner stared back at him as the ground shifted under his feet. "Oh. So you wanna go. And... who knows, maybe swap tonight if we can?"

Caspian stilled, pulling the protein powder to his chest as he contemplated the lid. The speakers blasted loud pop music, and other customers went about their business, but in the little corner of the healthy snacks aisle, clouds gathered over Gunner and Caspian.

"It only makes sense. You can't work as an accountant, and I don't want to lose my parents. It's only been two weeks, and I already kind of miss them," Caspian admitted in a soft voice.

All of a sudden, his boots became Gunner's focus. "Makes sense. And then there's your parents' party tomorrow. I wouldn't know which fork to use for what." He gave a nervous laugh, but a chill was already spreading through his bones. It didn't matter if they called each other boyfriends *now*, because this situation was temporary. If anything, he was postponing the inevitable by playing twink and indulging in piano-playing whenever he got the chance.

Maybe it would be for the better if they put an end to this fantasy instead of gradually forgetting that life wasn't about fun and pleasure.

They left the aisle and headed to the cash registers without uttering another word.

Chapter 20 – Gunner

Gunner's favorite burgers tasted bland. He and Caspian attempted to make conversation over food, but it was no use. The storm cloud that had descended on them after talking to Madge wouldn't lift, and every moment in each other's presence stretched, until Gunner longed to just go home and leave Caspian to handle this.

But he couldn't run from responsibility any longer, so he sucked it up, and they parked their vehicles in front of the bar half an hour before the live music performance was about to start.

Gunner stiffened when a man he vaguely recognized left the bar and lit a cigarette in front of the entrance, and realization made Gunner break out in goosebumps. For a moment, he tried to convince himself that the setting sun and the long shadows it cast fooled his eyes, but he couldn't be mistaken.

"Fuck. See that guy? He used to be a biker in my dad's club. The only one who survived the fire. He might recognize the face tattoo, so keep it cool."

"Doesn't *everyone* know about the face tattoo? It's kind of obvious, don't you think?" Caspian asked and offered Gunner a stiff smile. At least he was trying to make this easier. "What's his name?" Caspian asked.

"Roach. I don't know how he's really called. A grim bastard, so stay on your guard— Wait." Something clicked in his head when a tall, long-haired man with a guitar stepped outside seconds later.

He'd seen them kissing.

Two weeks ago when he'd parked here, too upset to go home. It had been too dark for Gunner to recognize Roach's face, but it clicked into place now.

The new knowledge made as little sense as the smile emerging on Roach's features when the handsome stranger approached. Gunner couldn't remember ever seeing Roach smile when the Rabid Hyenas MC still existed.

He'd always been so grim, so subdued, but there was a lightness to his posture now, as if he were a normal guy who worked nine to five and didn't have to look over his shoulder all the time.

The guy with long hair put his arms on Roach's shoulders and moved, prompting the former biker into something akin to a clumsy slow dance.

"Doesn't look grim to me," Caspian said with a chuckle as the couple swayed in the orange glow of the flickering neon above the bar entrance.

"I don't get it. He's... gay?" Gunner asked flatly as his mind worked at full speed, trying to come to terms with what this meant.

Roach had been approaching thirty when all his club brothers had perished in a sudden fire. Tall, broad in the shoulders, he'd been a 'man's man', and the fact that he was touching another guy in Grit, Ohio, was like an explosion to shatter everything Gunner believed.

Mike Choi was a masculine guy, but one who owned a legit store, and had a business degree. He didn't need to cater to scumbags in order to survive another month. Roach, however, was the kind of person Gunner had imagined himself growing into, had the motorcycle club not crumbled.

If *he* could be open about his affection for another guy, if *he* wasn't afraid to be openly gay, they maybe it wasn't out of reach for Gunner either? Was the future really not set in stone?

"Evidently. They look hot together," Caspian said, stretching in the seat.

Gunner burst out with nervous laughter, rubbing his stomach when it twisted in a cramp. "Seriously?"

"I actually know them. Well, not personally," Caspian said and showed Gunner his phone, which featured a photograph of a very naked Roach holding the other guy in his lap.

"Jesus fucking Christ! What the hell?" Gunner flinched so violently he hit his head on the window. "Where did you get that?"

"They do amateur porn together. Been watching them for a while," Caspian said with a shrug and stuffed the phone back into his pocket. "So yeah, your old friend is very gay and doesn't hide it."

Gunner's head boiled in confusion, as if it didn't have the capacity to process all this, but Caspian remained chill and unbuckled his seatbelt. The two men stepped farther away from the building when several cars arrived, full of people dressed with way more elegance than a night out at a shabby bar warranted.

"Let's talk to them," he said and stole a kiss off Gunner's parted lips.

That did trigger him into motion. "Okay, okay," he said and jumped out of the car to the dull sound of Metallica playing inside the venue, even though he'd rather kiss a rat's balls than face Roach and his... paramour..

He was intent on dealing with this as fast as humanly possible, so they could move on from the silly notion that Mad Madge hadn't just imagined her story, but as he took a step closer toward the loud music and the couple hugging in the faint glow of the neon, Caspian's heavy arm dropped to his shoulders, and the agitation Gunner had felt moments ago turned into something else. He was wary of showing this side of himself to a former friend of his father's, but if Roach not only was gay but even did porn, what was there to worry about?

His heart pounded when the long-haired guy spotted them over Roach's shoulder.

"You here for the bachelor party?" the musician asked in a deep, southern drawl. "I'll be playing in half an hour."

Roach looked back, and his widening eyes had Gunner's stomach plummeting as if it was being filled with lead. Of course he'd have recognized a friend's kid, even after so many years.

"Roach, right?" Caspian asked with a friendly wave. "We've got an inquiry."

"It's Reed, actually," Roach said, squaring his shoulders as he turned to face them, and there was no mistaking his inquisitive gaze for anything but danger assessment. He focused on Caspian for a moment too long but pointed to his partner. "And this is Zane."

After coming to the conclusion that Alex had purposefully tried to make him into a caricature, Gunner was still looking for fashions to suit him. He'd kept the gray jeans on the tighter side, and stuck with the lilac sneakers, but went with a looser fit of clothes that many cute young guys favored. Due to his size, he'd begrudgingly bought the short black leather jacket in the women's section. This style felt more like him than the sweet print tops he'd gotten before.

Caspian grinned and squeezed Zane's hand before doing the same with Roach. "Right, sorry. It's been a long time, and I forgot," he said, petting Gunner's shoulder.

Despite Roach still holding his lover, Gunner had a hard time shedding the sense of discomfort over being embraced in public. He used to look up to the bikers from his father's club. They'd been rowdy, aggressive, and made their money in ways outsiders shouldn't ask about, but they had been the masculine ideals of Gunner's youth, and facing one of them with a man on his arm made shame creep up his back like a parasite.

Roach had changed. In fact, he looked better. His short hair was shinier, and the shallow wrinkles he'd had even as a young man were now barely visible.

"What do you want?" Zane asked, shifting to face them alongside Roach. He wore a leather jacket and thick, dark locks of hair cascaded down his chest in messy waves.

Gunner could see what attracted Roach—Reed—to this guy.

"So we... um... This might be a strange question," Gunner said, but his brain was fizzling and all he could think of was that he had a man's hand on his shoulder in public, wordlessly professing that he was *taken*.

"You want to get into porn too? All you need is a smartphone," Zane said with a wave of his hand and embraced Roach, squeezing his hip.

Gunner's face must have gone the shade of a ripe tomato. *No. No no no!* The filthy things he did with Caspian were for them only, and he'd never share them with strangers. "No! Nothing like that!"

Roach groaned and took a long drag of smoke, focusing on Caspian with a grim expression. "We don't do guest appearances either."

Caspian smiled. He not only used different words than Gunner but his body language had changed. Politer than his exterior suggested, he confused the hell out of people. And while it seemed to reassure many strangers who'd normally act anxious around Gunner, Roach went stiffer with every passing second, as if he sensed a bullseye on his forehead and didn't know where the snipers were.

"Oh, no, I know you're perfect together," Caspian said, betraying that he watched Roach and Zane's content. "This is about a thing Mad Madge told us about."

Enough was enough.

"The magic thing?" Gunner tried, kicking the butt of a cigarette across the asphalt.

"What 'magic thing'?" Roach asked.

"The one where one of you gets cut, and the other bleeds in the same place," Caspian said, and Zane stared at him, his brows rising ever higher.

"You two need to stop smoking whatever it is you're smoking," he said with a shake of his head.

Gunner took a deep breath and stepped up to Zane with a frown. It was in moments like this that he really wished to be a bit taller, because he needed to rest the back of his head on his nape in order to meet his gaze. "Hey, man. This is serious. Might sound messed up, but we need to know if there's something you know about this shit."

Roach choked on smoke when chuckles came from deep in his throat. "Chill, boy, I don't know what—"

Gunner pulled out his switchblade and swung it at Zane's arm. He'd either prove those two bastards were lying, or find out it was a fluke, but it was high time to find out.

Roach stepped in front of Zane, his eyes wide, but before he could have dashed forward, Caspian captured Gunner from behind and lifted him off the ground.

"There, there. No reason for all this anger!"

Gunner's chance to test out Madge's theory was gone the moment his feet flew into the air.

"The fuck's wrong with you!" Roach yelled, keeping Zane back when he tried to step forward. "Keep that chihuahua on a leash, for fuck's sake!"

Caspian exhaled, holding Gunner high up, so he couldn't attack anyone. "Yeah, yeah, sorry. He's just a bit on edge. Because of magic—"

"There is no such thing. Grow up," Zane growled, once again restrained by Roach's gesture. His mane floated in the breeze like that of a lion about to launch an attack on its rival.

Roach scowled and showed them the middle finger but didn't attempt to use force in order to chase them off and nudged his boyfriend toward the bar. "Come on, it's your time to play."

Zane hesitated but then met Roach's gaze and didn't protest.

Gunner sighed deeply as they watched them walk away, but Caspian let him down once the two men disappeared inside the bar.

"Why did you stop me? We would have known if it's true!" Gunner whined, but kinda realized he'd taken it too far. Sometimes, he only understood what position he put himself in once the burning wheel of destruction he'd pushed off the hill could no longer be stopped.

"What the hell were you thinking?" Caspian asked, spinning him around with a deep frown. "You could have hurt somebody with this!"

Gunner stilled and let Caspian pluck the knife out of his hand as if he were a parent pulling a child's hand away from the electric outlet. "I... That was the point."

"You stab a guy like that, and he'll break your neck. What the hell, Gun?" Caspian roared, his face flushed a deep red.

Gunner spread his arms in frustration, but his stomach was sinking ever deeper. "I don't know! It made sense at the time!"

Caspian shook his head, folded the knife, and instead of giving it back to Gunner, he shoved it down his own pocket. "I'll get you some pepper spray."

Gunner lowered his head in shame. "Sorry, I got carried away. So that was useless. We should have known not to listen to Mad Madge."

Caspian frowned but glanced at the entrance to the bar when a girl walked outside with a stepladder and a rainbow flag, which she swiftly hung high by the door.

"Didn't know Grit has gay club nights," Caspian said when disco suddenly blasted from inside, replacing the earlier rock music. His lips crooked. "Maybe they'll still let us in, if you behave."

"What?" Gunner couldn't be more confused. "I mean... they host events. Why would we go? Those guys won't tell us shit."

"What do you mean why? We could have some *fun*," Caspian said and swayed his hips in a way Gunner never would have in this hulking body.

Gunner sucked in beer-scented air. "I told you I'm not out, and you want me to go to a gay party? Seriously? No."

Caspian's arms dropped. "It's not a big deal. It's not like your friends are gonna be here. I won't have this body for long. I just want to go to a club and for once be the one people check out, not the other way around."

Gunner looked Caspian up and down. He was so damn hot even in simple jeans and T-shirt combination.

Would they? Would they check him out?

"You didn't go to clubs? Didn't you say you were out at University?"

Caspian scowled and averted his gaze, folding his arms over his chest. "I did, but I've never been... you know, noticed. Never the kind of guy people wanted to pursue.

Always the fucking ugly duckling," he said and kicked a bottle cap resting by the tip of his shoe.

Gunner wanted to answer, but a huge white limo, of the unnaturally long variety, drove into the parking lot and stopped a stone's throw away. Its doors opened, letting out a flood of people who'd already infused themselves with alcohol.

He swallowed when the two bachelors stepped outside in matching denim suits and denim cowboy hats to a rain of confetti thrown by their friends. The bouncer let them all through as Caspian and Gunner stood watching with tension sizzling in the air between them. The music inside became louder when the guests of honor arrived, and Gunner shoved his hands into his pockets.

He glanced into a side mirror of a nearby car. "But I'm not ugly," he mumbled.

Caspian swallowed. "No. You're so hot, and so cute. It's just that... I never wanted to be *cute*."

"Okay." Gunner took a deep breath to calm his nerves. He could understand the sentiment in reverse, so he wouldn't deny this to Caspian, but he was growing nervous.

What if Caspian's experience was universal, and he wasn't nearly as cute as he thought he was? How would he feel if Caspian got all the attention while he remained ignored? And what if that wasn't the case? How would it even feel to be seen as available by a lot of people?

But while opposing fears gathered in his skull like a storm cloud, he didn't want to be selfish. If it was Caspian's dream to have this experience, Gunner wanted to do this for him. They'd have a drink, enjoy some music, and go home. What was the worst that could happen?

"Yeah?" Caspian asked softly as two women arrived in a Volkswagen Beetle and entered the bar holding hands. He licked his lips and reached out for Gunner. "I'd never pull someone as cute as you without those broad shoulders you gave me."

Gunner snorted. "I've seen you're good at bondage. And now you've got a knife too. Easy-peasy kidnap-easy."

Caspian chuckled and leaned in, stealing a quick kiss before pulling Gunner toward the entrance. Their hearts pulsed in unison, faster than the loud, joyful music inside, but just as Caspian was about to step through the door, a massive guy blocked their way and eyed Caspian's face in all-too-familiar judgment Gunner had almost forgotten in the past two weeks.

"Hey, friend. I don't think it's your kind of party tonight. We don't want any problems," the bouncer said with squared shoulders.

Caspian mimicked his movement. "It *is* my kind of party," he said and squeezed Gunner's hand.

Gunner's instinct was to pull away, to deny everything, but while he remembered how important this was to Caspian, it also hurt him that this stranger made assumptions about his body, and by extension—him. The man assessed his size, his clothes, at his inked face, and decided Caspian—Gunner—didn't belong.

"You think he doesn't belong just 'cause he's big and tattooed?" Gunner choked out, squeezing Caspian's hand. "My boyfriend's not gay enough for you?"

Caspian looked down at him and swallowed before meeting the bouncer's gaze again. "Dude, you don't want to know just how gay I am."

The bouncer's lips twitched before spreading in a wide grin. He let out a roaring laugh and stepped aside. "Fair enough. Enjoy yourselves."

Gunner's heart rattled like a cup of dice, but for once those fell in his favor, and he winked at Caspian, drunk on the freedom the declaration had given him.

Chapter 21 - Caspian

Roach kept giving Caspian and Gunner the stink-eye throughout Zane's concert, but the two of them left once the performance was over. The bar was relatively small, but so packed, all of the queer men and women from the area must have come for the party. With some straights mixed in, the crowd was huge and even included two glamorous drag queens.

Caspian felt as if they'd stepped into a venue in some big city. While the decor was basic and uninspired, the bright lights and fun music made up for the generic interior. And yes, he *was* being checked out. Often. But the face tattoo had to be scaring off most people who might have been interested otherwise, because no one was biting other than the odd fish who chose to see what he was about by making some small talk. He vaguely recognized a few of the guests, and those who knew Gunner from somewhere acknowledged him with brief nods but didn't seem keen on making conversation.

Then again... it wasn't as though he was searching for someone to flirt the pants off, because how was he to focus his attention on any of the other people when Gunner was *there*.

Drunk. Cute. Laughing. Dancing. The life of the party.

So maybe he'd never wanted to be the adorable shorty, but the attention his boy was getting hit home. He could have gone to more parties while at university. He could have made friends and not have been a wallflower so much if he hadn't been so obsessed with picking apart every flaw he saw in his body. He'd lost so much time in his own head, worried that his arms were too skinny, that his legs were too short, or what prospective partners might think of his naked body that he'd forgotten to *live*.

And seeing Gunner so comfortable in the skin he used to loathe so much didn't just unlock stuck windows at the back of Caspian's brain. Reality barged right through them, throwing open all doors until he had to face the fact that while his body wasn't the kind he'd always wanted, it shouldn't have been a hindrance. Those twinks he'd always stared at in secret on campus? Maybe they'd have gone for him, were he to make a move. Gunner had no trouble attracting the attention of all kinds of guys, and was currently back-to-back with a cute boy of the emo variety, who made very obvious attempts to lure Gunner into more than dancing.

The flush on Gunner's face suggested he'd had one or three too many, so Caspian kept his eyes on his cutie at all times, while giving him space to have fun. Gunner had had so many doubts about coming here in the first place that Caspian had expected him to sit in the corner, but as soon as the drinks had started coming, he'd loosened up and was loving his first non-straight party.

Someone blocked Caspian's view, so he got up without thinking, because losing sight of Gunner raised his blood pressure.

"Whoa! You're taller than I thought," the guy said, raising his hands. He wasn't as tiny as Gunner, but Caspian *was* six-foot-five now and towered over most people.

The stranger had a broad, handsome smile and wore a shirt that showcased his muscular frame. He wasn't Caspian's *type*, since that skirted more toward what Gunner currently represented, but the attention was flattering nevertheless, so he grinned and leaned in to speak, because the music was loud enough to make communication difficult.

"I drank a lot of milk growing up," he stated, cringing as soon as he'd said it. He wasn't used to flirting. Not in real life at least, where he didn't have whole minutes to come up with a perfect response.

The man leaned in too, looking up at Caspian. Up. At Caspian. The thrill of being taller would never get old. "I'd drink some of your *milk*. Your hands look like they have a good grip on a man's neck."

That was forward. Holding Gunner's throat and squeezing it, to let him know who was in control, had come naturally to Caspian, but he didn't quite think about it as *choking*, and having a stranger suggest this off the bat sucked all the magic out of the gesture.

Still, after making sure Gunner was safe, happily grinding back against a splendid dude with dimples, he decided to experiment and placed his hand on the stranger's throat. Blood rushed to his groin the moment he felt the man's Adam's apple bob against his palm.

"You'd have to find out." It rolled off his tongue, the perfect thing to say in response, yet despite the sudden excitement, he felt like a cardboard cut-out. Like a character he'd made up on Grindr rather than a real person. He always thought he wanted to be seen for who he was inside—a badass, dominant fucker who had all the confidence in the world, but that also wasn't *all* there was to him?

The handsome stranger stared straight at him, and the attention tickled Caspian's ego, but he didn't feel *seen*. They were in a bar, not on a hook-up app, where getting straight down to business made perfect sense, and it struck Caspian that this guy hadn't even asked for Caspian's name. He wanted a *type*, and he'd have taken anyone who fit the bill. *De gustibus non est disputandum*, and all that, but it was a bit too objectifying for Caspian's taste.

"My place? I've never been with a guy like you. I'm gonna choke on that D and rasp when I tell my bestie all about it tomorrow." The stranger chuckled, but his eyes were hazy, as if his thoughts were already in his bed, and his mouth—on Caspian's cock.

This was everything Caspian had wanted and fantasized about. For someone to submit to his strength and be his willing bitch. Maybe if this had happened on day one of his new life in Gunner's body, he'd have gone for it, no questions asked, but the muscles, broad shoulders, and thick dick weren't what he was. In fact, he'd only been enjoying them for two weeks, and while they felt like his own now, they were still a costume for the real Caspian to wear.

The handsome stranger didn't want *Caspian*. He didn't even care that the hot stud he desired was horrible at flirting. Maybe it shouldn't have bothered him, but it did, because there *was* a guy who wanted him knowing who he was, and who appreciated him regardless. A guy who watched trash TV with him, enjoyed learning sayings in Latin, and taught him boxing moves.

His gaze gravitated to Gunner again, who at this point drunkenly leaned on the man he'd danced with earlier. There was a bit too much familiarity in the way they touched for Caspian's taste, but Gunner had overestimated his drinking capacity. It would soon be time to step in, so he offered the stranger a smile and let go of his neck.

"I don't think I'm what you're looking for."

The guy snorted. "Are you kidding me? You look like you'd wreck me, and that's exactly what I'm looking for."

Throughout his life, Caspian had often been afraid to react the way he wanted to when people tested his boundaries or were rude to him. Small and physically weak, he'd often been worried about the fallout, but he no longer had such concerns.

"If that was what I was looking for, you'd be bent over the hood of my truck already."

"Why not then?" The guy asked with disappointment painted all over his face, but Caspian's attention lapsed the moment he glanced at the dancefloor again and couldn't spot Gunner anywhere.

"Because I'm taken," Caspian said to soften the blow of rejection, since he knew all too well how badly that could sting a man's ego

He tapped the guy's shoulder and pushed through the middle of the dusky bar, scanning the rocking bodies. Someone touched his hip, but he didn't even bother looking their way, on high alert as he sought anything that would point him to Gunner's whereabouts. But none of the faces within sight belonged to the boy, and he couldn't see his leather jacket or T-shirt either.

He walked from one end of the interior to the other and came to the conclusion that Gunner must have left, which meant that he was either outside or—Caspian's gaze trailed to the neon sign pointing to the restrooms. He followed the blue arrow right away, prompted by an urgency burning in the pit of his stomach.

Had he started caring about Gunner's safety when he'd stepped in and saved him from his old buddies, or when he'd realized Gunner didn't have his shit together in life? It didn't matter. What did matter was that he loved falling asleep with Gunner's cheek on his pec and holding his hand.

He walked into the grimy bathroom and frowned when a lightbulb blinked in warning, but only one stall was closed. That was where he was headed.

"Come on, you wanted it on the dancefloor," a man cooed to someone, and cold slime filled Caspian's stomach.

He didn't speak out or call Gunner's name and, with tunnel vision guiding him to the shut door, he banged his fist on the scratched wood, not even bothering to look inside through the wide gap. "Open up. The party's over."

"Fuck off, man! Mind your own business," the stranger yelled back.

"C-Cas?" That was Gunner. And the fact that he mumbled his name as if he had trouble pronouncing it correctly made Caspian's self-control dry up.

This was war.

"This is your last chance," Caspian growled and banged his whole palm on the door, fueled by growing rage. He should have known Gunner might drink more than his new, smaller body could take and watched him with more attention.

But despite offering the stranger a way out, Caspian didn't have the patience to wait. He stepped back and slammed his shoulder into the flimsy door. A part of him didn't expect it to work, but the lock gave and the door smashed into someone.

Gunner wasn't the one who cried out, which meant Caspian hadn't hit him by accident, but when he peeked inside rage turned his gaze red. The same fucker who'd been handsy with Gunner on the dancefloor held on to his face, staring at Caspian with eyes so wide they might've popped out of their sockets any moment.

Gunner was sprawled on the closed toilet, with legs spread wide and head rolling against the wall. Jealousy had simmered under the surface of Caspian's skin when he stepped in there, but Gunner was in no state to entice anyone but a disgusting opportunist.

Who the hell wanted to bang someone who was literally falling asleep?

Fury rushed through Caspian's veins like a wild river. He grabbed the bastard by the collar, tossed him out of the cubicle, and before he could have attempted to explain his actions, Caspian's fist collided with his nose.

Bone gave way. Blood trickled to the man's white shirt, and his head banged against the tiles like a basketball. He rolled to the floor with a shriek and climbed to his knees, one hand feeling up his rapidly swelling face while he supported himself with the other.

"What... the fuck? You broke my nose!"

"You should be happy I didn't break your neck," Caspian roared and kicked the bastard over for good measure. He was a shark tasting blood in the water, and instinct told him to split the fucker's lip next, break his legs, slam his head into the mirror and see whether his brain was pink or gray. But the soft whine coming from the stall was like a bucket of icy water thrown on his head.

Also, he wasn't a psycho.

Gunner was attempting to get up but slipped and dropped back on the closed seat. His face was flushed a pretty pink color, but his eyes were clouded in a way that looked like sleepiness rather than lust.

"Cas, I think I drank too much," he slurred, but Caspian was right by him and pulled him up by the armpits.

"We both forgot you can't take as much booze as you're used to. Don't worry, I'll take you home," he whispered and, after a moment's hesitation, picked Gunner up and cradled him against his chest while the bastard who'd tried to assault him crawled into the corner in an attempt to get out of their way.

Good. Maybe he'd learn something from this.

"Nn, *mea culpa*, right Cas?" Gunner grinned, and wrapped his limbs around Caspian as if he were a little monkey when they walked out to a few curious glances. The sooner they left, the better, because Caspian didn't want to explain himself to the police if the bathroom guy had the audacity to report the incident and claim he'd been the victim.

He nodded at the bouncer who'd let them in earlier and walked out into the cold night, heading straight for his fancy car. Gunner hummed against Caspian's neck but didn't protest when Caspian searched his pockets for the key and then placed him on the passenger's seat. He looked so adorable in the tight jeans worn with a loose T-shirt and leather jacket that temptation lured Caspian into placing his hand on the warm thigh, but he only gave it a squeeze and smiled at Gunner, who was still conscious despite the limpness of his body.

"Give it half an hour, and you'll be sleeping like a baby."

"What? Noooo... Let's go to the backseat." Gunner offered Caspian a silly smile and grabbed at Caspian's shirt, even though he could barely hold his eyes open. "I love you—your dick."

Caspian's heart skipped a beat at first, but he shook his head when the drunk boy corrected himself. "Wow, I'm touched."

Gunner giggled and leaned forward, planting his face in Caspian's crotch. "No, you *will* be touched."

Caspian could have gone with it. Gunner was hot, and they fucked around like bunnies, so it was unlikely Gunner would be unhappy over a bit of drunk sex, but it still didn't feel right, so he gently peeled the boy off him and buckled his seatbelt. "I'd rather you remember every time I come inside you."

"Cum." Gunner chuckled like an eight-grader and rolled his head over the back of the seat.

"I'll give you some tomorrow, to cure your hangover," Caspian said and shook his head as he took in the driver's seat, which had been adjusted to Gunner's size and wouldn't offer him enough space to fit in. So he rolled it back and sat in the vehicle, preparing it for the drive.

"I don't want tomorrow. The fucking garden party's tomorrow," Gunner whined, his voice suddenly betraying upset.

Caspian started the car and drove away from the bar just as the guy who'd tried to assault Gunner spilled out into the parking lot, holding a tissue to his face. Caspian had no regrets over breaking his nose, even though he wasn't a fan of solving conflict with violence.

"We can still meet up once it's over."

"Yeah, but like, everyone will see I'm a fraud," Gunner's breathing got louder as he stared ahead. "How am I supposed to fake being you, when you're so smart, and all the Latin I know is *Scio me nihil scire*."

Caspian bit back a smile, because that was actually a pretty good use of *I know that I know nothing* in a sentence.

"Just keep calm and you'll be fine. It's just a garden party with a buffet, not high tea with the queen of England. I'm sure you'll manage," he said, even though deep down he worried that Gunner might end up saying something inappropriate. Caspian's parents would then be embarrassed and never let him forget it, but it wouldn't be the end of the world. There was no point in making Gunner self-conscious about things he couldn't immediately change.

"And then what? I'll fail at your job, 'cause I'm too stupid to do it, and your dad's really putting pressure on me. I'm meeting his partner tomorrow." Gunner sniffed and rubbed his face.

Oh. So it was *this* stage of a drunken night.

Caspian headed toward the highway and placed his hand on Gunner's sweaty fingers. "You're not stupid. You just didn't study accounting. And by the time I need to start working, we might as well be back to normal. So don't worry."

A part of him dimmed at the thought of going back to life as he remembered it, but maybe it would not be the same? Maybe this experience changed him forever? It certainly affected the way he saw his body, as if he'd been wearing distorted glasses and the swap allowed him to see things clearly.

And then there was Gunner. *Gunner Russo.* The man he'd envied in some ways but loathed in others. In his head, he'd always framed Gunner as this confident meathead with an I-don't-give-a-fuck tattoo on his face. What he'd found was a man lost in his sexuality, regretting the ink he'd gotten while on drugs, and saddled with debt he couldn't handle.

Whether they were to swap or not, Caspian wanted to sort out as many of those problems for Gunner as he could and leave him in improved circumstances. While Gunner might not realize it, he'd already shown Caspian that his body hadn't been what held him back.

And if they couldn't swap... well, they'd make it work. Caspian knew Dad wanted to pay him generously enough to afford a modest living for two, and if Gunner agreed to that scenario, Caspian could do the accounting for him. They'd work it out one way or another.

Gunner looked like the cutest little peach when he fell asleep with his lips half open. They'd need to have the your-body-can't-take-as-much-alcohol talk, but that could wait until morning. For now, Caspian wanted to tuck Gunner into bed and kiss his sweaty forehead, wishing him an awakening without headaches and nausea.

But as Caspian approached his house on autopilot, he realized he couldn't just drop Gunner off at the doorstep like a booze-infused gift basket. He'd need to face his parents. Worse yet, Caspian had driven here in the Southfield, and since he didn't want to keep this one-of-a-kind car overnight anywhere that wasn't safe, he begrudgingly stopped right in front of the garage. He'd get back to the trailer park. Somehow. Eventually.

The lights downstairs were still on, and he didn't need to check Gunner's phone to know it was full of messages and missed phone calls. He scooted down to pull the limp body out of the cab and froze when the door opened behind him.

He knew he'd have to meet his parents tonight but wasn't prepared for it yet.

Dad's face stilled in mortification. "Who are you?" he choked out, hovering his foot in the air mid-step, likely assessing how fast he could call the police.

Caspian shouldn't have felt hurt, because Dad didn't know it was him, but the judgmental stare still stabbed him deeply. And what pained him even more was that he'd also been insensitive and judgmental of people in different circumstances, lacking the insight that it wasn't easy to pull yourself by the bootstraps if your bootstraps were torn from wear. He still cringed at the memory of expressing joy over the death of several people, just because he considered them social vermin. He used to be too free with his tongue in high school, calling others trailer trash, and the cruel things he'd said about Gunner's dad had been such an afterthought he'd forgotten all about it.

Maybe he wasn't as good of a person as he'd thought himself to be.

He rose, holding Gunner to his chest. "Mr. Brady? I went to the same school as Caspian."

Dad blinked as Gunner mumbled something and drooled a little on Caspian's shoulder.

"What—what happened?" Dad asked and finally made the step he'd intended to. "Is he okay?"

Caspian approached him, hunching over to seem that bit smaller. His dad was as short as *he* used to be, and he knew how intimidating someone like the current him was, even if one ignored the face tattoo. "He overdid it with alcohol. Better make sure there's aspirin and water on his side table."

"What's your name again? Caspian, can you walk?" Dad asked, and when he was close enough, Caspian helped Gunner stand. His legs were wobbly, but he managed to stay upright with Dad's help.

"I'm sorry," Gunner mumbled.

"Is he back? He better be fine tomorrow!" Mom yelled from the house but stilled just like Dad had the moment she peeked out.

Caspian missed her. He'd looked forward to a day in her company, having cake and lunch between shopping, but she no longer recognized him as her son.

"Good evening. I drove Caspian here," he said, gesturing at the car before stepping forward to offer his hand. "Gunner Russo."

His only saving grace was that he'd never told his parents about the bullying, too ashamed to involve them.

Mom hesitated, but when Dad nodded, she extended her arm. "Barbara. Thank you for bringing him home safely. But... who are you exactly? Are you friends with our Caspian?" the incredulity in her voice gave away what she thought of that concept, and Caspian couldn't blame her. Two weeks back, he couldn't have imagined it either.

"It's an old friendship, but we've reconnected when he came back home. I should have told him he couldn't handle what they were serving at that bar, but I've brought his car too, so... they're both safe," he finished awkwardly, staring at Gunner, who slumped against Dad like a mannequin. Neither of his parents could get him upstairs. "I could carry him to his bedroom, if you'd like."

Mom offered him a stiff smile and shook her head. "Oh, he can sleep on the sofa tonight."

"Don't want the sofa," Gunner slurred and Caspian cringed, torn between embarrassment and the itch to stroke Gunner's hair and make sure he was fine.

Dad rolled his eyes and took the car keys from Caspian. "Yes, sofa it is if he can't get up the stairs on his own. Thank you for bringing him here. Barb, please get Mr. Russo a taxi. It's the least we can do."

Caspian stared back at them, with a sense of doom weighing on his stomach. Of course they were afraid of letting him into their home. At least he wouldn't have to walk or try to hitchhike home.

"Thank you. Tell Caspian I'll call him tomorrow," he said, stepping back.

Instead of taking Gunner to the living room, Dad made some awkward small talk about booze and bars. That taxi couldn't arrive fast enough, because he had no doubt the reason they all stood there was Dad not wanting to leave Mom alone with a stranger. And while Caspian understood that, it still hurt to see them so wary of him

When he finally got into the car, Caspian pulled out his phone to text Gunner.

[*Sweet dreams, babe. Call me when you're awake.*] He sat on the message for five minutes, unsure whether it didn't sound lame or cheesy, but pressed send in the end and looked out the window, hoping they both survived tomorrow's party.

Chapter 22 – Gunner

Gunner had nursed a head-splitting hangover in the morning, but it cleared by the early afternoon, and he felt good as new. He was dressed in a fine blue suit, drank fresh orange juice, and gentle piano music resounded through the speakers in the sunny garden. He'd even enjoyed several salmon canapés.

He might have been an impostor, a big fat fast food burger among fancy sliders made with grass-fed beef and garnished with caviar guacamole, but despite earlier fears, he'd been enjoying himself so far. It wasn't like he'd be expected to do accounting at the party, so he pretended he knew who he was supposed to, and mingled with people, complimenting women on their colorful cocktail dresses, and even helped Barb hang up some fairy lights for the evening.

Caspian's parents weren't happy about last night, so he worked hard to get back into their good graces. He'd first judged them as snotty rich folk, but while they had their oblivious moments and insisted on only drinking organic milk, they were kind and had lots of love for their son. If anything, guilt filled Gunner whenever he thought that he'd taken Caspian from them. No matter how much he wished to have parents like that, it wasn't the case, and he would have been a different person if he'd grown up in this household. His thoughts drifted off to being brothers with Caspian, so he quickly dismissed the creepy brain vomit.

The lush garden was the size of half a football field, and while most of it was manicured grass, flowers Barb had chosen and took care of herself grew in several beds surrounded by smooth stone. Gunner didn't dare enter there on his own, for fear of damaging the lawn, but it wasn't a great concern of the Bradys, considering that they'd invited so many people.

Several guests had come with children in tiny suits and dresses. A small area in the far corner had been surrounded by a temporary fence and featured toys, a bubble machine, and was minded by two young women dressed as princesses. The reality those kids lived was a world apart from the trailer park he'd grown up in. Maybe if he stayed Caspian for a while longer, he could help Noah find a good job and set him up with people who wouldn't pull him into drug deals or put him down for his scars.

Gunner might have read the text message where Caspian called him babe a few times too many before he called him. He'd been filled in on the fuzzy details of last night, and the fact that he'd almost been abused while drunk put him off alcohol today.

But Caspian had been there, watching out for him. It made Gunner's insides all mushy and wishing to hug his boyfriend all day instead of interacting with all these fancy strangers.

Caspian's presence would have been a lifesaver, but he knew better than to discuss a last-minute invitation with the Bradys. While Barb and Thomas had expressed gratitude toward Caspian's high school classmate, he had no doubt a guy with a skull tattooed over half of his face wouldn't be welcome at a party like this, even if he did own a suit to fit his broad-shouldered body.

The cell phone buzzed in his pocket, and he hurried toward the edge of the garden, to a modern statue shaped like a wave, which Caspian's parents had received as a present from an artist they knew. With heat climbing up his back, he stood behind its stone bulk and peeked at the crowd of guests in 'cocktail attire', as Barb called it, and pulled out the cell phone when he deemed it safe.

It was Caspian!

A stupid grin spread on Gunner's face. "Hey, I think it's going well, but what's *foie gras*?"

A soft chuckle came after a moment's silence. "It's pâté made with livers of force-fed geese or ducks."

Gunner eyed the far-away table of canapés, spotting Barb speaking to a blonde woman in a flared knee-length dress. "Thanks but no thanks."

"I thought not. I wanted to check up on you, but seems you've got it under control," Caspian said in a warm tone that felt like a stroke to Gunner's nape. Oh, how he wished to be wherever Caspian was instead of stuck with all those people and their expectations...

"And how's your day going? No unexpected drama?" He leaned against the statue, feeling guilty over burdening Caspian with his shitty life and its demands.

"I've found some odd jobs for the day, and I'm having my lunch now. It's all good. I wanted to tell you that if you needed something, just call or message me."

"Can you come over, kidnap me and—"

"You'll be fine. It's just a few hours."

"I know, I know, it's just stressful." Weakness. Something he'd rarely admit to anyone in his old body but felt comfortable to disclose to Caspian.

"I can take you away once it's all over. Let's go somewhere quiet and have a little picnic."

Gunner chuckled. "A picnic? Like with a basket and shit? On a blanket?"

"Yep. I checked the forecast, and the sky should be clear throughout the night too. We could stay out until late."

"That's like... real sweet, Cas." Gunner had an urge to bury his face in Caspian's chest and tightened his hold on the phone. He'd dated women since his teens but never had anyone organize something for *him*. For some reason, Caspian believed he was worth pampering. And while neither of them used the word *date* in relation to meeting up, getting together had been increasingly about spending time with one another instead of trying to solve the issue that turned the world on its head. Some days it felt Noah was more invested in it than either of them.

They only ate at inexpensive places, but despite having less cash, Caspian had always picked up the bill, as if he were trying to make a point of it. And Gunner let him, more flattered every time.

"Can't wait to see you and hear all the gossip," Caspian said with a smile to his voice.

Thomas waved at Gunner from around the dessert buffet, indicating he required his presence. "I gotta go. But I can already tell you *Aletia* had pretended to take French lessons when she was really going to chess practice. Saucy stuff."

Caspian laughed louder this time, but ended up smacking his lips, as if he were giving Gunner a peck on the cheek. "Good luck keeping up appearances."

Gunner put the phone back into his pocket and made his way toward Thomas, hoping the luck that had kept him blunder-free so far would not turn away from him now.

"Hey, Dad, what's up?" He was toying with asking Barb and Thomas if he could start calling them by their names, because calling the man he met two weeks ago *Dad* was painfully awkward. But that could wait.

"I know you don't like those events, but now that you're out of college, you should start thinking of networking as part of the job," Thomas said, putting his hand between Gunner's shoulder blades and leading him through the crowd gathered in little groups all around the garden while soft piano music played in the background.

Gunner had only seen events like this on television, but as it turned out, some people really organized lavish parties featuring large chocolate fountains as centerpieces, staff to wait on the guests, and expensive clothes. He wondered if, unlike him, they were actually having fun, or if it was a performance for all other members of the local upper crust.

Gunner nodded. "Am I getting paid for the overtime then?"

The joke fell flat and Gunner cringed when Thomas cleared his throat.

"No, but I talked with John about starting you on the job as early as next week, so—oh, look, he's coming over," Thomas pointed out a graying man in a sharp navy blue suit. But Gunner was still processing what he'd just heard.

What?

What?

The older gentleman's gaze met his, and a small smile stretched his mouth, which seemed pale in contrast with his tanned skin. He looked as if he'd gotten back from a vacation in Florida very recently.

"Ah, Caspian," he said, putting a small plate on the edge of the large table housing the chocolate fountain and a buffet of foods to dunk in the dark liquid cascading down the tiers. "Your Dad said you've really grown up while in college, but I now see what he meant. It's been years since I've last seen you!"

Gunner forced a smile on his face, and he sweated bullets as Thomas's words jiggled in his empty skull, creating an echo. Next week? He was supposed to start work as an *accountant* next week? He could probably bluff for a few days, but that shit could only last so long. Would anyone believe him if he faked a concussion and claimed it caused brain damage that irreversibly erased his college education?

Caspian would have killed him.

He shook John's hand, clinging to the present. "I'm pleased to meet you, sir. I'm looking forward to a summer vacation. Those final exams really tired me out."

John stalled with his warm hand in Gunner's, but then chuckled and let go after a brief squeeze. "Your son shares your sense of humor, Thomas."

Gunner froze when his fake dad's fingers dug into the flesh on his back in warning, but there was no anger to Thomas's tone when he spoke.

"Caspian can't wait to start."

A familiar voice cut into their conversation, and Gunner's blood froze when he realized that it was Alexander. The fucking menace who'd put him in children's clothes and called it fashion!

The bastard came closer and offered his hand to John, looking as stylish as he had been when they'd last met. "Mr. Sadler? I thought that was your car in the driveway. I'm sorry to interrupt your conversation, but I just had to come over and ask where you got the interior upholstered. I need to update mine, and I'm looking for a good shop."

John smiled, and all his attention shifted to the damn party crasher, who very obviously came over to make Gunner's life more difficult! Since the shopping fiasco Gunner had learned all about Alexander and his frenemy status in Caspian's life. Gunner didn't know why Caspian bothered with passive aggression. If he slashed Alex's tires once, the fucker would be out of his hair forever.

"Ah, I know a guy in Pittsburgh, who specializes in customization. They make their own patterns and colors, and it's always flawless work."

For Gunner, cars had always been about their utilitarian use, even though he could do basic upkeep. Driving the vintage Southfield, a one-of-a-kind vehicle Caspian had apparently purchased from someone selling his late grandfather's belongings, was a whole different ballgame. That car turned heads.

Gunner didn't care about its value as a collectible, but what counted was that Alexander had been jealous of the unique car since Caspian had restored it.

"I'd love to get their number," Alexander said.

Gunner smiled stiffly, unsure where to go with this, but John went on.

"Tell me, Alexander, did you take the summer off after graduating?"

Alexander shook his head and pushed his fingers through his tidy blond waves. "No, why would I? Graduating means you're *ready*. Isn't everyone revving to get into things once they're done with education?"

Caspian wished he could squish his fucking face like an overripe peach. "Yeah, but, you gotta live a little too."

"You don't sound very excited," John said with a dry chuckle, and his gaze darted to Thomas, who stood next to Caspian, stiff as a statue.

"It's just performance anxiety. He's afraid he'll disappoint me, but I know he's talented, and intelligent, and has a stellar work ethic," Thomas said.

John nodded. "I understand, but you'll be fine, Caspian. My niece joined the team last month and already feels right at home."

"You'll be working closely with me at first, so you can get acquainted with our procedures and how we work with other branches," Thomas said in a reassuring tone that, unfortunately, didn't calm Gunner down in the slightest.

Alexander nudged Gunner with his elbow. "I bet Caspian's ready to mingle with everyone."

John laughed. "Well, my niece is a lesbian, so *that* kind of mingling is off the table."

Gunner gave a startled chuckle. This was a piece of information he needed to pass to Caspian. Maybe he wouldn't have to worry about coming out if the company when it already employed a gay woman.

But before he could have said something coherent, Alexander butted in with a wide grin. "Caspian and her will have a lot to talk about then. It's good to have diversity in the office."

John's blue eyes sharpened as they zeroed in on Gunner. "Oh. You're gay, Caspian? Your father hasn't mentioned—I mean, sorry, there's no reason for it to just come up."

"No. I—what?" Gunner's heart sped up and rattled like the engine of his old wreck of a truck. He was going to be sick.

Thomas paled while the white noise around them echoed in Gunner's ears. "Caspian?"

Alexander cocked his head as if he was a confused parrot. "You're not out? I'm so sorry, I just assumed... you know, when we went shopping, and you talked about wanting to look a certain way..."

Something cracked in Gunner, and he pushed Alexander's chest. "You know exactly what you're doing, you motherfucker!"

Alexander's lips widened into a sneer, and his eyes glinted with triumph, as if he'd already won, not only this confrontation but the whole war of piano contests and attention. He had no idea how wrong he was.

Thomas squeezed Gunner's arm, but rage had already overflowed deep inside him, and there was no stopping it. This was for all the shitty gossip Alexander had spread about Caspian in school, the sabotaged piano, the offhand shortness quips, and wrecking Caspian's seventeenth birthday party by organizing his own swimming pool extravaganza with Taylor Swift as the star on the same day. Taylor Swift had really been an impersonator with a cover band, but the damage had been done.

He kicked Alexander straight in the nuts. The bastard folded in half, uttering a comically high-pitched sound, and when he met Gunner's gaze, his red face was the signal for the bull that had been huffing with aggression inside Gunner.

He charged at the lying fucker, who couldn't even be nasty to his face and had had to resort to backstabbing. Alexander lost his footing, his eyes went wide, and they both fell onto the table behind him, crashing between the little bowls filled with fruit and candy, the chocolate fountain, and the marshmallow stand. Sweet brown goo sprayed everywhere, covering them both like a representation of the years of shit between them.

Alexander writhed under him with a squeal, but Gunner didn't hesitate and punched him in the face with all the force he could muster. The table shook, and the chocolate from the unsteady fountain splashed onto his face before spilling into Alexander's hair as it fell over and rolled to the grass.

The garden erupted with squeaks and shouts, but while he could see figures moving in the corner of his eye, he was grounded in this moment of violence and wouldn't stop punching the self-satisfied bastard's face until even his mother wouldn't be able to recognize him.

"You think you can just toy with people's lives?" he yelled despite his next punch slipping along Alexander's forearm when the snake covered his face.

"Stop, you psycho!" Alexander cried.

"No! Get the fuck out of my life!"

He didn't get to land the next chocolate-stained blow because two sets of arms pulled him back.

His knees hit the edge of the table as he rolled off, but moments later, he found himself facing Barb, who stared at him from behind hands clasped on her face. "Caspian! What are you doing?"

Thomas helped Alexander off the table, keeping him up when Alex almost rolled onto the ground, holding his beaten face. Gunner bet his ears were ringing too. Good.

It was about time someone taught the smug bastard a lesson!

"Me?" he yelled, spreading his arms. "Why does everyone think it's okay for this cunt boy to out me, huh? So yeah, I'm fucking gay!"

"Go back to the house, Caspian! This is unacceptable!" Thomas said through clenched teeth, his kind face stiff with anger.

"No, I won't! He fucking deserved a good thrashing!" Adrenaline boiled in Gunner's veins and poisoned his mind until he couldn't think straight.

"I am so, so sorry," Barb shook her head, looking at her guests. "Dessert will be served shortly. I'll soon be back with you," she said and approached Gunner, digging her fingers into his arm. "Into the house. *Now*."

She pushed him forward with surprising strength, but he gave up the fight, because it wasn't as though he was gonna attack Alexander again. He stared at his feet, the grass, and then tiles as they walked on, because while he wasn't sorry about landing those punches, he didn't want to confront the judgemental stares and whispers stabbing at him from every direction.

Staff occupied the kitchen, so Barb led him to a side door, into a utility area and slammed the door shut before grabbing his shoulders. "What do you think you're doing? I don't know what he said to you, but you need to apologize and make amends before he presses charges! And in front of Mr. Sadler? Are you insane? Do you want to ruin your future, or just our reputation?" she asked, so flushed he could even see it through her makeup.

Something balked inside of Gunner, and he squeezed his fists, looking up at her. "I don't even wanna be an accountant! I told you I wanna play the piano! I'm so done with all of this!"

She took a deep breath and pushed her fingers into her smooth locks. "Since when? You've been planning this for years. And if you changed your mind, there are better ways to tell us!" she said, hissing in an effort to keep her voice down without compromising on her anger.

One of the servers passed through the corridor, no doubt lured by the commotion, and Barb dragged Caspian farther from the kitchen, to the home office.

She continued when Gunner couldn't find the right words to respond. "You can't just bail on everything you've worked for on a whim! You're an adult, Caspian, so act like one!"

"Oh yeah?" Gunner fired up. "I don't fit into your plans? Then I'm just gonna fucking go!"

She stared at him. "G-go where?"

"I don't know! I'll figure it out!"

316 | Take My Body

Barb pressed her lips together. "Sure. Don't let the door hit you on the way out."

Barely able to breathe from the sense of doom sitting on his chest, Gunner stormed out of the office and dashed upstairs to gather some basics into a duffel bag and change out of the chocolate-stained suit.

But as he headed out with the few things he could carry, guilt and panic had already chewed their way deep into his flesh.

What had he done? What had he *done*?

Chapter 23 – Caspian

Caspian shuddered when the damp shower curtain stuck to his ass again. He'd gotten a new one, because there was no way he'd be dealing with the mold on the one originally hanging in the bathroom, but he still hated the cold sensation of it clinging to him. He barely fit into the stall with a showerhead that faced him instead of hanging above his head. He needed to twist his body in order to clean himself everywhere, and kneel for the droplets to fall on his head, but it was what it was, since he couldn't sneak into his real home during the party.

He'd gotten motor oil all over himself by the time he finished repairing two of his neighbor's cars and made some improvements to Gunner's truck, so showering was a must. Especially since he'd planned an outing with Gunner, to treat him after the stressful day.

It wouldn't be much, but he had more than enough time to pack a blanket and other necessities, and stop at the grocery store to get food. The menu he had in mind was simple, but everyone appreciated fresh sandwiches and salad, even on days when they'd had fancy canapés for lunch.

He walked out of the bathroom dressed in a towel and took in the main room. He hadn't been able to stand the mess he'd woken up to on the first day of their swap, but while he was still battling roaches, he'd gotten rid of all the trash and bought a potted plant from Mad Madge to put on the counter, which made the place way more homely.

He usually left the curtains drawn over the windows, but it was bright enough outside for the sun to seep through the fabric and color everything within sight a pleasant warm hue. He hoped Gunner would appreciate all the changes and see them as the improvements they were instead of an intrusion into his home.

Caspian bit his lip, thinking of the way Gunner's head had rolled to the back of his seat as Caspian drove him home. Gunner might have been a red-blooded guy with a short temper, but he was also a sweet creature who'd thrive in the right circumstances. He played the piano with a passion Caspian never had for the instrument, and had more intelligence than Caspian gave him credit for. He might be stubborn but was kind at heart, and taken out of the environment that gave him a reason to hide his true self, Gunner became a different person.

Someone Caspian really liked around, as unbelievable as that was.

He was whistling to himself as he caught Fluffer and attempted to apply eye drops the vet had prescribed him last week when a rapid knocking on his door scared the cat away.

"Who is it?" he yelled and approached the source of the sound in the towel-skirt. While he liked to think of himself as modest and understated, he couldn't help but enjoy the fact that he now had a body he itched to show off.

"It's me!" Gunner said, and the smooth sound of his voice lifted the corners of Caspian's mouth, making him unlock the door with more vigor. He grinned when it flung open, revealing the compact form dressed in casual jeans, a T-shirt with a gray snake, and the same leather jacket he'd worn last night.

"So you couldn't wait to see me," he said and stepped away to let Gunner in.

Gunner locked the trailer, and then stood on his toes to pull Caspian down for a kiss, as if he'd been suffering without it. His warm lips tasted of mint and strawberry, prompting Caspian to nip at them, imagining sweet juice drizzling down his tongue.

He chuckled, hooking his thumbs through the belt loops of Gunner's jeans and pulling him closer. "How did it go?"

"Later," Gunner hummed and pushed Caspian's towel to the floor, leaving him naked. "Oh yess..." He ran his palms up the tattooed chest and sides, provoking a sudden hunger for pale, juicy flesh.

If his cutie was too horny to chat and wait for the picnic, Caspian was glad to fulfill his wishes.

"So impatient. Gonna help you let off all that steam," Caspian whispered, dragging his hands up and down Gunner's chest, and exposing the rosy nipples under the T-shirt. He'd become slightly obsessed with them, as Gunner made the cutest little noises when Caspian squeezed and pinched them, or just rolled them between the fingers.

Gunner nodded, already unzipping his pants. "That's all I need. *You*."

Their eyes met, and the hunger burning in Gunner's eyes was the match to light a raging fire in Caspian. He pushed Gunner at the empty table and sat him on the edge before dragging the offending piece of fabric off him. "Then you'll get what you deserve, slut. My big, throbbing cock drilling you until you have to bite your lips to keep from screaming," he said and nipped on Gunner's nipple.

Gunner whimpered and wrapped his arms around Caspian's neck, already spreading his legs. His pliant eagerness was like a ripening fruit, sweeter each time Caspian bit in. Not only did he love the shape of Gunner and what his body did for Caspian's cock, but it was Gunner's wicked mind and filthy mouth that had Caspian revving from zero to a hundred each time.

"All yours," Gunner whispered.

Caspian pushed between his thighs, wrapping the slender legs around him as he loudly breathed in Gunner's scent, licking and kissing the soft skin until his prick was so heavy he needed to widen his stance.

"Come on," Gunner said between one gasp and another. "I need to feel your dick in me now. Give it to me hard. Give it to me rough. Give it to me like I'm your little bitch. Cause I am."

Caspian had been in the mood for a hot, passionate tumble, but Caspian's words triggered the right switches in his brain, and he grabbed Gunner's narrow jaw, staring straight into his eyes. "Is that right? You want me to bruise you too?"

He knew he was spot-on when Gunner's lip trembled, and his eyes turned into deep wells. "Bite me, scratch me, mark me, and leave me dripping," he whispered, and no dirty talk on Grindr could ever match the intensity in his voice. This was *real*. A handsome twink who loved to be around Caspian wanted to be marked by him. Wanted to submit to him. Wanted to take his spunk.

It was all Caspian had ever wanted, and in his mind he was already tattooing Gunner's skin with his name.

"You *are* mine. Do you even remember another guy was trying to take you from me last night?" he asked and slapped Gunner's cheek. His heart stopped when the boy's eyes widened, because maybe he should have asked if that was okay, but then Gunner licked the inside of his palm and Caspian roughly twisted his nipple, grinding his crotch against the supple buttocks.

"Vaguely. He was no match for you though, was he?" Gunner reached for Caspian's pec, but he was no longer in charge.

"Pass me the belt." Caspian pointed to the piece of leather resting on the chair, and his cock twitched when Gunner reached for it without question. As soon as the small hand squeezed around the loop, Caspian dragged him back to his feet, took the belt and bent Gunner over, pressing his naked chest to the smooth white table top.

Holding the leather strap between his teeth, he pulled the boy's hands back with enough pressure for it to feel like a threat yet not cause pain. "You followed him to the restroom, and he'd have had you over the toilet if I hadn't come to get you. You drank far too much, you reckless, volatile *slut*. From now on, *I'm* in control of your drinking, understood?" he said and pushed his knee against the backs of Gunner's balls as he prepared the belt cuffs in a way he'd seen online. Gunner wouldn't be able to get out of those so easily. He'd be trapped and at Caspian's mercy for as long as necessary.

"Yes. You're in charge." Gunner trembled, and his beautiful submission lured out Caspian's inner wolf.

He ran his fingers along the ridges of Gunner's spine. He loved being this massive guy, and Gunner's size only made him feel more powerful. He could do anything with the strength he now possessed, yet the trembling body under him gave in willingly. Caspian wasn't particularly sadistic, but it turned him on to no end that his lover allowed him to do as he pleased. So he scratched the side of Gunner's ribs, leaving red marks behind.

"I'm gonna fuck you here, then tie you to my bed and return once I want more," he whispered, pulling Gunner's wrists through the double loop made with the belt before tightening the impromptu handcuffs to make sure the boy wouldn't free himself. Heat climbed his face as he looked at the marks he left on the smooth skin and smacked the pert ass still hiding in denim. "And you know why?"

"Because I'm your bitch!" Gunner whimpered, and the submissive tone in his voice made not only Caspian's cock but also his gums tingle with desire. He ducked, pushing his crotch at the jean-clad buttocks, and bit down on the warm nape.

"Yes you are, and you're gonna be a good little slut, because you don't want me sharing you around, do you?" Not that he would, even if he had gay friends who were up for that kind of play. Gunner was his only to indulge in. Only his to use and spoil.

"No, your cock is the only one I need," Gunner said, spreading his thighs in invitation.

Could a boy be any sexier that this slutty twink, who opened his legs as wide as Caspian desired? So pliant. So *available*. Caspian had never had as much sex as in the past two weeks, but his lover was relentlessly greedy for cum and shameless about it. Gunner's snug hole had been trained well, and as Caspian's attention focused on the tight little butt before him, a sense of urgency diluted his patience until he had none left.

Caspian reached to the front of Gunner's jeans and opened them before dragging cotton and denim off his hips to expose the peach-like globes that promised him sweet release. But he'd spoil the perfection of Gunner's body first and slapped the left buttock with all his strength.

"That's for almost cheating on me!"

Gunner caught his yelp midway and bit his lips, huffing through the nose. "I didn't mean to."

The next stroke of Caspian's hand made Gunner rise to his toes, and he barely swallowed the cry pushing at his mouth.

"That's for thinking I'll care whether you meant it or not," Caspian growled, his mind clouded by arousal as he focused on the red marks left behind by his palm, and on the sexy jiggle that followed each of the blows. "And for not taking off your clothes the moment you crossed the threshold!"

In moments like this he didn't miss anything about his old life. His dick was stiff as a tire iron, and Gunner was here with him, ready to fulfill any fantasy Caspian might have. They were two dirty-minded fucks, and Caspian wouldn't have had it any other way.

Gunner clenched his fingers hard and rubbed his cheek against the table. He shifted from one foot to the other, and as his hips tilted, the buttocks moved too, offering Caspian a glimpse of the soft, wrinkled skin between.

"I'm gonna destroy your little hole," he purred and pushed his thumb into the crack, touching the pucker.

The flesh yielded to his touch, and Gunner's opening widened, as if it were sucking on his fingertip. Already hungry. Prepared to take a rough plowing and keep in his cum.

Caspian kicked Gunner's feet farther open, as wide as the lowered jeans allowed, and raked his nails down the flawless back, finishing their journey by squeezing the bound wrists. His cock was as eager as Gunner's hole was, and he looked around, trying to remember where he'd put lube.

"Don't you dare move, bitch."

"Don't go," Gunner whined despite surely throbbing with pain where Caspian had marked flesh with his hand.

It was the first time Caspian was glad for the size of the trailer, because the tube was just a couple of steps away. The soft, lustful mewl Gunner uttered scorched Caspian all the way to the tips of his ears. Gunner not only hadn't moved. He was calling his stud over, provoking him.

"Come on, beg for it," Caspian whispered as he drizzled lube down Gunner's crack, watching the clear gel slicken the hole and then drip to Gunner's fuzzy balls.

"Please fill my greedy hole," Gunner said with a gasp. "I'm a filthy piece of ass and I need to be wrecked."

Caspian's brain scrambled. He could barely think beyond dick, and cum, and hole. As he spread the pert globes and saw the anus winking at him, the need to *take* became the single loudest voice in his mind.

He slapped his erection against the slick crack, which had them both squirming in pleasure. "You're such a horny little thing. I should teach you a lesson and tie you to this table once I'm done, and then invite all the willing guys in this trailer park to have a go."

Gunner's breathing got so fast and hot it left steam on the table next to his lips. "No, I'll please you right, keep me to yourself."

Caspian grinned, pressing his cockhead against Gunner's eager hole. "Is that right? You better, because I'll be fucking until I got what I'm owed. So that tight little asshole of yours better milk me good."

He thrust his cock in when Gunner felt ripe for the taking, and the boy's muffled whimper went straight to Caspian's balls. Now that he was in, hugged in the heat of the other body, he leaned forward over Gunner's back, rested his forearm on the table, and grabbed that slender neck in his palm. He loved sensing Gunner's every breath, his quickening pulse and bobbing Adam's apple when they fucked.

"I will," Gunner rasped. "I'll be your pliant little sex toy. Use me."

"I *will* use you. I *will* make your hole burn," Caspian said, increasingly overcome by lust. It could no longer be stopped. He needed to fuck Gunner right. The fuck. Now.

He shifted back, grabbed Gunner's hips and pushed, watching the tender flesh swallow his throbbing prick inch after inch as he forced it in. Gunner's moans fuelled his fire, but the teasing squeezes of his ass told Caspian exactly what his boy wanted. The little sex pest even raised his bound hands to tickle Caspian's stomach, so he squashed the smaller body under his and slammed home, making his lover squeal and tremble.

Passion burned through his body, leaving his insides scorched and his mouth dry, but he was close to the well and closed his mouth on Gunner's shoulder, dragging his cock out, only to push back in. Gunner's body was so tight around him it felt as if he was being sucked back in each time, so he shut his eyes, dug his fingers into flesh and jabbed his hips at Gunner's ass. His balls vibrated when they slapped against buttocks covered by a peach-like fuzz, so he sped up, holding Gunner still for his pleasure as he rutted on top of him, ever faster and harder.

The muffled cries escaping Gunner's lips were the lure making him go faster with each passing second. He was where he was supposed to be, and Gunner's scent intoxicated him beyond the rush booze could offer. Every stifled moan was confirmation that he was the stud Gunner craved, and no one else would do.

"You're mine, you little tramp. From now on, I'll oversee how much you drink. I'll tell you when to go to sleep, and when to suck my cock. Is that understood?" Caspian asked, grabbing Gunner's throat just hard enough to briefly make him stiffen. But the moment of fear had the boy moaning a seconds later.

Caspian shut his eyes and moved faster, focusing on his own pleasure, because he'd take care of his lover's once he was done. For now, he'd give him the experience of being treated like a cumbucket, and he'd leave him with enough spunk to make that point clear.

"Yes," Gunner choked out. "I'll be on your call."

The channel of muscles hugged him so tightly, he wished he could fall asleep right after the fuck, with his dick still in Gunner. Under his fingers, his lover's flesh was sunshine hot, and the quick pulsing of blood in the neck reminded Caspian he not only had Gunner pinned down to the table and open for his spunk, but also held Gunner's life in his hand.

"Good. That. We. Understand each other," Caspian grunted, already chasing the pleasure promised by the throbbing in his balls. It didn't matter that they were in a shabby trailer and had to keep quiet for the sake of all the neighbors, because as far as Caspian was concerned this might have been a palace, and the scent of Gunner's sweat would still have been the one thing he cared about. His thighs trembled, and he rested even more of his weight on the boy as the pressure in his dick rose until he could no longer stop himself from jabbing into the tight hole at a frantic rate.

Cum shot out of Caspian in several spurts, coating the walls of Gunner's sensitive ass, and he moaned against his lover's warm flesh just picturing it in his mind. No guy ever had made him feel so wanted. So powerful. So validated.

And while he knew they'd have to find a way back to their own bodies, he secretly wished it wasn't a possibility.

He slid his hand up Gunner's throat, chin, and to the trembling lips that sucked on his fingers, as if they were a delicious lollipop. But there was also moisture on his cheek, too much of it to be explained with perspiration. Caspian stilled with his nose buried in the pale, cherry-scented hair, unsure whether he should point out the tears.

"I want you to come, babe," he uttered, kissing Gunner's temple. His hand moved down the boy's stomach and took hold of his prick, which was so hard they both shivered with discomfort. The hole squeezed around Caspian's softening cock, as Gunner shuddered, giving in to the touch.

"Yes, please, please," he mumbled around the fingers, already thrusting into Caspian's hand.

A devilish voice at the back of Caspian's head told him to deny pleasure, to bait and switch, and make Gunner beg with that filthy mouth of his, but his muscles were becoming heavy, and the cock in Caspian's hand felt so hot and swollen he didn't have the heart to torture his lover any further.

He trembled when his own dick left the tight body with a loud smack, but remained steady behind the boy and hugged him from behind while his fist worked the hard length, which he used to scorn so much yet now loved to touch and suck.

"You're such a dirty boy. Coming here and demanding cum, as if you were an addict," he uttered while Caspian trembled in his arms, jerking in throes of frantic passion.

"Maybe... I am," the last word turned into a moan when Gunner came, spilling cum between Caspian's thick fingers.

It was so hot it burned Caspian's skin, but instead of having a taste, he went with the same emotions that had guided him through this sex game and wiped the spunk on Gunner's face. "There, have more, you greedy thing," he said before spinning Gunner around to watch him.

A beautiful mess with flushed cheeks and cum-stained lips, he was barely catching his breath when he looked up at Caspian with angelic eyes. But no matter how much that blue gaze glinted with innocence, the boy had more in common with demons.

As Gunner licked spunk off Caspian's fingers, the soft light seeping through the curtains caught the damp stains trailing from his eyes, making Caspian's mind stall in alarm.

"Are you okay?" he asked, gently cupping the smooth cheeks and rubbing the tears off with his thumbs.

No boy had a prettier smile than Gunner. There was a vulnerability to it that set Caspian's heart on fire whenever he was graced with the sight of those pink lips crooking in joy. Gunner wobbled forward, with the pants pooling above his knees and leaned against Caspian, as if he were seeking his care. "I am now. That was mind blowing. Just... so intense."

Caspian relaxed, and while he felt like giving himself time to recuperate, he picked Gunner up into his arms and carried him to the bedroom. The little cum vampire had sucked him dry, and he was relieved when they rolled onto the bed.

"This was exactly what I needed." Gunner closed his eyes and settled his head on Caspian's arm, not even asking for the belt to be removed. He seemed thoroughly satisfied, and Caspian longed to give him everything he needed. Fulfill his every craving. Or just stay in bed together forever. For now, he claimed his lips in a kiss that tasted of spunk and desire.

"So how was the party?"

Gunner rolled his forehead over Caspian's bicep with a low groan. "Hmm... Would it be okay for me to stay here for a few days?"

Caspian blinked, and surprise quickly turned into worry as ice sank deep into his flesh.

The post-orgasmic bliss melted from his overheated body.

"What did you do?"

"I mean… it wasn't *that* bad, but I may have had an argument with your parents, and shit went a bit sideways."

The ice in Caspian grew colder as he sat up, his body awoken by adrenaline. "What kind of argument? Out with it!"

He suspected the reason Gunner rolled to his knees instead of sitting up, like him, was to seem taller, but that couldn't make him look dignified when he still had his pants down and hands tied behind his back.

"I said I was leaving, okay? I lost my shit with Alex, they wanted me to start in the firm next week, which I couldn't possibly do, and also, John Sadler now thinks I'm a psycho, but I'm not, I'm just not gonna bend over when Alexander Dickface wants to fuck me over!"

"You did *what*? Jesus Christ!" Caspian's chest sank, keeping his breathing shallow as he met the glinting blue eyes. He couldn't believe what he was hearing, nor understand it for that matter. "What do you fucking mean? All you needed to do was keep your head down for a couple of hours," he rasped, rolling off the bed, only to hit his elbow on the cupboard, because there was too little fucking space to accommodate his size! "What did you do?" he roared, imagining flames engulfing his family home, police arriving in great numbers, and John Sadler losing his temper when his relationship with Dad had been so good before. They were as close to friends as business associates could get.

This couldn't be fucking happening!

Gunner sat back on his heels with a huff. How could one man be so tiny, and yet wreck the world around him like a bull on steroids? "I didn't do shit! Alexander outed me in front of them! So I lost my cool! I was doing just fine before that, but no, he had to come over and throw me under the bus! So *I* threw him at a table. Big fucking deal! Would you fucking untie me?"

Caspian moved back and forth in the tight space between the bed and cupboards, his brain on fire. "What do you mean he 'outed' you? How the fuck would he know?" He yelled and flinched when he spread his arm and hit the wall.

"He made assumptions after the shopping we did. Asshole. After I broke his nose—"

"The hell?"

"I told you we had a fight. So I was buzzing after, and kinda... admitted it was true?" Gunner's shoulders dropped, but he offered Caspian a hesitant smile, as if he didn't realize that there was nothing amusing about his behavior. This was dreadful. Absolutely fucking worst.

"You admitted—?" But the fact that Gunner had come out *in his stead* to his parents and their entire social circle wasn't the worst of it. He'd also beat up another person severely enough to break bone, and there had been at least three dozen witnesses to back up Alex's story.

He couldn't fucking breathe.

"You need to go back. You need to apologize to Alex right the fuck now, and beg him not to press charges!"

"What kind of pussy is he? I barely fucking scratched him!"

"You said you broke his nose!"

Gunner pouted. "Potato tomato."

Caspian stared at him in horror. "That's not how the saying goes!"

"And I said untie me! I don't wanna be here anymore!"

"Yeah, you shouldn't be," Caspian yelled, raising his voice. "We'll dress and go together, so I can keep you in check, because clearly you can't control your fucking temper." He roughly flipped Gunner over and pulled on the right fragment of the looped belt in order to loosen the cuff.

He couldn't believe this was happening. This party had been very important for Mom and Dad, and Gunner had ruined it. The possibility of fallout was so great it was making his insides cramp with the stress of it all.

Gunner slid off the bed with a miserable expression and pulled his pants up. "I'm not going! What if they arrest me?"

"Then you'll be a good boy and go with the police, apologize, and tell them you panicked because he outed you in front of everyone," Caspian yelled, tossing the belt at the wall, before quickly putting on underwear and jeans from a pile of clean stuff. "How could you do this to my parents?"

Gunner hugged himself, looking lost, and for a moment Caspian wanted to give in and tell him everything would be all right. But what the fuck was wrong with his head? The walking disaster deserved a kick in the ass, not consolation.

"I'm just a bad fucking person, and you know this!" Gunner finally yelled as if a dam had broken inside of him, and secret truths could no longer be held in. He put on his

T-shirt but stilled with the jacket in hand when someone knocked on the door.

"Will you fucking shut it? My baby's trying to sleep!" Carla, one of his neighbors yelled.

"I will not shut up! Tell your baby to suck it up. It's the middle of the day," Caspian roared, banging his hand against the wall, out of fucks to give. It didn't matter whether people liked him, because at the end of the day, this wasn't his world, his home, or his neighbors. If Gunner couldn't respect those in *his* old life, then he'd return the favor.

Gunner put on the jacket, glaring at Caspian as if he had any right to be pissed off, and headed for the door. "This was a bad idea. I shouldn't have come here."

But Carla wouldn't give it a rest with the banging, splitting Caspian's overworked brain in half. "I'll tell my husband, you no good bastard!"

This was it.

Caspian pushed past Gunner and ran to the door, opening it into the woman's face. Dressed in a skater dress and an open hoodie, she stepped back, as if suddenly reminded who she was confronting. "You and your husband fart out of your mouths every other day, and I have to listen to *that*, so don't you fucking come in here and tell me when to argue with my boyfriend!"

Carla stared at him, for once stunned into silence. *Good.* But the other neighbors already peeking at the situation from nearby only angered Caspian further—as if containing his aggression on a daily basis hadn't been hard enough.

Gunner slipped out under his arm and faced Carla. "He's talking bullshit, we're not— It's not *that*."

"Yes, it fucking is," Caspian said, struck that Gunner had no problem ruining his life and, possibly, getting him a criminal conviction to stain the perfect record, yet for some reason expected Caspian to stay civil. "I'm fucking this guy, because I'm gay. All out in the open now," he finished, moving his gaze from Carla to Gunner's pale face, which was still stained with cum.

Nearby, Mad Madge got up from her sun chair and started clapping while her dog bounced around. "Good for you!" she yelled gleefully.

Gunner clenched his fists. "You really think you can do this?"

Caspian laughed and spread his arms as the dark fire of satisfaction ate through his chest. "What are you gonna do? Burn down my house?"

Carla's husband, a big bald bastard with a tattooed skull, walked up to them like a bulldozer looking for a building to demolish. "Russo's a queer?" he asked his wife as if Caspian wasn't there to hear them.

Carla crossed her arms on her chest. "Apparently."

Gunner screamed out in helpless fury, and for once Caspian was glad to see him suffer for what he'd done. There were consequences to actions, and it was about time Gunner learned that.

"Oh, you crossed the line!" Gunner said. "You'll regret this!"

"Oh really? How will you make me pay, you dwarf?"

Gunner's shoulders went rigid when a couple of people around burst out with laughter. "You sure liked fucking this *dwarf* ten minutes ago, so who's the joke now, huh?"

It didn't even make sense. As if Gunner couldn't see he was digging a hole for himself, not Caspian, because once they swapped back, this would be *his* life again. Forever.

"What's not to like? You're pretty as a picture. But that doesn't mean you aren't acting like a dick and refusing to take responsibility!"

Gunner grabbed the metal trash can outside Caspian's trailer, but wasn't strong enough to pick it up with all the stuff inside, so he ended up tipping it over in his rage. He kicked around the empty boxes and cans, then stormed off with another scream.

The gleeful satisfaction of outing him in revenge fizzled out fast, and Caspian stared at Carla and her man with no joy.

"Show's over," he said as he climbed back into his trailer and slammed the door behind him, suddenly so nauseated he wondered whether he shouldn't run to the bathroom to empty his stomach. But he managed to keep it down and sat on the floor, staring at the covered windows while his body cooled, leaving behind a dull sensation.

Gunner was crazy. Completely fucking nuts.

How could Caspian have even entertained the possibility that their relationship could have ever gone beyond sex?

Chapter 24 – Caspian

Caspian's skin was on fire, and no matter how quickly he paced around his cramped living room or how many times he'd rolled into bed and screamed into the pillow, the sense of failure wouldn't leave him, buried deep like a rusty knife that would soon cause gangrene.

A part of him wanted to jump into the truck and drive to his parents' place, do *something* to pick up the pieces of Gunner's mess, but the last thing they needed was a hulking stranger coming over to offer his aid. So he gave up, lost in the sense of failure.

He'd never smoked, but the moment he found an old pack of cigarettes at the back of the kitchen cupboard, everything inside him told him the tobacco would bring some relief.

And it did.

Caspian wasn't proud of it, but he smoked three in a row while sitting on the steps leading into his trailer and petting Fluffer, who reluctantly accepted his company after being offered a catnip snack. And while the air went cool as the sun set, he was so exhausted following the fight with Gunner and his neighbors that he stayed still, trying to absorb warmth from the cat in his lap.

He flinched when a silhouette loomed in the dark, because several people had casually strolled around his trailer in the past few hours to gape at the newly out Gunner Russo. But as the slender form approached, Caspian realized it was Noah. Gunner's brother didn't talk to him much, weirded out by the whole body swap situation, but Caspian had heard from Gunner that they kept in touch. Too bad Gunner refused to answer any of *his* calls and didn't reply to any of the messages Caspian had sent him, even though he'd read them all.

"Hey, I just finished work. Is Gunner here?" Noah asked right off the bat and adjusted his tie dye T-shirt.

"You should call him. Maybe he'll actually respond," Caspian said grimly and stepped on the butt of his cigarette.

Noah pushed back his hair and groaned. "Oh. So he's not talking to you either. Figures. You had a fight over the video?"

Something icy stabbed the back of Caspian's head, and when he stiffened, Fluffer jumped off his lap with a shriek, as if he felt threatened. "What video?"

Noah stilled and his eyes widened. "You... you *have* seen the video, right?"

Caspian rose, feeling faint. "What's this about?"

Noah pulled out his phone, fiddled with it, and then turned it to Caspian, showing him a paused video. "I'm... sorry. I don't know what he was thinking."

But Caspian could no longer hear Noah, freezing to the ground when the video started with indiscernible shouting. He recognized his parents' garden, filmed from the balcony above the kitchen. A young man in a shirt and bow tie, likely a server hired for the event, was posing for a selfie when shouting erupted on the lawn below. The image shook before focusing on the action.

It was chaos.

Caspian barely heard his own thoughts through the drumming of blood in his head. Alex didn't even sound like himself when he cried out following a hard kick in the nuts. Flooded by chocolate, with marshmallows flying from the falling table, the brawl was as brutal as it was glorious. Witnessing Alexander get his comeuppance was a pleasure as guilty as a marathon of *'90-Day Fiancé* with Gunner.

The camera zoomed back in on the server after Dad dragged Gunner off Alexander.

"All you need to know about the guy getting his ass kicked by the twink in the blue suit, is that he asked me about the origin of the cocoa because 'he only ate Trinidadian'," the server said with a pout and stared into the camera.

Of course he fucking did, the snob. Clearly, the Ecuadorian variety Mom preferred wasn't good enough for him!

Caspian was mortified. For his mom. For his dad. For the damage this would do to *his* reputation.

But seeing Alex put in his place after years of suffering the indignity of his snide remarks, and especially after the stunt he'd pulled *helping* Gunner shop, was too much of a treat to pass on. So he put the video on loop and chuckled every time Gunner, the rabid twink, kicked

Caspian's frenemy in the nuts. The moment when they both collapsed on the table, covered by splashing chocolate was *sublime*.

And just about the sexiest thing he'd ever seen.

"So... um... You don't think he's in jail, right?" Noah asked when the chocolate fountain on the screen collapsed for the fourth time.

Caspian choked on air and stared at him, suddenly frozen with fear. "He was here a few hours ago. Do you think they could have gotten to him?"

Noah raised his eyebrows. "I just asked *you* if you knew."

"What if they put him in a cell with some psycho? He's so small," Caspian uttered, rubbing the top of his head and once again choosing Gunner's number. Should he go to the police station and demand to see him, if he was there? Was that kind of thing allowed? Caspian had never even been to a police station. And while he wanted to advocate on Gunner's behalf if it was needed, he didn't wish to draw attention to the violent encounter between Gunner's fists and Alexander's face either. Which left him at a crossroads, and without any indication about which path was the better option.

After hours of ignoring Caspian's calls, Gunner finally picked up. "Don't fucking call me, I'm busy!" he yelled, and... hung up.

The audacity!

Caspian roared and punched the side of the trailer, shocked when its wall gave, creating a fist-sized dip.

"*You* call him. You ask him where he is, or I'm gonna kill him!"

Noah frowned and pressed his full lips into a tight line. "Did you beat him up? He's half your size now!"

Caspian raised his hands, because the accusation felt like a slap. "What? I would never! He told me he fucked up my parents' party, and we argued. That's it!"

Noah put his phone in his pocket and shook his head. "Okay, listen, I hoped he'd be here, but this is getting out of hand, and I know you really want to swap back, so we should write down exactly what happened to you on the night before you changed places and see what stands out. I wanna help, and I know my brother can be a bit... much."

Today's events proved that life couldn't go on until Caspian was back in his own body. He missed his parents, and Gunner wasn't equipped to handle the unfamiliar life, but still, he couldn't stop the deep sadness spreading through his chest like wine over white cotton when he thought of this adventure coming to an end.

"We need to find him. This guy he beat up? He'll do everything in his power to fuck me over, and now he has me by the balls."

Noah rested both his hands on his nape, pacing in front of Caspian. "But I talked to Madge. She told me how she remembered that night. You drank with her, but she never even saw Gun that evening. She said she's happy to—"

"I don't fucking care, okay? We need to find Gunner. He might be in trouble!" Caspian demanded and locked the door to the trailer. Fluffer escaped right under his feet, but he didn't have time to deal with the furball right now. If he wanted back home, the flap at the bottom of the door was all he needed.

Noah stared at him for a prolonged moment, as if he were trying to read his thoughts. "Are you worried about *him* or your real body?"

Caspian walked toward the truck, nervously glancing around. It was dark, and Gunner wasn't used to being in danger. He might walk into a bad situation without knowing, unless Caspian managed to locate him. "How can you even ask that question?"

Noah had to power-walk in order to keep up with him. "I mean... he told me he hadn't exactly been kind to you."

Caspian barely remembered it anymore, as if the old Gunner had been a different person, separate from the cute boy occupying too many of Caspian's thoughts. "I'm not gonna fault him for something he did in high school. We've both outgrown this."

"I'm happy to hear that you think so. He puts up a front, but he's—" Noah froze at the sight of Todd and his brother leaning against the back of Gunner's truck.

"Heard you got some news, Russo," Todd said with a scowl, casually resting a baseball bat on his shoulder.

Chapter 25 – Caspian

A baseball bat? Really? The instincts instilled in Gunner's body allowed Caspian to defend himself just fine against fists, but how was he to deal with a weapon when he didn't have one of his own? Still, the fire burning inside him grew when he realized those fuckers were yet another obstacle to finding Gunner.

"Not now."

Todd scowled, and his brother obstructed the way to the door on the driver's side, his eyes glinting like a coyote's. "Yes, fucking *now*. Or does your little boyfriend not let you talk to strangers, huh?"

Neither Todd nor his brother were strangers. But Caspian had no doubt this conversation would be going off the rails for reasons other than logical sentence structure.

Noah licked his lips. "Is he talking about...?"

"Not in front of my little brother, fuck face," Caspian growled, squeezing his hands into fists. His vision blurred at the edges, and he stepped closer, only mildly wary of the baseball bat. Something inside him told him to go forward. To confront. To punch first. He'd never experienced such impulses in his own body, but he loved the rush they gave him, and his confidence had soared after the daily boxing lessons with Gunner.

Todd cocked his head with a mean grin. "Why not? You told the whole trailer park you're a faggot. Why hide it now? Took you long enough to show your true colors, but I always felt there was something off about you."

Caspian stopped inches away from Todd and stared straight into his mean, squinting eyes. "Yeah, I don't fucking care. Is that all, or do you actually have something to say? Don't have time for idle chatter."

Todd pushed at his chest with the handle of the bat, but Caspian wouldn't budge. "Sure fucking do. You're out, fag. We do a man's job, so there's no place for you with us, get it?"

Which might just have been the best thing that happened today, yet it still hurt to be called a slur to his face. Todd had done it back in high school, and when Gunner and his buddies had ganged up on Caspian at the gym, but it was different this time. This time, Todd wasn't using it as a generic belittling remark but a weapon against a man whose sexuality he knew.

"Fine. Now get away from my truck," he said and shoved at Todd.

"You watch those hands!" Todd yelled and pushed him back. "We're done when I say we're done!"

The desire to destroy this fucker burned hot in Caspian, like a pile of paper covered in gasoline. The humiliating confrontation at the gym came right back, and Caspian wished to rip the bat out of Todd's hand and smash in his skull. "Fuck you. You want me out? Fine. Now get out of my way, or you'll regret it!"

Ralph stood behind his brother like a silent warning. They couldn't shun Caspian and be done with it. No, they *had* to make it a fight. Caspian didn't know if this was some gangster masculinity issue he didn't comprehend, or simply years of low-key animosity being let off the chain, but once more he was forced to see Gunner's life issues weren't a question of just changing jobs. He was in debt, entangled with these homophobic assholes, and a witness of the many crimes they'd committed together.

"No!" Noah yelled the second Caspian realized Todd swung the baseball bat at him.

He should have foreseen this and not been this slow, but as he raised his hand, trying to grab it, the weapon skidded over his arm and hit his ribs. Out of breath from the sudden pain, he slammed into the side of the truck.

The world trembled, its shades fading as he focused on movement and backed away right before the baseball bat collided with his body again. This time, it hit metal, and Caspian grabbed it with so much fury, the single, powerful tug not only ripped the weapon out of Todd's hands but also made him stumble.

Caspian brought the bat down on the fucker's back, knocking him into the dirt.

Ralph shoved him away before Caspian could have hit Todd another time, but the rush of adrenaline was enough to give him a high. Todd Brown was scum and deserved nothing beyond a kick in the nuts, broken bones, and years in prison.

So Caspian charged right back and smashed his boot into the bastard's stomach for good measure.

"Stop it! You're gonna kill him!" Noah yelled and tugged on his arm just as Ralph pulled out a switchblade.

Todd squirmed in the dirt, curled into a ball. "You'll regret this, Russo," he said through clenched teeth.

"Right back at you. Fuck the fuck off and out of my life, both of you!" Caspian roared, ignoring all the shadows appearing in trailer windows around them.

"Kill yourself, you damn faggot. It's gonna be mercy," Ralph hollered but didn't attack and instead dragged Todd away, constantly looking over the shoulder, as if he'd finally realized Caspian was a force to be reckoned with.

The baseball bat felt so right in Caspian's hand he swung it through the air for good measure before opening the truck. "Get in," he told Noah and tossed the weapon inside.

Noah shook his head with a pained expression, but did as told. "They won't let this go. Fuck!"

Well, at least Caspian had unleashed some of the pent-up fury.

"What can those troglodytes do? Fuck them. I don't deserve to hide all my life, and neither does Gunner," Caspian said and reached across Noah's body to grab the seatbelt. Gunner had told him in detail about the terrible accident that had left his brother with scars and Gunner— in debt, and while the boy wasn't really Caspian's relative, he needed to take care of him for Gunner's sake.

They didn't speak for a while as Caspian started the truck and drove off with a screech of tires. He didn't know where to yet, but he needed to be out of this shithole.

"So... Gunner's gay, isn't he?" Noah said quietly once they were out on the main road.

Caspian stilled, wishing he'd bitten his tongue. "Well... yeah. But you didn't hear it from me," he said, heading for the town centre.

Noah played with his seatbelt, his face hidden behind the mass of curls. "Are you two like... doing stuff?"

Caspian's face flushed with intense heat, and he focused on the headlights revealing the asphalt road ahead. He wasn't sure how much Gunner would have wanted him to say, but Noah seemed like a good enough kid, and Gunner would need all the support he could get once the two of them returned to their own bodies. "We're... dating," he said, realizing that he wasn't comfortable keeping that fact hidden. As crazy as Gunner sometimes made him, their relationship wasn't just about sex.

"Oh. Isn't that really weird though?" Noah cocked his head and scratched his nose, as if he were trying to remove a freckle.

Caspian scowled. "It used to be weird at first, but my face looks completely different when he's the one behind it."

Noah squinted. "Okay, I get it, 'cause your expressions are often different to Gunner's. It's freaking me out, to be honest."

"There you go. He's much cuter than I was. And he had this I'll-cut-you twink mode, which is weirdly hot on him, right?" Caspian asked with a weak laugh.

Noah's eyebrows rose. "I err... wouldn't know. Since he's my brother and all? But it's kinda funny that he's smaller than me and still has that stupid swagger. And then you're so put together in comparison. Fixed his car, cleaned the trailer... I heard you sorted out Mrs. Weller's plumbing, and she already recommended you to her brother. I'm sorry he's messing up your life, but we'll work out how to swap you two back eventually."

Swap back.

That was what Caspian *should've* wanted, but along with getting back his life, his degree, his parents, and possessions, he'd be losing a body that made him feel so comfortable. The cute boy who smelled of berries and had fluffy blond hair would be gone forever.

Caspian already missed him.

"I just want him safe. He's your brother. Where could he be?"

Noah listed several places around town and promised to be on the lookout, but the suggestion that Gunner was messing up Caspian's life wouldn't stop bugging him, and he was itching to set the matter straight.

So Gunner had made a scene at the party, but Caspian knew how hard he'd tried to fit in. He simply didn't have the same upbringing and made a mistake. "He's trying really hard. I shouted at him, and I shouldn't have, but he refused to apologize for the scene he made at the party, and I lost my temper," he said, kneading the wheel nervously as they passed the first location on Noah's list. Unfortunately, Gunner was nowhere to be seen around the closed video rental shop.

Noah snorted. "Sounds like him all right. Does he also disappear on you when he doesn't wanna deal with something?"

"That's Gunner. I need to re-educate him when it comes to this shit," Caspian said, shaking his head.

Noah twirled his fingers, swallowing several times, as if he were psyching himself up. "I was surprised he stuck around when our dad died. But... he's always there when it matters, you know? And I think *you* matter to him. You're all he talks about. And not just because of the swap. It's all 'Caspian was so good at boxing today', and 'Caspian knows all this fancy food'. Apparently you had him taste basil ice cream?"

A small flame flickered deep in Caspian's heart, only to grow, coursing through his veins along with blood. "Does he really? What else did he say?" Caspian asked, suddenly desperate to dig up every clue Gunner could have dropped.

Noah grinned. "I was laughing that you probably eat a burger with a knife and fork, and he got so angry on your behalf it was hilarious. He was all, 'he's nothing like that, he's nice, you don't know him'."

Caspian chuckled, feeling warm, as if Noah had served him a cup of hot chocolate with chili. He kind of knew Gunner liked him, but didn't expect him to be so serious about it and even defend him from such silly accusations, just because he thought they were an insult.

"Yeah... he can be quite sensitive when you know where to look," Caspian said, in disbelief, because this description sounded nothing like the guy he used to hate for so many years. The same one he'd hated only weeks ago.

"It makes sense now that you said you're dating. I teased him about it, but he wouldn't say yes or no. I don't know what he's scared of. I don't even..." Noah bit his lip, glancing at Caspian, "know where I stand on the sexuality thing."

Oh. Oooooh.

"He might freak out, but he'll understand," Caspian said quickly, passing the library and the café where he'd been humiliated over daring to flirt with the barista.

"Look." Noah straightened up like a meerkat and tapped Caspian's shoulder. "By the gas station. Is that him?"

He pointed to a figure occupying a bench with a bottle in hand, and while it was far from the roofing above the pumps, and its lights, there was a familiarity to the silhouette.

Caspian stepped on the gas pedal and cut through the other lane, passing right in front of a vehicle that rapidly slowed down. He ignored the sound of the horn and parked by the store, rolling out of the truck the moment its engine stilled.

His heart beat fast with worry, but when his gaze trailed to the bench and the hunched figure, he immediately recognized the lavender trainers and the pale hair falling into Gunner's face.

"Gun!"

Gunner looked up at him in the faint light that reached his sad little spot surrounded by random trash, and stiffened with a cigarette in one hand and a beer in the other. His car was parked in the shadows nearby, as if he planned to drive the expensive Southfield while drunk. Then again, he'd said he'd moved out so he probably meant to sleep in the car, or even on the fucking bench, since the night was so warm.

"What do you want?" Gunner asked, glancing to Noah, who stayed a few steps behind Caspian.

Caspian exhaled, determined to reassure him. "I saw you destroy Alex. That was quite something," he said with a small smile.

Gunner's shoulders relaxed a bit, and while Caspian was itching to pull the cigarette out of his hand, it could wait. "I shouldn't have done that. I..."

Go on, say it. Say you're sorry.

And then Caspian noticed it. Ink. Right under Gunner's collar bones, clearly visible under the loose white tank top. Caspian's anger came back like a tsunami and crashed over him. While Caspian had been agonizing about their argument for all those hours, Gunner had taken revenge against him by tattooing his body without Caspian's consent?

Un-*fucking*-believable.

He grabbed the collar with both hands and ripped it open in a powerful tug. "What. The. Fuck, Gunner?" He uttered, staring at the huge black letters on reddened skin. The fucker had even removed the dressing, as if he wanted it all to get infected!

Between the outlines of two guns, bold gothic script read *GUNNER*.

Caspian wanted to cry but no tears would fill his eyes.

Gunner yelped and his half-smoked cigarette fell to the ground, but the ripped fabric revealed not only the tattoo but also... pierced nipples. This was insanity.

Instead of fighting Caspian though, Gunner looked down his chest and... sobbed. "It made sense at the time."

"How did you even pay for this?"

Gunner bit his trembling lip. "I know a guy..."

What a fucking mess.

And the worst thing? The moment Gunner made that pathetic sound, the fury buzzing inside Caspian was replaced by worry. Had someone hurt him? Was he unwell?

And that was when Caspian saw something even more disturbing than the tattoo. Or the piercings.

A small piece of a Snickers bar remaining in an opened wrapper. It just sat on the bench, right next to the bottle of beer Gunner had been drinking from.

Caspian's head filled with red hot smoke. "Had... did you eat this?" he asked breathlessly and pointed to the bar.

Gunner rubbed his eyes. "What? Eating healthy is the least of our problems, isn't it?"

"You're allergic to nuts! Where's your EpiPen?" Caspian asked, squeezing Gunner's hips to see if he could feel the familiar shape in the jean pockets. Nothing.

"Am I?" Gunner looked up with dazed eyes. How much had he already drank? "Why do I need a pen?"

Panic filled Caspian from head to toe. He needed to take Gunner to the hospital, and fast!

"Yes, I fucking told you. What the hell were you thinking?" Caspian asked, pulling him up to his feet. A middle-aged couple watched them from inside the store, but he ignored them, focused on getting to the emergency room before the allergic reaction took hold.

"I don't know!" Gunner cried. "We've already established I'm a dumb fuck, who can't get anything right. How allergic am I? Am I gonna die?" He gasped and grabbed his neck, staring up at Caspian with reddened eyes.

"You're not gonna die, because we'll take you to the ER," Caspian said and took the car keys from Gunner before opening the passenger seat of the Southfield to help him in. His attention briefly lapsed when the damp blue eyes met his, and he wiped away a tear rolling down Gunner's cheek. "And you're not dumb. Now strap your seatbelt."

"Is he okay? What's going on?" Noah asked, approaching them quickly.

"I'm taking him to the hospital. Take care of my truck," Caspian said and tossed him the keys.

"But—"

"Noah?" Gunner rasped. "If I die, you can take all my stuff, okay?"

"He's not gonna die. I'll call you" Caspian said and turned on the engine as soon as he sat behind the wheel, determined to make it to the ER before the idiot living in his body choked to death. He stepped on the gas hard and drove onto the road, speeding toward the nearest hospital.

Chapter 26 – Gunner

Gunner went into full-on panic mode even before his airways started to swell, but Caspian had been there, holding his hand, rubbing his back, telling him when to inhale, and when to exhale. He'd felt sick and got an ugly rash. By the time they'd arrived at the ER, Caspian was so frantic he carried Gunner in and *demanded* help. It had all been a whirlwind after that. Eventually, the symptoms had subsided, and Gunner had fallen asleep with Caspian sitting at his bedside, exhausted.

A *ping* brought him back to reality, and he blinked, opening his eyes to see Caspian chewing on a rice waffle and typing something on the iPhone, which, theoretically, belonged to Gunner now. He had shadows under the eyes, but those couldn't make him any less handsome to Gunner.

The room was small and basic, with no decoration nor comforts beyond the blanket covering Gunner and the chair Caspian occupied, but it was where Gunner managed not to die, and that counted for something.

"Um… what time is it? Did you use my finger to unlock the phone?" Gunner asked, still a bit dazed.

Caspian looked up, blinking. "Uh… between two and three a.m. How are you feeling?" He asked, pulling the stool closer to the hospital bed and taking hold of Caspian's hand. He dropped the phone in his lap.

Gunner didn't deserve all this care after what he'd put Caspian through. He was an embarrassment. "Just tired, and a bit achy. Do I… do I have insurance for this?" He squeezed Caspian's hand even though he didn't know why Caspian would want to touch him after today. But he was needy, and he'd take whatever he could get.

Caspian offered him a weak smile. "Yeah, I gave them the insurance number, remember?"

Gunner didn't, but he'd been too frantic to notice such things. Caspian had taken care of everything.

"I exchanged some messages with Mom and Dad. They're worried. And they say they'll love me no matter what," Caspian said, and his smile broadened, as if there was a positive to this whole situation, other than Gunner not dying. "They seem to think you panicked because Alex outed you in front of everyone, so I guess that's why they're so forgiving."

Gunner fell back on the pillow with a deep sigh, painfully sober again and all too aware of what he'd done. "Well, it's not *not* true. You said there's a video?"

Caspian chuckled, grabbed the phone and rubbed the fingerprint reader against Gunner's digit. "Oh, and Noah also knows you're okay. He's the one who showed me this," he said, offering him the phone.

Gunner watched the video in growing horror. Had he really done that? At an elegant party? He was fucking rabid and didn't deserve to walk among people. No wonder others thought he was scum. He hid his face in his hands as soon as the video ended.

"Why am I such a shit? Sometimes I just can't think fast enough, and then I—I can't live your life. I'm useless."

"I wouldn't go that far, but yeah, you screwed up and didn't even say sorry," Caspian replied, a bit more harshly this time. "And that tattoo? And... piercings? What—?"

Gunner shook his head, overwhelmed by regret chewing through his insides. "I just wanted to feel more like myself. B-but I *am* sorry," he whispered from behind his hands. "I'd like to make things right, but I'll never be like you. I don't have your vocabulary, or skills, or brains. I love being in this body, but I can't *be* you."

Caspian exhaled, his shoulders dropping as he squeezed his own nipples through the T-shirt. "Last time I checked you didn't have them pierced. Was that just about getting back at me somehow?"

Gunner knocked his fist against his forehead. "I guess I... I was at the tattoo studio, and I remembered how you liked playing with them, and it was a bit of a spur of the moment kinda decision. Do you... like it?" Heat shot to his head when he realized how embarrassing that was. "Sorry. Don't answer that. I'm an idiot. I need to make things right for you."

Caspian sucked in his bottom lip. Chewed it. And then grabbed the sides of Gunner's collar, only to rip the top all the way to the bottom, making it into a flimsy vest. Cool air tickled Gunner's chest, and he froze in a moment of unexpected excitement when Caspian leaned in and placed his massive, warm hands on his skin, as if he were about to gather all the meat on Gunner's pecs.

The tender flesh ached, but when Caspian kept his warm palms motionless, the throbbing became oddly pleasant.

"It's... it's a good look on you."

Excitement tickled Gunner's skin, but this really wasn't the time to indulge in compliments. "How are you not smashing my face in?" He glanced down at those massive, tattooed hands, and while they used to belong to him, now they were Caspian's, and he wanted to kiss them all over.

Caspian rolled his eyes and scowled before meeting Gunner's gaze. "Mostly because you could have died. Also, you're so cute it should be considered a lethal weapon," he muttered and shook his head.

Gunner placed his hands over Caspian's and held them to his chest, imagining an alternative world where this man's strong arms would never let him go. It might have been a fantasy, but a beautiful one. "How can I make things better?" he asked, desperate to show Caspian that he wasn't a waste of space.

He half-expected Caspian to laugh, ask for a lap dance, or a blowjob, but he sucked on his teeth and looked at Gunner. "Noah keeps talking about ways to swap us back, and I... I want to see my parents again, talk to them like I'm not a stranger. And I was really excited about starting my new job."

The faint smile died on his lips, and he pulled on Gunner's hand, enfolding it in his massive paws. If Caspian's parents could excuse what Gunner had done earlier, then they must really love him.

"Yes, of course," Gunner said right away. "I'll do everything I can to make it happen. I'm so sorry I outed you, but Alex—and... yeah. We're even on that front." He dreaded to even think about the gossip that must have spread through the trailer park like wildfire.

"About that... I had a fight with Ralph and Todd. They don't want to sell drugs with you anymore," Caspian said quietly, his eyes turning as if he didn't dare look up.

Gunner couldn't blame Caspian. This whole mess was his fault, but how was he to pay off his debt without those two clowns? "Fuck. Fuck, fuck, fuck. Did it get violent? Are you okay?"

Caspian shrugged and lifted his shirt, showing off the bruises on his side. "Todd's hurt more. But don't worry, we'll think of something and work out a new status quo," he said with so much conviction a part of Gunner believed that his life might take a turn for the better, even once he was back in the body that had restricted him.

"Sure. I'm sure it will work out," he said, just because he didn't want to dim Caspian's optimism, but he'd already lost hope that his life could change course and avoid the eventual crash-landing in prison or in a body bag. They needed to find a way to swap back, but Gunner had no future plans or ideas beyond that. The vague dream of becoming a piano teacher would be dead in the water as soon as he was back in his hulking body, with fingers that didn't understand how to play and a brain that couldn't read sheet music.

"There's one more thing," Caspian said, moving to sit on the edge of Gunner's bed. Even so late at night, after carrying him to the ER, he smelled so good Gunner wished to open his pants and show him how much his help was appreciated. But Caspian squeezed Gunner's shoulder in a very non-sexual way and spoke. "Alex is here."

Gunner's stomach clenched in panic. "Oh no. You want him to beat me up so we're even?" He met Caspian's gaze, unsure if he could take that right now when so pumped out.

But the handsome face froze. Was he having a stroke?

"Er... no. I want you to go to his room and grovel."

Oh. Oh no. That was so much worse. Gunner's cheeks already heated up from the shame of it. His tongue tied in his mouth, as if it didn't want to produce words, and his expression must have made his opinion clear, because Caspian frowned.

"Gunner..." he said in warning.

"Okay. Okay. I'll do it. I just... I'll try not to mess up."

"You will not mess this up, because I'm *not* going to court over this," Caspian said in a stern voice that was annoyingly sexy.

Gunner couldn't even discern anymore if he was doing this for himself or for Caspian, but for Caspian's sake, yeah, he'd apologize, grovel, and kiss ass to Alex if need be.

He took a deep breath and sat up with a nervous smile. "Or we could like, go off the grid and never come back."

Caspian stilled, and his arm slowly rested on Gunner's shoulders. "It would be a dream, and we'd never have to wake up from it. But I can't leave my family. I don't want to."

And Gunner would have never demanded that from Caspian. He gave Caspian a quick hug, because fuck knew how much longer they had with the swap, and he'd squeeze as much joy as he could out of every second together. "Just kidding, I wouldn't leave Noah either. Let's get this over with. Where's Alex?"

Caspian's nose rubbed the top of his head as he breathed in, and the tickle of air moving over Gunner's hair was so pleasant he curled his toes, as if he'd been caressed deliberately.

"I don't think anyone's ever hit him like you did."

Gunner groaned but let Caspian lead him into the bright hospital corridor. "'Cause he was so fucking rude, and expected me to just take it. Is that what I should have done? Grinded my teeth and kept my mouth shut?"

Caspian shushed him by placing one finger across Gunner's mouth and gestured at the empty corridor. Right, it was late at night, and many patients were asleep.

"I still can't decide whether I'm angry at you or if I find the whole rabid twink thing sexy," Caspian whispered, herding Gunner by gently pushing his back.

Gunner bit back a nervous laugh. He sure hoped it was the latter. "I'm not very good at apologies," he whispered when they stood in front of a mint-green door. His hands were already sweating with unease at the upcoming confrontation, but Caspian didn't leave him a choice and knocked.

A dull sound came from inside, but Caspian didn't hesitate and opened the small room with several bouquets of flowers resting on a table close to the bed, as if Alex had suffered a serious accident, not a couple of punches to his face.

Wimp.

Gunner had to admit he barely recognized the man behind the dressing and heavy bruising, but Alex realized who'd walked in, because he went stiff and moved his hand toward a button on the wall, as if he were trying to suggest that he'd call for staff at even the smallest hint of hint of threat.

"What the hell are you doing here, dwarf? You have a henchman now?"

Gunner stuffed his hands into his pockets, simmering in the indignity of the offence he wished to punch off Alex's lips.

"No... that... he's my boyfriend," Gunner mumbled. "No need to alarm anyone. I came to say... to say..." Caspian nudged his back. "To say I'm sorry."

Alex stared at them, his arms folding across his chest. "You're just scared shitless of having to deal with the police."

Caspian spoke first, in a clear, stern voice. "No. He panicked because you outed him at a party. To his parents, their friends, and co-workers. That was really not cool, but *errare humanum est.* Let's work it out between the three of us."

Alex stared at him with more attention. "I know you."

"Impossible," Caspian said. "I don't move in your kind of circles."

But Alex was already bristling, and an oily lock of blond hair fell on his forehead and the massive dressing covering the nose. "You had a road rage freak-out at me two weeks ago or so." He glanced back to Gunner. "Like peas in a pod, the two of you, huh? Though I never actually pegged you for a gay man before, Cas. You never had any style."

Gunner had to bite the inside of his cheek to bear this. "Can we please consider this a misunderstanding between old friends? Look at me, I wouldn't last in jail." He laughed, hoping the self-deprecation would be up Alex's alley.

Alex exhaled, staring at him for the longest time. "No, you would not. Though you might end up with a whole collection of big bad boyfriends from the other side of the tracks if the judge decided not to let you off the hook with just a fine and some community service."

Gunner's face flushed at the threat. He couldn't bring himself to meet Alex's eyes, and was nervously pulling on his own fingers. It felt like being a teen again, and having to answer to his father for a job he'd fucked up.

"Is there anything I can do to make things better?" he tried.

"Sell me your car."

Just like that. It came out as if Alex had been keeping this sentence at the back of his throat and waiting for an opportunity to let it out.

Gunner wasn't sure how to answer, and his tongue tangled, because the vehicle wasn't *his*, but Caspian answered before Gunner could have decided what to do.

"Yes. He will sell it, won't you, Caspian?" he asked, glaring at Gunner, who at this point could only nod. He knew how much Caspian loved that car. He'd even insisted on washing it himself the few times Gunner came to visit him at the trailer park, because he didn't want it accidentally scratched by car wash workers.

He'd just sell it, as if it meant nothing?

Alex's gaze moved between the two of them, but when Gunner didn't protest, he spoke on. "For a hundred grand."

It was a ridiculous amount of money for a car so old and this unique, but Caspian spoke faster than Gunner again. "You gotta be joking. If you want to pay so little, get a 1930s Ford model A, not a unique vehicle like the Southfield. You'll need to pull at least twice that out of your pocket."

Alex raised his eyebrows, as if he knew he'd won. "*You're* the one haggling with me over your tiny boyfriend getting dragged through court and jail? My forgiveness is worth more than that car, but I'm willing to be kind for old times' sake…"

Gunner swallowed, glancing up at Caspian. This mess was *his* fault, and therefore he should've been bearing the consequences, but life wasn't fair, and Caspian would be the one to have his future put through the grinder once they swapped. It only made sense he wanted this over as soon as possible and without charges.

But he didn't flinch. "Three hundred and fifty grand and the car is yours."

Alex might have flushed under all the swelling and dressings, but he kept still, and for the longest moment, the room sunk in tense silence. And then, he shook his head at Gunner. "You know what? Keep the car. I'll see you in court."

Caspian's jaw muscles twitched, and for the longest moment the world stood still. And then he spoke. "Hundred and fifty then. You know that's dirt cheap."

Alexander grinned, and his gaze stopped on Gunner, as if he wanted to make a point of humiliating him. "I win."

"I guess you do," Caspian said and gently pushed Gunner forward.

Gunner gave a nervous smile and reached out to Alex. "I'm sorry. For the nose and shit."

Alex hesitated, but in the end gave Gunner's hand a brief squeeze. "I'll be calling you about the car once I feel better. You should really apologize to your parents."

Gunner groaned, eager to just be out of here as fast as possible. He wasn't looking forward to the conversation with Barb and Thomas, even though Caspian had already handled the worst of it for him through messages.

He mumbled a goodbye and an awkward "get well soon" as they left, but back in the empty corridor, he clung to Caspian with a tight hug. "I'm so sorry."

He couldn't believe Caspian would be losing his beloved car because of him, and to his arch nemesis at that!

Caspian patted him on the back, already leading the way down the hallway. "It's just a car. Don't worry."

Gunner rubbed his face. "How are you not angry with me?"

Caspian exhaled, staring at the exit ahead. "Honestly, I have no idea, but here we are."

Gunner snorted and dared to entwine their hands in public even though the only person to see them was a nurse behind the desk close to a double door. "Is it 'cause I'm real cute?" Something that would end as soon as they swapped back.

"Yeah, that could have something to do with it. Though I might use those pierced nipples to punish you once we're home," Caspian said with a small smile before segwaying to the desk in order to deal with a few formalities.

They were already in the dark parking lot when Gunner's phone rang, and he stilled, knowing no one called in the middle of the night, unless it was important, but his shoulders relaxed when he saw Noah's name on the screen.

"Hey, didn't Cas tell you I'm fine? You can't take my stuff," Gunner said as he picked up the call.

The silence alarmed him, sending visions of his brother beaten up and held hostage by the Brown brothers, but Noah finally spoke. "There's nothing left to take, Gun. They set your trailer on fire. I woke up to sirens. The fire is still going, but there's… there's nothing left. I've got Fluffer," he added quickly. "I'm so sorry."

Reality kept hitting Gunner's skull again and again, yet didn't seem to land a punch. He couldn't believe it. Couldn't comprehend it. He didn't have much, but the trailer had been his home for years. He had nowhere to go.

Caspian grabbed his hand and tugged him toward the truck. "Let's go!"

Chapter 27 – Gunner

Barely anything was left of Gunner's old life by the time they reached the trailer park. All the residents were up, frantically packing, in case the fire spread, or watching the firefighters deal with the damage. Gunner's place had been ground zero, but the flames had taken over several homes around it. It was over by the time the sky started to brighten.

The air still smelled of the fumes, and Gunner doubted anyone would get any sleep after waking up to face the fragility of their existence, but the reality that had burnt down didn't feel like his own anymore. His and Caspian's identities had been entangled so tightly he couldn't tell where one began and the other ended. At times, he wasn't even sure what to call himself.

But he knew for sure that Caspian was the one who'd have to live in the ruins of Gunner's life now—homeless. While Gunner could support him with the money earned on the sale of the Southfield, it wasn't his money to spend. For all they knew, Alex could call the transaction off come tomorrow, and then Caspian would be *fucked*.

Once it was clear that there was nothing left to salvage from Gunner's home, they'd ended up resting on a log set up in front of an old, charred barbeque grill by a neighbor's trailer. Deep in his self-punishing thoughts, Gunner hadn't noticed Noah's approach and flinched when a blanket dropped to his shoulders.

"I took Fluffer to my mom's," Noah said, rubbing his eyes.

It was such a relief to know that at least the cat survived. The fluffball had been with Gunner for over two years now, and Todd would find out the meaning of *war* if the pet had suffered.

Because he had no doubt that his ex-friends were behind the fire. Furious that the pair of them hadn't managed to intimidate and beat up a gay man, the arson was an expression of fury, homophobia, and a big fuck-you for the years they'd spent together. A voice at the back of Gunner's head told him that Caspian should have known some actions had bitter consequences, but the truth was that Caspian had no point of reference for this kind of situation. And while he shouldn't have outed Gunner in the first place, there was no turning back time.

Without a job or a roof over his head, Caspian was vulnerable in ways he didn't seem to understand, and if Gunner cared for him, he needed to do the right thing.

"Caspian said you had an idea for the swap? That you spoke with Madge?" Gunner said, looking up at his kid brother. It was still night time, but the horizon had already turned pink and blue.

Noah opened his mouth but didn't speak, his eyes fixed on a stretcher carried by two of the firefighters. There was a black bag on it, shaped like a person, and all three of them stilled, watching the dead body being carried away.

"Yeah. Just before—" Noah uttered and gestured at the stretcher.

Smoke filled Gunner's lungs and scratched his throat. "No…"

"Everyone else got away in time. But there was so much stuff in her trailer. She might have gotten blocked and couldn't get out."

Caspian exhaled and rubbed his face. "Shit."

Gunner had liked Madge. Sure, she was the wacky neighbor who asked uncomfortable questions and often listened to music too loudly, but she didn't deserve a death like this, through no fault of her own.

Gunner got up and handed Noah the blanket. His brother had even brought him a T-shirt he could wear for now. "Let's at least try to retrace your steps that night."

"Will it count if she's not with us?" Caspian uttered in a bland voice. "She appeared with her dog and talked to me, and we drank moonshine."

Gunner spread his arms with despair filling his heart. "I don't know. What else do we have left? Maybe if we at least found Dingo—do you know if he was in the trailer with her, Noah? And you, Cas, what else do you remember? All the details."

Noah's shoulders relaxed. "I saw him running around and whining while everything burned. He's either still here or someone had taken him in"

"We should find the dog," Caspian said, standing up somewhat shakily, as if he were in a daze.

Since it was safe, most of the residents had already gone back to their homes, so the three of them switched on the flashlight option in their phones and ventured out, determined to find Dingo. Noah managed to secure two jars of Madge's moonshine from a neighbor who was particularly fond of it, and made them pay premium for the questionable drink, but it wasn't the time to be stingy.

As they all wandered the trailer park, searching for a glimpse of orange fur, Caspian filled them in on everything that had happened on his last evening before the swap, including the panic attack outside the gym and Dingo constantly licking his hands while Madge fed him 'shine. Gunner's mind lagged at the brief mention of what caused Caspian's distress in the first place, but then shame scratched his back bloody when he realized Noah would now find out about the horrible things he'd done to Caspian. His younger brother didn't comment and just listened to the brief description of what happened in the locker room, but Gunner still cringed in silence.

Caspian spoke in a small voice, looking ahead as if he didn't want to meet anyone's eyes. "I don't remember if I said it, but I definitely thought a lot about wanting to have your body. That no one would hurt me like that if I was your size."

Gunner still didn't see affection between men as something normal in public, but despite Noah's presence, he slid his fingers between Caspian's, because that cat was out of the bag. "I could never make up for any of it. I'm sorry."

Caspian squeezed his hand, and as they faced the bushes on the edge of the trailer park, his warm fingers felt like the only thing anchoring Gunner to a world where he could become a better person.

"The longer I live in your skin, the more I grasp what you've been through," Caspian whispered.

Gunner bit his lips and nodded quickly, but he didn't want Caspian to understand. Born with a chip on his shoulder, he'd often thought that people like Caspian should try walking a mile in his shoes and fail at survival. But no one *deserved* a hard life just because the world as a whole wasn't fair. Caspian was a good person, genuine, caring, patient, and Gunner wanted him to have the best life. Loving parents, a good job, and better self-esteem, now that he'd seen his body from a new perspective. He deserved a boyfriend who wasn't a deadbeat loser.

Noah took a deep breath and moved his flashlight in a hurry. "Look. There he is."

The white beam snuck under a nearby trailer and reflected off a pair of eyes, turning them yellow, but the dog stayed quiet, as if it were still in shock after running for his life and having to leave his mistress behind. Gunner kneeled and stuck his head under the floor of the home, reaching toward Dingo as his heart beat in desperation. He needed to guide Caspian back where he belonged, even if it left him with nothing.

"Come here, boy. Don't be scared!"

Dingo made a quiet yelp and rested his orange head on his front paws, but when Gunner kept cooing, the dog started a slow, laborious crawl toward them.

Once Dingo was out, he whimpered and sat next to Gunner, licking his hands and face the moment Gunner settled his arms around the furry neck.

"I know, poor thing, I know. You'll be okay, boy." He looked up at Noah and Caspian, gently trying to pat the dog clean of the sand and dust he'd just dragged himself through. "Let's try it. Drink some moonshine, let him lick you, and make the wish."

Noah's eyes glinted in the first rays of sunlight. "Right. I can make a wish too. I want to win the lottery."

Gunner rolled his eyes. "Sure. Knock yourself out."

Caspian stalled, staring at the dog as if reality hadn't yet convinced him that going back to their own bodies was the only way forward. Their adventure had been fun while it lasted, but Caspian deserved more than Gunner's wretched existence.

And yes, he'd learned the word *wretched* thanks to Caspian.

"It probably won't work anyway," Caspian muttered but patted his thigh and whistled, prompting Dingo to follow him toward a set of benches made of concrete blocks and wood, where Gunner himself used to often sit around with his so-called friends, but the Brown brothers were likely away in order to secure an alibi, so Gunner didn't expect to see them around anytime soon.

"Still worth a shot," he said and took a few gulps of the incredibly potent alcohol before turning to see his brother with the other jar. "Noah! Don't drink it! Your mom will say it's my fault if you start puking." He frowned and was ready to wrestle for the 'shine, but Caspian was the one to take the container out of Noah's hand.

"You're seventeen. If you must drink, stick to beer."

Noah sucked in air, going red in the faint light of the upcoming morning, but he had the good sense not to argue.

Gunner met Caspian's gaze and imagined a future where it worked out between the two of them. Sleeping in the same bed. Going on picnics and to the movies. Like a normal couple. But no matter how much his heart yearned for it, he knew it was a pipe dream, so he let the liquor burn his throat again and rubbed his palm against the side of Dingo's muzzle. The dog hummed, responding to the touch by rolling his hot, damp tongue along Gunner's palm and down his wrist. And as Gunner closed his eyes, feeling the sticky trail cool, he wished with all his heart for Caspian to get his body back.

Because he was good.

Because he had a future that would be wasted on Gunner.

And because he deserved all the best things.

Caspian took two sips of the moonshine, and his handsome face twisted as he passed the jar back to Gunner. "Here goes nothing."

"Make sure to make the wish as he licks you," Gunner said even though warmth was already rushing through his head. Maybe he should have stuck to that first sip. His heart beat fast, as if fate was playing *staccato* in his chest while he watched Dingo turn his muzzle to sniff Caspian.

If this ridiculous plan worked, would they change right away, or wake up in the correct bodies in the morning, like last time? Technically, it was morning already, so would it only happen after they fell asleep?

Caspian's throat bobbed, but he extended his hand to Dingo. The dog licked his wrist in a couple of long laps, as if he were sampling the essence of who Caspian was.

"And... what now?" Noah asked in the dull silence that followed.

Caspian shrugged and put his hand on Gunner's shoulders. "We should go to sleep."

Gunner's throat felt tight, and the gentle touch on his shoulder only made it worse. "Where?"

Noah petted his head as if Gunner were *his* younger brother, not the other way around. "You can stay with me and my mom for a bit. She'll understand."

Caspian's fingers tightened on Gunner's flesh. His dark, attentive eyes focused on Gunner's face, and while he looked relaxed, shadows made the hyena tattoo seem sunken, as if the skeletal face was about to burst into tears. "I want us to stay together tonight."

Gunner was so afraid he'd fall apart that he closed his eyes and didn't utter a word.

Noah exhaled. "Right. 'Cause it's you my mom would expect anyway. You can both stay. She's got an early shift."

Caspian's chest sank, and he rose, pulling Gunner with him. "Thank you. For helping us out with this and... everything."

"Are you joking? He's my brother. He was there for me when I needed him, and I'll always be there for him too," Noah said and squeezed Gunner's arm before spinning around, as if he were afraid his face might betray too much emotion. Oh, how Gunner understood him. Living in Caspian's body gave him an excuse to express himself more, but he'd grown to enjoy it, and the perspective of going back to his real existence weighed heavily on his shoulders. But Caspian was still there for him, even if he'd be gone from Gunner's miserable life soon enough.

If this worked.

He was disgusted at a part of him that wished it would not.

Noah's home was a short drive away. They tried to stay quiet while parking in front of the pale single-storey house located in a quiet street close to the woods, but as they approached the door, it swung open, and Noah's mom, Zahra, stepped out in the black clothes she wore when working in a cafe at the mall, and a large handbag slung over the shoulder. Black box braids slipped across her shoulder when she moved her head, wary of the shadows standing in front of her home so early in the morning. But when she realized who they were, her body language relaxed.

Still, she raised her voice at Noah. "Why aren't you in your bed? Did you go out while I was sleeping?" She tugged on Noah's shirt, pulling him to the door. "We *will* talk about this once I'm back."

"It's my fault—" Caspian tried, but she glared back at him with a deep frown that pinched her round face.

"I bet it is." She wouldn't have been so stern if she knew about the fire, but there was no point in letting her know what happened when she was on her way to work. She stared at them before clicking her tongue in exasperation. "Food's in the fridge. Just don't eat from the red containers. That's for dinner," she said and rushed off to her car.

She didn't have the time to assess who Gunner was, but maybe he looked harmless enough to leave with her son and his half-brother.

Gunner would miss not being constantly perceived as a threat.

"Thank you," Caspian called out and waved at her, but she was gone two seconds later.

Since it was still quite dark, Noah switched on the light inside and invited them in with a broad gesture.

The house was small and modest, but it was always clean and smelled of Zahra's favorite spring-scented air freshener. The pale green walls of the living room were decorated with family photos and two framed posters depicting the Italian Riviera hung over a brown sofa with large potted plants on either side. The rest of the house remained dark, but Noah stepped through the nearest door, into the kitchen.

"I'm off to sleep. Do you want anything?"

"No, thanks, we're good," Gunner said, approaching the sofa. He'd stayed here enough times to know how to unfold it into a bed. "Where's Fluffer?"

Noah snorted. "On the counter by the microwave. He decided to fall asleep in the fruit basket."

Gunner exhaled, fighting off the instinct to run to his pet. This might as well be his last night in this body, and he wanted to spend it with Caspian.

Noah whistled at the dog, but Dingo stalled and stared at Gunner and Caspian with the eyes of a sage, who'd seen it all. Gunner froze, but Noah didn't seem to notice anything amiss and showed Dingo a piece of ham.

The *sage* transformed into a pet, immediately losing interest in Gunner and Caspian.

"Goodnight," Noah said before slamming the door of his room shut as soon as the dog ran inside.

Silence dawned on the living room, and Gunner rubbed his shoulders, suddenly cold.

"That was... an eventful day," Caspian muttered, gravitating closer with both hands down his pockets.

Gunner returned to setting up the bed. They'd touched and kissed since their argument, but he still wasn't sure where they stood or whether that mattered, if the dog saliva was to swap them back. "Too eventful, if you ask me."

He'd wrecked a fancy party, broken Alex's nose, got a tattoo and two piercings, argued with Caspian, got outed, outed Caspian, almost died because of a stupid Snickers bar, and was now about to sleep at Zahra's because his trailer had burned down.

Fucking mayhem.

At least he would have a sofa to sleep on until he managed to get a place of his own. Many people in his position couldn't count even on that.

The pregnant silence weighed on Gunner's shoulders, but he said nothing despite Caspian's eyes burning his back as he spread the bed sheet over the unfolded sofa.

"Can we... I mean, how big is the shower?" Caspian asked.

Gunner licked his lips, frustrated by the awkwardness between them when this could be their last morning together. He took a deep breath and turned around to face Caspian when he finished setting up the bed.

"Big enough for two."

The frown pinching Caspian's forehead relaxed. He placed his hands on Gunner's hips and pulled him in, as if this might not be the end of their dream.

"I'll give you a sponge bath," he said and flicked his finger against Gunner's swollen nipple.

Gunner chuckled, relaxing. "Dumbass. They're sensitive, okay?"

"How sensitive exactly?" Caspian leaned in, taking hold of the piercing and applying the smallest amount of pressure to the sore flesh.

"Very. Now come on." Gunner pulled on Caspian's hand, leading him toward the bathroom. "Will you keep them? If... you know, if we swap back?"

Caspian remained silent until they entered the dark room, which still smelled of the shower Zahra had taken before driving off to work. The bathroom had been designed without a shower stall, and instead had a floor that gently sloped toward the drain in the corner.

"Do you think we will actually turn? Because a dog licked us? I've gotten used to the fact that this fantastical thing happened to us, but still... wouldn't that be simply... too easy of a solution?" he asked and switched on the light.

Gunner shrugged as he peeled off his T-shirt. "We're kinda low on ideas, so magical dog it is. Who knows, maybe Noah will win the lottery too. Or did Madge's moonshine cause all this? We'll never know," he finished in a whisper.

Caspian hummed, and pulled off his top. "It just feels like déjà vu. Remember that first evening, when you convinced me we'd just wake up in our own bodies?"

Gunner didn't look his way as he undressed, flinching when the mirror showed him the tattoo he'd put on Caspian's body. Why was he such an impulsive shit? "I know, but we can only do trial and error."

Caspian shrugged, taking off his pants and socks next. "We can't tell my parents. They won't believe a word of it. So… yeah." He gave Gunner a tight smile and stretched, already naked.

Gunner hugged himself when his heart throbbed as if someone punched it. "I know I messed up for you today, but… can we be close one more time? In case we do swap back…"

Caspian shook his head and placed his hand on Gunner's cheek, with the rough thumb swiping along his lips, as if he were trying to memorize their texture. "Stop it with the apologizing. Very few things can't be undone," he said and moved toward the showerhead attached high on the wall in the other corner of the wet room. Gunner didn't know when he followed, as if the gentle hand was a leash.

How could Caspian be so calm? He'd be losing his beloved car, dealing with his parents' anger, and an unwanted tattoo all because of Gunner's thoughtless decisions, yet he was so understanding. As if Gunner deserved the second, third, and even fourth chance. It was so beyond Gunner's experience he could've cried. Nobody had been this considerate before. He was so used to fighting that he'd sometimes lash out just in case, before the other person could land the first blow.

Caspian was different. Kind. Loving. Compassionate. And a demon in bed.

Gunner took one more step and hugged him tightly, because he didn't know how to explain his emotions in words.

Caspian laughed. "I'm gonna miss this."

Words got stuck in Gunner's throat and tears stung his eyes, but then Caspian switched on the water, and the murmur of the shower replaced the uncomfortable silence.

He would miss this too. How could anyone ever compare to this guy who'd so quickly become his everything?

The water falling into his eyes gave Gunner an excuse to close them as he ran his hands up Caspian's chest, over the hard muscles and up the pecs.

"Stand back. We don't want your chest getting wet," Caspian decided and gently moved Gunner into the corner, away from the flowing water. But before Gunner could have answered, Caspian took two steps back and walked under the rain of droplets, which rolled down his muscular form in fat rivulets. He grabbed shower gel from a shelf right next to him and swiftly lathered up his chest, face, arms, as if he were in a hurry to get it done.

His body emanated strength, and while he used to resent the way it obscured the real him with bulging muscle and bold tattoos, Caspian had shown him that the strength it carried didn't have to be brutish. That was something he ought to remember for the future when he was back in the cage of his own flesh and bones. He'd let it stifle the real him in the past, but if Caspian could be both steady and wicked, maybe so could he? Maybe he too could use his strength to protect rather than lash out at whatever life threw his way.

Maybe with the ties to his toxic friends cut, and with the new outlook living in Caspian's shoes had given him, something could really change in his own? Maybe this short time would leave him with more than just the loveliest memories?

He stopped breathing when Caspian washed his cock and balls, and then rubbed his thighs in energetic swipes, but everything about those moves was utilitarian, and moments later, Caspian stepped out from under the water. The mirror had already fogged up, and moisture hung in the air, making it hot and dense. He picked up a bright orange shower gel with fruit and spices depicted on the package.

"Put both your hands on your nape."

That got Gunner's attention. He looked up into Caspian's eyes and followed the order without thinking, because letting him take charge left Gunner's shoulders light and his heart soaring. He trusted Caspian to make the right decisions when he was so prone to failing.

Caspian brushed back Gunner's damp hair and poured a generous portion of the gel into his palm before rubbing it between his hands. His dark gaze pinned Gunner to the wall before trailing lower. "That design. Did you want to make sure I never forget you?" he asked before tickling Gunner's exposed armpits.

Gunner laughed, but kept his hands in place, staring into the brown eyes watching him from the shadow of damp eyelashes. "You can get it covered with something else," he whispered even though he wished for Caspian to keep his name forever etched into skin, like Caspian's was into his heart.

His life would never be the same. And not just because he'd experienced living in someone else's shoes. Caspian showed him that real kindness and forgiveness existed. While his past set him up for failure, there were always people he could turn to for help.

"I have to think about it," Caspian said, rubbing the soap into Gunner's skin. His touch moved ever lower, past his belly button, and when he grabbed Gunner's cock and went down to his knees, staying still was no longer possible.

Gunner held his breath, closed his eyes, and focused on the slick fingers rolling his balls and prick with a gentleness that had him getting to his toes. A fire started at the base of his spine and then crawled all over, climbing his ribs and wrapping around his throat. But its hot tentacles dashed down his thighs too, and his cock stiffened.

"There I am, just helping you clean, and you're getting frisky. Such a dirty boy," Caspian whispered, staring up at Gunner while the pink dick rose, pointing at his handsome face. The big hands were in constant motion, drawing patterns all over Gunner's thighs, but it was when they settled on Gunner's ass that all and any thoughts in his head turned into vapor and leaked out into the steamy air around them.

Cooking on the inside, he looked at Caspian, already trembling, the reality outside the wet room forgotten. "I can't help myself," he rasped, confused whether he was more desperate for closeness or Caspian's mouth on his dick. But he didn't have to choose, because this moment wasn't just about pleasure. It was safe for him to let go. To be himself and *play*.

Caspian's lips stretched and as shadows danced over the lines tattooed on his face, it seemed as though his mouth became one with the hyena skull's sharp teeth. A jolt of arousal squeezed Gunner's balls when he thought about his lover's predatory instincts, but he was left to mewl as both of Caspian's hands moved, with fingers sliding into Gunner's crack and spreading the soap over sensitive skin.

"I bet. My pretty little slut."

He stirred against the fingers with a moan. "It's all your doing. I wasn't like this before." Oh, but he was. Deep inside, he'd always craved this.

Caspian grinned and blew air on Gunner's slick cock as he rubbed his fingertips over his hole, probing and teasing. It only lasted a moment, but by the time one finger dipped into the ring of muscle ever-so slightly, Gunner was ready to beg. He wanted to be on his hands and knees, taking Caspian's firm cock as many times as Caspian could get it up.

But instead of pushing the digit in farther, Caspian stepped back, leaving Gunner with an aching hard on. "Time to get all that lather off you," he said and pulled the showerhead off its attachment on the wall. "Turn around."

Gunner glanced at his needy dick, then to Caspian's growing erection. "You don't wanna—"

"Turn around."

Gunner bit his lip and did as told, unsure if the steam in the room came from the heat, or straight off his skin, because the fire coursing through his body became ever more scorching, and the droplets cascading down Gunner's back felt lukewarm in comparison. The gentle stream tickled his skin, and the fact that it was water, not hands that touched him now, stretched each second into an endless wait. But Caspian was the one in control, so Gunner bit his lip and waited while rivulets drizzled down his prick and thighs, and then snuck their way between his buttocks when Caspian opened them with one hand.

Overwhelmed by the gentle teasing, Gunner leaned forward and rested his forehead against the wall, but when the flow of water stopped, there was no certainty about what would happen next, so he stilled, breathless as all kinds of scenes played out in his mind.

Would Caspian drag him to the living room and fuck him under the covers? Would he do it here, rolling Gunner onto the wet floor? Would he—

His thoughts went awry when stubble scratched his buttock, and then Caspian's face rolled over it until his large nose dipped into the newly-washed crack.

"Oh my God..." he whimpered against the wet tiles, and arched his back as his mind blanked. In the time they'd been given so far, they'd never done *that*. He hadn't even dared to imagine that Caspian would—

He didn't have the brain power to control himself when the slick tongue teased his hole and he took his hands off his nape, to helplessly slide his palms over the tiles over and over.

Caspian was so hungry for him, and all Gunner wanted was to lie down on a silver platter and await consumption. When hot breath tickled Gunner's skin, every hair on his body bristled to attention.

Caspian exhaled, pulling Gunner's buttocks apart. He stopped moving, and the reason for it made goosebumps erupt all over Gunner's flesh. Caspian was staring at his butthole. Just watching it, while he stood with his legs parted, so very eager to give his man anything he might want. His insides felt so ready to stretch and accommodate Caspian's dick, but as embarrassing as this moment was, Gunner longed for more. To experience *everything* before unknown magic took this away from them.

Caspian started slow, as if Gunner wasn't eager enough already, but by the time he replaced his fingers with lips and tongue, Gunner's cock was so very hard he wished for something less gentle.

No such luck, because his lover seemed intent on taunting him until Gunner begged.

"Please..." Gunner uttered, with his cheek flat against the tiles.

"Please what?" Caspian teased and blew hot air at the damp skin of Gunner's crack.

That was it. There were limits to Gunner's patience, and right now, all he could think of was Caspian's thick rod spearing his hungry hole. He turned around, and just as Caspian opened his mouth in protest, Gunner pushed on his shoulders, forcing him to the floor. Technically, he didn't have enough strength to force Caspian to do anything, but the moment of surprise was enough to go through with his evil scheme.

As soon as Caspian's ass hit the tiles, Gunner straddled his hips and wrapped his arms around his thick neck, planting a kiss on his lips.

The broad mouth widened in a smile, and Caspian slapped his damp hands on Gunner's ass, making him arch at the flash of pain. "What is it, needy, greedy boy? You want my cock in your fuckhole this much? It's not like you'd die without it," he whispered and reached to the side, grabbing a bottle of baby oil Zahra probably used for her skin.

Gunner bit his lips, fighting the pinch of sadness that tainted his thoughts. He rocked against Caspian's slick fingers when they slipped against his ass. "I would," he choked out. "I'd die."

Caspian's smile froze, but he didn't pull away or chastise Gunner for reminding him of their situation.

"Come here, baby," he whispered instead, pulling Gunner's head to rest on his shoulder while he pushed one slickened finger up his hole, without any more preamble. They were both desperate for closeness, and Gunner hung his weight on Caspian's neck, then moved his legs around him and locked them behind his back.

"It'll be okay. I promise," Caspian said next and kissed his way up Gunner's throat as the digit went inside him up to the knuckle, spreading the oil.

Gunner nodded, too choked up to speak, and overwhelmed by the need to stay connected. He ran his fingertips over Caspian's nape, trying to remember every single hair, every inch of skin, because this body he knew so well was different when Caspian lived inside it. Gunner's perspective got turned on its head, and it didn't feel strange at all to make love to someone who wore his flesh. It was him, and it also wasn't.

None of it mattered when they moved as one.

Caspian pushed the bottle of oil away and must have been spreading the lubricant over his cock, because moments later, the tip pushed Gunner's buttocks apart and nudged his hole.

"Ready?" Caspian whispered, nipping on Gunner's lips, but he didn't wait for an answer and tightened his arm, holding Gunner steady as the pressure rose, until his body relaxed and let in the cockhead.

"Oh, yes..." might have slipped out of Gunner's lips when the hard dick made its way in, opening him up.

Nothing could compare to this closeness. The damp air smelled of orange and their arousal, and Gunner wished to explore every inch of Caspian's wet skin as Caspian's breath became more ragged. They moved in sync without having to discuss their needs, even though this gentle, more equal act wasn't the kind of sex they usually had.

Since Caspian sat with his legs stretched out and Gunner in his lap, impaled on the hard cock, the position wasn't made for vigorous thrusting, but now that the void inside him had been filled, Gunner felt much calmer and could think straight. He held on to Caspian with all his limbs while they moved, slowly rolling their bodies. The hard prick shifted within Gunner's body, fueling the lust burning inside him, but its flames didn't grow, keeping them both in that pleasant state of anticipation.

Caspian kept stroking Gunner's back, his arms, buttocks, he even rubbed the flesh stretching around his dick, but they were in a trance, grinding endlessly while their mouths played, passing warm air and sweet saliva until the continuous sensation teasing Gunner's prostate became too much, and his dick started twitching for attention.

He had no idea how long they lasted in the comfort of their sexual yet weirdly tender embrace, but once Caspian curled his hand around Gunner's dick, everything sped up. It only took several strokes for Gunner to whimper and clutch at Caspian's thick forearms as he came, clenching his ass over the stiff, hot prick inside him.

He writhed against Caspian, on the verge of crying, but Caspian was there to soothe him with sweet kisses and whispered words Gunner didn't hear through the blood thudding in his ears.

I love you. I love you, his whole being yelled, but he bit his lips, not daring to voice truths that would make their situation even more difficult.

He was hot, throbbing flesh, and bones made of liquid fire when Caspian repeatedly jammed his dick into him, shivering as he held on to Gunners hips. The thrusts were hard. And rough. And a wonderful contrast to the tender loving from before. By the time Caspian came, fatigue had already taken over and left them both in a mess of gasps and twitching muscle.

Caspian's cum was hot inside Gunner, and when his dick finally shrank, retreating from the tender hole, a strand of spunk rolled out, leaving a scorching trail down Gunner's balls.

Gunner closed his eyes, a boneless puppet still shivering from the intensity of the fuck, yet so safe against Caspian's wide chest. "How long can a person go without sleep?" he mumbled, already knowing they'd need one more quick shower before rolling into bed.

Caspian chuckled against him, and his stubble scratched Gunner's cheek as they kissed. "I'll take care of everything. Don't worry."

What Gunner tried to say was that falling asleep could end his time as the cute twink. That maybe if he prolonged this body swap for one more day... drank lots of coffee, had a Red Bull—-

But he was barely awake already, and the intense lovemaking had drained his energy even further, so he let destiny take its course.

Chapter 28 – Caspian

Caspian knew *it* had happened the moment he awoke.

His limbs felt light, and the presence behind his back—hot and massive, like a living shield. But he didn't want to face the reality of it just yet. So he kept his eyes closed and listened to soft footsteps followed by a muted whirring reminiscent of a kitchen mixer.

He should've been happy his life was about to go back on its usual rails. That he'd get to sleep in a comfortable home and once again talk to his parents. He'd even get to make sure they were proud of him and unfuck every single thing Gunner messed up.

But deep down, he wished to go back to sleep and wake up again, curled around the slender presence of *Gunner's* body instead of inside it, because while this body might truly belong to him, at the moment it felt stolen. But there was only so long he could pretend to still be asleep.

Even tucked between the wall and Gunner's form, he couldn't ignore the bright light shining into his face any longer. So he ripped off that Band-Aid and sat up.

Gunner groaned and rolled over to his back, but while his eyes remained closed, he was waking up too. A frown pinched his face when he stretched and ended up hitting the wall with his knuckles. His stern, masculine features were the same ones Caspian had looked at in the mirror for the past two weeks, and seeing them on someone else couldn't have felt odder.

Gunner opened one eye and stilled for half a second, but then sat up as well, patting his body as if he couldn't believe it was there.

"It worked." he stated the obvious.

He was so big, his face so masculine with strong, rigid features, and the tattoo covering half of it in a scary lineart, but despite being back in this body, Gunner no longer resembled a predator. His expression was soft, and the way he touched his massive pecs with wonder took Caspian right back to last night and the way Gunner had clung to him, asking to *be close*.

"It did," Caspian agreed, swallowing the rock forming in his throat.

Gunner wouldn't meet his eyes as he nervously scratched his nape. "Hm. So... this is weird, right?"

The old Caspian, the one from before the swap, would have never leaned in and touched Gunner's face for comfort, but the gesture had been so ingrained in him for the past few weeks, he'd done it without thinking.

Gunner glanced at him, and while they were dark brown rather than the blue he'd gotten used to, their gaze was familiar. Caspian froze and pulled back his hand, suddenly self-conscious. One look at his own chest reminded him why it was throbbing. Gunner's name was still etched into his reddened skin in bold black letters, and the metal balls squeezed his nipples like tiny torture devices. But while those additions made his appearance edgier, he no longer was the man Gunner wanted.

He was embarrassing himself by trying to comfort Gunner in a way that had felt so natural only yesterday. If he was to survive this day, his focus should be on keeping his shit together.

It was strange to sit next to this Gunner without it triggering a fight or flight response, but when Caspian took in his broad form now, all he could see was the man who'd craved his support and apologized for fucking up. The man who'd barely had a handle on his life, confused, in the closet, and constantly getting in trouble.

Gunner licked his lips, moving to the edge of the bed. At least both of them were wearing underwear, since this sofa bed wasn't a private space. "Do you need help removing those?" he muttered and pointed to Caspian's nipple.

Caspian cleared his throat. He wanted to say something funny and turn it all into a joke, but voice got stuck in his throat, and he shook his head instead, faking a smile. "Nah. I kind of dig this look. And it's not like clients are gonna see it under my ironed T-shirts, right?" he asked and joined Gunner on the edge of the bed, painfully aware of how much they differed in terms of size.

And the strangest thing was that when he looked at his slim legs dusted with just a bit of hair next to Gunner's tree trunk-like thighs, he no longer felt self-conscious. Yes, he was smaller. Yes, he'd never grow into the kind of hulking man Gunner was, but after seeing his own form as an outsider, he realized that there wasn't anything wrong with it. It was as if a deforming film had been peeled off his eyes, allowing him to see who he was.

He wasn't ugly, and never had been.

"Yeah? You gonna be that secret threat at the office? Undercover motherfucker." Gunner snorted as he got up, and towered over Caspian.

"Yeah, I think—I think things will change for me," Caspian said. His confused instincts told him to step closer and put his arms around Gunner's midsection. He no longer saw himself as unattractive, but Gunner wasn't into small guys. He wanted to be one himself, and regardless of Caspian's secret desire, he didn't want to make things between them any weirder.

So he stayed where he was and tried to focus on Gunner's face rather than his body.

"I'm sorry about the trailer. And your friends. I really messed up."

Gunner looked around for his jeans, because Caspian had been the one to take them off last night, but he'd found them before Caspian could have pointed out where they were. Just like he'd have to manage everything else without Caspian from now on.

"I guess they never were my friends in the first place. I'm really sorry about the tattoo. I wanted to retaliate, but it's permanent, and I wasn't thinking straight."

Caspian shrugged. "It's fine. It's just a tattoo. At least I'll have something to remember this crazy time by, right?" he asked with a small chuckle that left a scratch in his throat.

Don't fall apart. Don't fall apart. Don't fall apart.

"And you'll look like a badass at the boxing lessons. You'll still come by, right?" Gunner asked, and despite standing there, six-foot-five and so broad in the shoulders, Caspian could now see the vulnerability in his brown eyes. Gunner might have changed on the outside, but he was still shy in romantic matters, had few friends, liked fruity shampoo and classical music. Still, his exterior inevitably affected how people perceived him, and his sensitive side was in direct opposition to his appearance.

Gunner needed help reinventing himself, and Caspian would be there for him, no matter how awkward spending time together might prove.

"Yes. And I'll pay you for your time, of course. Do you—" He remembered last night's fire, and his heart tightened a bit when Gunner approached the windowsill and picked up Fluffer, who must have walked over there as they slept. The cat let out a little meow and rubbed his forehead against Gunner's when he leaned in toward it.

Caspian's heart tightened with longing, wishing Gunner would do the same with him, but it wasn't his place to make such demands anymore.

"I mean—do you have a place to stay? I know this is your family, but it's because of me that you lost your home."

"You did what you did, but it's not exactly your fault Todd's a pyromaniac psycho gay-hater." Gunner sighed deeply and kissed Fluffer on the forehead as the cat stretched, resting its paws on Gunner's shoulder. "Noah's mom will let me stay here for a bit, I'm sure. And then I'll sort something out. It's not like I'll need privacy to bring anyone over for a while."

The thought of Gunner going off to find a new lover hit Caspian like a red-hot poker in the eye. He had no right to feel jealous, because they weren't together, and the lust they'd shared had been caused by the crazy change in their bodies. But when he thought of some stranger climbing on top of Gunner—touching him, kissing him, clutching at the short hair at the top of his head—his brain went up in flames so scorching he could no longer think straight.

He didn't want to think about it.

And in fact, it was time for him to go.

Paws tapped against the floor, and Dingo came in, watching them with brown eyes that didn't look more intelligent than any other dog's. And yet, he'd been the one to fulfill their wishes, like a fucked-up version of a genie, one without a bottle and with way more fur.

Caspian needed to get out of here before he went crazy.

Gunner watched him intently, but remained physically distant, as if the air between them was too dense for walking through. "And um... Can I do anything for you? Like... go tell your parents it was somehow my fault? That I gave you drugs or something? You can throw me under the bus, I don't mind."

It hurt Caspian to even think about it, and he shook his head. "No. I want to stay in touch," he said softly and pushed his feet into the lavender-hued trainers Gunner had gotten during that first shopping trip with Alexander.

He might not feel like the cute, twinky style Gunner had adapted during his brief time in Caspian's body was *him* but had to admit that the new clothes Gunner purchased fit him much better than the plain, baggy stuff that still filled his wardrobe. It might take a while, but

Caspian would eventually find himself somewhere between the somber style he used to prefer and the youthful, colorful clothes Gunner favored.

Noah's head popped out of the kitchen, and he walked into the living room with a large smoothie in hand when he saw neither of them was naked. "So it worked."

Gunner smiled. "It did. Have you won the lottery yet?"

Noah's face soured. "No, still poor. Are you staying for lunch?" he asked Caspian. "Wow, this is so weird. I keep seeing you as Gunner."

Caspian did want to stay, but when Gunner looked at him in a way that felt all-too-familiar, he knew he might not keep himself together unless he ran. So he shook his head and shoved his hands into his pockets. "Thanks, but I need to talk to my mom and dad. I have your number, Gun."

Gunner finally met his eyes. "I'll make sure to delete your browser history." He winked, but Caspian could sense the awkwardness for miles, so with stiff knees and shoulders, he went straight for the door.

***

"So it was meds? All of it?" Dad asked, staring at Caspian with brows lowered to shadow his eyes. It was a peaceful Sunday, and while Caspian knew he'd have to personally apologize to all the guests who'd seen Gunner's outburst at yesterday's party, his parents seemed to have brought the situation under control. He couldn't feel sorry for something he hadn't done, but the sense of shame was still there.

"I'm sorry. I forgot I'd already taken one tablet, took another one, and it made me so agitated. And when Alex—I

394 | Take My Body

wanted to eventually tell you. But not like that, in front of everyone, and I just snapped."

Mom sipped coffee from her favorite mug. "Oh. So that part was true?" she asked, and her inquisitive gaze bore into him with the force of a drill. "Wait. Is this related to that man who'd brought you home drunk? Tell us, Caspian. Was it *meds* or *drugs*?"

Caspian's shoulders dropped as he breathed in the fresh air seeping into the bright, elegant living room through a window larger than the shower stall in Gunner's burned-down trailer. Life really wasn't fair.

"It's meds. I got nervous about all those changes, and that's why—" He exhaled and looked at them again, because he didn't want to remove Gunner out of his life. In one way or another, he'd always be someone important. And while Caspian could never have Gunner the way he wanted, he needed to make sure his friend was welcome here. "He had nothing to do with this. Gunner's a really good guy, deep down."

Dad frowned, and Caspian cringed at him, connecting the dots in his head. "That man, Gunner. Did he seduce you into this? We all experiment when we're young. It's okay—"

Caspian stood up. "No."

In fact, it had been the other way around.

Sweat beaded on Caspian's back, but it felt good to speak more plainly about things that were so important. "No, I've had... partners at university. Gunner and I... we reconnected when I got back. He might look like a thug, because he's been through a lot, but he's trying really hard to turn his life around."

Mom raised her hand. "Okay, okay, no need to raise your voice. So... Is *he* your boyfriend?"

Caspian swallowed the anger buzzing inside him when he remembered how wary his parents had been when he'd brought Gunner here some time ago. It still hurt. "You are so judgmental. You think you're not, but you are. So he has a tattooed face. And his dad was a criminal, and he dropped out of high school, but he really cares for people. Just yesterday, he took me to the ER after I had peanuts!"

It had been the other way around, but he was so confused about where he started and where Gunner began at this point that it didn't seem to matter.

Dad got to his feet, eyes wide. "Why did you have peanuts? You know you're not supposed to have them! Caspian!"

"I was upset after the argument with Alex and ate a cake without checking the label. But he was there, and he— took care of me," Caspian muttered, dropping back into the armchair, weighed down by his parents' scrutiny.

Mom rubbed her forehead, flushed behind her mug. "Okay, so, is this Gunner person a serious boyfriend?"

It was well-intentioned and softly-spoken, but the question still felt like a punch in the gut. Caspian swallowed and shook his head, his heart like a ball of lead dragging him to the bottom of a dark ocean. "We—we split up."

In that moment, he knew that he'd never get over his regret.

Tears filled his eyes all too quickly and spilled down his cheeks. He'd fallen for Gunner so fast, so intensely, but their relationship had been built on the foundation of snow that had now melted.

Mom reached him within half a second and pulled him into a hug. "Oh, honey, I'm so sorry. We had no idea what was going on with you."

Sinking into her arms was relief, but the embrace couldn't soothe the pain of knowing that he'd never get to hold Gunner again. Maybe his heart would cover the thorn there with hardened tissue, but it would always remain there, stuck with him for the rest of his life.

Chapter 29 – Gunner

This was worse than detox. Gunner had no idea he'd become addicted to Caspian's presence, but a week later, he was starved for his touch, craving Caspian's attention, and an overall mess of a human being. It didn't help that he'd been uprooted from his home, and his so-called friends had all turned their backs on him. A few acquaintances still talked to him at the gym, but Gunner was well aware that his life would be very different from now on.

He wasn't about to roll over and show his soft underbelly to just anyone, but he didn't want to be the old Gunner either, and planned to make amends for the shitty things he'd done in the past.

If he was to clean up his act, the first step was to bite the bullet and have a serious chat with Snowman. Whether he liked it or not, the unsavory business he was now attempting to escape had funded the debt payments, so there had to be a way to go around it. He felt like a fool even hoping for such miracles, because no one cared about his personal problems when money was involved, but there was no shame in asking.

He could only ignore reality for so long, so he promised Zahra he'd pick up some cookies from the amateur baker who lived at the trailer park and ventured out of her home, followed by Dingo.

Gunner was surprised Snowman hadn't knocked on his door already, but maybe the cokehead had enough decency left in him to give Gunner a few days' slack following the fire. He presumed the kindness wouldn't come cheap, but he didn't want to look as though he was avoiding the issue.

With a cigarette in hand, Gunner leaned down to pet Dingo's head when the dog whined, staring toward his former home, as if he could still smell his mistress. "I know, I know, Madge had you for many years— How old are you anyway?" He frowned, wondering how this strange magic worked. He and Caspian had swapped twice already, but Noah hadn't been granted the lottery win. Gunner had experimented with drinking Madge's alcohol in case that was the trigger, but he hadn't gotten his wish either.

Dingo barked at him and dashed forward, greeted by the brilliant laughter of two small boys playing in front of one of the trailers. A part of Gunner worried the children might accidentally wish on something and get stuck in a situation they couldn't comprehend, but Madge had never restrained her dog, so he left Dingo with the children and approached the gray box-like building close to the gate.

Snowman's office was at the back, but as he passed the windows of the administrator's quarters, one of them opened, and Phyllis's bright blonde head peeked out. "There you are! We need to talk about next month's rent!"

"Rent? My trailer's burned down," Gunner muttered, facing her with a deep frown, but Phyllis didn't miss a beat and raised a cigarette to her wrinkled mouth.

"It's still taking up space on my property. If you want to leave, you'll have to remove what's left of your home and clear the slot."

"You've got to be fucking kidding me—"

Gunner let Mozart play in his mind, because he'd vowed to become a better person, and violence wasn't the way to achieve that. He needed to control his impulsive behavior, because the last time he let himself go, his attack on Alex had almost ruined Caspian's life. And while Phyllis was being heartless, it was her right to demand payment for the services she provided, so he took a deep breath and, much calmer, met her gaze.

"I'll work something out. Is Snowman in?"

"I'm not his mother," she said and shut the window without saying goodbye.

Typical.

Gunner rubbed his face, adjusted his T-shirt to make it tidier, and walked around the building to find the office on the other side open.

Snowman looked up from behind his desk, as if some sixth sense told him he had a visitor. "Gunner! Long time no see," he said and pulled a folder off a giant pile next to him.

"Hey, I came to let you know I wasn't dodging you. It's just that with the fire, and the… general situation… you know how it is sometimes." He took a long drag of smoke, but the fire had reached the filter already. He really needed to quit. The habit was bad not only for his health but also his already-thin wallet.

Snowman stared at him and dropped the folder before swiping back the wispy hair covering the flushed skin at the top of his head. "Why? You missed me or something?"

Gunner put the cigarette out in Snowman's overflowing ashtray and stuffed his hands into his pockets, ignoring the stale scent of the half-eaten burger resting on a plate by the edge of the desk. "My payment. I'll get you something next week, okay?"

Snowman's eyes narrowed, red as if he badly needed to see a doctor about pinkeye. "Are you fucking with me, Russo? You've been acting real strange lately."

"No, I'm serious. I'm out of work, but I should be able to get some cash by the end of the week." He spread his arms for emphasis, because his patience was running thin.

Snowman leaned back and pulled at the front of his sweaty shirt, peeling it from his skin. "Are you on crack again? You already sent a guy. The debt's been cleared."

Gunner stared at him with the confusion of a drowning man who'd just realized his feet touched ground. "What? Who?" He knew the answer the moment his lips uttered the question.

Snowman exhaled and poured himself some coffee from a glass jug with lots of ice cubes floating on the surface and chugged half of the mug in one go. "This small guy. Short. With pink shoes."

They were *lavender*. Not that such details mattered when Caspian had taken the massive burden chaining Gunner to his circumstances off his shoulders.

Just like that, without asking for anything in return. Just because he could.

"S-so, we're good?" Gunner asked, fighting the tremble in his voice.

Snowman sighed. "Don't know what you did for that guy, but my lips are sealed. If you ever need more cash, my boss will gladly lend to you, since you've been so good about paying up this time."

Wow, so his credit score with drug dealers was on the rise. All thanks to Caspian.

Gunner left the building in stunned silence.

Two years—that was how long he'd been saddled with this burden. He'd taken it on to help the only family he had left, but the interest was so high he lost hope of ever paying the whole sum off.

He couldn't believe he was free. So his plans for the future were tentative at best, but he could actually breathe now, and reconsider his options.

His mind whirled with a thousand thoughts. His first impulse was to call Caspian and ask him about everything. From why he chose to pay off the debt, to why he kept the cute sneakers, but if Caspian didn't bother to tell him about the money, maybe he didn't want to keep in touch?

What if this was a way for Caspian to cut ties without feeling guilty about it? The closeness they'd experienced during their unusual relationship had been intense, but back in his own body, in his nice home, with his nice parents, and nice job, Caspian likely wanted to distance himself from that crazy period in his life. And from Gunner. Could it be that he no longer cared? After all the things they did with each other?

Gunner's face flushed with heat at the memory of Caspian holding him by the ears as he face-fucked him.

But that had happened in a different life. A life within a dream that was over and would never cloud their minds again.

Gunner was now free to start his life over. Get an honest job. Move somewhere safer. Never have to see Todd's fucking face.

But he didn't know where to start. His life choices had always been about responding to other people's actions, and now, faced with the freedom to forge whatever path suited him, he had no idea where to turn.

Caspian was so put-together in comparison. Thoughtful and smart, he was a man Gunner had learned to admire in their short time together. But while Gunner knew it would be best for them to stay apart, the Caspian-sized hole in his heart was there to stay. It might eventually stop bleeding, but the scars would forever be a reminder of the happiest time in Gunner's life.

Gunner once more itched to grab the cell phone and make the call. He wasn't too proud to take the money if Caspian had chosen to gift it to him, but such kindness should be repaid with words of gratitude at least.

With a strong conviction to contact him later in the day, Gunner whistled at Dingo and hurried back to Zahra's, because he'd promised to give Noah a ride to work. He could look at job offers at the mall. His ink shouldn't be an issue in a stockroom. And if there weren't any vacancies, he could ask Tiamat at the tattoo shop if they needed anyone for maintenance and clean-up. Gunner would take any position at this point, as long as it didn't push him back into crime.

Perhaps the universe had caused the body swap to help Caspian understand his worth, but Gunner learned a lot too, and he wasn't about to fuck things up again.

But what did he know of leading an honest life? He'd never had a regular job, and his brief life in Caspian's skin proved that he didn't know how to behave among *normal* people. He crossed unwritten boundaries without realizing, and would surely get himself kicked out of any job he might find. But what then? What if he met Caspian in town and revealed himself as a failure?

Just the thought of it had him breaking out in cold sweat.

"The truck's so much cleaner now," Noah said from the passenger seat, pulling Gunner out of his thought jumble just as they arrived at the mall. "You think you'll be able to keep that up?"

Gunner rolled his eyes. "Ha. Ha. So funny. I had more important shit to do than clean." Though in truth, his truck had ended up looking like a hoarder's dream because he'd been too lazy to clean or forgot to do it. Caspian left the truck in better condition than it had been on the day Gunner purchased it second-hand. He'd even managed to get the transmission to run smooth-ish.

Was there anything this guy couldn't do? Unlike Gunner, Caspian planned things, and didn't get so easily frustrated, so he must have found a solution and applied it with the same ease he'd cleaned crumbs from Gunner's car seat. Caspian managed to take care of him even without being there. The vehicle would eventually become messy again, and the pine-scented air freshener would hang off the rearview mirror after losing its smell, but the debt

Caspian had paid off for Gunner had been dealt with for good.

A parting gift.

Was it guilt that had prompted Caspian to deal with the debt, or did he still have feelings for Gunner? Like that time he'd covered Gunner's eyes, so cum wouldn't get into them. That had been so thoughtful.

"Gun, come on, we only have an hour before I start my shift, and I wanna get a sandwich."

"When I had his body, people didn't stare at me, you know?" Gunner said, sighing as he took a final glance into the rearview mirror. His left eye glinted, as if it belonged to a hyena, but he shook his head and stepped out of the truck, because some things couldn't be overcome with Caspian's money, and he needed to face reality at some point.

Noah licked his lips and approached him. "Is that why you've been so quiet on the way here? That's what you've been thinking about?"

Gunner shrugged. "Yeah, everything's different now. It's hard to get used to it."

"I mean, the tattoo is a bit of a bummer, but they're always looking for staff here. Try the notice board by the photo booths?"

His baby brother stuffed his hands into his pockets and looked ahead as a young woman went out of her way to avoid walking too close to Gunner. It was easiest to pretend neither of them noticed, but shit like this happened to Gunner all the time. It was hard to not take such things personally after the brief time in a non-intimidating body.

"Let's get your sandwich first, it's on me." Gunner forced a smile and ruffled Noah's curls.

He should've been happy. His heaviest burden, the thing that had kept him in chains, was now gone. And yet he'd never felt so lost.

He'd lived in Caspian's flesh for three weeks, but he was starting to think there was no going back from that experience. It had showed him there was more to life than survival and violence, but every gaze frightfully sliding off him proved that most people wouldn't give someone like him, with a tattooed face and bulging muscles, the benefit of the doubt and a chance to prove himself. He had no education, no skills other than boxing, and was currently wearing his only surviving T-shirt.

Noah whistled and nudged Gunner with his elbow as they approached one of the cafés. "Rolling in cash, huh?"

"It's not funny. I... I actually just found out Caspian paid off my debt." It sounded so simple when said like that. As if this didn't change both his and Noah's life for good.

Noah grabbed Gunner's shoulder and stepped in front of him, brown eyes wide. "No way! What the fuck? That's insane!"

Gunner chuckled. "Guess I gave good head, huh?" The dirty joke made him flush, because he was still getting accustomed to his brother knowing about his sexuality. But, damn, it felt so good to be open about this.

Noah wouldn't stop laughing, his smile so wide and pristine. "So what? You're his sugar baby now?"

"It's not like that. I told you we're not... you know, we're just *not* anymore. It's different now. I'm pretty sure he wants to move on with his life."

Noah frowned. "Come on, Gun! No one donates thousands of dollars to get on with their life. Have you actually talked to him since... *you know*?" he asked, pushing

Gunner at a bench adjacent to a decorative platform made up to look like a deserted island, complete with a fake palm tree and sand.

"Not yet. He's probably very busy with his new job and shit. He's like... really smart, and needs to unfuck everything I did." Gunner pulled on his thumb in frustration as his gaze drifted to the piano, where he'd first met Alexander Fuckface. Was there a chance that his *soul*, or whatever had travelled between him and Caspian, still remembered how to play? He'd been too afraid to check so far, but the vacant bench by the instrument tempted him even when he ignored its call and focused on Noah.

"Don't say that! Gunner, are you blind? This guy likes you. And I mean that he's *into you*," Noah said and dropped next to Gunner.

"He was into a tiny cutie with big blue eyes. So even if he still likes me as a friend, he doesn't—" Pain speared Gunner's heart as if it had been stabbed with an ice pick. "Fuck. Why are you making me talk about it?"

Noah rolled his eyes and grinned. "'Cause I don't have a love life? Mom's TV broke down, so how else am I to entertain myself?"

Gunner shook his head, once again looking toward the piano. "You're such a little shit."

Noah must have noticed where his attention went, because he pointed at the instrument. "Try playing. You knew how to when you were in his body. Let's see if your brain still remembers."

Gunner's back covered in goosebumps, but he wasn't a coward and wouldn't back down from a challenge. Yet as he neared the piano, worry snuck its way under his skin and whispered that he was being watched, and that every single person passing by knew he didn't belong behind the gorgeous instrument. That he was a brainless chunk of muscle no one wanted around. Still, he hovered his fingers over the black and white keys and tried not to panic when he realized how thick and inelegant they were.

But Noah was close, so Gunner swallowed his fear and sat, placing both hands on the keyboard. The speakers, which so far blasted pop songs, went quiet, as if leaving space for him to make music, but as the air thickened in his throat, he couldn't help but feel out of place with his sausage-like digits resting on the smooth keys.

Closing his eyes, Gunner shut out the white noise around him and remembered the first piece of music he'd played in Caspian's home. The desire to bring the beautiful melody to life kindled deep in his chest, but while he remembered its sound by heart, his hands remained still, like dead weights that couldn't recognize why they were on the keyboard in the first place.

The sound system came back to life, roaring about a sale in the department store, but the speaker's cheerful voice beat Gunner down farther.

He should have never touched the piano.

It wasn't for someone like him.

He pressed a few of the keys in hope that their sound would spark his memory, but he couldn't *remember* someone else's life and experience.

"You can't do it?" Noah whispered, as if he were afraid that he might shatter Gunner by talking too loudly.

A part of Gunner had stupidly hoped that if all else failed, he could try his hand at becoming a piano teacher. A pipe dream that could never come true now.

He shook his head, too choked up to speak, but set on not crying in public. Or at all.

That was it. He'd never play again, because he was a dumb ogre who hadn't even finished high school. Jobless. Homeless. With a murky past and no friends.

Without the man who made him feel so many things and took care of him.

His life was worthless.

"Look, I shouldn't have asked. Let's have lunch, okay?" Noah tried, pulling on Gunner's arm.

"He hasn't even texted," Gunner uttered, hunching his shoulders to keep the dark void inside him from spreading. "But I don't want to call first and bother him, you know?"

"He did pay your debt. What if he did it to give you a reason to call?" Noah asked, resting his hands on his hips.

"I should probably give back that money, but I'm in no position to reject it."

"Gunner. You've been taking care of me, helping Mom, and you even borrowed all that cash so I could get good treatment and physio. If you hadn't done it, I'd be limping and living with constant pain. I'm pretty sure you deserve to be treated for once. You don't have to do everything yourself."

Gunner chewed on that with sorrow squeezing his heart every time he glanced at the keyboard. "So you think it would be okay if I called him?"

Noah spread his arms. "Are you blind? I know it might be awkward now that both of you changed, but he does like you. Otherwise, the two of you wouldn't have been spending all that time together."

There were sexual matters Gunner wouldn't discuss with his seventeen year old brother, but he craved contact with Caspian too much to let go.

He took a deep breath. "Okay, I'll call him."

But when he pulled out his phone, it rang.

Caspian.

Chapter 30 – Caspian

Caspian's hands were sweating so much he might've considered rehydrating before the loss of moisture made his head spin. Gunner was coming over. Finally.

On the day they woke in their own bodies, they had decided to keep meeting up. He was meant to get boxing lessons that he even wanted to pay for, but his phone remained silent.

For a day, then two, then a week.

It hadn't seemed like that big of a deal at first, since he'd been so eager to reconnect with his parents and make amends for the things Gunner unwittingly messed up, but as time went on, it occurred to him that maybe Gunner had changed his mind about the whole thing. Maybe he wanted to move on, or didn't have the time to contact Caspian when so much of his life had ended up in pieces, but his silence had gnawed at Caspian even deep in the night, when he lay in bed, trying to remember how it felt to spoon Gunner from behind.

Things had changed since they'd last lain together. Gunner was no longer the cute, compact twink, and Caspian no longer had the broad chest Gunner used to curl up into, but the longing for the familiar touch was still there, like an infected wound at the back of Caspian's mind.

He'd driven by to check on Gunner but didn't trust himself to knock on his door. He'd *almost* sent out a dozen flirty messages, and tried to distract himself with his new job, but it was hopeless.

So he'd called and they had an incredibly awkward conversation. But Gunner had accepted the invitation to come over as it would make more sense to talk in person. When he'd mentioned it to his parents, they insisted they wanted to treat Gunner to dinner for saving Caspian's life by taking him to the ER. Caspian only agreed to all four of them having dinner together once Mom and Dad promised to keep their lips sealed about knowing of their relationship. But by the time their guest knocked on the door, he still wasn't sure if that was a good idea.

"Will you let him in, honey? We're busy in the kitchen," Mom said, but Caspian knew his parents wanted to give him and Gunner some privacy, and he wasn't entirely sure whether he was glad or about to have a panic attack. He glanced into the large mirror in the foyer and smoothed back the blond hair, which fit his coloring so well he hadn't yet decided what to do about it. He might have lived in Gunner's body for less than a month, but that brief time had changed everything, and while he wouldn't have been caught dead in the kind of cutesy, tight clothes

Gunner liked to wear, seeing his own form as an outsider convinced him that fitted clothes were the way to go. The emerald green pullover he was sporting tonight not only brought out his eyes but also accentuated the shape of his torso.

He looked good.

Not Gunner-would-have-eaten-him-up good, but definitely attractive. There was no reason to feel embarrassed in the presence of a man who had quite literally inhabited his body just over a week ago.

So Caspian manned up and opened the door, only to have his knees weaken a little. Not because he was all of a sudden attracted to buff guys twice his size, but because it was *Gunner*. While the eyes he saw in the handsome face were brown instead of blue, they reflected everything they'd done with each other, and every tender word they'd shared.

But they weren't a good fit anymore, no matter how much he wanted to throw Gunner over the shoulder and show him that he could still be the same guy.

"Hey," Gunner said in that low rumble of a voice, and scratched his chin, no longer intimidating, despite his size or the ink.

Caspian exhaled and took in Gunner's simple look of blue jeans worn with a white T-shirt. It had the faint rectangular creases that betrayed he'd just taken the top out of its packaging.

A lump got stuck in Caspian's throat, so he stepped aside, trying to gather his courage. "Welcome. It's been a while."

Gunner walked past him, and the banana & raspberry shampoo scent he carried with him triggered so many filthy memories Caspian held his breath in stunned silence.

"Yeah, I kinda thought you gave up on me. That this whole thing was just too weird."

Something inside Caspian balked at the accusation, but he calmed down by the time the door was once again locked. The air smelled of the meat roasting in the oven, but its familiar, homey aroma wasn't enough to soothe the storm raging inside him. "I mean… you said you wanted to give me boxing lessons, but you just lost your home, so I didn't want to bother you."

Gunner smiled and ruffled his hair as if they were buds not ex-lovers. "Just teasing. I was about to message you when you called."

Caspian's lips twitched, and while he didn't appreciate other people infantilizing him, he enjoyed the brief touch. "Someone had to make the first move. It's not like anyone else can understand what I've been through."

"No. No one would." Was that a faint flush on Gunner's tan skin, or was Caspian imagining things? "I got this for your parents…" Gunner held up a bottle of wine.

A part of Caspian was impressed Gunner was thoughtful enough to bring a small gift for his hosts, but another cringed over him feeling obliged to spend the little money he had on the present.

"They will really appreciate this." Such insignificant small talk, but the things Caspian truly wanted to say should be left unspoken.

Caspian no longer considered his body a hindrance when it came to dating, but it was painfully clear that he wasn't Gunner's type, and he needed to live with that, no matter how much he yearned for the messy guy who'd taught him so many things during their brief relationship.

"Are you sure they wanna meet me?" Gunner whispered, and it was time to admit why Caspian had invited Gunner instead of meeting him someplace else.

While Caspian had been craving to see him for reasons he wouldn't speak of, they were still friends, and he was set on pulling Gunner out of the tight spot he was in. Because Gunner deserved a helping hand.

Caspian cleared his throat and stepped closer, amazed that the hulking guy who was so much taller and broader than him smelled of the same shampoo the twinky Gunner had.

"They know you helped me when I ate peanuts, and they want to thank you, since you saved my life."

Gunner chuckled and bit his lip. "Only that I didn't. It was all you."

Caspian shrugged and winked at Gunner. "Tomato, potato, what's the difference, right?"

"Everything got kinda mixed up... But at least I came out of the whole experience knowing some Latin. Did you plant a dead rat in the car when Alex took it?"

Caspian chuckled and squeezed Gunner's shoulder, stealing a touch like some lecher. "It's not worth it. I'm actually happy I got rid of it. It was a beautiful car, but the truth is I don't need to have it right now, and the money went to something much more urgent and important," he said and met Gunner's gaze, wondering if he'd already found out that Caspian had paid off his debt, or if he'd have to tell him.

A month ago, he would have called his own actions crazy. He'd arguably been forced to sell the Southfield for a fraction of its value in order to appease Alexander. But the fact that he'd spent most of the money he'd gotten for it on the man who caused the whole mess made him a clown. He was at peace with that.

His time in Gunner's body had been short, but it had made the helplessness of the man's situation abundantly clear. A good person at his core, Gunner had fought a losing battle against the system and people around him since childhood. If Caspian could take some of that burden off his shoulders, he was determined to do so.

The truth was that he didn't need the money. Sure, had he kept it, he could have gotten a nicer car as a replacement, but he wouldn't have become homeless or hungry even if Alexander had taken the Southfield without paying anything. Gunner, on the other hand, might have fallen right back into crime, were he not offered help.

So that was what Caspian was going to do. He might not have a future at Gunner's side, but still had feelings for him, still knew they'd stay close forever, and he couldn't have lived with himself if he left the massive financial burden on Gunner's shoulders, when he had the means to deal with it.

It only now struck him that Gunner might take his gesture the wrong way and storm off, slighted by the charity, but he stood his ground and smiled.

Gunner kept his gaze for a while. "I'm sorry I didn't thank you yet. It's just so much money. I didn't know how to say it. I really hope it's not 'cause you felt obligated—"

Caspian grabbed his hand and squeezed it, his heart thumping. "No. I did it because I saw that you're in a bad situation and deserve help. You're my friend, and I want to do this. But let's keep that between us, all right?" he asked, because his parents surely would have balked at him giving away so much money when it could have gone toward something they considered sensible.

Gunner held on to the slender hand as if he were drowning. "Yes. We'll stay friends, right?"

"Do you want to stay *here*?" Caspian asked, because this was one of the reasons why he'd invited Gunner in the first place. It was his fault Gunner was now homeless, and it only made sense to offer him a comfortable bed to sleep in until he was back on his feet.

Gunner cocked his head in a manner painfully reminiscent of the way he acted while in Caspian's body. Even his squint was the same. "What?"

"As in, in our guest room. Sleeping on the sofa can't be comfortable in the long run, and it really is the least we could do," Caspian said as heat burned his cheeks.

Gunner slipped his hand out of Caspian's grip. "No, thanks, but, no, that's too much. And your parents live here. It would be awkward. I couldn't."

The floor was crumbling under Caspian's feet. "But my parents already agreed. And they're out for most of the day."

"No, really, you already did too much for me. But thank you. I need to take care of myself."

But he didn't. Every fibre of Caspian's being craved to take over and ensure Gunner was safe and comfortable. One step at a time, though.

"We can talk about this again later. I'm sure Mom and Dad are waiting for us already," Caspian said and cleared his throat, leading the way past the home office and into the bright dining room, which also served as Mom's green space and was filled with all kinds of potted plants and flowers arranged on shelves.

Mom was fantastic at making people feel welcome, and while Caspian expected awkwardness, the meet-and-greet went smoothly, even though the ice-breaker had been a joke at his expense about the time Gunner had brought him home drunk. Caspian wouldn't complain as long as it made Gunner feel more comfortable.

Caspian was intent on showing Gunner that he wouldn't be a burden for them if he stayed for a while. Without the pressure to take the first job available, he'd get to think through what he wanted to do with his future, not just survive. After a lifetime of not being given a fair chance, this was what Gunner deserved. A fresh start.

"You won't believe how patient this guy is," Caspian said, gesturing at Gunner while they ate his dad's signature tiramisu two hours later. "When I was trying to make changes to my wardrobe and went on that big shopping spree, he just walked with me and carried all bags so I could comfortably browse. And not a single complaint."

Gunner laughed and hid half his face with the massive hand. At least the wine seemed to relax him a bit. "It's not a big deal, I was happy to help."

The cake fork looked so tiny in his chunky fingers, and Caspian would have lied if he said he didn't miss being the big guy, but his size no longer made him feel inadequate.

Gunner was still the same person, with the same needs and a gentle personality hidden inside the rock-hard shell of muscle. If it weren't for Gunner's preferences, Caspian would have picked up where they'd started in a heartbeat. Now that he knew who Gunner really was, every single thing he did, even in this large, strong body, was too cute for words and made Caspian's heart melt. The desire to take care of him was still there, and Caspian wouldn't let go of it regardless of Gunner's pride.

"Actually, didn't you just lose a worker after he behaved inappropriately toward the bridesmaid at that wedding last weekend?" Caspian asked, glancing at his mother across the table.

There. Everyone had loosened up, and it was the perfect time to bring up another reason why he'd wanted Gunner to come over and show his parents that he wasn't a dumb brute.

Mom picked up on the cue with a smile. "Yes. Gunner, Caspian mentioned you're looking for a job right now, and you're strong and handy. Would you like a trial run with us? There's a lot of little odd jobs in event organizing..."

Say yes, say yes.

Gunner stilled with the fork in his mouth and took a moment to swallow. "Oh. I don't know if I'm what people wanna see at their wedding, or conference, or—" he mumbled and pointed to his face with an awkward smile.

Mom shook her head before Caspian could have butted in. "Nonsense. I'm not offering you a job at the reception, so it won't be an issue. But strong men are always needed to help with decorating, moving things, minor carpentry, and so on."

Gunner seemed lost, so Caspian smiled at him in encouragement.

"What do you think? I know you like doing practical things, and even if you end up finding something better in a while, why not try this for now? All the people who work for Mom are really friendly, and customers have different requests, so you'd be doing a variety of jobs," he said, trying not to sound pushy, even though he knew that Gunner should say yes to this. Because he was right about his tattoos putting him at a disadvantage when job-hunting no matter how unfair that was.

Gunner gave a slow nod. "Thank you. Yes, I'd love to. As a trial. I don't want it to be awkward if it turns out I'm not a good fit."

"Of course. You can join the team for a month, and we shall see where we want to go from there," Dad said, pouring the remaining wine into Mom's glass.

She clapped and shook her blonde locks. "I don't know about you, but I'm full. How about we move to the music room? Caspian has recently been playing the piano as if he'd been possessed by the ghost of Mozart. How about that, sweetheart?" she asked, smiling in a way that froze Caspian's blood.

She kept insisting on hearing him play, and had even asked Caspian to perform at an event—a first since he'd graduated junior high—so Gunner's dedication to playing the piano must have impressed her. And no wonder, because while Caspian was good at following sheet music, Gunner made music with passion.

Gunner offered to clean the dishes, but Mom wouldn't have it, and they ended up going to the music room, like she wanted. Caspian sat on the bench at the instrument without any more coercing, because he might as well get it over with. He had a set repertoire of five pieces, which he could play from memory, and once his mom was satisfied, they could all go back to their conversation.

He was almost done with the first tune when Gunner whispered something to Mom and left.

Caspian's first thought was that maybe he needed to use the washroom, but why wouldn't he have done that *before* Caspian started playing? Caspian's skin broke out in goosebumps, and he raised his hands off the keyboard, stopping the music abruptly.

"Is something wrong?" he asked.

Mom shrugged and was about to say something when Caspian rose.

"I'll be back in a second," he said and hurried out of the room, searching for a sign of Gunner's presence. He heard a door shut down the corridor, so he rushed over there, only to realize that he was being stupid, and Gunner really did go to the restroom, because there was light coming from under its door.

Caspian hovered his hand over the handle, but before he could have returned to his parents, a muffled sob echoed behind the door, turning his bones into ice.

Each was a stab piercing through his flesh and touching his heart with its freezing claws. Perhaps he should have backed away and given Gunner a moment of peace, but he stepped closer instead and spoke.

"Gunner?"

The gasp inside broke his heart, and made him want to break down the door just so he could be in there, comforting Gunner over whatever the problem was.

"Out in a minute!" Gunner said in a shaky voice.

Caspian banged his forehead against the wood, his hand already squeezing the handle while his heart raced. "No. Now. I want to come in. Please."

It took a while, but Caspian eventually heard the lock open, and he walked in so fast, he hit Gunner's foot with the door.

"Fuck!" Gunner hissed, rubbing his reddened eyes. "It's fine, really."

Caspian shut the door behind him, instinctively resting his hands on Gunner's ribs. "It clearly isn't. What's wrong?" Caspian asked in a soft voice, crooking his head to keep looking at Gunner's face, even when the stubborn bull tried to turn it away.

There was a dull moment of silence. And then—

"I can't play anymore," Gunner choked out. "I tried. At the mall. And I don't remember how to. I loved it so much." He tried to hold in another sob, but tears still ran down his cheeks and he leaned down to tighten his arms around Caspian.

The pain in his voice was so shocking that Caspian hugged him back without thinking, his mind ablaze with sympathy. For him, playing the piano was a skill, for other people it was a job, maybe a passion, but Gunner had only been able to play for the short three weeks he'd spent in Caspian's body, so it hadn't occurred to Caspian that he might have missed it.

Yet the massive man who had enough strength to turn people's faces into bloody steaks was crying over his inability to play an instrument, as if he'd just lost a dearest friend.

"I... I'm sorry, Gun. I had no idea you enjoyed it so much," Caspian whispered, pressing his face to the meaty chest in order to embrace him fully. He could sense every tremor passing through the firm body, and stroked Gunner's back to soothe him.

"It's... it's like magic to me. It takes me to a different world and brings back happy memories, like a light at the end of a dark tunnel. And when I played myself, I felt like I could reach that light and feel its warmth on my skin. Doesn't matter now, does it?"

Caspian knew Gunner had a romantic side to him, but he'd never expected he could be so poetic. With his throat tight, he gently wiped the tears off the stern masculine features and was on the verge of pulling him down, so their lips could meet like they used to. But he couldn't. Gunner wouldn't have appreciated it, and Caspian shouldn't use this moment of weakness to satisfy his selfish need. Regardless of how much he wanted to curl around Gunner and protect him from everything that might end up hurting his soft insides, Caspian shook off the silly notion of them maybe, possibly getting back together.

He cleared his throat. "I could teach you."

Gunner took a deep, raspy inhale, staring at the ceiling, as if he were afraid to meet Caspian's gaze. "I'd like that. But let's be real. It will take years. I even had this idea I could teach the piano if I learned to play, but who'd let me anywhere near their kid?"

Caspian's chest tightened, as if ribs were curling around his lungs and heart to protect them from sadness. But it was no use, because the regret twisting Gunner's face kept making him bleed. "I'm sorry," he said and offered Gunner the firmest hug.

Caspian's toes curled when warm fingers swept across his nape.

"It is what it is. I thought I was over it, but then you played, and I fell apart. I'm such a mess. But who knows? Maybe if I get the basics in five years or something, I could become a viral sensation on the internet? '*Looks like a thug, but plays Mozart*'," Gunner said with a bitter note to his voice.

He was joking, but Caspian knew him well enough to realize it was a ploy to hide Gunner's true feelings.

He needed protection. Maybe not his body but definitely his heart, and Caspian would do anything in his power to make life work out for Gunner in one way or another.

"You know, if you decided to stay here after all, we could have lessons every day."

Caspian could sense the battle inside of Gunner in the prolonged silence, and held his breath. *Stay, stay, stay...*

"Would that really be okay? With your parents and stuff?"

"Yes," Caspian said almost too fast. "This is a huge house, and they already agreed to it, because I told them about your trailer."

Gunner licked his lips. Caspian had liked him all small and cute, but the gentle giant wasn't any less adorable. "But you'll tell me if it starts feeling weird, yeah? I don't want to ruin this."

Caspian swallowed, entranced by the raw emotion in Gunner's eyes. He took his hands and squeezed them, standing a bit closer than just a friend should, but their intimacy had long gone beyond friendship. "You won't."

Chapter 31 – Caspian

A week had passed, but each night Caspian would step out of his bedroom and walk down the corridor, hoping Gunner might open his door and invite him in. It never happened, and Caspian didn't want to make Gunner feel pressured into anything just because they now lived together.

There was no denying facts, though—Caspian missed Gunner. Not his presence, because they spent lots of time together, but the kind of relationship they used to have, and which had been cut short by reality. He'd never been into big, tall guys, but Gunner was... well, he was *Gunner*, and while it made Caspian self-conscious that he was again so much smaller than his sort-of-ex, who very clearly told him he liked buff, dominant men, he couldn't shake off the thought that maybe he was overthinking things. Maybe their bond went beyond looks and wouldn't matter to Gunner either?

And if Gunner was the same lost boy with a bad handle on decision making, only packaged in a bulky body, maybe he was waiting for Caspian to make a move? Caspian could swear Gunner had rubbed his elbows against him on purpose when they had a piano lesson yesterday.

Fortune favored the bold, and while nerves were eating up Caspian's stomach like ants swarming a piece of cake, he was determined to make his intentions clear. Dressed in a dark blue suit with a slim tie, hair slicked back, and in a pair of fancy new brown oxfords with navy laces, he could barely remember the boy from two months ago, who wore oversized clothes, and ruffled his hair over his forehead.

Because he was hot now. Maybe not buff or tall, but the tailored clothes accentuated his narrow hips and shoulders that were quite broad for his size. Today was the day. Work finished early on Friday, and he hopped into his new car—a second hand blue Subaru Legacy he'd gotten with the money remaining from what Alexander had paid him for the Southfield.

Gunner was working on a rustic wedding his mom organized for a busy lawyer couple, and he'd surely appreciate a bit of leisure at the end of his day. So Caspian decided to bite the bullet, and drove all the way to the farm where the event was to be hosted.

He could see garlands of artificial flowers hung on wooden poles all the way from the parking lot, and he checked his hair a final time before stepping outside and marching toward the newly-built wooden barn.

He couldn't spot Gunner anywhere, but Lionel, Mom's assistant, was there with *his* assistant, Katie, both of them chatting over a clipboard in the bright sunshine.

Stylish as always, in a white T-shirt peppered with pastel polka dots, Lionel smiled at Caspian as soon as he saw him.

"Looks like this caterpillar's growing wings."

Caspian's mouth stretched into a smile, and he approached them down an aisle between rows of seats meant for the outdoor part of the ceremony. "I can't hold a candle to you two. Might have to try harder."

Katie laughed, and her lush brown curls bounced on her shoulders. With the large rainbow-colored glasses and a flared skirt, she was a dead ringer for Zooey Deschanel. "What's the occasion? You have to live up to your celebrity status now?"

Caspian struggled to keep on the smile, and discreetly looked around, but none of the two workers setting up fairy lights resembled Gunner. "It was a bad day."

"The jerk had it coming," Lionel said, straightening his back with an angry set to his lips. "You shouldn't out people under any circumstances."

"Unless they're a hypocritical public servant," Katie said, pretending she was browsing through her folder.

Lionel nodded. "Or a televangelist. Or a homophobic Fox News anchor."

"We can all agree on that," Caspian said, but his eyes were instantly drawn to a tall silhouette stepping out of the barn, and his heart drummed in anticipation.

Gunner looked great in black, even though his clothes were a bit dusty after a whole day's work. Lionel's gaze must have drifted the same way, because he stood closer to Caspian and lowered his voice.

"His name's *Gunner*. Don't know which ex-con reformation program your mom found him at, but at least he's eye candy, right?"

"He could have gone with more stylish tattoos on his face though," Katie said, twirling her hair. "Some celebrities make it look good, but that skull is so-so. Like he didn't want to commit to the bad boy aesthetic."

Caspian's stomach filled with ice, but Gunner noticed him before he could have responded, and when the ruggedly handsome face brightened, so did Caspian's. Lionel and Katie were excellent at their jobs, but they were so snotty he wondered what they said about *him* behind his back.

"Not everything needs to be an aesthetic."

"Well, I don't think he'll stay with us long, considering he didn't know what boho was," Katie continued.

"What is boho?" Caspian asked, just to fuck with her.

Katie frowned, but then Lionel winked at her and invited Gunner over with a gesture. "Gunner, tell our friend Cas what you thought boho style was."

Gunner glanced at Caspian with a slight pinch to his brows, and put his hands in his pockets with a deep sigh. "I thought it was *hobo*, and that people wanted to use trash cans for decoration..."

Katie burst out laughing, and when she patted Gunner's bicep patronizingly, Caspian wished to peel her arm off him out of pure jealousy. Instead, he'd make her squirm with embarrassment—the thing she probably feared most.

"Are you saying it's not? I thought hobo was for men and boho—for women?"

The little smile on Gunner's face was barely there, but Caspian noticed it. He hated the way Gunner slouched though, as if he were trying to make himself smaller.

Katie groaned. "Oh come on. You know what it is. Tapestries, rugs, saturated colors, long, floaty skirts..."

Caspian made sure to appear bewildered. "I have no idea what you're talking about."

She huffed in frustration, but Lionel stepped in to cover for the *faux pas*. "You done with the fire pit, Gunner?"

"Yeah, all done."

"You're sure you checked it twice?"

Gunner frowned. "I'm not—" He took a deep breath. "Yes, I checked twice."

Caspian was done with the mean kids attitude. "Gunner's reliable. I'm sure it's all done. Can I take my *friend* out for lunch yet, or is there something else you need him for today?"

"Oh. You know each other?" Katie straightened with, and Caspian couldn't help the satisfaction he felt at the terror in her eyes. He could only wonder what other shit Gunner had been put through so far.

"Oh yes, we've known each other since high school. Gunner's giving me boxing lessons," Caspian said and glanced at Lionel, who stood still, with a fake smile.

"I think we will be wrapping up for the day anyway."

"Fantastic. You up for some food, Gun?" Caspian asked, more than ready to rub their friendship into both those clowns' faces.

"Yeah, starving." The warm grin made Caspian want to kiss him, cuddle, and then stuff his mouth full of dick. How on earth did Gunner manage to look *cute* in his own body was impossible to tell, but his smiles made Caspian's heart skip a beat every day.

Katie's grin was so uncomfortably wide it almost reached her ears. "You should have said! Do you two want some cake samples to go? We've got orange, fennel, and vanilla, all nut-free," she babbled as if to make up for her blunder.

"Sounds delicious. We'd love to have some," Caspian said and, despite Lionel still standing close, rubbed Gunner's arm.

There was a moment of silence when Katie rushed off, but once she was gone Lionel cleared his throat. "To be perfectly honest, I didn't know what boho was until I got into this business. It's more of a girl thing. But it kind of goes with the barn wedding and all that."

So now he was trying to blame all this embarrassment and low-key bullying of Gunner on Katie. *Staying classy, Lionel.* "Maybe."

"The rustic wedding thing is so 2014 anyway. But the bride's in her forties, so that's probably why she chose this theme."

"I don't know. I think it's a nice style. Very warm and inviting," Caspian answered, to make Lionel even more uncomfortable. Was the guy sweating yet?

"You'd wear burlap for your wedding?" Gunner snorted and poked Caspian with his elbow.

Lionel laughed. "I'm sure his mother wouldn't allow it. Any husband on the horizon, Caspian?"

Caspian stilled, because Lionel had kicked his feet from under him without knowing. And the worst thing was that while he'd never thought of marriage or commitment, there was only one name that passed through his mind when he heard the question.

"I would consider it if someone offered to carry me over the threshold of a nice barn, like this one," he said and smiled at Gunner, freezing when their eyes met. Had he said too much?

Katie dispersed the tension by dashing toward them with a big paper bag filled with tiny boxes of cake samples. "Enjoy! The lemon and rosemary cupcakes are out of this world."

"See you tomorrow?" Lionel smiled at Gunner, squeezing the clipboard a bit too tightly. "You've done amazing today."

Of course he did. Here was to hoping Gunner's job would be more pleasant from now on. Caspian was extremely polite when saying his goodbyes, to keep Katie and Lionel on their toes, and then led Gunner back toward the parking lot.

"Hope that teaches them a lesson. You don't have to know everything from the get-go," Caspian said as they approached the Subaru.

Gunner shook his head. "It was a good day of work, but they don't like me."

"They're snobs. Just ignore them as long as they're being civil. And they should be, from now on," Caspian said and opened the door for Gunner before stalling when he realized what he'd done. Would Gunner notice?

Would he like it?

Or would he hate it?

He definitely hesitated and gave the door a prolonged look, but then he sat in the passenger's seat. In a way, Caspian was glad for the new car, because the old one was uncomfortably tight for Gunner.

"You look... *good* in the suit."

"Yeah? You like it?" Caspian asked, holding the door open, because as long as he wasn't in the driver's seat, something off-plan could still happen, and all he wanted was to lean inside and give Gunner the kind of kiss he used to when Gunner had been a sweet, tiny thing. "Seeing you in my body made me rethink my style choices."

Gunner snorted. "Has it now? I don't see you wearing lilac sneakers."

"Well, they're not *me*, but the way you dressed made me see wearing clothes that are actually my size makes me look better," Caspian said and finally shut the door before climbing into the driver's side.

"You look so put together." Gunner glanced at him with a little smile, and Caspian tried to assess whether it was flirting or not. He couldn't tell, and making the wrong move might wreck the fragile friendship, which he so desperately didn't want to lose. They had been joined in an experience they could only share with each other, so he never wanted them to lose touch.

"You think? Do I give off hot boss vibes?" Caspian asked and started the car.

Gunner laughed out loud, and... was he blushing? "You do. Already bossing me round. You haven't even told me where we're going, and I just follow your lead like a dumbass."

Caspian licked his lips, on the verge of suggesting that he intended this to be more than a casual lunch, but in the end, he shrugged and briefly touched Gunner's hand. "Food. Some tea. How about that café by the Grit library?" Caspian asked but stilled, suddenly remembering the rude way he'd been treated when he went there last time, while wearing Gunner's body.

Shit.

"Actually... we can't go there."

"Yeah, it's pretty expensive, isn't it?"

It wasn't expensive for Caspian, but he didn't want to embarrass Gunner so he shrugged. "It's more... look, I might have done something stupid there when I was still you, on the first day. There's this guy who works there, and I'd seen him on Grindr, and I might have come on too strong. And also might have thrown coffee beans at the manager," he added, fighting through the embarrassment twisting his insides.

Gunner laughed out loud instead of being mortified. "You did *what*? I didn't know you had it in you. Then again... you did break Alexander's nose," he teased with a wiggle of his eyebrows.

"We both made mistakes. But yes, the café is off limits for you, I'm afraid. What do you want to eat? Meat? Pizza?"

Gunner's face brightened. "Oh, hell yes! Pizza. Are we celebrating something?"

Just... being in each other's company.

Caspian, again, had the gnawing urge to touch Gunner in a way that would have made his intentions obvious, but what if it forced Gunner to reject him? They'd be stuck in this moving car.

"We can make it whatever we want it to be. Pick up a pizza and make it a picnic or eat indoors? Your choice."

"We missed out on a picnic. We should do that in this great weather. People always stare at me when I go places. I'm kinda used to it, but I just wanna eat in peace, you know?"

Caspian did know, and this time he squeezed Gunner's hand as they drove down the highway, heading to Grit. Gunner squeezed back, leaving Caspian in the limbo of not knowing what the touch meant. Were they two gay friends who were close enough to express their support for each other through touch, or was this a prelude to more?

After a while, Gunner spoke in a softer tone. "I liked that about being you. I could grab a strawberry Frappuccino at the mall, and no one stared at me because of it. But that's probably not what *you* want."

"No. Not really," Caspian said and sped up.

Soon enough, they arrived at the only pizza place in town, which branded itself with a jungle theme and had a lion mascot. Caspian had to let go of Gunner in order to change the gears, and the warmth of their physical touch was gone as if he'd dreamed it.

But he didn't want to cause any awkwardness, so he smiled at Gunner and led the way into the restaurant, which smelled pleasantly of dough and cheese. A roar accompanied their entry, and since Gunner didn't want to stay, Caspian went straight to a pickup station set up between two artificial palms. He was about to press the toucan-shaped bell when a familiar face emerged from behind the tacky decoration.

Adam, the infamous barista of all people, smiled at him with recognition. "Oh hey, haven't seen you in a while. I'm afraid we don't do flat whites here." He pointed to his hat, which bore the logo of the pizzeria.

"Oh, I haven't been at the café since my friend got thrown out because someone there didn't like him," Caspian said without losing a beat and glanced over his shoulder back, leading Adam's attention straight to Gunner, who'd just gravitated closer.

Adam's stunned expression was as delicious as Katie getting flustered earlier. Caspian was so done with people judging Gunner for his exterior.

"I was there, you know," Adam choked out and glanced toward the open kitchen, as if he were making sure he had backup. "That's not exactly how it went down."

"No? Then how?" Caspian asked and reached back to grab Gunner's hand again, because he now actually had an excuse.

Gunner, who must have realized who Adam was, rolled his eyes. "Come on, it's not worth it."

Adam bit his thumb, avoiding Caspian's gaze. "He hit on me and was very inappropriate. If he's your boyfriend, keep him on a leash."

"Oh, is hitting on people illegal now? That's new, considering that you flirt with most customers to get better tips," Caspian said, offended both for Gunner and himself. Adam's face might be pretty on the surface, but now that his judgmental nature shone through, it was oddly reminiscent of a rat muzzle. "You're not better than him just because you're a fresh-faced boy with a buzzing Grindr profile."

Adam flushed and leaned back behind the wooden stand. "No, I flirted with *you*, 'cause I thought you were cute. Excuse me for not being into tattooed meatheads! Maybe if you'd actually asked me out, we wouldn't be having this conversation!"

Caspian stalled, struck by the dissonance rattling through his head. Adam had been into *him*?

Gunner ran his fingers through his hair, never letting go of Caspian's hand. "We're not getting this pizza, are we?"

"No. And I'm happy I haven't asked you out, because you're a judgmental prick, *Adam*. This guy here has way more brains and heart than you," Caspian said and stormed out with his stomach twisted in fury. He couldn't believe this shit.

Gunner only slipped his hand out of Caspian's when they reached the car. "Are you okay? We still have lots of cake."

Caspian pushed his hands into his hair, trying to ease the burning heat inside him. "I'm fine. I'm just angry at the way he treated you."

"Yeah, I know, I'm working on not punching people myself." Gunner leaned against the vehicle. "He's your type, isn't he?"

Caspian stalled, at a loss. "His pretty face doesn't matter. I don't want him. And now we can't have pizza ever again because I can't control my anger," he said and slapped the roof.

"Were you too shy to ask him out before?" Gunner whispered, drilling his inquisitive gaze into Caspian. But standing in the parking lot gave Caspian nothing to do with his hands, and he ended up sliding into the car, with Gunner following suit.

Words were stuck in his throat, but when he forced himself, more came out, as if dragged by an avalanche. "I didn't think anyone would *ever* want me. I was small, and thin, and weak, and I thought my face was average.

Whenever I got sex I assumed the guys were just desperate for anyone, and... yeah, he's so cute that I assumed he was just being nice. I wanted to be a big guy. Someone who is immediately seen as masculine, and dominant, and it was killing me inside that I could never become that."

Gunner stroked Caspian's forearm as Caspian tried to work out the best place to sit down with the cakes, but his mind was a mess of upsetting memories.

"But you know you're not, right? People have different tastes. Just like that pizza barista liked you more than me."

"I know that *now*," Caspian hummed and hit the steering wheel. "But I used to look in the mirror and see this warped version of myself. And then, you were there, rocking the blond hair, and the tight clothes, and when I touched your... my cock, I realized there was so much to like about my body. It's thanks to you that I have the confidence to wear this suit."

He'd intended to go out of town, but the moment he spotted the library next to the school and the empty bleachers nearby, he took a turn into the parking lot.

Gunner exhaled. "You have no idea how much it means for me to hear that. I'll probably always feel guilty over being a shit to you back at school."

"Well, I didn't treat you that well when we'd first swapped, so let's call it even," Caspian said as soon as they left the car. He grabbed the bag of cakes and led the way to the school football field while shadows lengthened and the sun turned a warmer shade.

"And yeah, there's nothing wrong with your cock, just so you know" Gunner added with a chuckle. He followed without even questioning where they were going. "First thing I did when I woke up in your body was jerk off."

Heat climbed up Caspian's back, as if Gunner touched his bare skin. "I... you know you were my first. The first guy I topped. Because I was too self-conscious before."

Gunner pushed his hands into his pockets and slouched a bit as they got to the bleachers. "You shouldn't be. You were... err... really good at it. Not 'cause you had my body, but because of what you said and did with it. How you took charge and all. One day soon, you'll find yourself a pretty twink, and he'll worship the ground you walk on."

It should have felt better than it did, but Caspian didn't want just any pretty twink. The past month had changed him forever, and he chewed on his next words as they climbed the bleachers and eventually sat in the top row, watching the empty field.

"What about you? Now that you're out... are you *looking*?" Caspian asked with ants crawling under his skin. Wouldn't this be the perfect place to make a move? At the same school where they'd first met?

Gunner stared out into the football field as Caspian passed him a dainty cupcake. "Nah... I don't think I'm ready. I wanna sort out my life first. Make sure I can handle the new job, get a place of my own and all that."

Caspian had been wise not to say anything then.

While Gunner might not have realized he'd rejected him. The hope Caspian still held on to withered, and there would be no getting it back.

Gunner wasn't interested.

Not in him. Not in anyone else.

So Caspian might as well stop clinging to the illusion and move on, regardless of how much his heart balked at the thought of pursuing another guy.

But he wasn't a child and had long learned to hide his true feelings, so he picked up a cupcake of his own and bumped it against Gunner's, as if they were holding champagne glasses, not food. "To a bright future for both of us."

Chapter 32 – Gunner

After the first bumpy days of working for Barb, Gunner slowly eased into the job and got to know his co-workers. Even Lionel and Katie, who'd been distant at first, ended up warming up to him. While he didn't always get along with everyone, or grasp every joke, once people got to know him, they could see the man behind his looks and background.

He wasn't earning sacks of gold, but without bills to pay, he was able to not only help out Zahra and Noah but also replace the necessities he'd lost in the fire. The generosity of the Bradys overwhelmed Gunner at times, but he'd put his pride in his pocket, because any help he could get was a lifeline at this point.

Living at a house so lovely was a guilty pleasure, but any time he considered moving out, he stalled for reasons other than a piano and a kitchen that had two ovens. Leaving would mean seeing less of Caspian, and knowing it would eventually happen already gnawed at Gunner's heart.

A month on from the swap back, Gunner missed Caspian more than ever, despite them spending so much time together. They'd watch trash TV after work, and even when tired, both of them always made the effort to practice the piano. Gunner was making some extremely basic progress, but playing also meant sitting close enough to feel the warmth of Caspian's body and get a whiff of the cologne Gunner associated with the one man to ever give him what he truly needed.

Even if he found a toppy guy whose sexual taste aligned with his, that person would never understand him the way Caspian did. The experience they'd shared forged a bond that couldn't be broken, but each passing day reminded Gunner that the fantastical adventure was over, and that he should be satisfied with having a friend willing to go to such great lengths to help him out.

Still, each time they were alone, sitting close, or when Caspian looked at him with the slight frown that reminded him of the bedroom eyes he used to give Gunner while they were still in the wrong bodies, he got a glimmer of hope that maybe he wasn't the only one missing what they used to have.

"How's it going, Gun?" Lionel asked, approaching him in a maroon blazer that brought out the color of his eyes.

While a bit of an asshole at times, Lionel wasn't a bad events underboss. He was organized and on top of everything, even if a bit pedantic. Gunner had once witnessed Lionel losing his shit at a flower delivery company over the phone, and he'd been surprised at how persistent the fucker could be. They had those lilac roses delivered right on time.

"All good," Gunner mumbled with a nail between his lips.

He was putting together a donut station for the Candyland-themed wedding. The bride was a baker, and the groom, a pastry chef, which explained a lot, though Gunner still couldn't get over how much time, effort, and money some people were ready to spend on a single party.

The cost of this wedding could have funded a small house.

"I don't know if working in wedding planning makes me feel more romantic or resent the whole thing," Lionel said with a huff and waved his folder to produce a breeze. His mid-length hair made up the perfect pompadour and wouldn't fall out of place, surely held by some magical product.

Gunner hammered in the last nail on a board meant to hold donuts. "I guess it's nice that people want to celebrate their love and shit. If they have the money, might as well. *And* they get lots of gifts."

"You haven't been doing this long enough. And you're not actually seeing all the meltdowns that happen at weddings," Lionel said and opened his eyes comically wide. "Just a week ago, this one guy got so drunk before the ceremony his best man needed to step in for him at the first dance. Makes me wonder if he became the stand-in on the wedding night too."

Gunner whistled. "Maybe it's one of those throuple situations. You don't have anyone? Always the bridesmaid, never the bride?"

"Gunner. That's offensive. How about always-the-best-man-never-the-groom, huh?"

Gunner rubbed his face in embarrassment. "Sorry," he mumbled. "I just meant... you know."

Lionel grinned and robbed his smoothly-shaven cheek. "Just pulling your leg. There actually is someone, but I told him it's not gonna happen."

When Gunner stared at him in disbelief, Lionel shrugged. "I feel this pressure to have this perfect wedding all the straights would envy, but as much as I like nice suits and food, stuff like this doesn't speak to me," he said, gesturing at the garlands made of fake candy and macaroons, at the pastel-hued ribbons attached to table cloths, and the rustic booths meant for food and painted in all the sweetest colors.

Lionel went on. "All my life I heard that I shouldn't rub my sexuality in people's faces, so I low-key want to, but I also think organizing giant parties to celebrate that uh-we're-in-a-legal-relationship-now, is kinda tacky. And the presentation takes over what's actually important. I'd rather have my guy stay with me because he wants to, not because there's formalities involved in leaving."

Gunner hadn't expected such a thoughtful answer from a guy who usually needed to be taken with a grain of salt any time business wasn't the topic at hand. "How did you um... find him?"

Gunner's stomach tightened with the stress of inquiring about such private things, so he toyed with the hammer to occupy his hands. He wasn't out to the people he worked with, and none of them were the sort to have friends at the trailer park where Gunner used to live, so they didn't know about him.

Deep down, he knew he could come out to them and no one would bat an eye. There was Lionel, one of the women was bisexual, and last week Gunner found out their carpenter was a trans man, yet taking that step felt like crossing a canyon. Deep down he feared that everything would change if people knew. He worried they'd treat him differently or ask questions he wasn't ready to answer. Or worse, try to set him up with someone when he wasn't ready to meet another *someone*.

Lionel rolled his eyes. "I tell everyone I met him at a charity event, but the truth is we met on Facebook, in a group with memes about county politics. We bonded over mocking the previous sheriff, and now I'm stuck with a guy who sits on his ass all day and streams video games for a living."

Gunner snorted, surprised that a fashionable guy like Lionel would have looked at that kind of man twice. "I always kinda imagined you with a high-powered lawyer."

"Or a fashion designer, I know," Lionel said and, after a moment's hesitation, browsed through his phone before showing Gunner a picture clearly taken at a Halloween party. In the photo, Lionel wore a skin-tight bodysuit in a pearlescent white shade, fake hoofs, and a wig that incorporated horse-like ears and a spiral horn on the forehead. Next to him was a man of average size dressed in a My Little Pony T-shirt and a rubber horse head mask that could have been purchased at the dollar store.

"We were supposed to match and go as horses. Couple goals, right?" Lionel asked with a chuckle.

Gunner laughed with him, getting all warm inside. It felt like crossing a threshold in their relationship, as if Lionel no longer saw him as just a worker he spoke to solely about the job. Gunner itched to share that bit more about himself too, and since Lionel was gay, maybe even open up about his sexuality, but something inside him kept balking at the notion of others knowing his secret. As if he were trying to climb over barbed wire made of fear and inadequacy.

Admitting his sexuality in Caspian's body had been one thing. This one? Quite another. Even telling Noah the truth had been tough.

"I mean... he seems fun. Xbox controller wedding cake?" he teased.

Lionel pressed his hand to his chest in a theatrical gesture. "You, sir, are inspiring me! Ha, I might consider it if we kept the party on the down-low. Though if I surprised him with something like this, he'd surely cry. My guy's a big softie," he said and put the phone back into his pocket. He hesitated, but glanced at Gunner again. "And you? Any wedding bells on the horizon?"

He'd asked about that before, but it always came with a dose of teasing, which prompted Gunner to reply with vague jokes. But after Lionel had shared his story, Gunner's throat dried with the lies it didn't want to produce. He could ask Lionel to keep his truth to himself. Before the exchange they'd just had, Gunner assumed his secret would go straight into the gossip bin, but—

"Oh. Okay. The bride wasn't supposed to be here yet." Lionel turned his face to speak into the little device he used to communicate with Katie when she was far away. "Bride alert. I repeat, *bride alert.*"

Three people stepped through a gap in the manicured bushes surrounding the garden where the reception was to take place in two days' time, and while one of them was tall as a giraffe, it wasn't the groom.

The only man in the party was handsome, with a muscular chest and arms, but he looked extremely average between a woman in fishnet and leather, and a pink-haired stunner whose simple clothes couldn't hide her enormous height. She not only dwarfed her male companion but was twice the size of the goth chick.

"Aaand we might have to raise the wedding arch a bit more," Lionel said absent-mindedly before welcoming the bride with a smile.

The woman was taller than Gunner, yet she still wore high heels, approaching them in quick strides. "I just had to see it, you know? And this is the donut station? Oh, God... it's everything I've ever wanted!" She wiped the tears already glistening in her eyes, leaving Gunner bewildered.

It was just a board with rows of nails made to her specification. It hadn't even been painted yet.

"Yeah. Katie will apply the finishing touches later. You wanna talk to her... maybe?" Gunner didn't feel like the right face for a Candyland wedding, and he'd hate himself if Barb got complaints about him, but the bride nodded, offering him a broad smile.

"Oh, yes, I'd love to chat to her, but this is amazing!" She pointed to the board with a glittery nail before Lionel swooped her away.

The groom smiled at Gunner and patted his arm. "Great job, man," he said and quickly followed, leaving Gunner with a warm feeling in his gut.

The board hadn't been his idea, and he'd simply done his job, but being appreciated felt nice anyway. Working for Barb and living with the Bradys had opened his eyes to just how little of it he used to get. Every now and then, he'd hear Barb complimenting Thomas's tie, or Caspian telling his mom how much he liked her breakfasts. Gunner tried slowly adapting to that, yet still struggled with feeling awkward during such exchanges.

To express his gratitude for letting him stay, and as an excuse to spend more time with Caspian, Gunner was learning to cook. He hadn't tried making anything too fancy, but he was allowed to use any of the many recipe books and kitchen staples, and he found that he enjoyed transforming *ingredients* into *food*. In a kitchen as grand as the one in the Brady home, cooking wasn't solely a utilitarian task to fill his stomach, but a pleasure in itself.

Just like melodies consisted of single notes, elaborate food was made of many ingredients, which created a symphony of flavor only once he put them together. Without having to worry over wastage if he messed up, Gunner felt free to experiment and added his own flair to the culinary tunes. But there was one thing he enjoyed even more than the challenge learning to cook posed.

Feeding his hosts.

He'd served them pancakes for breakfast last Sunday. Since then, they'd acted as if he was King Sugar, Barb had bought him a book on baking, and Caspian had gifted him a jar of vanilla pods. At first, he worried they were patronising him, offering praise as if he were a dog that finally learned to fetch. But the truth was that the Bradys were genuinely nice and appreciated his efforts to give back.

Now that they knew him as a person, not a stranger with a facial tattoo and bulging muscles, they no longer saw him as a threat. While Gunner had experienced as much unreasonable hostility as kindness since he'd started working for Barb, he decided to at least try seeing people the way they were instead of making the same kinds of assumptions others made about him.

He was about to return to his work when he realized that the goth chick in cut-out leather pants that showcased the fishnet stockings she wore underneath stayed behind and was now smiling at him. She had unusual makeup, with lots of pink and peach hues on the cheeks, nose, even around the eyes, but the amount of piercings she managed to collect on her face would have set off metal detectors at any airport. There was even a silver chain resting across her nose, above the upturned tip, and unless Gunner's eyes were tricking him, it was attached to piercings in both wings of her nose.

He bit back a smile, because it made him remember the barbells in Caspian's nipples. Why he still wore them would remain a mystery, because Gunner didn't dare ask. "Can I help you with anything?"

"I was hoping you'd ask. What are you doing this Friday?" She grinned and knocked on the donut board Gunner had set up.

Gunner didn't think the Bradys had anything planned. "Don't know yet. Why? You need a piercing station made?" He winked, pointing to the board, but cringed on the inside. He shouldn't have said that. This was the bride's friend, and the last thing he needed was finding out from Barb that someone complained about his behavior. He kept working on his self-control, but sometimes his mouth spewed things and nothing could be done about it.

But she didn't seem offended and chuckled. "No. My plus one decided to run off to the other side of the country without telling me, and you look like a worthy replacement," she said, letting her gaze linger on his tattooed arms.

Gunner raised his eyebrows. "Oh. *Oh.* I do?" He wasn't used to women hitting on him. Usually, he scared them off with his looks even if they considered him attractive, and since he never made the first move, he lived in a happy catch-22.

But now was the time to make a decision, because he'd either reject her and risk the consequences, if she felt offended, or go with the flow the way he always did and—what—end up with another girlfriend?

"Big. Dangerous. Just the way I like them," she teased but didn't approach, as if she hadn't yet decided if he were the biting type or not.

Sink or swim.

"I... I'm gay," he mumbled with his heart pounding as if it wanted to launch into space.

She laughed. He stared. Her laugh died.

"Oh. You're serious," she said with wide eyes. "Sorry."

Gunner could hardly hear her through the blood thudding in his ears. "No, it's okay. You couldn't know. I... I could still go with you. Just... yeah."

The woman relaxed and waved her hand through the air. "It was worth a try."

They smiled at each other, and Gunner felt overcome by a weird weightlessness, as if the shackles he'd always worn had crumbled to pieces. But Katie sent him a message, asking for his presence in the main building, which kept him from agonizing about what he'd just done. He said his goodbyes to the goth chick and rushed off, ready to hear about whatever dramatic turn of events stressed out Katie this time. Chair covers arriving in a hot pink instead of pastel? The plastic pony sculpture having unwanted genitals? It had happened before, and it had been Gunner's job to saw off the horse cock, then sand down its crotch.

Katie waved at him from the wooden arch that had been custom-made for the occasion. He saw what the issue was from afar.

Lionel had been right about the size of the thing. Both the bride and groom fit under the contraption, but her head was too close to the highest point of the arch and would look terrible in photos.

"Gunner, do you think we can bring the arch up altogether? From the bottom?" Katie asked as soon as he approached.

Gunner shrugged and cocked his head. "Sure, we'll just need more wooden crates."

Katie sighed. "And more of the flowers to cover them..."

The groom smiled and kissed his bride's hand. "Anything for my queen."

A part of Gunner wanted to laugh at the image, considering their size difference, but their affection was kind of endearing. It made him imagine a world where it didn't matter to Caspian that Gunner wasn't a cute twink anymore.

If a guy didn't have an issue with marrying a woman who was so much taller than him, and Lionel dated a guy with completely different interests, then maybe he didn't have to feel ashamed about who he was?

Easier said than done, of course, but one had to start somewhere.

"We'll take care of it, don't worry," Lionel said and gestured toward a steep flower bed filled with red and pink tulips. "This is where we're planning to set up the photo booth. Katie, would you take them through the details?" he asked, and his assistant led away the happy couple.

That left Gunner with Lionel and Fay, an artist who often made custom decorations for Barb's company and had a penchant for flower crowns.

Gunner scratched his head and scooted to get a better look at the bottom of the arch. "I'd rather the carpenter did this, really. We don't want all this wood falling on them as they say their vows…"

Fay smiled, typing on her phone. "I'm texting him right now. Lionel? Guess who my brother has a date with tonight…"

Lionel gave a little gasp. "Is it *our prince*?"

"The very same," Fay said with a grin. "My brother is a stick of dynamite. Poor Caspian won't know what hit him."

Gunner stumbled to his knees, out of breath and confused. Caspian had a date? And hadn't told him? He was getting hot and cold all at once, as if his brain was short circuiting.

Lionel snorted, not realizing Gunner was about to crash-land and break all his bones. "He's actually cleaned up quite nicely last month. Breaking that guy's nose gave him all the big dick energy he's been lacking."

Fay laughed and pushed at Lionel's arm. "Stop it!"

"Stop what? It's true!" Lionel grinned. "He's a five-foot-three Don Draper now."

"W-who's your brother?" Gunner choked out.

Fay shrugged and pressed the tape measure to the side of the arch before making a note in her cell phone. "Don't think you know him. He's a graphic artist."

"And a hot twink. Just Caspian's type," Lionel mused, stepping away when Fay tried to slap his calf.

Gunner got back to his feet, dizzy from all the emotions hitting him like a hammer to the head. Caspian wasn't the kind of person to maliciously withhold information, so he likely didn't think it was a big deal, but being kept out of the loop still hurt, because Caspian was moving on while Gunner... was still hopelessly in love.

"I'm gay," he stated without even stuttering.

Both Fay and Lionel turned their heads to stare at him.

The silence went on for so long Gunner was starting to get chills, but Fay finally broke it with a chortle to Lionel. "Told you that's how Caspian knew him."

Lionel spread his arms, sizing up Gunner from head to toe. "Well fuck me sideways. My gaydar didn't even make a blip."

Fay rubbed her nose. "Is there a reason you're telling us? If you want a shot at my brother, you gotta stand in line."

"N-no. I just wanted you to know."

Lionel opened his arms but only hugged Gunner when given permission. "Thanks for telling us, big guy."

He'd broken a lot of barriers today, and the world hadn't ended.

Which meant it would remain standing even if he took one more bold step. One that was probably more sink than swim, but if he didn't at least try, he'd never know if he'd missed out on the love of his life.

Chapter 33 – Caspian

Caspian stared at the house through the open garage door but hadn't stepped out of the car since he'd parked it five minutes back.

The date with Finneas, Fay's brother, had gone well. Nothing explosive or life-altering, but they did have many topics in common, and the guy was a cutie with long black hair and a beautiful, tempting mouth. And while a bit taller than Caspian, their flirting suggested he was a bottom, and interested in what Caspian had to offer.

With Mom and Dad away for the weekend, Caspian could have invited him over for the night, but he didn't want to put Gunner on the spot. He could have also gone to Finneas' place, but when that came up, Caspian found himself stalling.

He did enjoy Finn's company, and found him attractive, and maybe something more than sex could have come out of this if he gave the guy a chance. But the truth was that no matter how much he wanted to move on from the past, his heart still beat for only one man.

So he came back, giving up on sex with a pretty boy in order to teach Gunner how to play the piano, and watch a movie with him. Because they were best buddies, and he really cared.

Caspian rolled his forehead against the steering wheel and left the car at long last. He relaxed his shoulders and entered his parents' home, hoping to at least change into something more comfortable before Gunner noticed his presence.

But the shuffling of a chair in the kitchen lit up by a couple of LEDs put an end to those hopes, and he faced Gunner, who watched him from the breakfast bar. The faint glow behind him cast a shadow on his face but also illuminated his broad shoulders and thick arms as he slid off the barstool, dressed in a simple outfit of blue jeans and a white T-shirt, which fit him *just right*.

"Hey," Gunner said, arching his neck, as if he wanted to see something behind Caspian.

Caspian glanced over his shoulder, but they were alone. "How was your day?"

Gunner exhaled and crooked his hips, drawing Caspian's attention to the way denim shifted on his crotch. "Oh, you know, the regular wedding drama. But... You know Fay right? She said you had a date tonight? How'd it go?" He lowered his gaze to the counter and swirled his finger over the marble.

Caspian stilled, but his heart thumped with unease, and he leaned against the wall, briefly avoiding Gunner's gaze, because this uncomfortable atmosphere was his fault. "I'm sorry I didn't tell you. It's just... it's weird, you know?

And I didn't know how it'd go so I figured there was no reason to say anything unless things got serious."

"And did they? Get serious?" Gunner looked like a wall of muscle, yet Caspian was all too aware of the fragility hiding in that big body.

And the question hiding behind the one Gunner had verbalized squeezed around his heart. They both remembered their brief relationship and longed for the sense of fulfillment it used to give them, but things were different now, and it wasn't healthy to focus on what was lost. "We had dinner."

"Soo..." Gunner stepped back to reveal two small plates on the counter. "Room for dessert?"

Tightness grabbed Caspian's throat. He shouldn't have been upset. It was a good thing that Gunner wasn't jealous of him and instead offered him a sample of yet another of his culinary experiments.

But he *was* upset. And the fact that he couldn't have Gunner had never before been made so clear.

"Yeah."

Gunner's smile twisted the knife in Caspian's heart. "I made us tiramisu," he said, presenting the slab of cake dusted with cocoa. "I made too much, but I'm sure your parents will enjoy some once they're back."

"Yeah, Dad keeps asking me what your secret ingredient is," Caspian mused and placed his blazer on a side table in the hall before joining Gunner in the kitchen. His gaze trailed down the muscular back and settled on Gunner's ass. He had such hard buttocks, muscular from all the physical exercise.

Caspian really should focus on something else.

"Better not tell him it's my *special* cream." Gunner wiggled his eyebrows when they both sat in barstools in front of generous portions of dessert.

Idiot. Caspian loved his crude jokes.

They always made him think of dirty things he'd told Gunner during sex. And the tiramisu was great. Satisfying, sweet, with some bitterness from the coffee, and having a mouthful allowed Caspian to keep his lips shut for a bit longer.

"Leave that kind of spice for a boyfriend," he said.

The silence that settled between them next was surprisingly uncomfortable. Had he overstepped? Gunner had no snappy comebacks, didn't turn the comment into a joke, nor attempt to make the conversation even dirtier.

Caspian's back itched, as if he were about to start sweating, and he swallowed a piece of cream and sponge. "You'll find someone very soon, I'm sure."

Gunner put his spoon down and took a deep breath. "Could *we* really not work? I know I don't look like the guys you're after, but I'm the same person, okay?"

Caspian stilled, and the spoon fell out of his hand, clattering on the plate. Hot fingers clawed at his shoulders and kept him still as he watched emotion wash over Gunner's stern, masculine features.

Was this… really possible? Had they both been thinking about this and not said a thing *for weeks*?

"Are you serious? I'm half your size," he said, hot at the humiliation of having to spell it out. But it was true, and there was no escaping it.

Gunner chewed on that, but then… got off the chair and went down to his knees in front of Caspian. And once he sat back on his heels, he tilted his head back and looked *up* with shiny brown eyes. "How about now? I wanna be your bitch, whatever your size is." His voice trembled, and just knowing he provoked such strong feelings in Gunner shot pure adrenaline into Caspian's system.

Fire exploded in the pit of Caspian's stomach and scorched his insides, traveling all the way to his head. His treacherous mind told him that this wasn't possible. That Gunner couldn't want this. That maybe he was lonely and didn't know how to approach another man now that he was back in his own body.

But his heart beat faster, and he slid off the chair, lured by the pleading eyes that watched him as if he were the only man left in the world.

"I like that," he found himself saying. "You look beautiful on your knees."

The tremble in Gunner's lips and the red tint flooding his face switched something in Caspian. He was now a predator, and he'd tasted blood in the water.

Gunner didn't even blink, his eyes following Caspian's every move, as if he too recognized the shift in mood.

"I'm not... 'beautiful' anymore, but I could be yours."

Caspian stalled, struck by the resignation in that statement. It was true that Gunner no longer looked like the pretty boys Caspian used to have eyes for, but he was handsome, and sturdy, and not in any way unattractive. He might not have been what Caspian considered *his type,* but it did not matter when Caspian saw him as so much more than the muscular body he wished to have.

"Don't say that. You're still the same person," Caspian whispered, cupping Gunner's face with both hands.

It blew his mind that he was in a position to reassure someone like Gunner.

"You can see that?" The brown eyes staring up at him were as needy and starved for affection as the blue ones had been when Gunner had worn Caspian's face.

Caspian nodded, for a moment too choked up to speak. "Gunner, I've never known another person more intimately. I see you how you really are."

Gunner took a deep breath, not moving an inch off the floor. "I love you."

He might have as well have swept Caspian off his feet and hugged him forever.

Caspian kneeled next to him and opened Gunner's mouth with a hard, demanding kiss, just like the ones he'd dreamed of since they returned to their own bodies. Gunner's skin was rough to the touch in a way it hadn't been, but he yielded with familiar ease.

"You told me you didn't want to date. I thought... it was over between us."

Gunner let out a whine, grabbing Caspian's forearms. "I didn't want to date anyone else."

"It's okay, baby. It's okay. I'm back with you," Caspian whispered, pulling Gunner close and kissing the top of his head. A sense of power burned through his core, telling him to claw at his reclaimed lover's flesh and truly make him his again. Despite the size difference, Gunner was already putty in his hands, and Caspian couldn't wait to *mold* him.

It didn't matter that Gunner was bigger when he wanted to submit to Caspian despite being so buff and strong.

When Gunner arched up for another kiss, it was in Caspian's power to tease him with denial, so he leaned back with a wicked smile. His mind soaked in visions of what could happen next, playing out hundreds of scenarios, and suggesting that he could demand things a smaller man wouldn't have been able to do for him.

"Take off your clothes. You belong to me now. And you will do everything I say," Caspian said, standing up and unwinding his tie.

The way Gunner's eyes followed him made Caspian stand even taller. The man kneeling before him saw him for who he was, and no one could ever replace him. When Gunner peeled off his T-shirt, showing off all that tattooed flesh, Caspian could see himself teasing this big guy, and slowly exploring how much the strong body could take. A faint aroma of fruit and flowers radiated from the newly bared flesh. Caspian had learned to associate it with Gunner during their swap and couldn't help but smile at how adorable it was that Gunner had showered before this impromptu date and used his favorite pink shower gel.

Had he *prepared* himself in hope of Caspian taking the bait? Had he played with his ass, inserting fingers, a smooth bottleneck, or some other phallic item? Did he want to be treated exactly like before, or had something changed?

Gunner didn't bother folding his clothes and dropped them to the floor. His hands shook, as if he were on the verge of a meltdown, and seeing him so nervous stoked the predator within Caspian, triggering thoughts so lewd he needed to adjust his package.

"Did you jerk off thinking about me?"

Gunner rubbed his hair, and even though he was so much taller, when he stood naked in front of Caspian, he couldn't have seemed more vulnerable.

"Hell yes," he admitted in a raspy voice. "Every fucking day. A few times I even drifted off at work and had to take care of it in the bathroom. I'm fucking obsessed with you."

His words caressed Caspian's balls, forcing him to spread his legs, because the last thing he wanted was to get overly excited too soon. He'd never thought anyone could want him this much and so shamelessly, but maybe the fact that he was small and short didn't matter with the right person. He stepped closer, twisting both of Gunner's nipples until the handsome face creased with pain.

"How come those aren't yet pierced like mine?"

"You want them to be?" Gunner bit his lip, and covered his growing erection with his hand. Caspian knew that body inside and out, yet couldn't wait to learn all the new things he could do with it.

He wanted to see whether Gunner would produce as much pre-cum as he used to in the other form, or whether he was as reactive to teasing. After a month of thirst and longing, he was entering the candy store, and he could reach into all the jars, taking whatever struck his fancy.

Caspian had to rise to his toes in order to grab Gunner's jaw, but he made sure to dig his fingers real hard into flesh. "Hands back. You don't have the right to modesty when you're with me."

Gunner's breath tickled Caspian's fingers, but it was the speed with which he followed the order that made Caspian's dick harden. Gunner didn't have to listen. Caspian wouldn't be able to force him. But Gunner *wanted* to submit.

All of Gunner was on show and his to touch. The hairs on his forearms bristled at the sight of Gunner's cock twitching, and he knew he would take his time tonight until both of them couldn't stand it anymore.

He opened a drawer in the kitchen island and pulled out two plastic clamps used to reseal packages. "I do want them pierced. Mine are still healing, but they're so sensitive, and whenever I feel something rub against them, I remember that you put them there," he said and pulled on one of Gunner's nipples before mercilessly closing the clamp on the tender flesh.

Gunner gasped, and his face relaxed, expressing the insecurities and nerves that still plagued him. He didn't need to wear a mask when he was with Caspian, and his openness made Caspian want to push him further than ever before.

"I liked you teasing me there," Gunner said, but his chest rose and fell ever faster as he breathed in and out. He held his hands behind his back submissively—a bull of a man, yet willing to be at Caspian's mercy.

Caspian put a clamp on Gunner's other nipple and flicked them both, cooking on the inside when tension passed over Gunner's handsome features. This guy could've broken Caspian in half, yet he chose to put himself in his care.

Caspian had never been interested in burly men, so he'd considered his recent attraction to Gunner as seeing *beyond* his exterior. But watching him kneel brought out a new kind of thirst. "I won't spare you. It's not like I could break someone so big and strong," he muttered and slid his hand over Gunner's flesh as he walked behind him. The massive hands were clasped together at the small of Gunner's back, but Caspian still twisted Gunner's arms to make his point. The fancy silk tie would be the perfect thing to ensure Gunner knew his place.

Anticipating a submissive lover in his future, Caspian had spent some time last month learning knots, and while Gunner wasn't going anywhere, a bit of bondage would enforce the notion that he wasn't the one in charge. Moments later, both thick wrists were secured.

"You can always try," Gunner said, and the teasing in his voice prompted Caspian to slap his ass. Muscular, yet with enough give for a good squeeze, the buttocks had Caspian staring. And they were his to play with.

He kicked Gunner's feet apart and pushed on his back, wordlessly forcing him to bend over. And before Caspian could have lost the benefit of surprise, he grabbed the meaty cheeks and spread them wide.

Gunner's hole looked so snug with the delicate, wrinkled skin around it, and when Caspian smelled musk and soap, he leaned in and let hot spit drizzle to the vulnerable flesh.

Gunner whimpered, strained by the uncomfortable position, but he was fit enough to take any challenge Caspian wanted to put him through.

The soft flesh felt good against Caspian's finger when he ran it down Gunner's crack, and it was only then that he realized Gunner had shaved that entire area.

Sweat beaded on Caspian's back.

"I see you've prepared for this," he whispered and rubbed his crotch against Gunner's thigh.

Arousal was a constant pressure in his balls, but he wanted to make this last. To tease Gunner into oblivion and deny him release for hours. Just because Gunner had given him the reins.

Just because he could.

"All smooth," Caspian said, rubbing his saliva all around the hole while Gunner squirmed and clenched his bound hands. He was big, strong, yet so helpless and *open*.

Gunner didn't dare try to pull his legs together or protest. "I... I thought you might like that. In case. In case of this."

Caspian didn't find hair in any way repulsive, but the fact that Gunner was willing to shave his intimate parts for him made his dick so rigid he couldn't wait any longer and spat at the hole again before screwing in his thumb. Gunner was tight. But despite flinching at the sudden penetration, he didn't protest. And his passivity was so damn hot Caspian could barely stand still when his brain clouded with lust.

Maybe they should have talked about limits, but Caspian was positive he couldn't come up with anything Gunner wouldn't have wanted to at least try, so he moved the digit inside the snug channel and slapped Gunner's buttock, grinning when the sphincter tightened around his thumb.

This ass belonged to him now.

And he wanted Gunner to know.

"I want to come before we keep on playing. You'll get to your knees, you will put your cheek on the floor, and you'll let me use you."

Never in his wildest dreams would have Caspian imagined that *this* was what he'd be doing with Gunner Russo, and yet here they were.

Gunner shivered when Caspian pulled the digit out of him, but didn't hesitate and lowered himself to the floor. "I... I've never... I bought a dildo, but I didn't—"

Right. Gunner's body had never been penetrated. In a way, Caspian would be taking his virginity for the second time, and that thought forced him to frantically open his pants as pressure in his balls rose. "Okay. So you want to go slow after all?" he asked, because as much as he liked the idea of using Gunner for his pleasure without any foreplay, he wanted Gunner to have a good time and crave the things Caspian wanted to unleash on him.

"No. Just need you to know. I wanna feel you in me," Gunner mumbled and lowered the front of his body until his cheek met the cold tiles. All his muscles strained to keep him from falling on his face, and he awkwardly spread his legs wide in a bid to compensate for the bound hands and achieve greater balance. It paid off, and watching him in this compromising position had Caspian gasping for air.

Gunner was *so* showing the dildo to Caspian later, but he wanted to load his lover with cum first, so he pulled out a packet of lube, which he'd taken with him in case the date went well.

"It's your lucky day, Gun. I'm gonna pump you full of cum, and you'll have to just take it," he whispered, trying not to lose his mind as the cool lubricant covered his shaft. Even the way he saw his own dick had changed now. So maybe it wasn't massive, but his average cock was more than enough to take a guy for a ride. And because it had a nice girth to it, he'd have to be careful with Gunner's virgin ass.

"Christ. I've had so many wet dreams about this. I never knew how much of a slut I was," Gunner mumbled, arching his ass back, as if he wanted to tease Caspian into going for it without any more preparation.

"Only for me. Otherwise you'd be giving out freebies behind the Karma motel already," Caspian said and smeared some more lube over Gunner's entrance. He pressed his cockhead to the tight opening and waited, breathing slowly to resist the urge to just push on.

"Sounds like me. Go on. I want you in me. Wanna know what it's like," Gunner muttered, and Caspian could hardly believe they'd taken the plunge.

It felt so right no matter which body he was in.

Gunner would always be his.

He squeezed the back of Gunner's neck as the sphincter yielded to the pressure and let him in. The heat inside him made Caspian vibrate, and he worried he might come right away, but when he bottomed out, and his balls rested against Gunner's ass, they were still full of cum.

"That's it. Your cherry popped again," he muttered, moving his limbs until almost all his weight rested on Gunner's hips and back. He would ride him like a bull. Because he could. "I'm not gonna touch your dick, because *this* is about me. But I'm gonna use you to deposit all the cum I've saved this past month."

"Oh, yeah..." Gunner whimpered in a broken voice, and when Caspian moved his hand to the front of Gunner's neck, his Adam's apple bobbed against the sensitive palm, as vulnerable to pressure as anyone else's.

"Yeah, you like that? You like being my boy?" Caspian whispered, shivering with pleasure the moment he said that, but he didn't wait for an answer from Gunner and leaned back, grabbing his lover's meaty hips.

A soft gasp escaped Gunner's mouth when Caspian pulled almost all the way out before slamming back into the vise-like grip of that hot channel.

It felt so good. Heavenly.

"Yes," Gunner choked out. "I'm just your greedy hole. Yours to use whenever you're horny."

Gunner's thighs trembled, and he presented the picture of total submission with his ass in the air. So Caspian squeezed the flesh of his buttocks and rode. Rode him as hard and fast as he could, not even trying to last longer as dirty fantasies spilled out of his mouth. "I'm gonna come over on your lunch break, I'm gonna fuck you like this, and leave you with cum up your ass, so you can't stop thinking about me until evening. Maybe I'll even plug you."

"Oh yeah, you'll have me on the fucking bathroom floor," Gunner moaned, and Caspian got a glimpse of his face—red and twisted in pleasure. He'd even drooled a little. Caspian would make him lick it off the tiles. Or rub the floor dry with the flushed cheek. But regardless of how hot it made him to speak of such dirty deeds, those fantasies took second place to the pleasure of sawing into the tight hole. Gunner remained pliant and moaned as Caspian fucked him at full speed, slamming his hips against the firm buttocks until his balls flooded Gunner's hole with spunk.

They both gasped when Caspian twisted the meat of Gunner's ass, entering him a few final times. He had no idea how much time it took him to come, but it didn't matter, because the fact that he used Gunner's body solely for his pleasure excited them both.

"There you go, bitch. Drink it all."

Gunner let out a soft whimper as Caspian pulled away, still trembling with his orgasm. There was something deliciously obscene in a big guy like Gunner being left hanging, and he craved to see that pink pucker dripping with creamy spunk.

Gunner's rigid cock swung between his legs, but he wouldn't dare ask about his own pleasure, just kneeled there, gasping for air, with his ass on show and pleading for a picture.

He was so hot. The very essence of what Caspian desired, and Caspian chose to pet his back as reward for doing his job well. "Where's that dildo of yours, cream donut?" he asked with a lewd smile.

Gunner hesitated, so Caspian gave his ass a little slap. The way his slick ass clenched, letting out a drop of cum to slide down to his balls, made Caspian want to fuck him again, but climax had temporarily taken the edge off his urgency. He'd make Gunner wait for more. Maybe even beg.

"In a box by my bed."

Caspian twisted his fingers in the hair at the top of Gunner's head and licked his cheek, savoring the saltiness of his sweat. The shivers going through the big, muscular body were the perfect spice.

"Stay like this. I'm not done with you," he promised and rose, walking off on invisible wings. He wanted to keep teasing Gunner but couldn't wait to see what kind of toy he'd purchased. He ended up stopping in the bathroom, where he'd washed his dick in the sink, before going straight for the elusive box, which he opened with a hurried heartbeat.

The dildo was of an average size, made of purple silicone threaded with swirls of glittery pink, and had a wide suction base. Just the thought that Gunner owned it, that he'd bought it at some point in the last month because he missed being fucked made Caspian grin.

And yet he'd needed Caspian to pop his cherry. How sweet was that?

There was an unused tube of lubricant in the box too, and Caspian took both the items downstairs, shedding his remaining clothes on the way. A part of him wondered whether Gunner adhered to his orders, but finding him in the same submissive position Caspian left him in sent a pang of pleasure to his balls.

"Look at this pretty thing," he said, lifting the sex toy. "Couldn't help yourself? It had to be pink?"

"I... I mean, might as well get a cute one." Gunner's cock was a stiff baton between his legs, and it had dripped enough pre-cum to make a small pool under him.

Gunner's gaze followed him, as if he were a hungry dog dependent on its master for food and water.

"You should have a taste then," Caspian said, squatting next to Gunner and roughly pulling his head up by the hair. "Tell me if it tastes like candy," he ordered, rubbing the toy against Gunner's lips.

Gunner opened his mouth without protest, and Caspian stuffed the toy in, aroused by the way it spread Gunner's lips. Their eyes met as Gunner sucked on the silicone without prompting, and Caspian already knew he'd be getting his dick sucked by that greedy mouth before this night was over. He just hadn't decided if he wanted Gunner to swallow, or if he'd come all over his face.

"Good boy. That's where you belong. On your knees. With at least one of your holes filled. You're gonna take so much of my cum," he uttered in a low voice and pushed the dildo in until Gunner choked.

Despite his eyes watering and drool trailing down his chin, he still nodded. Even now, he kneeled with his legs spread to avoid touching the fat dick hanging between his thighs, desperate for attention.

"I almost wish there was two of me to spit-roast you," Caspian said and gently removed the toy out of Gunner's mouth. It was going in up the other end, so he opened the tub of lube and squirted a generous amount over the pink silicone.

Gunner watched his every move, gasping for air with damp lips. A perfect mess with his bound arms, drool on his chin and dripping with spunk. "Maybe you should invite a friend," he teased with a silly grin.

Desire clawed into Caspian's flesh when he imagined a faceless stranger fucking Gunner against the wall, but while it was an exciting vision, he didn't want to share what they had with anyone else.

"Greedy slut," he said and slapped Gunner's ass. "Get up and bend over the counter."

Caspian kinda enjoyed watching Gunner struggle to rise with his hands bound, but made sure to be close enough in case Gunner's legs cramped. His lover managed to get to the breakfast bar on his own and leaned against it, presenting his ass with a little sigh.

"It's your fault. Leaving me all needy."

"That's because I enjoy it," Caspian said and placed the slick toy between Gunner's buttocks. There was no need for further preparation after the rough fuck, so Caspian put his hand between Gunner's shoulder blades and pushed until the tight hole opened up and sucked in the colorful silicone.

He already knew they'd be getting more toys, because they gave him so much more control. When his own cock was inside Gunner, he found it hard to focus on much beyond the sheer pleasure of this tight body milking his dick, but dildos would be perfect for then he wanted to tease Gunner and watch his pucker swallow a fake dong. Gunner had no idea what was coming. Maybe Caspian could buy one of those vibrating plugs with a remote and watch him squirm in public?

Gunner moaned at every slow thrust, pliant and sweet despite the aggressive ink that singled him out as dangerous.

"Good boy. How do you like that?" Caspian whispered and changed the angle at which the toy entered Gunner's hole, on the lookout for the perfect way to torment Gunner's prostate. He knew he'd succeeded when his partner hummed and arched his hips in a way so pleading Caspian bit one of his buttocks, leaving a bitemark.

"Oh fuck! Oh fuck!" Gunner whimpered, sliding his legs apart, as if he wanted to take in more. He even tried to thrust against the the counter, so Caspian moved the dildo again, carefully pumping it in and out as if he didn't notice that his lover was going crazy from the direct stimulation. Caspian needed to get one of those dedicated prostate massagers and tease bucketfuls of pre-cum out of Gunner before letting him come. He'd buy cuffs. And nipple clamps. And have Gunner lie on top of Twinky while fucking his ass.

He loved the control toys offered and continued thrusting with the dildo until Gunner's face reached the color of raspberry juice. He pushed the toy in all the way to the flared base and grinned. "Hold it, or I won't let you come today."

It was an empty threat, since he didn't actually want to have this kind of power over another person, but saying such things out loud made his cock stiffen again. Oh, he was getting ready for the next round.

Caspian must have broken Gunner's smart mouth too, because he wasn't spewing any stupid talk and just lay there against the counter with little moans coming out of his lips as he squeezed the toy with his ass.

Happy with the result of his threats, Caspian took hold of Gunner's shoulder and pulled until the firm body stood straight, with impromptu nipple clamps still on his chest. He made a delicious sight, but Caspian wasn't sure how long they should sit there, and opened one, releasing the flesh.

Gunner let out a pained grunt and clenched his thighs, which prompted Caspian into hugging him. His lips closed around the tortured flesh, and he gently teased it with his tongue, holding on to one of Gunner's bound hands. The thick fingers instantly grabbed him when he reached for the other clamp. The massive chest heaved, and the nipple he soothed with his tongue burned with heat.

"It hurts," Gunner whimpered but didn't otherwise complain or ask to be released.

There was no anger in his voice, only pleading.

"It still needs to be removed, baby. I can go slower this time," Caspian whispered and licked the freed nipple, which felt so hot and swollen he wasn't sure whether Gunner's discomfort made him aroused or sympathetic.

"Uhm. Slower." Gunner took a deep breath as Caspian took his time with the other clamp, replacing it with his lips as soon as he pulled it off. He licked the sensitive flesh, then blew air on it and gave Gunner a firm hug.

"You still can't come. And you won't until I say so," he said and reached to the open drawer with kitchen utensils. The silicone spatula he so often used would work perfectly for what he intended.

Gunner shifted from one leg to the other, watching Caspian with a hazy gaze that only reminded Caspian of the dildo stuck in Gunner's cum-filled hole.

"Please," he uttered, so the teasing must have sweetened his filthy mouth.

"No," Caspian told him and slapped the wide end of the spatula against one of the damp nipples. Gunner stiffened but didn't protest when Caspian repeated this several times.

Caspian felt odd about deriving so much pleasure from Gunner's pain, but this wasn't what truly got him going. The reason why he liked watching his lover squirm was about Gunner submitting to his will, even when he didn't quite enjoy the process. They'd have to discuss this in the future, but since Gunner wasn't protesting, Caspian went with his gut and delivered fast, loud strikes all over Gunner's body. To his back and the buttocks tightened around a sex toy. To his chest and thighs. And then, Caspian squatted in front of Gunner and tapped the stiff prick hanging between Gunner's legs in the gentlest way possible.

His lover fidgeted, backing into the counter, but Caspian had all of his attention when he looked up into the wide eyes on a tattooed face that anyone else would have found threatening. But not Caspian. Not anymore.

This was the face of an overgrown puppy. The cutest he'd ever seen. But a puppy needed training as much as cuddles, so Caspian held on to Gunner's nape and slapped his balls next.

"Poor thing. This must be torture."

Gunner got to his toes with a loud moan. "I just wanna come," he pleaded. "Please let me come."

He was shivering and sweating, yet tightened his legs to keep in the dildo and sobbed, as if he'd truly given up the right to make decisions about his own pleasure.

Caspian loved it.

This man was the fulfillment of all his dreams.

"You'll get to come when you suck me off."

Caspian had to stop Gunner when he almost dropped to his knees.

"No. Stay here."

Instead, Caspian climbed the bar stool and sat on the marble counter. He spread his legs, inviting Gunner to feast on the stiff cock throbbing between his legs, ready for more action.

Gunner didn't say a word and leaned in, happy to get his mouth around a juicy dick. Caspian slid his fingers into the short hair on top of Gunner's head with a groan of satisfaction. He could get used to this. Not just to having an eager lover with a hot and ready mouth, but to Gunner being his.

Pleasure pulled him right back to reality, and he lay on the cool surface, with heels digging into the edge of the counter, and hands pushing Gunner's head down until all of Caspian's cock was buried in the heat of his throat.

His cock wasn't big enough to injure someone like Gunner, and seeing him take it all like a champ, Caspian forced his head up and down, hypnotized by the sight of his dick gliding in and out while streaks of saliva coated their skin.

Just imagining that at the same time Gunner was squeezing his ass around the dildo, all because Caspian told him to, brought Caspian to the edge of orgasm. He couldn't have felt more fulfilled as a man. Even in this body, which didn't come with the inbuilt benefits of height and size, he could top Gunner, and be the center of his universe.

To master him. And care for him.

Caspian came, setting the countertop on fire as his burning body shook violently in pleasure. Gunner's face flashed at the back of his eyelids when he shut them, and as tension left his body, the warm head between his thighs was the one thing keeping him from drifting into sleep.

He willed his eyes open and sat, bringing Gunner up for a spunk-flavored kiss. Gunner was eager as if he'd never tasted anything better. He arched into Caspian, but with his arms bound, he could only rub against him like an over-excited Labrador. He even licked along Caspian's jaw to express his appreciation.

A deep shiver ran up Caspian's body as he finally slid to the floor while still keeping his hand on his giant's throat. "Let's see if I can take your dick as easily."

"Oh, God... yes, please," Gunner whispered with bloodshot eyes focused on Caspian.

That loving gaze gave Caspian such a sense of power even as he dropped to his knees and faced Gunner's massive cock for the first time. It was dark, dripping with pre-cum, and he didn't expect this to last long, but in the future, he'd take his time exploring the length and caressing Gunner's balls. Now though, he reached between his man's legs and grabbed the dildo, moving it out the moment Caspian flicked his tongue against the salty cockhead.

Gunner moaned, and when he jerked his hips, the hard cock slid along Caspian's cheek.

"Oh fuck, oh fuck!" He was a restless, beautiful puppet, and Caspian would be pulling his strings however he liked.

He loved the sense of power it gave him and opened his mouth, looking up as the cock rode his tongue until Caspian hollowed his cheeks and sucked.

Gunner's flesh was so rosy now, and he shook so violently Caspian feared he might fall over, but that didn't stop him from pumping the pink dildo against Gunner's prostate and playing with his tool. So he was teasing instead of going for the hard stimulation that would have brought Gunner off in no time, but he also wasn't denying his lover anything, dedicated to giving him all the pleasure he needed.

When the fat dick twitched in Caspian's mouth right before spurting cum, there could be no greater satisfaction than Gunner's sobbing. Everything about Gunner, from the scent of his arousal, to the pliant way he took cock was perfection.

Caspian embraced Gunner, holding him still as spurts of cum flooded his mouth, but he swallowed all of it and held the dildo still, soothing his man with gentle petting.

"It's all right, baby. You did good," he whispered when he finally leaned back, letting the spent cock drop out of his mouth.

Gunner struggled to catch his breath, but his expression was so bare and open. The damp streaks running down his face made Caspian want to kiss the tears away and make sure Gunner knew he'd be taken care of. Because Caspian would do anything for him.

"It's... it was more than—" Gunner struggled to find the right words to describe his experience, but Caspian understood him anyway.

He gently removed the dildo, and, for lack of better options, placed it on the floor. His parents weren't coming home until next evening, so there would be more than enough time for cleanup. "I know. I loved it too," Caspian said, climbing Gunner's body until he stood straight. The knot tying Gunner's hands together unwound with a single tug, and Caspian pulled the freed arms around him. It felt strange to find himself in an embrace of a man so massive yet still feel like the one *giving* support.

He had no doubt this was a defining moment in his life. With Gunner's help, he'd kicked his insecurities in the face, because he'd never again let his size stop him from reaching for what he wanted.

"I have one more request, Gunner. Carry me to my parents' bathroom," he whispered, petting Gunner's muscular pec in appreciation.

This would work out. The swap had changed the way he thought about his body in the first place, but *this* proved that he didn't have to look a certain way in order to have the relationship and sex he wanted. For the first time in his life, he could have it all. All thanks to Gunner and the silly orange dog, who might or might not understand the magic he caused.

Gunner's gaze was still hazy, but his breath evened out. He pulled back from Caspian and glanced at him, as if assessing the best way to pick him up, but then turned around and offered his back.

"Hop on."

He was so delicious, with all those firm muscles under tattooed skin. Caspian grinned and climbed on, giddy like a kid getting to ride a pony for the first time. "This is the life." He didn't need to feel self-conscious about his boyfriend—because they were back together—carrying him. Who was to tell Caspian what made him a man when only he and Gunner got to decide the rules in their relationship?

Gunner chuckled as he left the kitchen, arching his head with pleasure when Caspian kissed his ear. "Are we gonna take a long bath?"

"Mhmm, you deserve a nice bath bomb, and lots of foam, and cuddles," Caspian whispered, winking at Dingo, who peeked at them from his bed in the corridor and slammed his tail against the padding, as if he were letting Caspian know he was happy for them. Or maybe he was just a dog being a dog. One could never know with him.

Gunner climbed the stairs without trouble, despite carrying additional weight, and walked toward the master bedroom. "I would have never admitted in the past that I loved shit like that. But like… why wouldn't I, right?"

Warmth filled Caspian's chest when he showered gentle kisses all over Gunner's bare shoulder. "No. No reason not to. And I never thought I'd feel comfortable dominating a big guy like you, or really anyone, but it felt so natural. Like we were made for each other," he added, tightening his embrace around Gunner's neck.

"You think the dog knew this?" Gunner snorted, but then smacked his lips a few times, and the sound of paws thudding on the floor resonated in the silent house.

"I think he knows everything, and we should start making homemade organic food for him," Caspian muttered, enjoying the steadiness of Gunner's body.

His parents' bathroom was big, with a large window, which was currently hidden behind a curtain, and lots of plants surrounding the big corner tub that would fit two people, even if one of them was Gunner-sized.

Dingo squeezed past Gunner's legs in the doorway and sat on a plush green rug by the sink.

Caspian slid off Gunner's back and went straight for the taps, making sure the water was warm before grinning at Gunner. "How do you feel?" he asked, reaching for a basket where his mom kept her bathing supplies.

Gunner slouched a little and petted Dingo's head with a smile. "Tired. But happy. I've never imagined I could feel like this in the body I have now. I thought my chance was gone the moment we changed places."

Caspian took his time chewing over what Gunner had said, and eventually chose the rose-scented bath bomb he knew Gunner would love, before tossing it into the filling tub.

"You are perfect. The way you are, and in my body both. You are still the same person to me."

"I worried you'd only want a little cutie." Gunner met Caspian's gaze with a shy smile.

Caspian reached for his hand and pulled him closer, caressing the front of Gunner's torso, overcome with warm feelings. "You *are* a cutie. And if you want different clothes, we can go shopping together, find something that fits your taste more."

"Will you... take care of me?" Gunner whispered and stroked Caspian's shoulder. "I've always been taught I have to do everything myself. As a *man*, you know? And you just seem to have it all figured out. Would it be so bad if I wanted you to take charge? Even if just a little?'

He couldn't have said anything more perfect. Caspian took hold of Gunner's hands and looked at him while the flowery aroma spread in the air. "I love you, Gunner. I will always take care of you."

The gentle smile spreading over Gunner's features was worth all the effort Caspian would have to put into this relationship in the future. "I don't wanna be a burden on you, but I love you too much to let go," he said as Caspian urged him into the bubbly water.

"Don't be dumb. You're *not* a burden. I like this. I want to be *the man* and make you feel safe. And you made me realize today that I don't need to change to offer you all that. You have no idea how happy this makes me," he said and picked up a new natural sponge, which he drizzled with Mom's shower gel, the same Gunner liked so much.

When Gunner slid into the water, the level rose so much that no more was needed. Caspian's giant smiled at him and washed his face. "I've never been in love before you," he said, so enamoured with Caspian it bordered on sappy.

But Caspian liked it, and each word from Gunner's mouth made his heart fuller. "Me neither. But you are exactly what I always wanted, even though I didn't know," he said and rubbed the sponge over sweaty skin that still kept some of its flush. He was careful around the nipples, since he expected them to be still very tender, and lifted Gunner's arm, lathering him up.

While surprised at first, Gunner tuned into the touch and let Caspian take care of him. "I just miss the piano, you know? A different life seemed within my reach when I had your fingers."

Caspian stilled, meeting Gunner's eyes. He'd expected Gunner to long for being small and cute, or having Caspian's secure financial situation, not this. "You really love playing, don't you?"

"Yeah. But you're teaching me now, so it is what it is," Gunner said, looking away. "Do *you* miss anything about being me?"

Small things. The pleasure of being seen as strong and potentially dangerous without needing to establish his position every single time he met new people, but his newfound confidence made up for the loss in pounds of muscle. Life had given him a priceless lesson, and he could from now on be the master of his fate, with a body he no longer resented, a man who loved him, caring parents, and a good job. He could have it all.

But Gunner wanted to play the piano.

Music lived in his heart, but he could no longer make it and it would take years until he became proficient in the same way Caspian was. If it was even possible, because while Caspian didn't want to dampen his enthusiasm, he did notice that Gunner wasn't as good at feeling rhythm or hearing nuance in sounds. Whether it was because of lack of early exposure, or because his body was just built that way, he would never become a teacher or performer. And knowing this became an instant weight in Caspian's heart.

"I liked being big and tall. It made carrying you around easy-peasy."

Gunner smiled at him, and leaned in for a little kiss, but then grabbed Caspian's arm hard and pulled him into the rose-scented water with a splash that reached Dingo.

Caspian snorted, shaking his damp hair like a dog. "You're the worst!" he said and gently punched Gunner's chest before sliding into his lap. But Gunner's words stayed with him, and no matter how happy he was, the thought of Gunner truly missing something from the brief time of their swap remained a thorn in Caspian's heart even as they kissed and joked around while Fluffer graced them with his presence and settled on the closed toilet seat.

Caspian had promised to take care of Gunner. So he would.

Chapter 34 – Gunner

Gunner woke up surprisingly not-sore, but when he patted the soft bedding next to him, he realized Caspian wasn't there. It took several big yawns for him to open his eyes wide, and he frowned at his outstretched fingers.

They were slim.

Pale.

"Caspian?" he uttered, sitting up in panic. This couldn't be happening. Not again. Not when they'd re-established their lives.

"Cas!" But Caspian was nowhere to be seen, so Gunner jumped out of the bed and pulled on a pair of shorts.

The bedroom door was open, and the sweet scent of frying batter pulled him into the hallway. He stalled, wondering whether Caspian's parents hadn't returned home already, but they wouldn't have driven all night without letting them know that something had cut their weekend trip short. So he took a deep breath and looked down the staircase, feeling naked. A part of him wanted to run back for a shirt, but they were alone, and the sound of sizzling oil lured him onto the steps. Once the cool wood touched his bare feet, he walked all the way to the first floor.

Dingo spotted him first and got up from his spot at Caspian's feet with a short bark that got Caspian's attention. To Gunner's bewilderment, Caspian smiled at him, grabbing the front of his black T-shirt and fanning himself with it to cool his broad chest. The kitchen was quite hot, due to the sun shining in through the windows, and the steaming pancakes on the stove.

He was once again in Gunner's body.

"Morning."

Gunner's heart rattled when he entered the kitchen. "Why are you so calm about this? Why didn't you wake me up?"

Caspian cupped Gunner's face and leaned in, kissing both of his cheeks before claiming his lips with a soft groan. "It's all right. You needed the rest."

"What do you mean?" Gunner's shoulders relaxed, and he reached for Caspian's hands as the dog sniffed around them, tapping its paws over the tiles.

Caspian pulled him into a warm hug that smelled of soap and the maddening cologne he liked to wear. "Why don't you play for me, hm? I'm almost done with breakfast."

Gunner stilled in the warm embrace, overwhelmed by being back in the form that allowed him to be so small next to Caspian. But most of all... "You did this? You just asked Dingo?"

Caspian's teeth rolled over his tongue, but he ended up nodding. The rays of sun made his brown eyes brighter, and his features were so relaxed even the stark lines of the tattoo on his face couldn't have made them look threatening. "I did. You can change back, if you like, but I wanted to surprise you. Needed to see if it works when I'm the only one to make a wish. Didn't want you to be disappointed if it didn't work out."

Gunner bit his lip, glancing down at his elegant hands when he stepped away from Caspian. "And you... want to hear me play?" Joy filled his heart already. Maybe once a month or so, they could take the risk and swap for a day? And he could play? Also, they could *play together,* but that was a different ball game.

"Whatever you like. Beethoven. Mozart. Chopin. Or improvise," Caspian said and unexpectedly pulled on Gunner's pierced nipple while the air heated, dense with fumes of fried dough and love.

Gunner laughed out loud and returned the favor. "How does this body feel in the aftermath, huh?"

A flush climbed Caspian's neck, and he turned around to flip the pancakes. "Well... I'm quite sore, actually. You sure I wasn't too rough?"

Gunner stalled for a second, then laughed out loud when he realized Caspian wasn't talking about his nipples. "I like it rough!" he yelled, walking off, because the piano was calling to him.

"Duly noted," Caspian said, but Gunner was already in the music room and lifting the keyboard cover. His gaze swept over the collection of sheet music gathered on shelves close by, but he didn't need any of them today and gingerly sat on the bench, placing his hands on the white and black keys.

He inhaled the sweet, sun-spiced air and looked at his thighs, dusted with faint, golden hairs, his chest, marked with the tattoo he'd put on Caspian's body in an act of thoughtless revenge, and at the blue veins at the tops of the graceful hands he'd missed every day since he got back the coarse, meaty paws given to him by nature.

But the boy he so loved being was back, and he let his inner voice come out in a series of fast, joyful chords. He jumped between one melody and another, between composers decades apart, and then added his own little twists with the same ease he improvised in the boxing ring.

Caspian's generosity took his breath away, and he fought the tears of happiness while his fingers danced across the keyboard. He'd never felt more loved, and let the instrument boast about his happiness. The piano he'd barely started making any progress with, was once more an extension of him, not an object of wood and string.

His whole body moved as he played, and by the time he froze, finishing his improvised mashup on a strong note, warm hands gently squeezed his shoulders. "You have such talent. It's amazing."

Gunner's grin could split his face in two as he looked up. "You liked it?" he asked, greedy for appreciation. "You taught me all I know after all."

Caspian pulled Gunner up. "I can't play like that. You use what I know and take it to another level."

"Are the pancakes ready? How do I deserve such an amazing boyfriend?" Gunner took the opportunity to hug Caspian again. He still couldn't get over last night. He'd risked their friendship by putting all his cards on the table in front of Caspian, and it couldn't have been more worth it.

They were together. In love. And for the first time, he could rely on someone else's care instead of trying to keep himself afloat in the stormy ocean of life.

"Everything for you," Caspian said and pulled Gunner along, to the dining room, which smelled so *green* because of all the plants heating up in the sunlight. The table was crowded with little bowls full of fruit and other toppings, but there was also coffee, juice, and a huge stack of steaming pancakes as the centerpiece.

Caspian sped up and pulled the chair back for Gunner. Always the gentleman. Gunner laughed and gave him a kiss before sitting down. He couldn't have felt more pampered. "Am I a prince today? You must have really enjoyed yourself last night."

They'd been too tired to fuck again, but made out in bed so late into the night, Gunner didn't even remember when he'd fallen asleep.

Firm arms settled around Gunner's neck as Caspian leaned down, pressing his stubbly cheek to Gunner's with a soft sigh. It was as if he couldn't bring himself to stay physically distant. "You'll always be my little prince. If that's what you want."

His words hung in the air, stealing Gunner's breath away when their meaning sunk in. The concept of *staying like this* shimmered in Gunner's mind with thousands of colors, but he held back his enthusiasm for Caspian's sake, and distracted himself by grabbing a pancake.

"I would, but also, I get it that we couldn't. Your job, your parents— it's okay, Cas."

"I wouldn't be offering if I didn't want to do it," Caspian said, his voice sounding a bit sterner this time.

Gunner glanced over his shoulder, out of breath. "You're serious." His mind went blank. He'd already made peace with his future and didn't know how to deal with this nuclear bomb of an offer.

Caspian kissed him on the cheek and sat in front of the other plate. "I've thought about it all night," he said and took a pancake from the platter in the middle.

Gunner absentmindedly poured some maple syrup over his own, still too confused to think straight. "You know I want you no matter which body you're in, right? I meant that."

"Me too," Caspian said and reached across the table to squeeze Gunner's hand. "I realized that last night. But you can only play the piano as you are now, and you love that so much. I couldn't look at myself in the mirror if I took that away from you."

Gunner's eyes filled with tears. This was so thoughtful. So selfless. "And... and how would it work? When Dingo dies one day, there will be no going back."

Caspian shrugged and drizzled syrup on top of his pancake. "Then we better not swap often. I'm happy being in either body, but you need those hands, and I want you to have them." He swallowed, briefly looking away and pretending he was too focused on the choice of fruit to meet Gunner's gaze.

"Cas? This has to be the best thing anyone's done for me. I won't let you down, won't ruin your reputation, and I'll try my best to make it work. But you know I can't be an accountant, right?" He rubbed his eyes with a napkin and added more toppings on his pancake as his mind raced with the possibilities opening in front of him.

Caspian grinned. "No. You'll be a piano teacher. And if you want, maybe you'll even perform. And I'll finish high school and think of my options. We're still very young."

Gunner chewed his sweet breakfast, watching Caspian with so much love it threatened to break his heart open. "First of all, the pancakes are amazing. Other than that, are you really okay with taking on the job I do for your mom?"

"I'm not a snob, I hope. And I like DIY, so it'll be perfect for now." Caspian added a dollop of whipped cream and cut a piece of his pancake, smiling at Gunner. "But you have to promise you'll make my parents love me like their own, okay?"

"I will. I promise. They won't be happy about me quitting accounting, but they'll swallow it, won't they?" Gunner didn't want to seem ungrateful and filled his mouth with food but couldn't stop looking at the perfection that was his man. Caspian would carry all that baggage, and put in so much effort, effectively starting his life over, just to make him happy. But he seemed adamant to do it, as if he'd considered all the pros and cons, and no longer had any doubts. If he wanted this, who was Gunner to reject such a generous offer?

Caspian shrugged. "Yes. But you really need to grovel. My education cost a lot of money."

Gunner nodded so eagerly a berry fell off his fork. "I will. I'm gonna make it up to them. I'll—wait. Are they gonna lose their shit about us dating?"

Caspian grinned. "They know we used to date, so I don't think it'll come as that much of a shock. But it will probably be a bit awkward for them, so we should look for a place of our own soon."

The pancakes tasted even sweeter. "It's really happening? We're gonna make it work?"

Caspian leaned back in the chair, the food forgotten on his plate. "Last night was transformative for me. I understood what I really wanted. I want you. And I want to give you everything you deserve but couldn't get. We will find a small home, and move in with Fluffer and Dingo. You will play, I'll try to get a qualification, so I can make use of everything I already learned and earn decent money. I really wanted to go to Italy for our honeymoon, but feel free to come up with a counter-suggestion."

Gunner dropped his fork. "Say what?" He cleared his throat, staring at Caspian with his face on fire. "Did you just propose to me?"

Caspian froze and quickly hid his hand under the table when it shook. "Um... I figured it was obvious, since we share everything. Don't you want to?"

Gunner laughed, and just had to get up. He pushed into Caspian's lap and kissed his sweet lips. A forever with Caspian. Who could ever say no to that? "I do. I totally do. This is it. I wanna be with you. You know your mom will organize the most lavish wedding ever?"

Caspian smiled with relief and hugged Gunner. "I count on it. Need to let everyone know what a hottie I scored."

"No, I'm the one who got myself a sugar daddy." Gunner kissed Caspian all over the face that was no longer his.

They didn't just swap this time. They somehow melted together and each held a piece of the other in their heart.

Epilogue – Caspian

3 years later

Caspian's balls throbbed as he slammed into Gunner's tight body, rolling his hands over his lover's slender mid-riff. His fingers snuck under the pink T-shirt, slid over the sweat gathered between his shoulder blades, and settled on the nape, just below the knot of pale hair.

"Go on. You still haven't filled the page," Caspian uttered, breathless and focused only on his lover, who helplessly held onto the side table and scribbled on a large piece of paper while Caspian railed him from behind.

"B-but I'm... almost done," Gunner whined, filling the sheet with crooked letters.

Caspian slapped his ass hard, and the boy barely managed to bite back a cry. "No buts. Write it down: *Caspian has the hardest dick*," he uttered, increasingly breathless. The game they were playing both amused and aroused him, and he wasn't about to let his bitch off the hook.

There was a tiny bit of real satisfaction to role-playing the bully who fucked Gunner and demanded his homework done while it happened, but no one needed to know that. Especially since Gunner was eating it up.

"I'll report you!" Gunner warned between one moan and another, knowing very well he was waving a red flag in front of a bull. Up for some rough play, then.

Caspian grabbed him by the hair and squashed Gunner's face against the desktop as he sawed into him ever harder. "No one will believe you, little bitch, because I'm not leaving any DNA inside you," he grunted, referring to their use of a condom. No one wanted to deal with cum-stained pants on a six-hour drive.

Gunner cried out, gripping the sides of the desk, and when his tight hole twitched around Caspian's cock, there was no doubt that he'd come. The way he still writhed and wiggled in Caspian's grip only made fucking him more delightful.

Caspian grabbed his hips as if they were handles and let his head drop to his nape, no longer focused on the angle of his thrusts, and let his instinct carry him.

Gunner braced against the table and whimpered. "Fuck, you're so good at this..."

Caspian came, bending over his lover as he pumped a few more times. "Damn, you're so... so hot, baby," he uttered, burying his face in the folds of Gunner's T-shirt.

"We're so fucking late," Gunner groaned but kept his eyes shut and rested atop the desk. His skin was scorching to the touch, and Caspian didn't want to let go yet, but Gunner wasn't wrong about the clock ticking away precious seconds.

Caspian held on to the condom as he withdrew from Gunner but kissed his nape, breathing in the scent of fresh perspiration and the sweet aroma of Gunner's fruity body spray.

"It's okay. Don't want to be married to the schedule now that I finally got a few days off," he muttered and finally tied the condom before tossing it into the trash can on the other side of the hallway.

Their home was modest, nothing like the villa owned by Caspian's parents, but the neighborhood was nice and safe, and they didn't need that much. Three years on, Gunner was still the sweetest little slut of a boyfriend Caspian could have wished for. He'd secretly worried whether he made the right choice by offering Gunner the permanent swap, but as strange as the whole experience had been, he had no regrets.

After some growing pains and tense months with Caspian's parents, Gunner got their support to pursue his dream of becoming a piano teacher. He got a certification for it while Caspian graduated high school in his stead. Their wedding, while lavish, had been small and featured no chocolate fountains. Mom and Dad hadn't been thrilled about Caspian *"rushing into things"*, but once all was said and done, they'd slowly warmed up to 'Gunner'. Caspian did everything in his power to make sure they saw him for who he was, and while things would never be as they used to be, he was always welcome in their home and often chatted to both of them.

Life had been tough for him, since he needed to not only pass his high school exam again but also restart his further education while *also* working, but now that he'd gotten a secretarial job at Dad's firm, things were finally looking up.

Impressed by how well their 'son's' ex-delinquent partner had cleaned up his life, Caspian's parents gave him more support than he could have anticipated, and if he kept up his hard work, he could count on a promotion and a job more suitable to his education. Gunner also contributed to their budget, but earned less, and Caspian couldn't help feeling proud that he supported Gunner no matter how heteronormative that was. It suited them both, so he didn't care about the opinions of others.

But working so much pumped Caspian out, and he was eager for a weekend getaway with his boy. They'd be staying at a nice hotel, but since there was nothing he loved more than pampering Gunner and seeing the awe on his face whenever Caspian managed to surprise him, he'd also booked tickets for *Don Giovani.*

Gunner, on the other hand, was happy to take on most of the house chores. He'd expanded his cooking repertoire and never failed to prepare dinner for them like a good little house husband.

Some days were harder than others, but Caspian wouldn't change a thing in their relationship. He absent-mindedly petted Dingo on the way to the bedroom where they'd left their bags, when the doorbell rang.

They finished just in time.

"I'll get it," Gunner called out and ran down the corridor while Caspian scratched Fluffer's head goodbye and carried their luggage toward the entrance.

Caspian looked around the bedroom once more, to make sure Gunner's little brother didn't find any sex toys while he stayed with their pets, but it seemed all the naughty boxes had been tucked away in the closet.

Caspian stilled as he glanced at the tall mirror. He still sometimes caught himself surprised by the reflection staring back at him. He had a bit of a flush left from the sex, and wasn't nearly as buff as he used to be when he'd first taken over Gunner's skin, but his silhouette was imposing thanks to his height. Three years were a lot, so he'd grown out his hair to a mid-length, which he liked to slick back, and wore clothes that were way more stylish than Gunner's original wardrobe. A series of painful laser treatments ensured that while the face tattoo remained visible up close, it was no longer so stark against his flesh.

He was tall and handsome though, and glancing into the mirror never stopped being a delight. He'd had to learn to navigate attention from women which was a surprising minefield he'd never walked into before, but when the wedding band on his hand didn't do the trick, revealing that a *husband* waited for him at home was usually more than enough.

"Hello, Noah," he called out.

Noah cooed at Dingo before yelling a 'Hey!' He was the only person who knew the truth about them, and they'd grown close thanks to that. Noah was also the one person they trusted with Dingo, despite his constant attempts to encourage the dog to grace him with a lottery win.

Gunner was talking to his brother when Caspian approached with their bags. "So you've got food in the fridge, and I bought the ice cream you like, but remember—"

Noah rolled his eyes. "I know, *don't bring peanuts into the house.*"

"Have fun. Call if anything's wrong. And don't invite strangers over," Caspian added and pressed a little kiss to the top of Gunner's head on his way out.

Gunner grinned back at him, the blue eyes sparkling with so much love Caspian got a happy tingle in his chest. Moments later, Gunner was running to catch up with him by the car.

"I can't wait to see New York!" he said, putting his sunglasses on. In the knee-length shorts and a pink T-shirt, he couldn't have looked more relaxed.

"I can't want to see *you* in New York. I suppose we both win," Caspian said and squeezed Gunner's hand as soon as they both sat in the car.

Gunner gave him a toothy smile. "You make my dreams come true."

Caspian grinned. "This whole life is a dream. But we're not gonna wake up."

The following hour passed on listening to Gunner's favorite playlist of classical music remixes, but when Caspian's gaze briefly focused on his husband's pink fingertips, his mind was taken right back to the quickie they'd had just before leaving.

"Fuck! The paper."

Gunner pushed his shades down his nose, and Caspian groaned.

"The paper where you wrote *'Caspian has the hardest dick'* a hundred times. We left it on the desk."

Gunner started laughing so hard tears glistened in his eyes. "Oopsie."

The End

Thank you for reading *Take My Body.* If you enjoyed your time with our story, we would really appreciate it if you took a few minutes to leave a review on your favorite platform. It is especially important for us as self-publishing authors, who don't have the backing of an established press.

Not to mention we simply love hearing from readers! :)

Kat&Agnes AKA K.A. Merikan
kamerikan@gmail.com
http://kamerikan.com

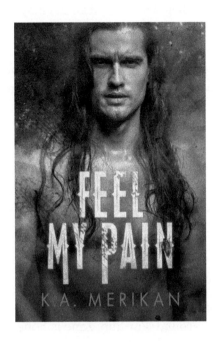

Feel My Pain
K.A. Merikan

—Two enemies cursed to feel each other's pain.—

Zane. "I will burn your life to the ground."
Roach. "I'm a cockroach. I'll survive."

Two years ago, the Rabid Hyenas MC ripped Zane apart like a pack of starving wolves. But he's not only a survivor, he took revenge that same night.

Turns out, one of the bikers is still alive, and as long as that's the case, Zane will not know peace. Especially since

Roach is the dirtbag who caused all the mayhem in the first place.

When an act of revenge meant to close that chapter of Zane's life takes a shocking turn, all hell breaks loose.

Roach's pain is his.
When Roach bleeds, he does.
When Zane suffers, Roach screams.

So until Zane can figure out how to lift the curse and kill Roach, he's stuck caring for the dumbass who drinks too much, works like a dog, and hasn't moved on an inch since he lost his motorcycle club.

But Roach has other plans for the man twisting his miserable life around. For him, Zane is hope, lust, and love combined, so Roach will gladly stay bound to him forever.

Even if it kills them.

Dirty, dark, and delicious, "Feel My Pain" is a gritty M/M dark romance novel with magical elements and a happy ending. Prepare for violence, intense jealousy, and scorching hot, emotional, explicit scenes.

Themes: Enemies to lovers, forced proximity, magical bond, revenge, poverty, disability, small town, vulnerability, versatile lovers
Length: ~110,000 words (Standalone novel)
WARNING: This story contains scenes of violence, offensive language and morally ambiguous characters as well as sensitive topics of child abuse, addiction, and suicide

AUTHOR'S NEWSLETTER

If you're interested in our upcoming releases, exclusive deals, extra content, freebies and the like, sign up for our newsletter.

http://kamerikan.com/newsletter

We promise not to spam you, and when you sign up, you can choose one of the following books for FREE. Win-Win!

Road of No Return by K.A. Merikan
Guns n' Boys Book 1 by K.A.Merikan
All Strings Attached by Miss Merikan
The Art of Mutual Pleasure by K.A. Merikan

Please, read the instructions in the welcoming e-mail to receive your free book :)

About the author

K.A. Merikan are a team of writers always eager to explore the murky waters of the weird and wonderful, K.A. Merikan don't follow fixed formulas and want each of their books to be a surprise for those who choose to hop on for the ride.

K.A. Merikan have a few sweeter M/M romances as well, but they specialize in the dark, dirty, and dangerous side of M/M, full of bikers, bad boys, mafiosi, and scorching hot romance.

FUN FACTS!
- We're Polish
- We're neither sisters nor a couple
- Kat's fingers are two times longer than Agnes's.

Website: http://kamerikan.com

Milton Keynes UK
Ingram Content Group UK Ltd.
UKHW022340080923
428326UK00012B/1355

9 798749 980479